Never a Dull Moment 1973

John M. Tallon

Copyright © John Tallon, 2014

Cover art, Adam Tallon, copyright © 2014

All rights reserved in all media. No part of this book may be used or reproduced without written permission, except in the case of brief quotations embodied in critical articles and reviews.

All characters and places are entirely fictitious. Any resemblance or similarity to persons living or deceased is purely coincidental.

Also by this author:
Something to Do – 1972
Available on Kindle and in Paperback
at Amazon.com and Amazon.co.uk

Find us on facebook @

https://www.facebook.com/pages/Something-to-Do-1972/427764967346581?fref=ts

To
Maria and Dave
for always being there

CONTENTS

PREFACE

CHAPTER 1 – Horse With no Name **1**

CHAPTER 2 – Mamma Weer All Crazee Now **17**

CHAPTER 3 – Bonny Bunch of Roses O **53**

CHAPTER 4 – Why Can't We Live Together? **84**

CHAPTER 5 – John Barleycorn Must Die **102**

CHAPTER 6 – Dazed and Confused **140**

CHAPTER 7 – Take a Walk on the Wild Side **168**

CHAPTER 8 – Something in the Air **194**

CHAPTER 9 – Broken Wings **215**

CHAPTER 10 – Silver Machine **240**

CHAPTER 11 – Streets of Laredo **268**

EPILOGUE **298**

MUSIC and GLOSSARY (**End Pages**)

Preface

This is the continuing graphic story of a disparate group of working class youths, who initially are all loosely unified by their membership of a large, urban, Skinhead gang. Set in the Liverpool of 1973 and located both on a number of bleak, sprawling housing estates and the City Centre, the action ranges from the seemingly innocuous to the extremes of sadistic violence, including that of a sexual nature.

Their circumscribed world is depicted throughout, reflecting; the fashion, the music and the aggression. This is the period immediately after the close of the idealistic 1960s; the 'Summer of Love' has ended and there will be several 'winters of discontent' to follow during the transitional epoch at the beginning of this pivotal decade.

The youths follow a particular stylistic trend, they like the look of the Skinhead fashion popular at the time, the opportunities for aggression that it offers and the respect they believe they receive from other members of society. There is no racist, neo-Nazi, Fascist agenda, overtones or undertones, they are a working class proletariat group and identify themselves more along social class lines than any other differentiation.

From the start there are references to the prevailing cultural mores and perceptions of that time. There is no attempt to glorify them in any way but rather to reflect the formative climate in which the youths have developed and, find themselves living in. The atmosphere is essentially machismo-driven, homophobic and misogynistic and, by today's standards would be totally unacceptable but arguably renders a true portrait of that time, 'warts and all.'

In the previous book, the opening tale **'Something to Do 1972'** Jay Mac, the central character, his friends from the Crown Estate and his enemies from the vast Kings Estate all adhere to their original Skinhead style, even though they are increasingly aware that their distinctive look is rapidly becoming outdated. As they evolve from Skinhead through Suedehead to Boot Boy so too a new deadly trend begins to emerge, the widespread use of increasingly harder drugs. Ultimately once this 'genie' is released from the bottle it can never go back, with dramatic consequences for all those involved, whether friend or foe.

Chapter 1

A Horse with No Name

Sunday 14th January 1973

The sound of a loud, insistent knocking on the weather-worn front door of his present, single-storey abode roused the weary Jay Mac from a deep slumber. This brief period of relative tranquillity had finally overtaken his exhausted body and freed his troubled mind from the otherwise restless captivity of dark and disturbing thoughts.

"Alright stop bangin', there's nobody in." he lied then settled back down, pulling the coarse, dark brown, army surplus blanket up over his head. Even as the youth attempted to drift back into the surreal landscape of his recurring dream, which appeared to be populated by a race of menacing gigantic statues, whose penetrating gaze constantly observed his every move, a new sharp sound of rapid tapping on his bedroom window left him with no choice other than to deal with this irritating nuisance.

"This better be somethin' important. If you're Jehovah's Witnesses, fuck off while y'still can!" he shouted angrily whilst pulling on his twenty-two inch, parallel, well-scrubbed, blue denim Flemings jeans and slipping the red half-inch elasticated braces over his shoulders.

Standing in the gloom of his tiny box room, he could see by the weak grey winter's light that barely penetrated the dirty, yellowed, threadbare and similarly worn, tattered net curtain, stretched awkwardly on its string line across the small grimy window, that it was in fact day though he had no idea of the time, whether morning or afternoon. The sound of laughter had greeted his irate warning and the window-tappers had now resumed their banging on the front door; Jay Mac concluded that this was most likely mischievous neighbourhood children.

"Fuckin' kids, pissin' about" he muttered to himself as he stepped into his gleaming cherry-red Airwair boots. "I'll give them a kick up the arse, if it is."

He moved from this room into the small living room of his mother's hastily constructed, corporation, prefabricated, cardboard box of a maisonette. Passing through into the hall he strode down the dark, narrow lobby with its single paned, louvered, badly-fitting, fan light window and swiftly by the bedroom door of his sole parent, as she lay in her usual alcohol induced semi-comatose state. After sliding the chain from its fastening, he unlocked the latch and wrenched the front door open, ready to deliver a scathing torrent onto his tormentors

"Fuck me! Y'not dead then!" exclaimed a familiar voice.

"I told yer, the bizzies couldn't kill 'im" followed another instantly recognisable cheery rejoinder.

Jay Mac rubbed his bleary eyes while the cold frosty air rapidly restored his senses. Standing in front of him was the tall rangy, dishevelled, dour figure of his long-time friend, Irish, accompanied by the somewhat smaller rotund, dapper, ever-smiling Blue. It was the first occasion that Jay Mac had seen any of his Crown Skins team mates, since his arrest towards the close of the previous December.

As he looked in surprise at both of his friends dressed in their dark blue-black Crombies, blue Flemings jeans and Airwair boots, he experienced a range of mixed emotions but was genuinely pleased to see them.

"Shit, who would've thought it? Laurel and fuckin' Hardy back from the dead." Jay Mac said with a wry grin. "To what do I owe the honour of this unsolicited and unwelcome visit, might I ask?"

"We'll tell y'that in a minute, any chance of us comin' in for a brew, its fuckin' freezin out 'ere?" Irish requested in his usual surly manner.

"It's not much better in 'ere. The crappy heatin' system packed in years ago." Jay Mac advised as he led his two friends through the small lobby and into the dingy, cramped living room.

"Take a seat and I'll make a brew," their host offered graciously, before disappearing into the tiny kitchenette.

Irish, who had previously visited the small prefab several times during his and Jay Mac's first year's incarceration in *The Cardinals' School for Catholic Boys*, sat down in a battered old armchair situated on one side of an equally aged wooden table nearest to the kitchen entrance and began lighting a cigarette. However, an uncomfortable Blue was a little more reticent before seating himself in the heavily stained, worn fabric-covered item positioned on the opposite side of the table. Finally he chose to perch on the very edge of the chair and began studying the interior of the dilapidated room.

Apart from the two armchairs on either side of the table that he and Irish were occupying, the room contained a large, ebony, late-Victorian sideboard which dominated the area with its considerable, incongruous bulk; a spindle-backed rickety, dark stained wooden chair and, fixed precariously to the wall adjacent to the kitchen entrance, was a well-used dartboard replete with three arrows of oddly coloured plastic flights. Just as Blue was completing his brief inspection, having noted the excessive mould and damp ingress stains on the faded, cream distemper coloured walls, he spotted a small transistor radio amidst the cheap bric-a-brac ornaments that clustered on the old sideboard's principal shelf.

"Is this piece of crap workin'?" he enquired, whilst fiddling with the control dials on the front of the radio. Suddenly between the hiss and crackle of static, the smooth dulcet tones of Mr Tony Bennett could be heard singing the classic *I Left My Heart in San Francisco.*

"Leave that on Blue," Jay Mac shouted returning from the kitchenette, balancing a tray with two glass tumblers, an old china cup; a dark brown teapot and a bottle of milk. After he had placed the tray on the table and poured the tea, Jay Mac pulled the wooden chair over and sat down. Blue felt obliged to give his considered assessment of their present surroundings.

"No offence mate but this *really* is a shit-hole and..., what is that, it smells like cat piss?"

"Thanks Blue don't spare me feelings like" Jay Mac replied, smiling, "Yer not far wrong. Me mum seems to let stray cats in 'ere all the time, they're the only ones that can stand the stench."

"I think one of the little fuckers must have died." said Irish in his droll manner.

They all laughed but Jay Mac knew only too well from past, painfully embarrassing experience that the powerful odour of cat urine was all pervasive, not only throughout the tiny dwelling but also within the very fabric of any garment that became a feline resting place. He recalled how his own school blazer, which he 'grew into' and then rapidly out of, had proved particularly attractive to one old incontinent, resident Tom. Once, having been caught in a heavy rainstorm on his way to school, Jay Mac made the mistake of placing his saturated blazer onto one of the old iron radiators to dry. His classmates became increasingly aware of the powerful, pungent aroma and subsequently traced its source; Jay Mac had to wrestle the item free before it was torn to pieces, after being kicked around the entire class.

"'Ere drink this, mister fuckin' house critic" Jay Mac said passing Blue one of the glass tumblers filled with dark brown tea, before giving Irish the china cup. He noticed the circumspect Blue curiously sniffing his drink and advised "Don't worry; it's not the one she keeps her teeth in."

Seemingly reassured Blue took a sip of the tea, which he instantly spat out.

"Fuck me! What's this, not more cat piss?" he blurted, before checking his 'cup' once again.

Jay Mac and Irish laughed.

"Look at the bottle, its sterrie, y'fuckin' prick, gerrit down yer." Irish instructed after casually blowing two consecutive smoke rings.

Blue had never experienced sterilised milk before and its distinctive taste did not appeal to him. "I think I'll pass on that Jay Mac, thanks. Is there any food goin'?" he enquired, ever conscious of his stomach's demands.

"Don't yer fancy the sterrie Blue? I understand mate, it's an acquired taste. There's some mouldy crackers in the kitchen but I wouldn't recommend them to a connoisseur like you." Jay Mac replied, before taking a drink of his 'stewed' tea. "Now that everyone's sitting comfortably, what the fuck is it you two want, comin' all the way off the estate down into this forgotten part of the city?" he asked curiously, whilst studying Irish's impassive expression.

His former school friend and Crown Skins team mate explained how wild rumours had been circulating around the Crown Estate, concerning Jay Mac's last arrest and subsequent withdrawal from gang activity. He also advised how he and Blue had risked life and limb, by entering the Kings Estate to try and apprise him of the situation by visiting him at his aunt and uncle's flat. However, having been turned away from there, they pursued their quest to the only other place where Irish expected to find him.

"So one way or another Jay Mac yer've got to go back to the Estate, show y'face and put everyone straight." Irish finished his summary of the situation with his well-meant advice.

Jay Mac considered his response carefully. "I was in court at the Magistrates on Monday, just so yer know. Thee've put me on bail until thee get a probation officer's report, then they're gonna sentence me, so I don't need any more trouble and I don't give a fuck about what anyone thinks on some shit-hole of an estate."

Irish stared at his friend for few moments then spoke.

"Do y'really want to stay 'ere? This is worse than the fuckin' Nick. If a probation officer comes 'ere they're definitely goin' to tell the Mags to put yer away for yer own good." He paused, letting his words be fully understood, "Yer've got to get back t'yer aunt and uncle's place, if yer don't wanna get stuck down."

Blue, who usually only thought of his own immediate dietary needs, suddenly made a surprising gesture. "Tell yer what, until y'can sort things out with yer aunt and uncle, y'can stay at ours for a bit. Me mum won't mind and me dad's always workin' shifts, so he won't even know yer there."

After a few moments of silence except for the sound of the barely audible radio, where a BBC announcer was delivering the four o'clock news with perfectly clipped annunciation, Jay Mac, who was genuinely moved by his friend's kind offer, finally responded.

"Alright Blue, I'll take yer up on that. I'll get me gear together an come back for it in a couple of days, if yer mum's ok with me stayin'. Thanks mate, I owe yer one."

Irish was in the process of lighting another cigarette when he spoke "Thank fuck for that! Now let's get out of this dump and away from this shit area. Its goin' dark outside and no one wants to be round *here* after dark."

"Why's that?" asked a curious Blue, "What are thee all round 'ere, vampires?"

"No Blue, fucking *well* worse than that, they're L.O.L!" Jay Mac replied with a grin and both he and Irish nodded knowingly.

Blue, who had only ever lived on the Crown Estate, in the overspill housing district outside the city at its northern boundary, knew nothing of the ancestral, sectarian divisions of its inner core. While Jay Mac was putting on his Levi's denim jacket with bleached collar and pocket flaps, followed by his blue-black Crombie, both he and Irish provided a potted history from their Catholic biased perspectives, of the principal causes of the 'Troubles' and its consequences.

"So y'see Blue, not everyone got moved out the city in the slum clearances of the early sixties, some people like me mum and me got moved further in. The only problem was we ended up here, right in the heart of the Loyal Orange Lodge district, not really a good place for a Catholic, y'know what I mean?"

Jay Mac finished his preparations by giving his gleaming Airwair several wipes with his soft polish-stained cloth, until he was satisfied with their appearance and then the three youths departed.

Mrs Mack the errant mother of Jay Mac slept on; unaware she had been in receipt of visitors or of her son's departure. The small transistor radio had not been switched off and in the cold darkness of the now empty living room, continued to play faintly as its weak batteries began to fail. Bing Crosby's melodic version of *Beautiful Dreamer* serenaded the collection of cheap ornaments displayed on the antique sideboard and an old Tom cat asleep in the airing cupboard stretched languorously, dreaming of where next to leave his scent.

◇ ◇ ◇

Immediately on stepping out of the small maisonette, all three Crown team mates were struck by how cold the temperature had become. A thin grey veil of frosty fog, hung in the narrow spaces between the prefabricated dwellings and across the old cobblestone road to the other side of the street, where the few remaining original Victorian terraces stood like a row of broken teeth. On the corner of this particular row, directly opposite Jay Mac's mother's residence was also located one of the original public houses, a sole survivor of a myriad hostelries that had been the social hub of each small enclave of dedicated patrons, now long gone. Appropriately named The White Horse, it was a pale shadow of its former Victorian self.

Loitering in the lounge bar doorway, were a dozen or so youths aged between thirteen to sixteen years, similar to the Juniors of the Crown Estate. They were bored, frustrated and looking for an outlet for their anger. Self-styled, the 'Billy Boys', or 'Billy Skins', they were the younger siblings of the far more dangerous '1690s Skinheads'. Jay Mac's visitors' arrival had been noticed and now the departure of the three companions, dressed in full 'uniform' required some immediate response.

It was a long walk to the top of the street where it met the main road at its brow. Jay Mac knew it well; he had run the gauntlet of various adversaries from an early age, not always successfully. He knew that just past the midpoint there was a plot of waste ground, euphemistically called the 'playground' that contained a couple of rusty swings; a broken see-saw; a static round-a-bout and a dubious sandpit. It was in this stimulating play area, that he had first learnt the painful results of giving the wrong answer to the question of his religious denomination. A similar sized but entirely vacant plot, except for being strewn with various pieces of builder's rubble, faced its rival on the opposite side of the street. As the three Crown Estate Skins were approaching this mid-section, fully aware that they were being followed at a short distance to the rear by this motley collection of local youths, Jay Mac was considering the possible avenues for flight and the probability of the success of such a venture.

"'Ave yer clocked the gang of pricks trailing us?" Jay Mac said chiefly to Irish but also as a nod to Blue.

"Yeah, which way d'yer wanna play it, run for the main road at the top, or turn round, grip the biggest ones and give them a dig?" Irish asked.

Confident that he could out sprint any of their followers and that Irish, despite his heavy smoking, could probably make a good attempt, he was also acutely aware that Blue had no chance of escape by running.

"Let's just stroll on and let them make their move but be ready." Jay Mac said to his friends.

"Good idea Jay Mac" said Blue nervously, "Am not runnin' from a bunch of kids, y'know what I mean?"

"We fuckin' know exactly what y'mean Blue, just be ready." Irish said, echoing Jay Mac's warning.

At that very moment the apparent leader of the trailing youths shouted his instructions.

"Hey you three dickheads, stop where y'are, we wanna word with yer!"

The three Crown Skins walked on without response through the thin mist of the freezing fog. A shrill whistle sounded and suddenly half a dozen more similarly aged youths ran down from the top of the street, blocking any escape route in that direction. The original followers now ran up behind their intended prey.

"Billies or Papes?" the leader demanded.

"Are you talkin' to us little feller?" Jay Mac asked, turning toward the ginger haired, pasty faced questioner.

Irish moved to his friend's right flank and Blue hesitantly took up the left position.

"Billies or Papes, what are yer? C'mon, fuckin' answer!" 'ginger' demanded again.

Then stepping closer to Jay Mac his gaze fixed on the Crown skin's open-necked Ben Sherman shirt.

"What the fuck is that round your neck?" He had spotted Jay Mac's small silver crucifix and the oval medal of St Michael that he wore on a short chain. Reaching forward slowly he made to take the items from Jay Mac.

"That fuckin' hand better come no closer or I'll snap your scrawny wrist, yeah?" Jay Mac warned, never taking his intense gaze off the ginger youth. The latter decided to err on the side of caution and withdrew his outstretched hand.

"So what have we got here then, three fucking, stinking Papes?" he sneered shifting his stare from Jay Mac to Irish and then settling upon the clearly nervous Blue.

Unable to hold his composure, the portly youth blurted out, "I'm not a Pape, these two are. I go to that Lodge place all the time.

"Shut the fuck up Blue." Irish warned.

"Blue don't say any more, yer makin' a mistake." Jay Mac added but it was too late, Blue was afraid and would offer anything to save himself.

"Are y'now and what Lodge is that? Where is it?" asked the ginger questioner, who wore a cruel grin on his thin lips.

"It's round by ours, you wouldn't know it." Blue answered cautiously.

"That's alright mate, if yer are one of the boys let's see yer L.O.L ring, or maybe yer've got somethin' on a chain round yer neck." As he spoke he gestured for Blue to step away from his two friends and over to *his* companions.

"Blue, stay where yer are!" Jay Mac tried to warn.

"Don't let these two fuckin' Papes tell y'what to do mate, come over 'ere yer alright." Ginger coaxed slyly.

Blue was now in the midst of six of the Billy Boys, who placed their hands on his arms and shoulders.

"Take him over there to the 'Oller' and check him for a chain or a tattoo. If you're lyin' we'll give yer a free tattoo and a little reminder not to fuck around with the Billy Boys." The sinister warning of the ginger leader sent a chill through Jay Mac, having previously heard of their penchant for a particularly sickening torture. He turned to look at Irish and he nodded his silent agreement in return.

"No, please don't do anything. Look, me name's Billy, Billy Boyd, I'm one of you, honest." Blue pleaded desperately, shaking with fear.

"Get his kecks down, we're gonna do a little bit of 'Jap's eye' roastin'." the ginger leader stated with a broad smile, whilst reaching into the right hand pocket of his grubby Crombie for a box of matches.

Blue's six captors laid hands on him in earnest and began to try to take off his clothing.

"Please no, fuck off, no." he cried in terror.

At that very instant the three metal darts with their hand-filed razor-sharp points and odd coloured plastic flights, which Jay Mac had been searching for in the left hand pocket of his Crombie, were brought out in a thrusting arc into the pasty face of the ginger leader. Irish's dirty, wooden-handled craft knife, which he had also been searching for, slashed across the upper lip and under the snotty nose of the Billy Boy facing him. He followed this with a powerful thrust kick to the gut of the youth next to his original target.

"Fuck you tits, we're Crown Skins!" Jay Mac shouted, his face illuminated with a vicious delight as he struck another victim on his left.

The remaining youths were, for a few moments, frozen in static pose not sure how to respond. In that short space of time both Jay Mac and Irish had leapt forward, to where Blue was standing with his intended torturers, all similarly motionless and, having stooped to pick up half bricks from the building rubble on the waste ground, they proceeded to strike their closest opponents in their respective faces with these impromptu weapons.

"Come on soft lad, fix y'strides and run like fuck!" Jay Mac shouted, catching hold of Blue by the arm and turning him round in the direction of a brick archway passage, in the old derelict tenements, barely visible in the thickening fog beyond the waste ground to their original right.

Both Jay Mac and Irish had successfully reached the opening to the vaulted passageway, which promised some hope of escape but despite his best running efforts, Blue failed to arrive unscathed. The Billy Boys had resorted to launching volleys of mixed rubble at the three runners, whilst awaiting the arrival of reinforcements in

Never a Dull Moment 1973 ▪ 10

the form of their older siblings, the '1690s Skins' whom they had sent for.

Blue was almost at the archway entrance when a well-aimed piece of half-brick struck him on the back of the skull, knocking him to the ground. Jay Mac and Irish had themselves been hit by a hail of ballast but were relatively unharmed; they immediately ran forward and dragged the fallen Blue into the dark, cavernous passage.

"They don't seem to be too arsed about chasin' us any further." Irish observed peering through the hazy fog, trying to discern their attacker's next move.

Jay Mac, who had gone further along the dark, dank passage, now returned with the results of his foray.

"Yer know why thee've not bothered gettin' any closer yet? This fuckin' tunnel's blocked by loads of rubble at the other end."

"Shite, I thought you knew all round 'ere?" Irish asked angrily.

"Yeah Irish, I'm always runnin' round checkin' which archways are open or blocked. Light a couple of matches will yer and let's have a closer look, before those little fuckers are joined by their big brothers." Jay Mac replied curtly.

Blue was on his hands and knees trying to crawl forward over the rough ground of the floor surface. Blood was streaming from a gash at the back of his head and his blond hair was becoming matted with the sticky, scarlet fluid.

"What the fuck is that?" he shouted in alarm. "Shit, I've put me hand on a cheesy, wet Johnny."

"Save that Blue, we might pick up some birds later" Jay Mac called back to his friend, while he scrambled over the obstructing rubble, looking for any opening.

Irish had lit two matches and was also studying the 'cave's' interior. "Fuckin' Hell, will yer look at the walls? This must be King Billy's knockin' shop."

By the brief flickering light they glimpsed a primitive mural of the famed monarch on his white stallion and the proud accompanying slogans *'1690's Skins'* and, *'Fuck the Pope'*. They noticed also that the floor was littered with used condoms, cigarette butts and empty beer bottles.

"Hey Jay Mac this is the place for you isn't it? I heard you like havin' a shag anywhere like this." Blue shouted, sitting still for a few moments, trying to staunch the flow of blood from his wound with the dirty checked handkerchief that Irish had passed to him.

"No thanks Blue, I couldn't manage one now I'm busy but thanks anyway" Jay Mac called back as he pulled away some of the looser debris.

"Come 'ed, gerrup 'ere, we can do this!"

A gust of freezing air dashed in through the small aperture Jay Mac had forced open, extinguishing the tiny flame from Irish's second collection of illuminated matches. All three Crown Skins scrambled up the pile of rubble and began desperately tearing away lumps of brick, stone and cement.

"You Pape fuckers are dead, I'm gonna cut your fuckin' balls off when I get hold of yer!" screamed the leader of the 1690's Skins as he charged headlong towards the passageway were they were presently entombed. At six foot two and built like a brick outhouse with a shock of firey red hair, which had long since grown out of his last 'Number One' crop and his battered countenance, the nineteen year old William George McGrath, the older brother of the dart-wounded Billy Boys leader, looked like he could dispatch all three Crown Skins himself, without the aid of his six accomplices and the rag-tag Junior followers in his wake.

"For fuck's sake pull!" a terrified Blue implored, while both Jay Mac and Irish, who had already scrambled through the small opening they had managed to create, attempted to drag him through also.

"There's some sort of fuckin' gorilla comin'," he warned in earnest.

Even as the remaining Crown Skin was wrenched through the tight brick portal and out onto the top of the rubble mound, which thoughtful council employees had recently forced into place with a JCB, to stop anyone being injured by trying to gain ingress to the former passageway though the condemned tenements, the 'gorilla' bounded forward and caught hold of Blue's right ankle.

"Come 'ere you little shit, you're goin' nowhere!" William George shouted triumphantly.

His elation was a little premature; Irish thrust his arm through the gap and slashed a deep cut across the back of the restraining hand, which immediately released Blue's ankle. Whilst the three Crown Skins scrambled down the 'mountain' of rubble onto the waste ground below, the wounded 1690's leader clutched his pouring wound and raced back to his comrades.

"Come on, run round the side of the tennies, we'll catch them fuckers on the oller." he commanded.

The whole crew raced towards the far end of the crumbling building, thirty yards further on. Even as the 1690s Skins and Billy Boys were turning the corner of the old housing block, the three Crown Skins had reached the end of the two-hundred yard stretch of rubble-strewn waste land, known locally as 'the oller'. Jay Mac and Irish had hold of Blue by the shoulders of his Crombie and were literally dragging him as fast as they could towards the narrow road in front of them. For once Blue was not complaining about the pace and was making a determined effort not to stumble and fall.

"You three fuckers stop right there!" commanded a strong voice, directly in their escape path.

"Fuck me, not again." Jay Mac said aloud.

Under the yellow lights of the high rise tower blocks, the exhausted Crown Skins could see at least three dozen youths gathered in a tight throng. Their leader stepped forward abruptly and caught Jay Mac by the lapels of his now filthy Crombie.

"Are you Billy's or what? You look like fuckin tramps so y'could be." There was the hint of a smile on his lips as he spoke.

Jay Mac quickly scrutinised his captor and realised that he was in the grip of a powerfully built individual, about six feet tall with thick dark hair cut in the new 'feathered' style, short on the top and sides but more than collar length at the back. In the few brief seconds while he stared at the acne-scarred face in front of him, with its off-centre badly broken nose, some faint glimmer of recognition was desperately trying to rise to the surface. Before Jay Mac's synapses could produce a sufficiently clear memory, the other youth spoke.

"I fuckin' know you, John Mack isn't it?" he said with a broad smile lighting his previously sinister looking visage. "It's me, Mozzer, Morris Kirwin yer mate from St Francis' infants and juniors. By the way that Crucifix and St Michael medal is a bit obvious for round 'ere." A palpable wave of relief washed over the three weary companions. Jay Mac felt obliged to offer a brief explanation.

"I've been stayin' at me mum's for a bit, but I live out on the Kings estate, these are two of me mates from the Crown Skins. We've just had a bit of trouble with some of the Billy Boys and now they're leggin' us with some of the 1690s."

His rapid, garbled explanation was sufficient and presaged the imminent arrival of the bloodied William George McGrath and his motley crew, who could clearly be seen even through the mist, running at full pelt across the two-hundred yard stretch of barren waste land. Mozzer, whose crew were dressed in an eclectic mix of Crombies and leather coats of varying lengths; white bib and brace jeans, or twenty-four inch parallel blue Flemings; dark woollen skull caps or tartan Slade caps, smiled at Jay Mac and shook his hand.

"You can tell y'from out of town, yer kit is played out. Nice to see yer all grown up mate, say 'ello to Jimmy McCoy next time y'see him, I hear he lives out on the Crown Estate, when he's not in the Isle of Man. Don't worry about the 1690s; we'll deal with these fuckers." Then he turned to face his rapidly approaching enemy.

On seeing the massed ranks of the J.F.K Boot Boys, now visible through the thin screen of fog, William George wisely brought his troops to a halt. He focused on the enemy leader and addressed his comments to him.

"Alright Mozzer! This isn't between us tonight. Give us those three queers back that's all we want."

"Why d'yer want these three, what's so special about them, haven't y'got enough of yer own queers over there?" Mozzer shouted back, much to the amusement of his own crew.

The furious 1690s leader reached inside his dark Crombie with his blood soaked handkerchief-bandaged hand and drew out a steely blade, which he held aloft for all to see.

"This is me old feller's dirk, right? Send those three cunts over here now, so I can gut them, or else!" McGrath stood rooted to the ground with the blade proudly displayed, as he waited for Mozzer's response.

"Sorry lad, I can't help yer and y'can put yer dad's weapon away, nobody's impressed.

He turned to the three Crown Skins, "Go 'ed, fuck off. Y'can 'ave this one on the J.F.K's, it's not your fight." With that the leader moved forward with his troops to do battle with his ancestral enemy.

"Come on McGrath, you ugly Orange bastard, you know yer don't come on to the oller. Let's have it!" he shouted.

"This is our ground by right, you Papist shithouse, yer time's up Kirwin, come on." was McGrath's bitter response.

The exchange of insults continued as custom required for a few more moments, followed by volleys of missiles from both sides and then the torrent of sectarian hatred compelled both opposing forces ineluctably, to crash into each other. Friend and foe merged into a maul of insane bigotry, punching, kicking, gauging, slashing and biting with frenzied energy.

The three Crown Skins were redundant spectators and made good their escape while the madness raged on. Jay Mac now had his bearings and led his two friends up the hill to the junction with the main arterial road. When they reached this point of relative safety, where Everton Brow met Netherfield Road, the clamour of the mayhem below could still be heard. Angry shouts and shrieks of pain mixed with thuds and the distinctive sound of breaking glass as the desperate struggle raged on. The freezing fog did little to deaden these noises but it did obscure the bloody spectacle, adding to an uncomfortable eerie feeling that the three companions each experienced. It was as if the wraiths of historic combatants had joined the struggle and were cloaked in a spectral mantle of ethereal mists.

A city centre bound bus was travelling towards them and they raced to the nearest stop to ensure they did not miss it. When they had boarded the vehicle, the customary ten pence fare was thrown down on to the small tray by each youth. The driver played the established game, he asked no destination questions and issued no tickets, he knew that if an inspector got onto his bus, the dirty, dishevelled youths would be his problem. A glance at their grimy faces, sullen expressions and filthy bloodied hands, convinced the driver that any challenge would not be worth the risk. None of the three Crown Skins spoke a single word during their journey to the city centre but instead blankly stared directly ahead of them, as if a backward glance would bring the insane, sectarian spectres after them.

◇◇◇

One hour and a couple of hundred years later the youths were sitting in the comparative comfort of the States Bar, clutching their pints of Newcastle Brown and casually studying the early evening trade for potential entertainment. Despite having each previously devoured full plates of the finest greasy fare, that the Punch and Judy Cafe, at the corner of Lime Street and Skelhorne Street could provide, with Blue taking full advantage of his below street-level window seat to observe unwary female passers-by, they all felt the need for copious amounts of salted snacks to complement their drinking. Whilst refreshing themselves and waiting for the 'show' to begin, each was locked in his own thoughts, until Jay Mac broke the uneasy silence.

"That's the place for me, I've got to get out of this shit-hole and start living" he announced while studying the stock poster images of New York's iconic buildings, juxtaposed with the faded photographs of local boxing legends, whose prime had long passed.

"What, yer gonna become a boxer?" Irish asked sarcastically.

"No smart arse, I'm talkin' about the States" Jay Mac replied sharply, "Y'can be whatever yer wanna be there, it's up to you. Not only that thee've got space, lots of fuckin' space."

"Yer make it sound like the 'Promised Land'." Irish responded. "Why don't yer get the fuck over there, if y'like it that much?"

"I will do mate. Give us the fuckin' cash and I am gone!" Jay Mac replied in an angry tone.

Blue felt the tense atmosphere required a change of direction and, returning from the jukebox after making his selection and from the bar with another armful of salted snacks, he suddenly asked "What do yer think they were goin' to do to me?" He was clearly still shaken by the incident.

"You dont wanna know Blue." Irish advised. "It would have involved yer 'Jap's eye' and two matches, let's leave it at that."

"Yeah it would've been the end of Blue, the 'Bird Bandit'." Jay Mac added.

"I tell y'what, I'm gonna get one of them Crucifixes and an L.O.L ring, then I'll be safe." Blue announced naively.

"Y'might as well get a Star of David while y'there. Y'don't really think it was about religion do yer, fightin' over two hundred yards of shite? It's just another game to them, like the one we play on the estate, it doesn't really matter who yer are, if y'not one of *them* you're the enemy. Thee don't really know how the trouble began but even if any of them did thee couldn't care less." Jay Mac concluded.

"Hooray for Jay Mac, president of the United Nations!" said Irish sarcastically. "Now, more importantly, it's your round Mr President."

Jay Mac ignored Irish for the moment then, as Frank Sinatra's *My Kind of Town* sprang into play on the jukebox, he stood up from his seat to go to the bar.

"One thing's for certain, I am never goin' anywhere near that fuckin' part of town ever again." Blue stated emphatically.

Jay Mac turned and said "Yer jokin' aren't yer Blue? I'm expectin' you to help me pick up me gear from me mum's tomorrow." He strolled over to the bar with a wicked grin on his face.

Chapter 2

Mamma Weer All Crazee Now

Friday 19th January 1973

The bitterly cold though sunny, brief daylight hours of Friday 19th January, had slipped away to be replaced with a clear frosty evening by the time Jay Mac arrived at his temporary lodgings ready for his 'tea'. For the past five days he had been enjoying the considerable hospitality of his friend and Crown Skins team mate Blue, or rather the comfortable surroundings of his parents' house and in particular the home cooking of his mother. Ever the realist, he knew full well that this pleasant hiatus could not last and that his host's warm welcome was wearing thin.

Even as Jay Mac sat at the kitchen table salivating and ready to eat whatever sumptuous fare was placed before him by the ever-smiling Mrs Boyd, whose short stumpy legs, corpulent figure topped with an equally fleshy red-cheeked face and whose culinary efforts were prepared and served by a pair of brawny arms and meaty hands, leading the youth to see her as the archetypal farmer's wife, a clear reminder of his imminent departure was also delivered.

"Well, hasn't that gone over John, your last night with us here already." Mrs Boyd said smiling pleasantly.

"Yes who would've thought a week could go so quick." Jay Mac replied with a broad grin.

"You must be missing your aunt and uncle and I'm sure they're missing you. So it will be nice for you all when you go back, wont it?" She paused for a moment then added, "We will be sorry to see you go of course."

"Thanks Mrs B, I mean, I suppose I could always stay for another week...." Jay Mac's tease was cut short as Mrs Boyd, whose cheery smile had momentarily frozen, quickly interjected.

"Yes, much better back with your aunt and uncle, much better for everyone. Now enjoy y'tea."

Two large plates overloaded with huge portions of steaming Irish stew, were placed before Jay Mac and Blue and instantly they were set upon by the two youths. Before retiring to the comfortably furnished living room, Mrs Boyd also set out a dozen slices of thickly buttered bread, two bottles of sauce both red and brown and the usual condiments held in novelty mini Blackpool Tower replicas. Standing on the stove nearby was a large dark brown, glazed teapot and part way through their ravenous assault upon their evening meals, Blue disengaged temporarily in order to breathe and pour out two mugs of scalding tea.

As he was adding the Channel Island's gold top milk to each brew, he turned to Jay Mac, "Hey I bet you're missin' that cat piss sterrie from yer Mum's aren't yer? Do y'want me to nip outside and see if I can milk the neighbour's cat?" He laughed at his own witty remark, though Jay Mac simply raised two fingers in victory salute and carried on with the serious business of ensuring no morsel was left unconsumed. Pausing finally for breath himself and casually wiping his plate clean of any last trace of gravy, with his fifth round of bread, he now felt able to speak.

"What's for afters mate?" he enquired greedily.

"There's two custard slices from Sayers over there in that cardboard cake-box if y'fancy one of them." Blue replied placing the mugs of tea onto the Formica-topped dining table.

"*If* I want one, fuckin' hell Blue is the Pope Catholic or what? Lash one over." Jay Mac said enthusiastically. "I might have them both if you're not quick; after all it is me last night 'ere"

It transpired that during the week Jay Mac's mother, on seeing that her son was no longer present, had decided he must have returned to his aunt and uncle's flat on the Kings Estate. She had found his belongings in the plastic bags where he had previously placed them and had been only too pleased to deposit them at her sister and brother-in-law's residence with the words, "Here's his stuff, tell 'im 'good riddance' when y'see 'im."

Jay Mac's aunt became distressed as she did not know his exact whereabouts and to add to this she had received a letter from the local police probation office, stating that a home visit had been arranged. Knowing that Mrs O'Hare, the mother of Irish, had a telephone, she contacted her via a neighbours' phone, to enquire about her nephew's current location.

A meeting was arranged the following evening between Jay Mac and his aunt and uncle, with the result that they finally agreed he could return to live with them, for the short term at least. This *rapprochement* of sorts presented his uncle with the opportunity to deliver a stern, earnest, ultimatum.

"You step out of line once, just once mind and your kit goes in the bin and yer out on the street for good. Is that fucking crystal clear?" Jay Mac had answered in the affirmative and as was customary with his uncle, he shook hands acknowledging formally a gentleman's binding agreement.

After finishing their evening meal both youths left the kitchen and went to the front room, where they set about the next vital task with equal gusto; polishing their cherry red Airwair to the highest standard. Whilst Jay Mac was sat on the old comfortable sofa with its new mustard coloured stretch-covers and Blue was sitting in a similarly protected aged armchair, they were listening to a selection of Motown tracks, either from the popular Chartbusters LP series or the individual artists' 45rpm singles hits. Just as *I Wish it Would Rain* by the Temptations, began to play on the turntable of the teak veneered stereogram, Jay Mac spoke.

"I hope it doesn't fuckin' rain, I've just about got these right. It's taken a week of polishing to sort them out, after scrambling through all that brick rubble with the Billy Boys chasin' us."

Blue didn't respond or even look in his friend's direction but carried on polishing his boots with increased vigour. A number of loose broadsheets from both the local *Liverpool Echo* and the national *News of the World* newspapers, where scattered across the heavily patterned rectangular carpet that extended over a sizeable part of the linoleum covered floor. Noticing that the entertainment page of the former was nearest to him, Jay Mac changed the uncomfortable subject.

"Lookin' forward to Sunday night Blue? That'll be a good one, don't y'think?" He was referring to an advertisement for forthcoming cinematic attractions which proudly declared, that the Liverpool premiere of the notorious Clockwork Orange film, would be taking place at the ABC Lime Street on that evening. Reputedly having narrowly escaped the national censors only to fall foul of some local home counties, blue rinse, public decency committees and currently being hyped as far as possible by the media's sensationalist reporting of alleged copycat crimes, box office success was guaranteed.

"Too right I am mate everyone will be there, all the crews and their birds." Blue said smiling in anticipation.

"Well I don't know about their birds but you're right about all the crews being there." Jay Mac partially concurred. "Y'never know yer might even get to meet yer old mates, the Billy Boys again." he added cruelly.

"Piss off arsehole." Blue replied before announcing that he was taking a bath.

◇◇◇

Half an hour later having collected Irish from his home, further along the same row of small council terraces where he and Blue lived, all three were entering through the gap in the low brick wall which surrounded the perimeter of the Eagle public house on two adjacent sides.

"Fuckin' hell Blue that's strong, is it that Brut stuff?" Irish asked, clearing his throat.

"Yeah mate, y'know the birds can't resist it. 'The great smell of Brut' never fails." he replied, smiling.

"You used to say that about Old Spice didn't yer? Anyway, yer supposed to splash it on, not take a fuckin' bath in it." Jay Mac observed.

"I hope this bird's worth it." Irish announced much to Jay Mac's surprise. During the entire time that he had been staying at Blue's, his friend had made no mention of a new love interest. He decided not to ask any questions for the moment, his immediate concern was what sort of reception he would receive from his assembled team mates.

Fortunately for Jay Mac on this occasion he was about to learn that the heightened anticipation of an event, often far exceeded the bland actuality of its realisation. The heaving lounge bar was almost at capacity and his arrival was barely noticed by his team mates, seated at the far end of the smoke-filled 'cauldron'.

After forcing their way through the tightly packed throng at the bar and being continually jostled, Blue was eventually served.

"Double up Blue, get another round in now it'll be like this all night. 'Ere y'are, here's some cash!" Jay Mac shouted above the ferocious din.

Gary Glitter's *Rock and Roll part 1 and 2* was currently playing on the jukebox but this was barely audible in the present circumstances.

Carefully threading their way through the maze of tables, each one surrounded by the maximum number of raucous drinkers, the three struggling companions, precariously balancing two pints of amber liquid each, finally reached the twelve-strong cohort of their Crown team mates.

"Bunch up lads, c'mon, we can squeeze in there if y'move up." Irish insisted, before Jay Mac, Blue and he wedged themselves into the centre of their crew, who were as usual fully occupying the semi-circular seating arrangement at that end of the lounge. Johno, the blond haired, immensely strong farm labourer was present on the trio's right alongside Terry (H) an old school friend of Jay Mac and Irish; the two diminutive boxing brothers, known respectively as Ant One and Ant Two were sat next to the now one-eyed Brian 'Brain' Dent and the permanently unemployed Joey 'Tank' Turner. Several members of the 'old guard', the absent Tommy (S)'s usual coterie, where positioned to the three new arrivals left.

"Yer back then?" Terry (H) observed casually.

"Not fuckin' dead after all" the somewhat slow witted Brain acknowledged.

"I don't think so Brain." Jay Mac replied, smiling.

"It's good to see yer mate." Johno said honestly. "Am glad the bizzies didn't kill yer." he added.

"I am meself, it would've ruined me evenin'." Jay Mac responded.

Some of the 'old guard' were a little more circumspect. Gaz, one of the eldest members of the team, rapidly approaching his twentieth birthday, wanted a little more specific information.

"How come the bizzies let *you* out? Yer see we heard that they was gonna charge you with Yad's murder, so what fuckin' happened there, like?" He stared at Jay Mac while he spoke, then looked away and took a drink of his pint.

Jay Mac was beginning to feel uncomfortable with the notion that he had to explain himself and replied "I don't know where yer 'heard' that, Gaz but whoever told yer was a fuckin' liar and I'll say that to their face, if y'point them out."

Gaz didn't say anything further and finished drinking his pint, then downed his whiskey chaser in one gulp. After a few moments when no one spoke, the group resumed their conversations as normal. Jay Mac noticed that even though he had been missing for only a few weeks, not only had the atmosphere changed within the team but also everyone's hair appeared to be considerably longer, making his present Suedehead style seem like a recently grown out crop.

Looking around the disparate group of young males, he realised that although they almost all still wore their old Crombies, denim jackets and Airwair boots, the original, core-unifying feature, their hair or rather their very specific choice of cut, a number one crop with razored trench, had disappeared entirely. That particular distinctive element of the Skinhead look was gone and except for random isolated outbreaks amongst a dwindling number of diehards, or archaic behind-the-times parochial teams, it would not be seen again in significant numbers for many years.

For the Crown Team one other vital ingredient was also missing; leadership. Their long absent, seriously injured courageous commander, Tommy (S), only recently discharged from hospital, was a pale shadow of his former self, requiring constant attention. The severe beating that he had taken for the sake of the team in their last major battle with their arch rivals, the Kings Team Skins, had left him almost dead and the Crown Team lifeless without direction.

Jay Mac, whose only other interest than his passion for Americana, particularly superhero comics, was military history, felt that in the microcosm of their circumscribed world, this present situation was analogous with dozens of historical examples, none more so than the rapid implosion of Alexander the Great's Empire that followed his death and his generals' divisive, individual bids for power. He himself had been forced reluctantly into the power vacuum, only to lead the Eagle crew into a futile skirmish with some renegade Kings Team Skins, which ended in multiple arrests on both sides.

After an hour or so spent drinking and swapping exaggerated tales of violent combat and equally vigorous sexual encounters, the atmosphere had become more relaxed and the lounge bar began to clear of some of the older 'retired' or 'semi-retired' ex-team members.

"Where are all these arl arses gettin' off to?" Jay Mac enquired as most of the twenty years plus aged drinkers departed with their female companions.

"The council runs an over twenty-one's disco for them every other Friday night now, over at Central Way Hall, so that's why it's more chocker than usual in 'ere tonight." Johno who was sitting on Jay Mac's immediate right, advised "Gives the arl ones a bit of a night out I suppose" he added.

A few moments later, with Blackfoot Sue's *Standing in the Road* playing on the jukebox, three new arrivals entered the lounge bar. Through the pale blue-grey cigarette smoke haze, the remaining Eagle crew members could see that sauntering towards their group, were three of their opposite numbers from the Heron Public House Team; Macca (G); Weaver and Crusher. The convivial atmosphere chilled a few degrees, as the trio stood directly before the table where Jay Mac was positioned with Irish and Blue.

Gaz put his pint down then leaned across to Jay Mac.

"Y'know you were sayin' y'would tell someone to their face that they were 'fuckin liars', well now's y'chance. It was Weaver who told us all about you grassing to the bizzies to save y'self."

Jay Mac's blood ran cold and the colour drained from his face while his stomach churned realising what he had said in his anger, as he stared up at the menacing figure of the crazed hammer-wielding psychopath.

"Got somethin' to say Jay Mac, 'ave yer?" Weaver asked with a sneer through his almost lipless mouth, all the while fixing his small steel grey, triangular shaped eyes upon the clearly nervous youth.

"What I said was, Weaver..." Jay Mac began, trying to regain his composure "that whoever said the law was gonna do me for Yad's murder was lyin'."

Macca (G) the cruel sexual sadist and co-leader of the Heron Crew also smiled, adding his comments.

"That's not good Weaver mate, sounds like some cunt's callin' you a liar, y'cant be havin' that."

Weaver stared directly into Jay Mac's pale face, trying to make eye contact.

"Is that right lad, are you callin' me a fuckin' liar?"

"Listen Weaver, no one's tryin' to disrespect yer but that is a pile of fuckin' lies. I dont know where yer got it from but it's not true, right?" Jay Mac was trying his best to answer calmly and to couch his words carefully, when unexpectedly Weaver offered him a glimmer of hope.

"Y'see Jay Mac, I was pulled in that night as well an while I was gettin' done over by the pigs, *they* fuckin' told me they had you banged to rights. Y'know what else, thee said you was signin' all kinds of fuckin' statements to save y'self."

Jay Mac felt his time was up and he had nothing to lose as he stated "Well y'right, I did sign a statement, after thee threatened to work me aunt and uncle over and trash their place. I signed a confession that I was the only person who was fightin' with Yad before he died and that was *all* I fuckin' said, alright?"

Weaver seemed momentarily phased by Jay Mac's vehement response and before he could say anything further the youth continued.

"...and just for the fuckin' record, those three little shitbags from your crew Nat, Pezza and Tommo, had all grassed me up and tried to say it was me who actually stabbed Yad to death. The bizzies even showed me their fuckin' signed statements."

Again Weaver appeared uncertain of what action to take.

Terry (H) a formidable scrapper in his own right, suddenly interrupted, "Leave it now Weaver. Jay Mac's given yer his answer, and I know he's talkin' straight."

A number of the old guard, including Gaz also added their similar judgement.

Weaver appeared resolute, unmoved "Stand up, we'll take it outside. I'm not havin' you talk to me like that." he ordered.

In the microseconds before Jay Mac rose to his feet, his brain desperately scrambled for a strategy that he could employ, to at least survive his imminent brawl with Weaver. Instead all his memory would provide were stark images of blood soaked victims that the crazed psychopath had previously dispatched with his famed toffee hammer, or permanently scarred with the glistening Stanley knife he weaved with lightning fast dexterity.

"I don't wanna fight yer, Weaver." he heard himself say now standing facing the glaring mad man. "But it doesn't look like I've got much choice, so come 'ed, outside." then he stepped round from his side of the table. Medicine Head's *Pictures in the Sky* had replaced Blackfoot Sue on the jukebox but no one was listening.

"'Ave 'im Weaver, fuckin' hurt 'im." Macca (G) urged smiling slyly. Others, however, more sympathetic also added to Terry (H) and the old guards' plea for leniency.

With the two potential protagonists standing toe-to-toe, Weaver struck without further warning. He gave Jay Mac a sharp, stinging slap with his cupped right hand and a rare smile cracked his grim visage.

"Sit down y'mad cunt, forget it." he announced in an uncustomary magnanimous gesture.

Jay Mac's circulation instantly improved and the adrenalin began to vacate his veins. He smiled with a mixture of relief and disbelief, before resuming his seat with his team mates, who almost all laughed at the unexpected reprieve, all except for Irish who retained his usual dour expression.

"Fuckin' disappointin' but no 'ard feelin's Jay Mac, some other time, hopefully." said Macca (G) as he and the immeasurably strong, ever silent Crusher turned to walk towards the lounge exit, where Weaver was already standing.

"I'll be seein' yer Jay Mac." the crazed psychopath called back still smiling. Elvis Presley's *In the Ghetto* was now playing as the three Heron crew members left the building.

Once again after a brief moment while individuals gathered their thoughts, conversations resumed as if nothing had transpired. Sitting drinking his pint in silence, Jay Mac was the one soul who appeared removed from the hubbub around him, although he had been at the centre of a potentially dangerous challenge that would be the subject of serious debate for some time. Lost in his own reflections on what had occurred and how lucky he had been to escape unscathed, he was suddenly snapped back to the present by Blue.

"Fuckin' hell mate, I've gorra give yer credit there. You stood 'im off, the nutter backed right down."

"Blue do me a favour, shut the fuck up and never say that bollocks again, to anyone." Jay Mac snapped angrily. "Stood 'im off? He fuckin' let me off, for some reason. Who knows what goes on in his head?"

"That's right, he let yer off, for now, nothin' else." Irish added sceptically.

Placing his pint glass, which was almost empty, down onto the table, Jay Mac leaned across to his old school friend, Terry (H).

"Thanks mate, I won't forget that." he said.

"Fuck it, Weaver's a tit, someone's gonna bring him down, it won't be long now." Terry (H) replied calmly.

For the second time Blue made an uncharacteristic gesture, where his motive was not entirely self-gratification.

"Listen, I'm gettin' off now but ...er... if y'fancy it, y'can come with me, an you as well Irish" he said without giving too much information.

Intrigued and not wishing to remain in his present surroundings, Jay Mac replied "Alright Mystery Man, I'm sure there must be some birds involved, so am up for it, what about you Irish?"

Irish had just lit another cigarette and still had some dregs of Double Diamond left in his glass, "Nah, I'd rather stay here, I've had enough excitement for one night."

A few minutes later Jay Mac and Blue were outside in the freezing night, heading in the direction of the eastern side of the Crown Estate.

"Where are we off to Blue? The only person I know that lives over 'ere is Floyd and he doesn't usually share his birds." Jay Mac enquired.

"What happened was, on New Year's Eve, me and Glynn went to a party at a house of one of Mary's mates..." Blue began his lengthy, convoluted explanation of how the unfortunate Mary, Glynn's girlfriend at that moment in time, had naively introduced him to one of her more attractive and flirtatious school friends. Glynn, who never required much encouragement, other than the lightest massage of his ego, was instantly enamoured with the result that by the first stroke of midnight, Mary's New Year replacement was firmly ensconced and firmly entwined in a passionate embrace with her now former boyfriend.

Blue finished his lengthy preamble then came to the principal objective of his tale.

"So y'see Jay Mac, this bird, who Glynn's definitely pokin' has got a couple of half decent mates, and I'm tryin' to get in there with one of them." He paused then added, "Maybe one of her mates might even fancy *you*, y'never know."

"Thanks Blue, I could do with a bit of relief, especially with all that shite in the Eagle before. Just as long as none of them look like that big beast Niamh, that Glynn tried to set me up with last year, the cunt." Jay Mac replied with a grin.

Finally they turned into a road that was bordered on one side by the old, uncultivated farmer's fields and was familiar to Jay Mac. He knew the ultra-cool Floyd, his former 'business associate', small-time thief and son of a long-serving policeman, lived near the top end of this very road, he also knew that they had 'borrowed' a number of items from the few cars, that the residents at this part of the estate owned.

"Here we are mate, just remember the one called Susan is mine," Blue warned only partly in jest, recalling how the previous object of his desire, Julie Quirk, had preferred Jay Mac's charms to his.

Blue rang the doorbell of a neatly painted, small mid-terrace house that had a similarly well presented, tiny patch of grass to the front. Standing proudly on this mini lawn, on either side of the deep blue gloss front door where two painted white wagon wheels. Jay Mac began to feel a little uneasy on observing these items and was certain that he and Floyd had visited this distinctive property before.

"Classy, don't yer think?" he said to Blue.

"Don't fuckin' start Jay Mac; we're not even in yet." Blue replied.

The door was opened, not by their female hostess but by their former team mate, Glynn, who Jay Mac was pleased to note looked fully recovered from the near fatal beating, he had received at the hands of the vicious, late Heron co-leader, Yad.

"What the fuck is *he* doin' with yer?" a startled Glynn demanded. "Yer know Lorraine doesn't want any trouble".

"Nice to see you too Glynn," Jay Mac responded. "It's just with me birthday comin' up in a couple of weeks, Blue asked me if I wanted to come round and see if there was any birds I wanted to knob. Is that ok?"

"Y'can come in but don't fuckin' start anything, these are all decent birds." Glynn answered reluctantly, before leading them into the front room, which in this particular house had unusually been 'knocked through' to the rear.

"Very nice" said Jay Mac, "it reminds me of me mum's place, what d'you think Blue?"

His team mate did not respond, having already spotted his new love interest standing with three other girls by the large teak veneered stereogram, against the far wall in this extended lounge. Jay Mac stood with Blue just inside the doorway, as if waiting to be formally received by the hostess. The former was scrutinising the room and its contents, in much the same way that Blue had done at his mother's prefabricated box residence.

Signs of relative prosperity were visible all around, including the largest television the boys had ever seen, which bore the logo *Colourvision* on its teak veneered cabinet. Two lava lamps both displaying an undulating range of colours and a huge illuminated tropical fish tank, supplemented the selection of lamps that lit the extended room. There were black leather couches at each end, with additional seating in the form of matching swivel armchairs. Jay Mac noted that even the random patterned carpet that covered most of the floor space in each living area, felt deep and plush. Just as he was completing his inspection and studying the two ubiquitous framed prints of a pale blue faced oriental crying girl and a Spanish senorita revealing more enticing olive shoulder than modesty should allow, he heard Glynn telling Lorraine and her friends who he and Blue were.

"So I know you've met Blue before and this is Jay Mac, he's another friend of mine." He paused before quickly adding "but I don't see much of him now."

Jay Mac finally disinterestedly looked in the direction of the females, knowing they had been friends of the deadly serious Mary and having been set up with the heavyweight Niamh previously, he was expecting the worst. On this occasion, his fears were soon dissipated. Standing in front of him, in line were four smiling females with pretty faces and attractive figures, instantly his full attention was restored. When they responded to Glynn's introduction of him and Blue in unison with "We all know who Jay Mac is." his libido went on full alert.

Blue had said Susan was his intended target and told Jay Mac that she had dark hair, the only problem was, of the four girls facing him one was blonde and the other three were varying shades of brunette. Fortunately when their names were reeled off by Glynn as Lorraine; Karen; Colette and Susan, Jay Mac noticed the latter's other more memorable feature, she had by far the largest breasts of all four, he knew he would easily be able to remember her.

These girls were dressed unlike the regulars at the Wednesday disco, whose mini dresses and hot pants literally left nothing to the imagination. They wore smart satin blouses, knee length checked or patterned skirts, their make-up, although heavy was not plastered onto their faces but just sufficient to cover teenage blemishes and reveal their natural beauty. What struck Jay Mac most was their footwear. Three wore platform shoes of considerable height and the fourth wore similarly elevated knee-length pink suede boots. This gave them all the appearance of being taller than they actually were.

"I'll get some drinks, what would you like boys?" asked a smiling Lorraine, suggesting a wide variety of wine, beers and spirits were on offer. As their choice was in fact limited to beer, wine or sherry, all four opted for the former. Lorraine disappeared with her giggling friends into the adjoining kitchen.

Jay Mac looked at Blue then at Glynn and began shaking his head, "What's all this then, you two and four birds? I know what's goin' on here, nudge, nudge, wink, wink. I've just been readin' about this in the News of the World when I was polishin' me boots;

it's one of them fuckin' orgies isn't it?" He paused for a moment before summing up the situation. "Oh eye, and what am I 'ere for, just to watch, and then next thing am gettin' dragged in and I don't know whose Arthur or Martha, is that what yer plannin' – yer kinky bastards."

"Piss off Jay Mac, I told yer these were decent birds. I've only had a couple of good feels off Lorraine so far, I'm goin' fuckin' nuts and me balls are burstin', so behave will yer?" Glynn replied.

Before he could provide any further details, Lorraine reappeared with their drinks and some salted snacks in brightly coloured plastic bowls on a tray of the same material.

"I don't know where they've got to" she said cryptically then joined her friends who were stacking records onto the turntable. *Hot Love* by T-Rex was the first selection and as the obliging Lorraine turned up the volume sufficiently to annoy the neighbours, the boys and girls began to relax.

Within half an hour, while the beer and wine flowed freely, three couples had formed. Glynn and the hostess Lorraine were already an established item. Blue, after exhausting all of his clichéd pick up techniques, appeared to be having some degree of success by resorting to pleading. Unfortunately, artificially aided by her platform shoes, Susan was considerably taller than his five foot eight stature, which put him at a pleasurable but disingenuous looking vantage point, level with her considerable bosom. Sitting very comfortably in one of the leather swivel chairs, was a contented if surprised Jay Mac, with Karen and Colette perched on each arm rest. The notoriety which had preceded his unexpected arrival had raised several notches when Blue chose to reveal with advantages, as an ice-breaker, the events that had occurred earlier in the Eagle.

"You should've been there, it was dead quiet, no one moved, then Jay Mac walked up to Weaver and said 'Fuck you'," he paused letting the anticipation build. "Then Weaver said 'No hard feelings mate', and totally backed down."

Jay Mac was livid and strenuously denied what Blue had said but that was only perceived as false modesty, somehow adding to his allure.

Now Karen and Colette seemed to be vying for his attention. Unfortunately in the perverse way that nature sometimes operates, Jay Mac's gaze kept wandering to the curved, nubile form of Blue's intended paramour, Susan. She in turn had to cover her mouth with her hand several times to avoid Blue noticing her yawns of boredom, on each occasion her eyes darted furtively to where the intriguing rebel was seated. Sadly for Blue it appeared lightning was about to strike twice in the same place.

"I'll have to nip up to the gents, Sue, me guts are killin' me. Sorry about that, I might be there for some time. I must have had a dodgy pint or somethin', if yer know what I mean." Blue announced apologetically.

"Take as long as you need, don't worry. By the way my name's Susan not Sue," she replied smiling insincerely.

Even as Blue ascended the first couple of steps, Susan swept over to where Jay Mac was being entertained by Colette and Karen "alright girls let Jay Mac have some air" she said in half jest but firmly enough for them to stand up.

"I'm fine thanks, no need to worry about me." Jay May advised

"Lorraine's just making some sandwiches, I think she would appreciate a little help." this time she employed her sixth form school prefect tone and both girls complied, although Karen, the wearer of the knee-length, pink suede platform boots tarried long enough to lean over Jay Mac and kiss him lightly on the cheek.

"Won't be long, don't go anywhere", she said with a pleasant smile on her pretty face.

"Is this seat taken?" Susan enquired.

"D'you want me to stand up, 'cause I don't think I actually can." he replied honestly.

Without any further warning Susan hitched up her knee-length skirt and promptly sat on Jay Mac's lap.

"My, you have been enjoying talking to Karen and Colette haven't you?" she said smiling.

"You should see me when I'm excited. Is there something you can help me with, or is this just your way of saying hello?" he said placing his right hand on her right knee. She made no response, gave no sign of objection; emboldened he pressed on.

"I've got to say, that's some leg!" As he spoke he slid his hand part way along her smooth warm thigh.

She was wearing sheer dark tights and shiny black platform shoes, which accentuated the shape and extended the length of her already long legs.

"I've got two actually, they go all the way up to my ..." she broke off leaned forward, affording him a generous view of her deep cleavage, as her well rounded breasts strained against the remaining unopened buttons of her revealing, satin blouse. Their mouths met simultaneously and locked together in a lingering passionate kiss. Jay Mac surprised and elated, felt her tongue in his mouth and immediately slid his hand to the top of her soft round thigh to where he could feel her flimsy panties over her tights. Instantly Susan broke away, recoiled and caught his probing hand by the wrist with her left hand.

"That's as far as you're going Jay Mac, for now." she smiled coquettishly then stood up straightening her skirt as she did.

"Is that what yer wanna be when y'grow up, some kind of prick teaser?" a frustrated Jay Mac asked, wisely remaining seated for the moment.

"Think what y'like ..." As Susan gave her reply, Blue having temporarily relieved himself, was making his way down the stairs.

David Cassidy's *How Can I be Sure* was playing on the record turntable.

"Y'not bad looking Jay Mac, now if you had hair like David Cassidy, it might be another story." Susan teased, stepping away from the exasperated youth.

"Fuck, I'm definitely growin' me hair now. Would a wig be any use in the meantime?" he laughed, then the door opened and Blue stepped in.

"Who needs a wig?" he asked naively.

"Jay Mac's just thinking of how he could improve his looks" Susan answered smiling sweetly.

"Right, am feelin' a lot better now I can tell yer, I needed that. I wouldn't go up there for a bit though," Blue warned.

Glynn who had not left the room during the entire time Jay Mac was enjoying Susan's company, stared at his gullible former team mate in dismay as he stood in front of Jay Mac, totally unaware that anything was amiss.

Lorraine and her two kitchen assistants had just returned with another selection of snacks, including that exotic classic cheese and pineapple on cocktail sticks, when the doorbell rang.

With Blue being the nearest to the front door he obliged by offering to open it.

"Thanks Blue, it'll be the boys, I hope." their hostess announced without any further explanation.

"Watch out stumpy, there's hot birds waiting for us in there!" Blue was roughly pushed aside and suddenly four large stocky males burst into the room.

"Who the fuck is this?" asked Glynn momentarily lapsing back into his old character.

"It's alright this is Keith and Tristram, we met them at a Sixth form conference, I told you they were coming but I don't know the other two boys." Lorraine advised, looking to the lead male Keith, for some explanation.

"Oh yes, cripes, should've said really Lorrie. This is Reggie and Neil, bloody good guys in a scrum. Thought they could come along for any spare totty, not a problem is it?"

Jay Mac still seated, was studying the new arrivals, as he always did in these situations. Keith and his three companions were of a similar height and build, reminding him of the 1690's leader W.G. McGrath. All four had collar length mops of hair of no distinct style. They were also uniformly dressed in black blazers with a decorative badge and accompanying motto on the breast pocket; dark grey flared trousers and black platform shoes. Apart from the large 'kipper' ties of different hues and random patterns, which hung at half-mast from their deep collared, open-necked, brightly coloured shirts, their generally similar appearance hinted they were members of a particular club, or school. There was a strong smell of alcohol and tobacco all about them and their demeanour suggested they had been drinking heavily before their arrival. To someone like Jay Mac who spent his first nine years living with an alcoholic, the signs were unmistakable and he took this factor into account as he considered how best to deal with them, when the inevitable trouble erupted.

"Right, first things first, where's the booze?" a smiling Keith demanded.

When Lorraine led him into the kitchen to show him the available alcohol, he was not impressed. "Not to worry boys and girls we've brought some extra supplies. Reggie, catch!" he shouted, throwing a set of keys to his friend. "Get the goods my man before we die of thirst."

The four new arrivals had travelled to the Crown Estate from the more affluent leafy suburbs several miles from the city, by car which Keith had borrowed from his father for the evening.

"We had a hell of a job finding this place. All these bloody little houses look the same. Don't know how you tell one from the other." Keith announced as Reggie returned with the essential refreshments.

Neil had made his way to the stereogram and was examining the pile of records laid out on its wooden veneered top, his eyes lit upon the David Cassidy album cover that happened to be most prominent.

"What's all this then? Is this the sort of music you boys like?" he shouted in derision.

"What's the matter lad, is the Osmond's more your thing?" Jay Mac casually called back from where he was sitting.

Reggie, who was nearest to him, leaned over and belched loudly into his face. "Are you a little funny man, are you?" he asked wiping his mouth with the back of his hand, before taking another swig of the frothy bottle of ale Tristram had thrown to him.

"There's only four fuckin' clowns round 'ere and I'm talkin' to one of them now." Jay Mac replied staring up at the overbearing Reggie.

In an instant he was dragged to his feet and face to face with the furious drinker.

Lorraine screamed "Please no trouble, not in here, please!"

Keith also added his judgement "Come on Reggie put him down, you don't want to get blood on your best togs do you?" he laughed as he spoke then continued, "Let's have a dance ladies. There's four of us and four of you, so you don't need to worry, no one will be left out".

Karen, Colette and Susan quickly transferred their affections to the new arrivals, with Tristram grabbing hold of Susan for himself.

"Susan isn't it? I remember you from the conference. You're the kind of girl it's difficult for a bloke to forget, with those great big ... eyes."

Susan giggled moving in close to her prospective dance partner, as her two friends happily took to the floor with their new beaus also.

Al Green's *Let's Stay Together* was playing on the turntable and the three couples began a slow, stimulating dance. Jay Mac looked across at Blue, watching for his response when Tristram placed a large, sweaty hand on Susan's curved bottom and began squeezing it firmly. He had been looking in the wrong direction as over in the corner nearest the front window, Keith made his move towards Lorraine.

"Sorry Keith, I'm with Glynn, he's my boyfriend. I invited you and Tristram to meet my friends." she said loyally.

"Oh come on Lorraine, don't be a tease, 'Glynnis' doesn't mind do you?" With that he pulled the pretty blonde towards him.

Glynn exploded in a paroxysm of rage.

"Take your fuckin' hands of her, you cunt!" he demanded, reverting fully to his former Crown Skins type.

As he stepped forward to free the struggling Lorraine from the encircling arms of the leering Keith, the latter placed his heavy right hand over Glynn's face and pushed him backwards, causing him to stumble and fall onto the floor.

"Sit down you little oik, these girls want real men, not boys!"

Jay Mac leapt forward forgetting his natural cowardice and put a headlock on Keith, dragging him away from Lorraine and the downed Glynn.

"Fucking leave him yer cunt, he's not up for it!" he shouted thinking of his friend's long period of convalescence, after the severe beating he had suffered some months earlier.

At that same moment Blue's fury overrode his usual caution.

"Get off her, that's my fuckin' bird!" he shouted enraged.

Tristram, engrossed in his groping of the curvaceous Susan, who was becoming increasingly frightened, looked at Blue and laughed.

"Oh piss off, you sad little fat boy."

Before Blue could make any response, Reggie released his dance partner and grappled him around the waist. Keith, who was far too strong for Jay Mac, stood up fully with the strangling youth on his back and slammed him hard into the wall behind them, causing the Crown Skin to release his grip. Neil joined in the 'fun' catching hold of Jay Mac, pinning his arms behind him and leaving him an open target for Keith's thumping straight right, which smashed into his face like a flesh covered house brick.

The girls were all now screaming and Susan was pleading for rescue.

"Blue, please, I don't want to go out with you but please help, get him off me."

Tristram laughed loudly, "Be quiet you slut, don't advertise the goods then say they're not for sale." He withdrew his right hand from between Susan's thighs where he had tightly clamped it and placed it on her breasts, before pushing her violently backward onto the nearby black leather settee.

"Sit down and wait there. I'll give you a good rogering in a minute." then he strode over to where a wildly struggling Blue was being carried around at shoulder height by a very amused Reggie.

"Hold him still Reggie." Tristram ordered delivering a sickening right hook to Blue's groin."

"Lovely shot, Trist! Right in the family jewels." Reggie said as he released the agonised youth, dropping him to the floor where he collapsed like a crumpled sack of meat.

"How's this for a conversion?" Tristram asked, stepping back before booting the kneeling Blue viciously in the face.

Jay Mac was struggling to break free from Neil's vice-like grip and threw his head backwards to strike his captor hard in the face. It was a futile gesture; too many collapsed scrums and hard tackles had left him with a badly broken nose and a blossoming cauliflower ear.

"That's not very nice is it?" asked Keith who proceeded to punch Jay Mac in the face twice more, splitting his lip and opening his old nasal injury.

A shaken Glynn was trying to rise from the floor, looking desperately for any item to use as a weapon. Keith turned his attention towards him, slapping him hard across the face with his right hand.

"Sit down on the floor like a good little boy, or else." he warned, waving a raised index finger in front of his face.

"Stay down Glynn, don't give this bum-boy an excuse for another sly dig." Two straight punches to Jay Mac's stomach, first a right then a left marked Keith's return to his original victim.

"This is becoming a bore and the totty's waiting for us. Let's show them the door." Tristram announced with a wicked grin.

"Get out of this house now or I'm going to call the police," a terrified Lorraine screamed,

"You're not calling anyone and we're not going anywhere missy, not until we get what we came for. You don't think we drove all the way to this bloody awful place for a dance and a quick feel do you?" Keith warned ominously.

A ferocious struggle then ensued with Jay Mac being dragged toward the front door by Keith and Neil, closely followed by Blue who was being carried by his arms and legs by Tristram and Reggie. Glynn tried his best to intervene and block the open doorway but was quickly forced to one side, becoming the first of the three Crown Skins to be ejected. He was swiftly followed by his two companions, who were thrown unceremoniously onto the strip of lawn outside, landing awkwardly next to each other.

"Now don't try to come back, or we'll *really* hurt you. Oh, and don't worry about the girlies, we're going to give them a good seeing to." Keith shouted laughing, then slammed the door shut.

As soon as they had all regained their feet, a distraught Glynn's initial response was to try to kick in the front door. The music had been turned up but even above the sounds of Little Eva's *The Loco-Motion*, they could all still hear the girls' terrified screams.

"Fuck this." said Jay Mac "Glynn stop kicking that door, we don't want anyone calling the bizzies, not yet". He paused for breath then continued "Y'know what thee say? If the odds are against yer change the fuckin' odds. Blue, make sure he doesn't do anythin' stupid, I'll be back as quick as I can, right?"

Within minutes of leaving his frustrated team mates, Jay Mac acknowledged as one of the fastest runners of the Crown crew, had arrived in the doorway of their customary watering hole, The Eagle public house. Bursting into the lounge bar, his bloodied face said as much as his urgent entreaty.

"Anyone fancy givin' four snotty bastards a good kickin'? Cos I know where yer can find some." No further explanation was needed and moments later a thirteen strong rescue party, including Jay Mac in the van with Terry (H) and Irish, were racing towards the eastern side of the estate for a grudge match with Keith and his pals.

On arrival Terry (H) assumed command. Though not yet considered as a serious replacement for his close friend their usual commander, the critically injured Tommy (S), the whole crew acknowledged his awesome fighting prowess. He had been trained from an early age by his own father, a tough, hard-labouring docker, who supplemented a basic daily wage with his winnings from brutal, unlicensed boxing bouts that he regularly engaged in. Losing was never contemplated, to win by any means was all that mattered, rules were for those battered failures who lay bleeding in their own shame.

Keith, Tristram, Reggie and Neil, proud members of the all-conquering first fifteen, were facing a different team tonight; no referee would call foul here. All the rescue squad were loaded with their usual glass ale bottle 'ammunition' stuffed into every possible pocket and carried in their hands.

"Everyone, line up ready on the road." Terry (H) shouted, then turning to Johno the Eagle crew's strongman. "Put that fucking door in Johno, then get back over 'ere."

The blond haired, immensely strong farm labourer charged up to his target and with one powerful kick took the well painted, blue gloss front door nearly off its hinges. Standing in the centre of the assembled crew, Terry (H) issued his challenge.

"Come out you bags of shit, if you've got any fuckin' balls. Don't have us come in and drag yer out like a bunch of queers."

Other than the sound of The Animal's *House of the Rising Sun* blaring out from the fully open front doorway, there was no immediate response; then Keith and his friends emerged casually fastening their trousers and tucking in their shirts. They stood still next to each other on the mini lawn, a couple of feet in front of the small mid-terraced house.

"C'mon then you dirty little toe-rags." Keith challenged in return. "You're four best tough's against us how's that, sound fair?"

A cold tense silence spanned the distance between 'Crown Skins' and 'Rugby Chums', before a new record from the stack began to play from within, then a harsh laughter erupted spontaneously throughout the ranks of the former.

"Let them have some." Terry (H) said, smiling. "And when they're down, that cunt's mine, right?"

A withering hail of glass projectiles was immediately launched and poured onto the four game public schoolboys, striking them mainly on the head, shoulders and upper body, or shattering against the wall of the house immediately behind them. Some bottles landed on the thin strip of turf and did not break. Unwisely Tristram and Reggie bent down to retrieve these, only to be hit in the face by a second wave of similar missiles. Like the over confident mounted French aristocracy at Agincourt, these arrogant, well-born youths were quickly cut down by the contemporaries of the villein archers that had also been held in disdain.

Reduced to four kneeling, bleeding targets, the players were about to receive their reward for tonight's performance. The rescue party, supplemented by the furious Glynn and Blue, swarmed around them kicking and punching with painful accuracy, like a multi-limbed mechanical monster. All four tried to rise to their feet at different moments and to throw wild punches but they were quickly overpowered with their flailing arms ensnared.

Jay Mac and the revived Glynn identified Keith and reached him first, despite Terry (H)'s orders, whilst Blue allowed Irish to assist him in delivering appropriate retribution to Tristram. Even as they were savagely kicking the faces and torsos of their chosen victims, they witnessed their temporary leader fully occupied, enjoying brutally stamping on the already blood-drenched face of Reggie, while he lay on his back moaning trying to mouth a plea for mercy. Neil somehow managed to struggle to his feet and staggered forward a short distance, while Tank and four other members of the team stepped back to watch in amusement.

"Please, I just want to go home," he managed to say before Tank jumped forward and delivered a devastating head-butt directly onto the bridge of his already broken nose, the shock of which caused him to stumble and fall to his knees with blood pouring from the wound. All five youths surrounded him at once punching and kicking him from every possible angle.

When Jay Mac and Glynn stepped back to catch their breath and admire their 'work' the bloodied wreck that was Keith, tried to crawl away on his hands and knees, even though his vision was almost totally obscured by his matted blood and sweat-soaked hair. He fumbled for something in his pocket while the youths watched curiously; then he produced a set of keys.

"My dad's car, my dad's car." he repeated over and over progressing a few inches in no specific direction.

Jay Mac looked at Glynn with a broad smile; neither of them had even considered the vehicle, which was badly parked at an awkward angle, partly on the kerb outside the next-door neighbour's residence.

"A nice little bonus there mate." Jay Mac said looking at the pale blue Ford Anglia.

"Irish, d'you fancy doin' a bit of drivin' mate?" he shouted to his friend, who together with Blue had seated Tristram against the front of the house and was taking turns booting the latter in the face, body and groin.

"What a fuckin' great night, four Hooray Henrys to give a kickin' and a free car." he called back to Jay Mac.

Irish was in his element, always considering himself a member of an oppressed underclass, a proletariat warrior ready to rid the world of privilege but without actually doing anything about it, this was the nearest he had gotten to fulfilling his ambition.

"Hello Keith, can you hear me?" Jay Mac began, studying the crawling heap, "Thanks for the car, we'll bring it back later, tell daddy thanks from me." With that he delivered a bone-cracking boot to the left side of Keith's face fracturing his jaw and eye-socket then he bent down and took the bloody keys out of the still twitching hand of the unconscious prop forward.

Amidst the feral frenzy of the packs' wild attack, no one had noticed that the four girl victims of the upper sixth rugby stars had emerged from the house. The music had stopped abruptly and almost as suddenly, so did the beating; the whole crew turned their gaze towards the quietly weeping females with their torn clothing and badly laddered tights.

"Step back lads," Terry (H) ordered, "give the girls some room." Silently each broken figure walked to where her attacker lay and spat either in their face or on the back of their head.

Away in the distance the unmistakable sound of police sirens conveniently gave advance warning of their imminent arrival. In a last act of vengeance Glynn and Blue picked up the white painted wagon wheels and slammed them down onto Keith and Tristram.

"Get in the fuckin' car!" Jay Mac shouted to them both and they quickly turned and ran to the vehicle, joining him, Terry (H) and Irish, the getaway driver.

"Everyone fuck off home!" was the last command of the night from Terry (H) before they all disappeared from the scene.

◇◇◇

The police did arrive eventually, followed later by the ambulances they had sent for. Statements were taken first from the distraught girls and then when they had recovered consciousness, the unapologetic boys; the neighbours of course had heard and seen nothing.

According to all four girls they had met two of their attackers at a sixth form conference; they had never met the other two before that night. They agreed that they did invite Keith and Tristram to Lorraine's house for some drinks and to dance, nothing more. All four said matters had quickly got out of hand with the boys trying to ply them with additional drink, which they had brought, before attacking them. Some local boys, whom none of the girls knew, were passing by, heard their screams and tried to rescue them but it was already too late. They insisted they had no idea of the identities of the youths. The girls' parents were all very supportive, although Lorraine's mother and father were almost as equally annoyed about the damage to their home as to their daughter.

It was a very different matter for the four boys. Their parents expressed indignation, outrage, in fact it was a wonder that questions were not asked in the House. From their perspective four innocent, hard-working academics and naturally gifted sportsmen, with potentially highly lucrative brilliant careers ahead of them, had been enticed onto a disgusting, degenerate working-class housing estate by the guaranteed promise of sexual relations of four worldly-wise, very experienced common girls. Furthermore, even while their sons were being cruelly duped by these harlots, their actual boyfriends, with the aid of at least a dozen accomplices, were engaged in stealing one of the boys' father's prized motorcar. When their sons had bravely attempted to prevent this criminal act, they were set upon by the mob receiving a savage beating, though they acquitted themselves like gentlemen in the encounter. They considered that the girls' parents should think themselves fortunate, that their own children were not the subject of major criminal charges.

The boys' Headmaster, the Head of House and the Head of Games provided glowing testimonials; after all was it not just a case of high-spirited young fellows letting off steam and sewing a few wild oats? Nothing to make a stink about.

Jay Mac, Irish, Blue and Glynn doubted that if they had acted in like-manner, committed such a heinous cowardly act, the law and its representatives would have viewed their actions quite so benignly.

Several weeks later after extensive police searches, the burnt out shell of Keith's father's pride and joy, was found on the field of overgrown grass and weeds where the Crown Skins normally fought their rivals from the Kings Estate. After just a few hours of joy riding, the boys had become bored and finally crashed it through a gap in the railings previously made by another car thief and abandoned it fully ablaze to burn through the remainder of the night.

When he received the distressing news, Keith senior wept at the despoliation and for the loss of innocence of his previously immaculate vehicle.

Sunday 21st January 1973

"What's the name of that bloody film you're going to see tonight, John?" Jay Mac's uncle asked curiously whilst running a hot iron straight from the gas burner on top of the stove, over the youth's twenty-two inch parallel petrol blue trousers.

"*A Clockwork Orange*, I've already told yer half a dozen times." he shouted back, lazily fiddling with the control dial of the small transistor radio, trying to find the 'Radio One Chart Show'.

"What sort of name is that? It's not about fuckin' queers is it?" the ex-soldier, proud former member of the Royal Horse Artillery and now long-serving postman, asked raising a concerned eyebrow.

"Why would it be about fruits?" Jay Mac asked, unable to make the link that seemed glaringly apparent to his uncle.

"'Clockwork Orange', 'Nine-bob note', something that's not right, not natural, d'yer know what I mean?" he replied, believing that he was stating the obvious. Like most of his generation, he was notoriously homophobic.

"Hangin' is too good for them." was one of his favourite stock expressions. When the 1967 Sexual Offences Act decriminalised homosexual acts in private between two men, he announced, "That's it, I'm leavin' this fuckin' country, before they make it compulsory."

Jay Mac laughed and turned up the volume when he finally found his chosen station, *Nights in White Satin* by The Moody Blues had just been introduced by Alan Freeman, everyone's favourite disc jockey. Though he prefaced nearly every selection with "Hi pop pickers", thousands of youths never tired of hearing his rich smooth voice on a Sunday evening revealing the top 40 hits of the previous week.

"When that shite's finished I'm changin' channels. I've told yer before, I'll iron y'kecks but I'm not listenin' to that," his uncle said then took a long puff of his old briar pipe, making the tightly packed strands of Ogden's St. Bruno ready rubbed tobacco, glow red with a mellow, sweet, spicy smelling aroma.

Jay Mac was clearing some of the dinner plates from the table after he and his aunt and uncle had finished their evening meal of cold roast beef slices, with *Bisto* gravy, boiled potatoes, boiled carrots and the dreaded, overpowering boiled cabbage.

"Thank fuck for y'pipe smoke." he said smiling. "That cabbage stench could seriously damage everyone's lungs."

His uncle made no response but leaned over and turned the dial of the radio until he found something more to his taste. The melodic sounds of Ann Shelton singing *Arrivederci Darling* filled the small space of the tiny kitchen, mingling with the thick grey pipe smoke and the distinctive smell of a hot flat iron travelling firmly across fabric.

"Now *that's* a singer and a fine figure of a woman as well." his uncle announced, making his pipe erect itself at a forty-five degree angle as he spoke.

"Who's got a fine figure?" his impaired-hearing aunt shouted from the living room, her selective deafness somehow momentarily miraculously cured.

"Bloody hell woman, fix y'aid will yer." his uncle shouted back. "I said you're still a fine figure of a woman." Feeling that his quick response had sufficiently addressed his wife's query, he passed Jay Mac his freshly ironed trousers, with their razor sharp creases and began humming along with the 1955 hit ballad.

Jay Mac quickly completed his usual preparation ritual ensuring finally that his highly polished cherry-red Airwair were at their gleaming best. He was surprised at how easily he had slipped back into his old established routine and how, for the moment, his aunt and uncle appeared to be almost pleased to see him, perhaps he thought, they preferred to focus their simmering frustrations onto his shortcomings and avoid the 'elephant in the room' of their loveless relationship. Either way, after several weeks 'enjoying' his mother's non-existent maternal care and hospitality, searching for food, some clean bedding, or even a clean plate or cup, he was equally pleased to be back in his frugal yet comfortable surroundings.

As he was checking his appearance in the 1920s Art Deco 'Sunrise' style mirror, with its distorting bevelled glass side panels, positioned above the fireplace, Jay Mac's uncle entered the room where his aunt was already sitting smoking one of her Embassy filter-tipped cigarettes, whilst re-reading a well-thumbed Agatha Christie murder mystery. Turning on the small rented black and white television in the corner by the window, in order to watch and sing along with *'Songs of Praise'*, he casually looked across at the youth and asked "When are you getting a haircut anyway? It's not like you to have a scruffy head, yer not becomin' a fuckin' hippy are yer?"

"As if! There are no hippies now anyway, we've hunted them all down." Jay Mac answered grinning. "Am growin' this for a bit so I can get it cut in a different style. The Skinhead Number One's had it."

His uncle re-lit his pipe and took a few puffs then sat down. "All this talkin' about hairstyles, it's a bit worryin'. A good short-back-and-sides is all yer need, nothin' else. Anyway, 'ere, take this". He passed the youth some loose cash without his usual furtiveness. "It's alright; she's got her aid turned off. Daft old bat, can't hear a thing." Pausing he puffed again on his old briar. "Don't forget; always stand y'round and no fuckin' trouble, alright?"

"Thanks, I'll probably stay over in Irish or Blue's, see yer." With that and a nod to the old mongrel dog, Patch, asleep on the faux fur rug in front of the two-bar electric fire, he departed from the first floor council flat.

"Who can't hear a thing?" his aunt asked without lifting her head. "I can hear you passing wind all the time and blaming the poor bloody dog."

Jay Mac quickly descended the two flights of stone stairs, unlocked the heavy wooden, sheet-metal faced door and stepped into the street outside. Walking across to the crumbling old, precast concrete slab bus shelter, with its dark glassless windows, he glanced to his right to see if any of his former enemies the Anvil Crew were about. As usual a small contingent of youths were gathered in and around the space beneath the two-storey tenements, next to the chip shop, some yards further along from where he lived with his aunt and uncle in their flat above the TV and Radio Store. Danny (H) the leader of this crew was present that freezing, clear evening and stood up on spotting Jay Mac.

"Alright Skin?" he called then sauntered across to talk to his once bitter rival.

"I 'erd yer was dead." he announced on joining the Crown team player, outside the dilapidated bus stop.

"Yeah? I've heard that a few times meself." Jay Mac replied. "The bizzies gripped me in the middle of our last scrap with Mono's crew, just before New Year's Eve. Thee slapped me around for a bit, then said thee were gonna come 'ere and do the same to me aunt and uncle and turn their place over."

"Fuckin' bizzies, they're all cunts." Danny (H) concluded. "Mono got pulled that night as well as a few of his crew but he's back out now and even more cracked."

While they were talking, exchanging news, each youth was studying the other. Both still wore denim jackets with Crombies over them and parallel trousers with the obligatory Airwair but neither had skinhead crops anymore, with Danny (H) now possessing the new 'feathered' haircut.

"I'd like to have seen that scrap with you an Yad, I heard it was a fuckin' good one. Pity the cunt's dead." the Anvil crew leader announced to Jay Mac's surprise.

"Why's that?" he asked.

"I always wanted to do him meself, y'know what I mean? I'd love to have gutted 'im but too late now. Y'never know I might get a chance to have that cunt Macca (G)." Danny (H) said, concluding his brief fantasy disclosure.

"I'll mention it to him next time I see him." Jay Mac said with a grin. "What about Weaver, d'yer fancy yer chances with him?"

The Anvil leader looked at Jay Mac incredulously, "Are yer mad? That is one crazy fucker, I'd rather have had a go at Macca (G) and Yad together than that nutter." He laughed at the very idea.

Jay Mac had noted a number of major new graffiti additions to the already crowded panels of the bus shelter; the largest depicted a huge chevron with a capital K in its centre and a capital B on either side, below which was the inscription 'Anvil Crew'.

"What's all this about Danny?" he asked curiously.

"Everyone's doin' it now, all the teams, I'm surprised your boys haven't got on to it yet." He paused then added, "it means Kings Boot Boys, no one's callin' themselves 'Skins' now, that's totally fuckin' played out."

Jay Mac recalled how his old primary school friend Mozzer, had referred to his crew as the J.F.K Boot Boys and that he had seen similar logos with J.F.K in the centre of the chevron on the walls of the tower blocks where they were gathered.

"Here's me bus, I'm off. A few of us are gettin' into town to see that Clockwork Orange film." Jay Mac advised on seeing a green Atlantean vehicle making its way down from the ridge, at the top of the road. "Aren't you boys goin' t'see it before some council twat bans it?"

"Nah, not tonight, we've got a bit of business with the Brow team." Danny (H) advised, moving away from the bus stop then shouting back finally to Jay Mac, who was about to board the vehicle, "Watch out in town lad, Mono is defo goin' with his whole crew and he fuckin' hates you."

The short journey from the huge, expansive Kings Estate to its much smaller rival the Crown, was uneventful and within a quarter of an hour Jay Mac had alighted from the bus at the old municipal depot and was walking along the western edge of the urban housing development. His usual route past Mal the Pig's house also brought him close to the residence of the Heron Crew's sadistic co-leader, Macca (G). On this freezing brilliant moonlit evening Jay Mac was surprised to see the tall, rangy, sinister youth standing in the open doorway of his parents' mid terrace. Unlike the majority of dull grey, utilitarian, indistinguishable properties, the exterior of Macca (G)'s home was painted in a bright, fresh magnolia hue and had a huge incongruous, carbuncle of a white-pillared portico extending across the front door and ground floor window. Suddenly he pulled the door shut behind him and walked forward to intercept Jay Mac.

"What d'you want?" Jay Mac asked angrily.

"Nothin' am waitin' for Weaver, he'll be 'ere in a minute, we're goin' into town with some of the Juniors, to see that Clockwork Orange film." he replied, smiling.

'Fucking great' Jay Mac thought, 'I'll have to warn the others, so we don't bump into them'. "Right! Thanks for the warnin', we'll probably give it a miss if you's are goin' tonight." he said openly.

Macca (G) laughed then said "I'm glad I've seen yer Jay Mac, there was somethin' I wanted to talk to yer about..."

"No thanks not interested." Jay Mac interrupted.

"Come on, let's be friends, what have I ever done to you?" Macca (G) asked disingenuously.

"Nothin' much unless y'count gang rapin' me mate's mum, then nearly beatin' him to death and kickin' the fuck out of me with Weaver, when I tried to stop it." he replied.

"Yeah but apart from all that, we're mates, we're on the same team. Anyway that business with Glynn's Ma, that was down to Yad, it was his idea and I've gorra say the old bird was well up for it. Look everyone knows you've got brains, y'not one of those thick fuckers, yer just like me, we've got it up top, y'know what I mean? We're a pair of sharp cunts, on the ball, yeah?"

Jay Mac gave his considered response, "Yer right, I'd say we're both pretty quick but that's it, I'm nothing like you. You're a sly cunt, I wouldn't trust yer as far as I could throw yer."

"Fair enough, that's clear but that doesn't change things. We should be runnin' this team. Times are changin' and there's gonna be money to be made, big money. Once you've got dough, you've got it all, smart gear, good booze and all the snatch you can manage."

Jay Mac had heard this speech before from his lugubrious one-time business associate, Floyd, less than six months earlier.

"What about yer best mate, that fuckin' psycho, Weaver?" Jay Mac asked.

"Don't worry about him, Weaver does what I say, I can handle him. He just needs to think he's the top dog and to be fed little rewards now and then." Macca (G) said with a sly smile.

Jay Mac made no response but turned away and walked on.

"It'll keep for now, I'll catch yer again." Macca (G) shouted after him.

After a brisk ten minute walk Jay Mac had collected Irish from his house and they were now standing outside Blue's residence further along the same street, waiting to be admitted.

"Come in lads, take a seat in the front room. I'll just give me boots another quick wipe." the ever chirpy Blue announced.

On entering the room, where they could hear The Supreme's *Automatically Sunshine* already playing on the stereogram, they were both surprised to find their former team mate Glynn waiting for them.

"Alright Glynn, what's goin' on 'ere?" Jay Mac asked smiling.

"Am comin' with yer t'the pictures, is that ok?" he asked rhetorically.

"Sure that's fantastic Glynn but how have yer got away? Has Lorraine let yer off the leash for a night?" Irish asked tactlessly.

"Lorraine who?" Glynn replied coldly. "I don't know any Lorraine."

"Yer know the fuckin' bird you've been tryin' to hang out of?" Irish continued, making matters worse.

"Oh her, yeah, that's all finished right, she's damaged goods." Glynn answered firmly.

Jay Mac looked at his friend and sensed he did not wish to say anything more on the matter.

"That's a bit harsh Glynn, nothin' that happened that night was *her* fault mate." he said intending to ease his team mates anguish but Glynn snapped "She fuckin' invited them to *her* house; she might as well have said 'do yer fancy a shag'? Right?"

Just then Mrs Boyd entered the room with a tray containing a pot of tea, four cups and a pyramid of Jacob's club biscuits. In part Blue's popularity and his 'physique' were due to his mother's part-time employment at the famed biscuit factory in Aintree.

"Here you are boys; I thought you might like a quick snack before you go to see this 'orange' film." She said quaintly. "Seems a queer thing t'me to make a film about, whoever heard of a clockwork orange? I don't know, young people today what are thee like?" After putting down the tray she left the room and all four youths smiled. While they were drinking their tea and eating their biscuits, Jay Mac told his friends about his conversations with both Danny (H) and Macca (G). When he had concluded his brief summary he added "So let's gerroff quick and hope we don't get on the same bus as 'psycho', or worse meet them in town."

Irish raised an eyebrow and took a drag on his first cigarette of the evening. "Why's that then? Are yer fuckin' scared that he won't let yer off next time y'see him?"

Jay Mac stared coolly at Irish, this was the second instance that he could recall his team mate making such a provocative remark and he was not pleased.

"I think you've said somethin' like this before haven't yer? Is there somethin' on yer mind; don't hold back, we can sort it out now, yeah?"

Both Blue and Glynn felt the tension as Irish and Jay Mac the two old school friends and Crown team mates stared intently without blinking at each other. Blue decided that he did not want his front room, or prized record collection destroyed.

"Right, so everyone's had enough tea and biscuits, let's gerroff. There's bound to be loads of birds in town tonight lookin' for a bit of action. Come 'ed."

All four youths stood up and departed, heading in the direction of the nearby bus stop.

After completing their forty-five minute journey to the city centre on a heaving, crowded bus, the four youths made their way along Lime Street past the Empire Theatre with its splendid six columned facade and then the Victorian grime blackened Gothic revival Railway Hotel, until they reached the junction of that main thoroughfare and the steeply climbing Skelhorne Street.

"Fuckin' hell, look at the size of the queue, will yer?" Glynn announced as all four observed the snaking line of expectant cinema goers that ran from the entrance of the art deco theatre along Lime Street and beyond.

"I think we better jib having a drink until later, or we've got no chance of gettin' in to see this film." Glynn continued.

Although he was notoriously mean with his money, on this occasion they all agreed that Glynn's suggested abandoning of their usual pre-film drinking session, was probably practically motivated and decided to join the end of the lengthening queue immediately. As they continued along Lime Street then turned the corner at Ranelagh Street, with Epstein's monumental statue of a naked male standing on the prow of a ship, entitled 'The Spirit of Liverpool Resurgent' but known locally as 'Dickie Lewis', a proud feature of the frontispiece of the quality goods department store, facing them on the building opposite, they studied the composition of the waiting crowd.

"Every team in Liverpool's 'ere." Blue noted remembering his crew mate's remark about the Billy Boys and cautiously checked to see if they were present. Jay Mac had a morbid fascination with identifying different teams and particularly their more prominent members. Tonight, although there were 'civilian' punters with their female companions dotted about in the extended queue, they were almost invisible to him. Instead he gauged the size of each rival contingent and noted their stylistic differences.

Crombies with denim jackets were still the popular norm, outnumbering the leather coats of varying lengths, worn with twenty two or twenty four inch parallel jeans or similar styled petrol blue, cream, or Prince of Wales checked trousers; there was a considerable showing of the earlier eighteen or twenty inch parallel white Baker's trousers also. The latter were worn with black Airwair as opposed to the more conventional, ubiquitous red variety and in some instances the wearers had their Baker's trousers tucked into their boots.

Jay Mac and his friends were amused to note that a few of the more adventurous crew members were also sporting bowler hats, although there were only isolated incidents of the appearance of this headgear, for the moment.

"I tell yer what, Blue's right; I've seen crews from nearly all the big teams so far." Jay Mac said, pleased with his successful 'gang-spotting'. "Speke, Breck Road, The Swan and the Dingle, they're all 'ere. It'd be a fuckin' hell of a kick off if anythin' started tonight; no wonder there's so many bizzies hangin' around."

Jay Mac was referring to the large, visible police presence that they had begun to notice as they approached the cinema and which followed the extended line of the queue all the way to its end, half way along Charlotte Row, where the Crown team mates joined it and took their places.

"No sign of Weaver, so you're alright Jay Mac." Irish said slyly, trying to niggle his friend.

Before he could respond, Glynn suddenly said, "Listen Irish, I don't know why y'keep goin' on about Weaver but do yer think y'could drop it? I don't wanna see that rapist cunt or the other one, Macca (G), yer remember what thee did to me Mum don't yer?" Irish decided not to reply and fell silent.

The cinema doors opened, and the leviathan began to shuffle forward. A long time later the four youths were finally admitted to see the X-Certificate tale of a young man whose 'principal interests were rape and Beethoven', as the lurid advertisement posters had proudly proclaimed. Amongst some of the last fans to be admitted before the doors closed and the house was declared full, were the Heron Crew commanders Weaver and Macca (G) with their Juniors and finally the bowler-hatted Mono leading a dozen Kings Boot Boys.

After almost two and half hours, as the final bars of Gene Kelly's rendition of *Singin' in the Rain* were playing to a rapidly emptying auditorium, Jay Mac, Irish, Blue and Glynn were trying to force their way through the tightly packed throng heading for the exit doors. One pressing thought was on the collective minds of the shuffling majority, to reach the nearest public house before 'last orders' were called.

"Shit! The towels will be out before we get through these doors." a concerned Blue complained. "Whoever is out first get over to the 'Mansion' and get a couple of rounds in." he added.

A few minutes later Irish and Jay Mac were in the process of complying with Blue's urgent request and both shouting at the top of their voices, amongst the clambering crowd at the bar of this more salubrious drinking establishment. Eventually they were joined by the anxious Blue and Glynn; the latter of whom was no longer comfortable pushing through anywhere, fearing he might slip or worse receive an accidental or intentional blow to the head.

A barely audible Roxy Music's *Virginia Plain* was playing on the jukebox in the background.

"Where's me roasted peanuts?" Blue demanded.

"D'you really want an answer to that Blue? Piss off to the bar and *you* try and get served, if yer that fuckin' desperate." Jay Mac replied.

"So, the usual question, Jay Mac, where's that one goin' in y'top ten films?" Irish enquired, before taking a drink from his pint of brown bitter, then a drag of his cigarette.

Jay Mac was pleased that his friend seemed to be more amenable than earlier in the evening. "Well that's a good question mate. McDowell was brilliant as Alex, he nailed it in his own way and the action was good for the first half hour or so but am not sure what to make of it over all."

His view appeared to be reflected by the majority of cinema-goers present on that premiere evening. Other drinkers nearby were expressing similar opinions. Despite its notoriety and the anticipation of trouble erupting during the performance, the audience had been remarkably subdued with only the odd cat-call, or observation being shouted at random intervals. It was as if no one was quite certain what they were watching and were concentrating their minds to allow an opinion to form.

Irish as usual adopted his own unique film critics considered stance. "Not enough shaggin' for one thing, some good violence but again, not enough. I'll give it four maybe five out of ten." He paused, blew a perfect smoke ring then continued, "I tell y'what it shows how the fuckin' state can mess with y'mind whenever thee want."

"I don't think you need to worry then Irish, your mind's already messed up." Jay Mac said smiling.

"Time gentlemen, please!" the bar staff began to call followed by the usual, "Empty y'glasses!" and then the rhetorical "Have y'got no homes to go to?"

On finishing the last of their ale and the salted snacks that Blue had bravely acquired with his 'round', the four youths fastened their Crombies, turned up their collars and stepped out of the boiling pub into the frozen night.

Making their way along Lime Street then turning down Elliot Street, past the ABC cinema where a short time before they had watched the long-awaited film, they were in deep conversation discussing whether to get hot dogs from the nearby greasy vendor or wait until they reached their destination, the Pier Head bus and ferry terminal and purchase some 'pigeon/seagull' pies there. They failed to notice that the heavy police presence of the early evening had completely dissipated, leaving the climate perfect for any number of malcontents, stimulated, energised and excited by the actions they had recently witnessed on the silver screen.

"Fuck off! Brilliant shot." Jay Mac heard just as the well-aimed brown ale bottle smashed across the right side of his head.

"He's the one, fuckin' grab 'im!" the same voice shouted.

A hail of glass bottles struck the four Crown team mates from all directions and Glynn desperately tried to cover his head with his hands. Suddenly bursting out from the darkness under St John's Shopping Precinct's concrete steps came a seven man crew who were quickly joined by half a dozen others from across the road. Booted, punched and repeatedly struck by bottles used as clubs, the battered youths had been taken by surprise, without warning and were completely surrounded by the ambush.

Jay Mac felt a strong arm around his neck and he was wrenched away from his beleaguered friends. Dragged backwards by three of their attackers into the Stygian darkness of the stairwell, he fumbled desperately in his left hand Crombie pocket for the three darts with their oddly coloured flights that he now carried in the absence of his knife. He had no idea who his captor was and at first could not discern any distinguishing features.

"Hi, hi, hi, little Jay Mac, time t'get one in the yarbles, if you've got any that is." said the ever theatrical, Clockwork Orange obsessed, bowler hat wearing Mono, now trying to paraphrase his version of Alex the main character's dialogue, as well as his manner. With his eyesight straining to adjust to the darkness Jay Mac could just see the smiling face of his attacker, though his two 'droogs' were as yet only silhouettes.

"Am gonna cut you bit by bit, after what you done to me." Mono announced referring to an incident the previous year in which Jay Mac, as a member of another 'rescue' party had struck him across the face with a four foot aluminium bus pole, leaving a permanently visible diagonal scar. Knowing that pleading for mercy would be useless and only add to Mono's pleasure, instead he closed his hand tightly around the three sharply pointed darts in his pocket, waiting for the opportunity to strike.

"I do the cuttin' round here." a familiar, sinister voice shouted and then Mono was gone, dragged to one side, as were his two assistants. All was now agonised screams of pain in the dark, confusing sounds of blows being struck and furious kicks being delivered to yielding flesh and breaking bone. Jay Mac joined in the madness catching hold of the nearest of Mono's crew, who had just released his hold on him. Maddened with rage and relief he struck with his triple-pronged weapon into the back, neck and face of the desperate youth in front of him. The tumult of struggling boot boys stumbled out into the glaring neon light of the shop fronts and tall street lamps and Jay Mac could finally see his saviour, holding the limp, bare-headed form of Mono by his blood soaked matted hair, striking over and over with his infamous toffee hammer.

"I'm Weaver, I done this to yer, don't forget, I'm Weaver." he howled in an orgiastic climax of delight, continuing long after his victim was past hearing.

A few moments later the still shaken Jay Mac was reunited with his bloodied friends and recently arrived rescuers: the now bowler hatted Weaver, Macca (G) and half a dozen Heron crew juniors.

"Fuck me, this turned out to be as queer as a clockwork orange night, after all", he announced with a grim smile.

"This calls for pies all round down the Pier." said the ever chirpy Blue smiling in anticipation.

"Nice one Blue, yer first thought is yer gut." Jay Mac observed smiling before the whole mixed cohort of Crown Team players set off for the infamous eatery, leaving their bloodied Kings Team rivals where they lay.

Chapter 3

Bonny Bunch of Roses O

Sunday 18th March, Wednesday 21st March and Friday 30th March 1973

Time moved on and the seasons changed, a long freezing winter finally relinquished its icy hold in favour of a cold, wet spring. After a favourable report from his probation officer Jay Mac had appeared again before the Magistrates and received a suspended sentence, a £5 fine and a stern warning to avoid any further trouble. Since his last narrow escape from the crazed Mono that warning had been superfluous, as not only did Jay Mac make a concerted effort to evade any potential incident, generally there had been a total dearth of gang activity on the Crown Estate.

Following the *Clockwork Orange* premiere evening and having become acutely aware that stylistically his appearance was becoming outdated; the fashion-conscious eighteen year old Jay Mac had begun an overhaul of his wardrobe. He may be classed as a deviant, albeit an intelligent deviant but he was determined to be a sharp-dressed one. Working in the City Centre in his menial office junior position gave him one distinct advantage over his factory-hand and building labourer Crown team mates, every day he was able to visit the latest trend setting shops. 'Eric's' stores on Commutation Row and Manchester Street and 'Tony Harris' on Lime Street were his favourite regular venues but he also began to make speculative forays into the relatively recent alternative fashion Mecca 'Cape' situated in Williamson Street. Of these four retail outlets Jay Mac felt slightly uncomfortable and out of place in the latter with its long-haired, bearded ex-hippie sales assistants and some of the more outlandish, new glam-rock influenced styles on display.

Having already decided that his definitive behavioural role-model must be Alex, the lead character from *A Clockwork Orange*, he had also been considering a number of influential stylistic icons to emulate in order to stand out from the crowd. On a cold, wet, dreary midweek evening in late February, sitting in the lounge bar of the Eagle public house with the core members of that eponymous crew, David Bowie's *Jean Genie* suddenly made its dramatic entrance, courtesy of the old jukebox and instantly dominated the clammy, smoke-filled room causing Jay Mac to pause mid conversation as if a Damascene moment had occurred.

Almost a month had past and, on an equally rainy, dismal Sunday evening, sporting a *Ziggy Stardust* style haircut and wearing a blue jumper with yellow sleeves and two diagonally positioned white stars on the front under his old Crombie; and twenty-two inch white parallel trousers with his usual gleaming cherry red Airwair, Jay Mac was strolling with Irish toward the home of his long-time friend. The youths had been playing snooker with the older members of the local Catholic Church parish club and were making their way back to Irish's house for something to eat before embarking on a night's drinking.

"We could've beaten those two arl bastards if you hadn't miss-cued and potted the white. What happened?" Irish asked brushing some loose strands of his unkempt hair away from his eyes. Although he had allowed this to grow much longer as a nod to the prevailing fashion, he still had yet to pass a comb through it. As one other concession to the changing youth fashion, he was wearing a faded purple and green patchwork jumper under his food and cigarette ash stained Crombie.

"What happened? Miss-cued? I was lucky I could even see the ball, never mind hit it, after drinkin' that fuckin' potato stuff last night." Jay Mac replied, referring to several glasses of Poitin that they had been generously allowed from Irish's father's personal supply, as a formal acknowledgement of St Patrick's Day. The considerable amount of bottled Guinness that they had quaffed under the same pretext, had also left their senses somewhat impaired the following day.

"What's that, did you 'ear something?" Jay Mac asked as they passed a dilapidated two story tenement block, near the central road of the estate.

"It sounds like someone gettin' a good kickin'," Irish replied, as the moans and groans grew louder and were interspersed with agonised screams of pain.

"Fuck, we better check it out, it could be one of our crew gettin' done." Jay Mac announced then ran up the path with Irish and booted the old metal swing doors open.

They quickly traced the source of the distressing cries, after stepping over a number of displaced refuse bins that were lying on their sides with their stinking content spread across the dark concrete floor. Amidst the tin cans, bottles, food remains and other reeking detritus, was a young man holding his stomach and vomiting violently. Irish and Jay Mac leaned down to see if they could identify the 'victim' in the darkness of the bin storage alley, beneath the stone stairs of the flats.

"It's fuckin' Gaz!" Irish shouted in surprise, looking down at the barely recognisable spew-covered face of the old guard member and personal friend of Tommy (S).

Jay Mac realised Irish was correct and said "What's happened to 'im? I know I haven't seen 'im for a couple of months but he looks like a fuckin' skeleton, he used to be a big, fit bastard." Both youths were astonished at the deterioration of their senior Crown team mate and his present condition.

"Fuckin hell, he's pissed 'imself and by the smell of it he's shit his kecks too." Irish announced in disgust.

Just then the seriously ill youth vomited another heavy stream which completely covered his chest and splashed onto the floor, adding to the stinking content already present.

"This fucker's dyin'" said Jay Mac, "he needs an ambulance quick-style or he's gone."

Irish was reluctant to agree. "Who made you a doctor? He's probably had a bad pint that's all."

"Irish stop bein' a prick, look at him, he's shiverin', white as a fuckin' ghost and there's blood comin' up with that puke. Leg it round to yours and ring for an ambulance, I'll hang on 'ere and stick 'im on his side or somethin'." Jay Mac snapped then knelt down to put his 'patient' in the recovery position. Having been saved from drowning as a young boy, it was the one useful memory he had of that experience.

Irish ran as fast as his cigarette smoke-damaged lungs would allow past the tenement blocks, the terraced row and the totally vandalised, useless red telephone box that now served only as a free-standing, convenient urinal. Twenty minutes later Jay Mac had just finished explaining to the ambulance men how he and Irish had found their team mate Gaz and what action they had taken.

"You probably saved his life, lads. Whatever he's been takin', this is one bad trip he'll never forget, if he ever comes round from it that is."

Irish and Jay Mac watched in silence as the former super-fit Crown team founder member was placed onto a stretcher, then lifted into the back of the ambulance. Within minutes the speeding vehicle with its urgent alarm sounding, disappeared from the estate. Neither of the youths knew that they had witnessed the first signs of an epidemic that would lay waste to the young people of their territory and far beyond. Like the plague carrying rats that decimated medieval Europe with the legions of fleas that bloated themselves on their diseased blood, the drug dealers had 'slipped ashore' just as inconspicuously and the consequences would be equally devastating.

Within an hour of finding their elder team mate collapsed amidst the midden of collective filth and covered in his own vomit, Jay Mac and Irish having ravenously devoured their evening meal of mixed fare provided by Irish's mother, Mrs O'Hare, were ensconced in the heavily worn but relatively comfortable surroundings of the Eagle Public House lounge bar. Positioned near the centre of the semi-circular seating arrangement, at the far end of the long rectangular room, they were casually discussing their discovery of Gaz and his condition, with those members of the Eagle crew who happened to be present on this less crowded than usual rainy Sunday evening.

"I'm tellin' yer, he'd pissed and shit 'imself," Irish revealed, enjoying unfolding the tale in graphic detail.

"Go way, what the fuck would make yer do that?" asked Johno the farm labourer incredulously.

"L.S.D, acid. Sent 'im on a bad trip, y'can always tell the signs, y'know what I mean." a perceptive Irish concluded.

"Fuckin' hell Irish, I never knew you were such an expert on hard core drugs." Jay Mac began. "The bizzies could do with you helpin' them out." he added, before taking a drink of his pint of Guinness, which he had just topped up with another bottle of the dark stout.

Terry (H), Tank, Ant One, the marginally elder of the two boxing twins and Brain were also present and listening intently to the story, though Jay Mac noticed that the latter seemed very uncomfortable.

"You alright Brain?" he asked turning to his team mate positioned immediately to his right. "Yer look like yer on edge mate, the way y'keep watchin' the door, y'not waitin' for a bird are yer?"

"Nah mate, I fuckin' wish I was." he replied nervously before taking a drag of his cigarette and swiftly downing his whiskey chaser.

Pappa was a Rolling Stone by the Temptations had just begun playing on the jukebox when the swing door to the lounge opened and stepping in with the cold damp night air was the tall, rangy figure of Floyd. The uber-cool lone player, apprentice chef, small time thief and long-serving police officer's son, swept over to their group of tables with the tails of his expensive calf-length, black leather coat flaring open.

"Move up there my man." he said pushing his way in between Jay Mac and Brain.

"I'll get yer a drink in." said the latter jumping up from his seat in order to make his way to the bar.

Floyd suddenly caught Brain's left wrist with his right hand, "Bourbon on the rocks, just a splash of soda." he said with his usual beguiling smile.

"You've got him well trained, Floyd." Jay Mac observed while studying his former 'business associates' heavy, gleaming gold watch. "Looks pricey Floyd, is it one of them Rolex jobs?" he asked.

"Fuck no man, that's not my style. Breitling, yeah? It's a one-off." the lugubrious Floyd replied lifting his wrist to allow the assembly to admire his luxury timepiece.

"More like knock-off." said Irish cynically but quietly.

Floyd dropped his usual insincere smile. "Irish, be careful what you're sayin' my man. People could get the wrong idea about me and I wouldn't like that." His trademark smile returned and he added "When you've got the bread y'can buy whatever gear you like. It's only povo tramps that have to go round theivin' yeah?"

Irish knew not to reply; Floyd was a capable scrapper in his own right and used his heavy brass knuckle duster to tip the odds in his favour, if needed.

"Speakin' of cash, if y'fancy earnin' a bit of spare ... Jay Mac ... and you, Irish, my offer's still open." Floyd added, referring to a business opportunity he had put before Jay Mac in the autumn of the previous year. "Not interested lads? That's ok, I might have a one-off that yer fancy, comin' up, I'll give yer a nod."

Just then Brain returned with Floyd's drink and after passing him the glass tumbler, he squeezed back into his former position. A few moments later the increasingly nervous Brain took something from the inside pocket of his Crombie and passed it quickly to Floyd.

"All there my man, am not goin' to find any mistakes am I?" Floyd asked rhetorically. "'Cos mistakes can be very painful."

Brain said nothing but stared directly ahead of him with a cold sweat visible on his pale brow.

"What's all this I've heard about an ambulance and some fucker bein' found lyin' in the bins, in the old tennies on Central Road," an apparently mildly interested Floyd asked.

Jay Mac provided the details in a brief summary of how he and Irish had found Gaz, the old guard member, earlier that evening.

"Fuck man, that's a pity I'm sorry to hear that." Floyd said, appearing concerned about the welfare of his chronological peer.

"Yeah, he's a decent lad Gaz, I hope he pulls through." Jay Mac replied.

"That's what am sayin' me too. He's one of my best customers; it would be a real shame if anything happened to him." Floyd responded as he casually lit one of his long dark cigarillos and took a leisurely drag.

Wednesday 21st March 1973

Travelling towards the city centre on the graffiti covered backseat, of a litter strewn, virtually empty green Atlantean bus, Jay Mac and Irish were busily over-writing the existing names and slogans with their own and the new Crown Boot Boys emblem. It was an unseasonably mild evening and both youths were wearing Harrington style jackets instead of their usual Crombies, Jay Mac in his classic black version and Irish in his grubby dark blue.

"Are *you* sure there's gonna be some birds at this fuckin' place? It's a Wednesday night, there's no one about and it's not even a proper club that we're goin' to is it?" Jay Mac asked as he completed an extensive decorative work across the previously unmarked white ceiling of the vehicle.

"Birds mate, like you've never seen before." Irish replied while diligently engaged in adding appropriate comments to the names of other crews. "Legs up to their armpits, massive tits and great arses, I'm tellin' yer."

"Yeah, is that right? How come we've never been 'ere before then and, why did Glynn and Blue jib it as soon as you said the name?" Jay Mac persisted.

"Fuck them, it's their loss. Anyway, they wouldn't fit in." Irish responded intending to close the discussion.

Jay Mac knew exactly what his friend was referring to by his cryptic comment, Irish felt that both he and Jay Mac had deep Celtic roots and, in addition although they had lapsed they were also baptised Catholics. Jay Mac accepted the latter as fact but dismissed the former notion as nonsense. He decided for the moment not to challenge his long-time friend's assertion and changed tack instead.

"What about that other guaranteed shag nest you recommended last month, the fuckin' Grafton? Chicken-in-a-basket and grab-a-granny night." Jay Mac asked smiling.

"Did yer get a shag? Just answer me that?"

"Yeah, thanks, am still wakin' up with fuckin nightmares about it now." Jay Mac replied.

"Did yer get fed, tell me that?" Irish continued

"Yeah, I rented some underdone chicken and then spent most of the night lettin' it go free." Jay Mac agreed.

"There y'go then, a shag and a feed, what are y'complainin' about?" Irish concluded, case closed.

Shortly after alighting from the bus outside the Empire Theatre on Lime Street, the two youths made their winding way past the famed eponymous nineteenth century railway station; the varied collection of public houses; the ornately fronted Adelphi Hotel and began the gentle climb up Mount Pleasant towards the Georgian elegance of the neo-Classical Wellington Assembly Rooms, contemporarily known as The Irish Centre. Standing outside the place that he regarded as the beating cultural heart of the Celtic community, Irish began fumbling in his jacket pockets for the prized tickets that he had managed to obtain for the 'young people's swinging discothèque and Ceili band', being held as part of the week-long celebrations of St Patrick's Day.

"Fuckin' hell, where are thee?" Irish asked while removing a varied assortment of toilet paper, bus tickets, mixed coin and partially smoked cigarettes.

"Let's hope yer haven't lost them and we have to miss out on a wild night." Jay Mac said hopefully, then added, "It's a crackin' lookin' buildin' though, I'll give yer that. I hope it's as good inside, if we ever get in."

Finally Irish located the missing tickets and they were admitted. Sadly from Jay Mac's perspective the dowdy interior was only a dismal reflection of its former glory and although original stylistic elements were still visible, successive unsympathetic decorative overlays had almost obliterated its restrained Regency splendour.

Once they had given in their tickets and signed the non-members' visitors book, they made their way to the wooden fronted John F. Kennedy bar with its welcoming gold-lettered slogan above which read, *Céad míle fáilte* and then to a small round Formica-topped table with their drinks, four bottles of Guinness and two pint glasses.

Jay Mac began to survey the poorly lit room with its scattered irregular selection of worn chairs and tables, situated randomly on either side of the wooden floor. He particularly focused on the clientele who were almost entirely male of varying ages, engaged in serious drinking and heavy smoking with some more energetic members playing stimulating games either of draughts or dominoes.

"I don't wanna say nothin' mate but except for the odd old brooster, there's no fuckin' women in 'ere." he announced with genuine disappointment.

"It's only early yet, you wait. When the Ceili band gets goin' the birds will all appear from nowhere." Irish said in a less than convincing tone.

After close to an hour of almost uninterrupted drinking, both youths had all but abandoned the hope of any appearance of females that night. Added to this a group of young male drinkers who were becoming rapidly intoxicated, began staring across at the two Crown Boot Boys dressed in their distinctive 'uniform' and particularly their Airwair boots.

"Doin' some labourin' are y'boys?" One acne-faced, wild-haired youth shouted.

"No, they're a pair of gardeners, up hill gardeners." said another with a mop of black curly hair, parted just above the left ear and plastered into place with a more than generous helping of Brylcream.

"Fuck this." said Jay Mac, "I'm not takin' shit from some half-wit bog trotters." he continued, letting the alcohol induced bravery override his natural cowardice.

Irish began to rise from his seat and gestured towards the hecklers. "Now lads, come on, we're all Irish 'ere, y'know what I mean? We're celebratin' St Patrick just like you; we don't want any trouble, ok?" He paused and raised his pint glass, with the word "Slainte!" This nationalist sentiment and salutation appeared to settle the rowdy youths and they responded in similar fashion. The brief period of calm and extension of bonhomie was instantly shattered by the arrival of six pretty, giggling girls. Making a sweeping entrance to the shabby room with its stale atmosphere smelling of tobacco and ale, the stylishly overdressed and heavily made up sextet breathed an effervescent life back into the tired chamber and stirred the loins of all those males, whose potency had not yet been fully sapped.

Within an instant they were surrounded by the younger revellers, with offers of drinks coming from all potential suitors. The girls, however, declined this spontaneous hospitality preferring to buy their own refreshment and sat at two tables that they had pushed together.

"Things are lookin' up." said Jay Mac with a grin.

"What did I tell yer?" Irish said both equally pleased and surprised.

At that moment a tall male in his early sixties and wearing a badly fitting, double-breasted dark grey flannel suit crossed the room and stepped onto the small stage. He brushed his loose thinning grey hair back from his sweating brow and announced "Now boys and girls we're all having a grand time I know but I do have a little bit of bad news for yer." He paused and let the assembly take stock of his words. "I'm sorry to tell yer, that Gerry O'Malley and the Galway Stars won't be playin' tonight, they've been delayed by a bit of a rough crossin'."

Once more he halted waiting for the expected protestation which failed to materialise, except for Jay Mac calling out "Thank Christ!"

"I know yer all disappointed but don't worry Kevin's got his record player all ready to go. So without further ado, let's get started with the discothequing."

"This'll be fuckin' good," said Jay Mac slyly smiling at Irish.

DJ Kevin's first selection was the rousing *Black Velvet Band* by the Dubliners which, although it drew universal approbation from most of the drinkers who joined in the chorus with gusto, including Jay Mac and Irish, it failed to attract any dancers to the floor. Several ballads of similar nature followed in succession but the dance floor remained empty save for an aged lone drunk who shuffled aimlessly about within a circle of varying radius whilst continually singing *When Irish Eyes are Smiling* irrespective of the song being played.

Jay Mac looked at his friend and said "Someone's gonna have to speak to that DJ tit and tell 'im to put somethin' decent on."

Irish nodded his agreement.

Before anyone else took some positive action, two of the recently arrived girls stood up and teetered across on their platform shoes to speak to Kevin.

"They're about the best lookin' of the six, I'd say." Jay Mac commented having made his assessment partially based on their pretty faces and well rounded figures but also, for him, that key deciding factor, the quality of their legs. This decision was made easier for him on this particular occasion as two of the girls wore flared trousers and two wore full length, though considerably revealing maxi dresses. Only the pair who were trying to charm Kevin into playing some more contemporary hits, wore skirts above knee length, allowing the young connoisseur to make an informed judgement.

"Yeah, I think we'll make a move there, ok?" he asked Irish, as he watched the girls return to their table.

Irish had drunk enough to remove his usual uncomfortable reticence and agreed "You give the nod and I'll steam in with yer."

Unfortunately for the Crown team mates the law of supply and demand meant that they would be facing stiff competition, as the young male revellers had also made their individual verdicts.

Elton John's *Crocodile Rock* suddenly and incongruously began to play next and all six girls immediately took to the floor.

"Alright, me name's Jay Mac, nice to meet yer," the youth began after rapidly positioning himself in front of an attractive deep-auburn haired shorter skirt wearer, with Irish following his lead and joining her partner.

"You don't waste anytime do yer? I'm Lucy by the way." she smiled pleasantly and moved slightly closer to him. "What are you and your mate doin' in this place?" she asked curiously.

"That's a good question comin' from you. Tell me why are six hot, well-dressed birds hangin' out in this dead hole; is it for a bet or somethin'?" Jay Mac was studying her curvaceous figure clearly visible through her close fitting white satin blouse. Lucy ignored his question and asked another of her own.

"So y'think we'er *all* hot do you?"

"Oh yeah but especially the one called Lucy." he quickly replied, smiling.

Lucy laughed and said "I'll save you a dance later."

With that offer secured, when the record ended Jay Mac returned to his seat to discuss the joint plan of action with Irish. His friend had obtained similar favourable results and additional information.

"Yeah, her name's Gaynor. They're all sixth form girls and, y'see the one with the curly hair in the checked flares, she's called Roisin, it's her dad who's a member and he got them the tickets". He paused took a drink of his pint then lit a cigarette. "I think we're well in there."

The local competition had other ideas and for the next five dances Jay Mac and Irish were constantly pipped-at-the-post on four occasions, having to withdraw partner-less and shamefaced from the floor.

"Thank God you're back, what happened to you?" Lucy asked when Jay Mac next managed to take his place in front of her, with Irish similarly positioned with Gaynor.

"That greasy-haired pig calls himself Brian, keeps putting his hands all over me and he won't take no for an answer." she said with an expression of genuine concern on her face.

Jay Mac instantly felt the hairs on the back of his neck stand up as a wave of righteous anger rose within him. Conscious of recent events that he had failed to prevent on the Crown estate, he now experienced a distinct sense of obligation to stop any repetition.

"Don't worry about him, he's a no mark, me an my mate Irish, won't let anything happen to yer." he heard himself saying not really thinking of the potential consequences of his words.

Lucy leaned in closely and lightly kissed him on the lips "Thanks, I feel a lot better now." she said with a smile.

Fate, however, was about to conspire against them. When their dance ended Jay Mac returned to his table and Lucy to hers. Irish left the room to use the toilet, intending to get another round of drinks on his return. He was enjoying a lengthy urination when he heard the slow tempo of Jimmy Helms *Gonna Make You an Offer* begin in the adjoining room. Even before Jay Mac could cross the floor, the girls, who were already standing, were surrounded by over eager partners with Lucy immediately ensnared by the amorous Brian.

Forced into being a reluctant spectator, Jay Mac was becoming increasingly frustrated as he watched the tall, excessively greasy-haired youth, pawing the struggling Lucy. Irish returned from the toilet and abandoned any idea of going to the bar for the moment when he saw what was happening on the dance floor and Jay Mac's reaction.

"Fuck this Irish; I'm stoppin' that cunt now." he announced angrily.

"Jay Mac, listen to me there's way too many of them, you'll get fucked and I'm not jumpin' in for some bit of strange that I've never met before." Irish said coldly and pragmatically, then added "I'm goin' to the bar, don't do anything fuckin' stupid."

With those words playing over in his head, Jay Mac recalled how he had given the same advice to Glynn on that fateful night in January. Looking across at the desperate Lucy in the invasive clutches of the grinning Brian, the Crown team player watched enraged as he pulled the girl even closer with his right hand on her bottom, shoving his left under the hem of her skirt and up to the top of her thighs. Lucy screamed and slapped the tall, sweating groper hard in the face. Brian laughed and pulled her tightly to him intent on continuing his assault.

Jay Mac's powerful straight open-handed palm-heel strike smashed into the left side of the drunken fumblers head, knocking him sideways and instantly releasing the tearful Lucy as he did.

"Gerrout the way, quick!" Jay Mac managed to shout, pushing Lucy to one side, before the furious Brian returned a hard right of his own, which caught him just below the ear.

Both youths now faced each other and exchanged a flurry of wild punches to the head and body. A swinging right hook whisked over Jay Mac's head narrowly missing its intended target, as he dodged underneath before delivering a lightning fast combination of a short range left jab to Brian's gut, followed immediately by a devastating right upper-cut that caught him perfectly under the chin, snapping his head back violently.

Jay Mac stepped back as his lanky opponent dropped to his knees, then fell backwards unconscious onto the weathered boards of the dance floor. It was normally at this point he would have finished off his 'kill' with a swift kicking but as he stood panting and filling his lungs with revitalising air, he realised that by fortunate accident or grand design, he had produced a knock-out coup de gras which required no further action.

Suddenly he felt a strong hand on his right shoulder and at the same moment another gripped his left arm firmly.

"You'll need to be returnin' to yer seat now young feller."

As he was being marched back to his table he glanced to his left at the battered meaty face, edged with thick dark sideburns and crowned with a heavy black, greased back D.A style thatch of hair, of the stocky bouncer who was escorting him. A similar individual had retrieved the fallen Brian and, after having sat him in an upright position, was administering first aid in the form of slapping him across the face and forcibly encouraging him to take sips from a pint of Guinness, which he had picked up from a nearby table.

Once he was seated, Jay Mac glanced over to where the six girls were sitting and could see they were clearly arguing amongst themselves. He was at first surprised that Brian's companions had taken no reprisal action but when he saw the huge 'first aid' giving bouncer gesturing to them, he assumed that was the reason for their passiveness.

"Some nice digs there wee man, yer sparked 'im with a lovely upper-cut." the massive ex-Teddy Boy bouncer said with a warm smile momentarily lighting his warrior's countenance. "With a bit of training for y'footwork and timing you could be a useful scrapper."

"Thanks that's er... decent of yer mate." Jay Mac replied totally bemused by his kindly response, having fully expected to receive a severe beating from the doormen in some dark alley behind the building, or in a designated room used for that purpose.

As the friendly giant walked away, Jay Mac noticed his suit which was well cut, dark blue in colour and had a certain sheen about it. He placed the swarthy male as being in his mid thirties and felt there was something familiar about him. Looking across at his equally large and similarly dressed companion who had now joined him at the bar, he experienced a momentary disquiet.

"I tell yer what these are the politest bouncers I've ever met. What the fuck is goin' on?" a perplexed Jay Mac asked Irish.

"Well y'see, what happened was, I was at the bar and thee started askin' me about you, thee'd seen yer name in the visitors book and wanted to know if yer was related to the 'Gerard Boys', thee thought yer looked like one of the younger ones." Irish paused and took a drag of his almost finished cigarette then continued, "I told them you was their favourite cousin.

"Fuckin' great." Jay Mac replied not certain whether to be pleased or worried.

His cousins of the same surname as him, were a thirteen-strong vicious clan, who specialised in robbery with extreme violence, sometimes referred to as the 'Gerard Boys' even though they included within their ranks their equally formidable sisters. Jay Mac avoided them whenever possible, with good cause.

Before he could consider the matter any further his original escort returned to their table and placed two tumblers with a couple of generous measures of whiskey in each in front of the Crown team mates.

"Finish y'pints and drop these, then we'll have to ask yer to leave. Those boys over there are members and we can't be havin' their night spoiled, no hard feelings. If yer happen to see Tommy, Francis or Niall, tell them Eamon and Sean from the old crew treated yer right... Slainte." With that he turned and walked back to his partner and they remained casually watching the room for any commotion, whilst drinking their pints and enjoying their cigarettes.

A few moments later the dusty old compere crossed the room carefully carrying his pint, stepped gingerly up onto the small stage and began a new announcement.

"Well wasn't that grand? A couple of young fellers lettin' off some steam, settlin' their differences like gentlemen and who can blame them with all these lovely girls about? Why, if I was ten years younger meself..."

"You'd still be sixty", shouted an anonymous wag unkindly.

Unphased the compere continued, "Anyway enough of that for now. If y'want to carry on boys yer'll have to take it outside, we haven't got the facilities in here, more's the pity." He paused and gathered his thoughts, "So, if y'can stand anymore excitement don't forget the raffle's comin' up shortly but don't panic there's still time t'buy yer tickets." Again he paused this time to take a sip of his pint. "We've got some great prizes..."

"Yeah, first prize a week in Belfast, second prize two weeks." another aspiring comedian advised.

Again the aged compere soldiered on "...and it all goes to a good cause, we're sendin' our team of wee dancers off to Dublin for the All Ireland final."

"Fuckin' hell!" declared a third and final disbeliever.

Finally the ever-smiling compere completed his routine announcements. "So I'll hand yer back to Kevin for a few more records. Take it away Kevin."

The stalwart DJ knew what the audience needed to restore order and decided to abandon his foray into the world of contemporary music for the time being. Next on the turntable... *It's not the leaving of Liverpool*.

"I think that's our cue to get off." Jay Mac said before finishing the dregs of his pint and then downing his whiskey in several swallows.

The disgruntled Irish followed suit and stood up to leave also, without speaking.

"Seeya ladies, enjoy the rest of yer evenin'," a smiling Jay Mac called over to the six females seated at their tables, still arguing amongst themselves.

With the final bars of the classic folk ballad playing, the two Crown team players stepped into the cool night air.

They had only walked a few yards when Irish stopped and lit a cigarette. "Fuckin' great, thanks for that, thrown out of the Irish Centre!" he shouted angrily after Jay Mac, who stopped and turned round.

"What's yer problem? I've done yer a favour. Fuck! Yer might as well climb into yer coffin now than spend any more time in that dead-hole!" he shouted back in reply.

"Dead-hole? That's our place, we're Irish, it's the only place we've got. Me Da got us those tickets and now we've been chased out of there", Irish snapped back.

"Patrick, listen to me lad, *we're* not fuckin' Irish, we was born 'ere in Liverpool, *not* Ireland, so drop that shite." Jay Mac responded, becoming increasingly angry.

"Don't you ever say that to me again or..." Irish warned, throwing his freshly lit cigarette to the ground and about to raise his fists, when suddenly they both heard a shrill whistle coming from the doorway of the club they had just left.

"Hold on! Hold on for us boys!" a smiling Lucy shouted as she and Gaynor tried to catch up with them, as fast as their platform shoes would allow.

Both males looked at each other and nodded as if agreeing that their personal dispute would keep for the present, now that a more stimulating opportunity had just presented itself.

Lucy caught hold of Jay Mac by the arm and Gaynor repeated this friendly gesture with Irish.

"Where are we off to then?" Gaynor, the pretty brunette asked, staring expectantly up at a bemused though pleased Irish.

"I think it's got to be the 'Mansion' for these ladies, don't you Patrick?" Jay Mac said with a smile, after a reticent Irish had failed to respond to Gaynor's question.

"Sounds great, better than that place any road," he said, finally managing a smile.

The two couples walked arm-in-arm, down the gentle slope of Mount Pleasant then on to Lime Street, until they reached the opulent Victorian drinking establishment, the Orchard, known locally because of its size and numerous rooms as the 'Mansion'.

Being a Wednesday night the most splendid imbibing chamber within the plush hostelry, 'the Cocktail Lounge' was closed and they had to settle for one of the comfortable, discreet booths in the ornately decorated parlour of this magnificent late 19th Century public house.

"Two brown bitters and two rum and blacks, when y'ready." Jay Mac asked politely, not having to shout, with only limited clientele being present on this mid-week night.

When he joined Irish and the girls who were sitting in a cosy corner of the virtually empty parlour and passed everyone their drinks, Lucy repeated what she had just told his friend.

"Yeah, I was just sayin' Roisin knows those lads and she said that slimy Brian was a bit of a bully to them as well, so they weren't bothered when y'knocked him down. They said he thought he was a hard case, now their sayin' you must be a tough guy."

Irish laughed when he heard this, "Tough guy? You should've seen him in school, most of the time he ended up on his arse." He laughed again as he poured his brown ale into his pint glass already half filled with amber bitter.

Jay Mac didn't respond as Lucy turned towards him and kissed him on the cheek saying, "Well I don't know about then and I don't really care, he's my hero."

Irish said no more but reached into his jacket pocket for his cigarettes and matches.

Jay Mac announced "This could be a good night after all." His feeling of elation did not last for long.

"Here y'are, try one of mine." said Gaynor, generously producing a freshly opened pack of ten filter tipped John Player Specials. After Irish had taken a cigarette, she passed the pack to Lucy who also withdrew one, much to Jay Mac's dismay. When the pack was offered to him he declined and said, "I never smoke but thanks anyway."

Irish grinned as he lit all three cigarettes in turn with one match; he knew his friend hated the smell of smoke on a girl and particularly on her breath.

The Detroit Emeralds' *Feel the Need in Me* was playing in the adjacent bar.

Several rounds of drinks and one empty packet of cigarettes, supplemented by Irish's Woodbines later, last orders had been called and the two couples made their way to the exit. As the parlour had remained almost empty for most of the evening and with the spirits flowing freely, increasingly amorous clinches had been enjoyed by each pair.

Laughing, joking and stopping in shop doorways at regular intervals for further passionate embraces, they eventually arrived at the Pier Head bus and ferry terminal. After walking across from the bottom of James Street where it met Strand Street, the main thoroughfare, their route took them past the rear of the Art Deco Mersey Tunnel building into George's Dock Way facing the elegant Mersey Docks and Harbour Board topped with its magnificent cupola.

Slowly strolling through the relatively silent darkness that hung in the chasm between these two structures, both couples stopped and without saying a word took sheltered positions within two obliging doorways situated some yards apart. Mysterious, unspeaking, anthropomorphic, ebony statues of the Sun and Moon stood guard on either side.

While Irish and Gaynor eagerly fumbled in their stone alcove, Jay Mac and the willing Lucy explored each others body with relish. The knee length grey woollen coat that Lucy was wearing, similar in style to her friend's dark brown version, had been flung open and Jay Mac was holding her close to him inside its warm enveloping fronts. As they kissed passionately he squeezed her ample breasts, first over her soft satin blouse and then after she had obligingly opened several buttons, through the lacy material of her straining bra. For the moment his rising ardour was helping him overcome his repulsion at the taste and smell of his partner's smokers' kiss. Sensing that she was also becoming increasingly aroused, especially as he teased her hardening nipples with his right hand through the flimsy garment, he slipped his left hand under her rouched-up skirt and began squeezing her curved pert bottom over her tights and panties.

Emboldened, he swiftly removed his right hand from her breasts, which he had assisted in tumbling out from her bra and placed that also under her skirt and began gently massaging her between the top of her legs, over her moist underwear. A breathless Lucy broke away from their kissing and caught his hand with her left, Jay Mac thought this was to be a repeat of his frustrating encounter with the unfortunate, voluptuous Susan earlier that year.

"Am not that sort of girl." Lucy announced coyly.

"Come on, I bet you say that to all the boys." Jay Mac quipped insensitively.

"No, I'm serious, I've only ever done it once and I didn't like it." she replied becoming angry with his flippant dismissal of her honesty.

"Look, let's see how it goes. I'll stop anytime you want, you just say." He paused fearing his throbbing erection may be denied. "Try it again with me, you might just like it." He had resumed his sensual rubbing of her most private parts while they were talking and could tell that her body was responding, even if involuntarily.

Lucy yielded to her hormones and burgeoning desire. "Alright, hold on, I'll take these down." she said then leant on him for support, while she rolled down her panties and tights, removed one shoe and stepped one leg out of her underwear, leaving herself fully exposed to his stimulating, exploring hands.

Jay Mac felt the spasms of delight pass through her body as he tenderly brought her to a point of no return. With his left hand he quickly unclipped his red half-inch elasticated braces, unzipped his Prince of Wales checked parallels, pulling them and his underwear down in one desperate wrenching movement.

"Have y'got something?" Lucy gasped. Her breath coming in short excited pants.

Jay Mac froze; he could hear the Durex machine standing forlorn in the toilets of the 'Mansion,' laughing at him for ignoring his wares when he had the chance to purchase a pack of three, as if to say... "Who needs my rubbers now then? Well it's too late, the shop's closed."

"It'll be alright, I can pull it out before I come, honest, nothing will happen." he desperately pleaded now entirely led by his pulsating erection. "Yer can't get pregnant if I pull it out; no one's ever got pregnant like that." he lied partially but also in part naively believing in his lack of sex education, that he may be correct.

"Ok but pull it out before anything happens, please." she acquiesced, allowing him to raise her naked left leg, with his right hand under her knee.

Forcing the tip of his erect member into her quivering, yielding flesh, he paused briefly to gauge her reaction. Lucy was past caring, rational thought had long abandoned her judgement, sensory pleasure was all that mattered. She kissed him passionately and he pushed himself fully inside her. For the next few minutes they moved as one, writhing and mounding, pulsing together enfolded in the physical act and reason liberating sensation.

Thrusting harder and harder with each stroke, drawn on by Lucy's soft moans of delight, Jay Mac knew he was close to climax and a fleeting pang of ethical anxiety of potentially fathering a bastard like himself almost caused him to withdraw, voluntarily as promised. In the end a more prosaic reason interrupted their lovemaking and brought it to a deflating, frustrated halt.

From the next stone booth the sounds of violent retching could be heard, growing louder and more urgent with each spasm.

"Fuckin' hell girl!" Irish shouted, equally frustrated as Gaynor let forth another rum and black perfumed stream of vomit. "Shit! That's gone all over me, try and hold it in will yer." he requested unsympathetically and to no avail.

"What's happening to Gaynor, what's he done? Oh no!" Lucy shouted, dismounting herself awkwardly, causing the orgasming youth to ejaculate his seed onto her rounded belly and exposed loins.

"Fuckin' hell, I don't believe this!" Jay Mac shouted, as he struggled to put away his still throbbing member, while his partner clumsily pulled up her underwear, after dabbing her semen-covered parts with her handkerchief.

"What's wrong Gaynor, what's he done to you?" she cried stumbling post coitus towards her retching friend.

"I don't think I've done anythin' to her, I hardly had the chance." Irish answered in the absence of an intelligible response from the bent-double, Gaynor.

While Lucy assisted her stricken friend, wiping her face with the same cotton handkerchief, telling her to "Get it all out," Irish was commiserating with his slightly more relieved team mate.

"I'd just about got it up her, when she started burpin' like fuck an sayin' she felt bad. Next thing she's throwin' her ring up." He paused while he dabbed at his stinking clothing with a dirty checked handkerchief that he always carried."Let's jib them and get a cup of tea and a pie over at the shop before the last bus." he concluded coldly.

Jay Mac agreed, there was nothing to be gained by tarrying any longer and both he and Irish escorted the two girls to their bus stop in silence, apart from Gaynor's random violent burps.

"Nice to 'ave met yer, we'll probably see yer again in town." Jay Mac lied as they prepared to depart when the girls began to board their bus, which was already waiting in its allocated bay.

Gaynor didn't speak but carefully stepped up onto the platform, Lucy turned and passed Jay Mac a scrap of paper containing her telephone number, then kissed him on the lips before saying, "Please call Jay Mac, we can go out on a proper date."

The smiling youth raised a thumb on his right hand to signify his formal agreement, then waved goodbye as the green Atlantean vehicle pulled away from the terminus. Both parties knew they would never see each other again.

A short time later after finishing their dark brown 'stewed' tea and having flicked the rock hard crust and gristly meat remains of their pies at a sleeping tramp, the youths made their way through the dirty glass cloisters towards their bus stop.

"Y'do know that was a lucky punch don't yer?" Irish began, "I thought that lanky fucker was gonna do yer but y'had a bit of luck and sparked him."

Jay Mac didn't respond for the moment but he could feel his anger beginning to rise.

Irish pressed on "Shameful that, gettin' thrown out of our own club. We'll have to go back there in a couple of weeks and sort things out."

Jay Mac stopped walking and stared at his friend in disbelief then said, "Irish, let me tell y'straight that won't be happenin'. As for that shit-hole, I defo won't be goin' back there ever. It's not *my* club an it's not *yours* either, so fuck them."

Irish now stood still also and looked directly at his long-time friend. "Y'know what, y'right, y'not Irish, y'nothing. At least I know who I am, I've got a name". He turned and walked away to board a vehicle bound for the Crown Estate, leaving seven years of friendship behind on the filthy bus station floor.

A silent Jay Mac sat downstairs on the backseat of his bus destined for the Kings Estate; he warmed himself against the seat with the heat escaping from the engine and studied the graffiti covered red leatherette seat in front of him. There was a faded Crown Skins logo with his name and several others of their crew including Irish just discernable; it had been all but obliterated by the new Kings Boot Boys emblem. Times were changing he thought then casually pulled out the piece of paper that Lucy had given him with her telephone number on it. He crumpled it up without a glance and threw it with the rest of the litter on the floor.

Friday 30th March 1973

A fine rain was falling steadily as Jay Mac, against his better judgement, was making his way across the lower edge of the Crown Estate in the direction of the Heron public house. During the ten day period since their visit to the Irish Centre, Jay Mac and Irish had been in each other's company with their crew, on a number of occasions with barely a word passing between them. After one of their heavy drinking sessions a number of the Eagle Boot Boys, including the two former friends, had made their way to their favourite eatery, Mr Li's Golden Diner, considered the best fish and chip shop in the area.

The intelligent, perceptive, deviant Macca (G) was also present with some of the Heron crew and their Juniors. It was not long before he became aware of a rift between the usually 'close' Irish and Jay Mac and he considered how he could best profit from this.

So it was that on this evening a circumspect Jay Mac, whose ego had been sufficiently massaged by the obsequious Macca (G), approached the entrance doors of the Heron his rival crew's headquarters. Not since the previous November and the issue of his fatal challenge to Yad, the former Heron leader, had he entered this hostile hostelry. Walking through the low walls that surrounded the ever-empty car park, he immediately encountered some of Molly 'Skank' Brown's younger business associates who were taking a break from bartering sexual favours for money and cigarettes, to enable them to chase one of the Heron Juniors around the forlorn tarmaced grounds of the public house, before pulling down the unfortunate youth's trousers and underwear. While they amused themselves cackling and shrieking with their embarrassed, wildly struggling captive, Jay Mac stepped up into the entrance then passed through the lounge bar swing doors.

Unlike the Eagle which was usually packed to capacity at the weekend, particularly on a Friday night with the recently introduced 'Over Twenty-One's Disco' taking place in the nearby Central Way Hall, it's sister public house was comparatively empty. With only the regular old curmudgeon patrons dotted about in small enclaves playing cards or dominoes and swapping tales of unlikely sexual encounters, the Heron Boot Boys and Juniors dominated the far corner of the long rectangular room with the bar conveniently close to them and the jukebox directly opposite. Stevie Wonder's *Superstition* had just begun to play as Jay Mac approached the cluster of tables where Macca (G) and Weaver were seated in the middle of their peers.

"What the fuck do you want Jay Mac? Yer in the wrong alehouse, unless yer wanna challenge me or Macca to a go, is that it?" Weaver asked, grinning menacingly as usual.

Before he could respond Macca (G) interjected, "Behave Weaver, I invited Jay Mac, he's a good lad he knows his own mind." Then he kicked the stool of one of his junior followers "Gerrup shithead and get this man a pint, show 'im what it's like in the Heron Crew."

Jay Mac pulled the vacant stool over and sat in front of the central small, circular table, where Macca (G) and Weaver were directing operations.

"What's on yer mind Macca? Y'said yer had somethin' that I'd be interested in?" Jay Mac asked curiously.

"That's a good question Jay Mac, an I'll tell yer what's been botherin' me, Weaver and the Heron Crew," he paused took a drink of his pint then continued, "Those cunts on the Ravens Hall Estate, thee done Mal 'the pig' last New Year's Eve, yeah? Put him in hospital, one of our own." Pausing again he looked around the assembled youths ensuring they were all listening to his words. "Tell me what 'ave we done about it? Fuck all that's what. Well even if your Eagle boys are shit scared to go over there, we're not. We're gonna teach them a fuckin' lesson." Macca (G) stopped speaking and basked in the positive response from his crew members, particularly the Juniors.

Jay Mac was aware that Macca (G) had been talking nonsense. Mal 'the pig' as he was known because of a facial disfigurement he had suffered after crashing a stolen car, was an unpopular loner who everyone, from both teams, considered to be genuinely weird. His severe beating, received on New Year's Eve, whilst literally trying to raise the dead in the local municipal cemetery, had largely passed unnoticed and those who were aware of it had no intention of taking reprisals.

Macca (G) was renowned for his devious nature and Jay Mac suspected that his actual ulterior motive had nothing to do with the attack upon the unfortunate Mal. For the moment, however, he decided to follow the Heron leader's direction.

"Yeah, that sounds fair to me Macca, I'm up for it" he replied, smiling insincerely, then continued drinking his pint.

Macca (G) beamed, it appeared everything was going according to his plan. "Good lad Jay Mac, it'll be a fuckin' gas." He paused and prepared to outline his strategy. "First thing is, we've got to get them out from behind those fuckin' big walls. No team can go in there without gettin' jumped. So me, Weaver and you Jay Mac, are gonna get right inside their estate and spray their main walls, cover them with our names, really fuckin' wind them up and that'll bring them out to us, with our crew waitin' in the cemetery for them." he smiled slyly at Jay Mac, "The question is have you got the balls to do it, just three of us in the middle of their ground?"

Intrigued and supremely confident in his own running ability, Jay Mac felt it might be an interesting venture, where he could test himself; avenging Mal 'the pig' was furthermost from his mind.

"Macca, like I said I'm up for it but get this straight, if they spot us in the middle of their estate, we're fucked. So if we've got to leg it, I'm not stoppin' for anyone. You two boys are gonna have to move yer arses." Jay Mac delivered his considered opinion and said no more.

Macca (G) smiled and nodded his agreement but Weaver had his own comment to add. "Just you remember Jay Mac that I saved yer fuckin' skin when Mono had yer, it won't be happenin' again."

With that he produced his prized, solid steel, toffee hammer and spat on it for good luck. This action of the crazed psychopath prompted Macca (G) to give one final instruction.

"Make sure yer all tooled up. When they come after us we want as much blood as possible, leave yer mark on them."

The crew finished their drinks, stood up and prepared to leave; Thin Lizzy's *Whiskey in the Jar* was playing on the jukebox in the corner as they departed.

Just as they were exiting through the partially glazed swing doors, Macca (G) was confronted by the eponymous Molly 'skank' Brown. Jay Mac had not seen her for several months but could not fail to note that her usual dishevelled appearance of dirty white blouse, ridiculously short skirt with frayed hem, badly laddered dark tights and down-at-heel, worn, red sling-back shoes were no longer the main items that made her so conspicuous earning her title, she was now heavily pregnant.

"Gary, we've got to talk, I need some money, please." she pleaded, catching hold of Macca (G)'s right hand.

"Fuck off, 'skank'. Don't you ever put one of your filthy claws on me." He pulled her hand from his then shoved her forcefully away from him.

"Please Gary, it's yours and you know it, you're the only one who didn't pull out when yer came." Again she tried to catch hold of the Heron leader.

Macca (G) was insensed, everyone knew Molly and how she made a pathetic 'living,' particularly her speciality of engaging groups of males in a long continuous session.

"Listen you smelly bitch anyone on this fuckin' estate could be the father. You've been poked by every feller who could be arsed, even some of the arl gits in there." He slapped her across the face with his right hand then took a handful of change from his coat pocket and flung it into the empty car park area. "There y'go, I hope that helps yer out." He laughed cruelly then walked away with his crew, never once looking back.

Jay Mac experienced a wave of nausea and considered abandoning their planned mission. Alone of the whole group he turned and momentarily glanced at the pitiful figure scrambling about on the dark, wet, tarmaced surface trying to retrieve some of the lose coin, while her younger protégés competed for the same.

Half an hour later the motley crew dressed in an eclectic mix of Crombies, leather coats of varying lengths, denim jackets, blue twenty-two inch parallel Flemings jeans or white Bakers trousers with red or now predominantly black Airwair, were climbing over the low moss covered, aged sandstone crenellated walls of the municipal cemetery.

They had made two stops en route, the first where Weaver had ran into his tenement block to collect his new headgear, the bowler hat he had taken as a trophy from Mono and the second, where Macca (G) collected a bag full of aerosol paint sprays and a white cardboard shoebox.

Jay Mac had asked about the latter at the time "What's in the shoebox?" to which he had received the edifying reply from Macca (G) "Fuckin' shoes, what d'yer think?" echoed by Weaver "Fuckin' shoes." Although he thought this was a peculiar item to take to a potential gang fight, he decided not to pursue the matter, for the present.

The twenty-strong crew quickly made their way through the dank cemetery, with a thin sheet of rain blowing towards them on a light cool breeze, the unseasonably warm weather of the previous week had disappeared and most of the youths had returned to their old warm Crombies or new leather coats.

When they had reached the southern edge of the cemetery Macca (G) deployed his troops, leaving the awesomely strong Crusher in command.

"Everyone get in out of sight behind the walls and let them come to us. When enough of them have jumped in 'ere, twat them hard, then it's everyone away before they can get any extra help". He paused then reminded them once again, "Me, Weaver and Jay Mac will be runnin' like fuck, once we've come back over these walls, we won't be stoppin'. Cut anyone else who lands by yer, then gerroff. We'll meet up back at the Heron, Crusher take over mate."

The six foot tall, fifteen stone apprentice drayman nodded his acceptance, maintaining his usual brooding silence.

"Fuckin' hell, he's even more quiet than he used to be." Jay Mac said as he, Macca (G) and Weaver climbed out of the cemetery, before strolling nonchalantly towards the sprawling walled estate of Ravens Hall.

The nearer they came to the enemy territory, with its ten foot high enclosing perimeter walls, covered with the new Ravens Boot Boys emblem and team names, the more daunting their task appeared.

Once they had crossed the main arterial dual carriageway, they arrived at the brick entrance opening and gateway to the dystopian kingdom of the Raven team, a landscape of dark grey, high rise tower blocks amidst long rows of equally sombre three-story tenements. The condescending high-minded architects and city planners had felt that a staggered, off-set ground layout would be far more stimulating for the 'fortunate' residents, making their regular mundane journeys a mini adventure as they tried to find their way to essential shops and services. This resulted in a confusing concrete maze where the bewildered human guinea pigs often lost their way, with painful consequences.

At the centre of the 'maze' was a magnificent eyesore of modern art, a bizarre construction of dark grey concrete with abstract cogs of iron, placed at aesthetically chosen intervals and appropriately entitled 'Industry', although other less heroic names had been suggested by those same fortunate residents. Four equally large narrow brick walls surrounded this ugly edifice and mercifully obscured its presence, although they were intended to provide interesting vistas, depending on the chosen approach route.

The three disparate companions now drew near to this graffiti covered heart of the bleak 'gulag'. Through the opening nearest to them they could see one lone youth with long feather cut hair and dressed in the Boot Boy style, with a dark brown leather coat over a patchwork jumper, Bakers trousers and black Airwair, he appeared to be waiting for them.

"I've got a bit of business to do." Macca (G) suddenly announced stepping through one of the spaces between the narrow walls that guarded the central monolith.

"You two get on with yer sprayin', I won't be long."

Weaver immediately set about the task in hand without a second glance at their wily companion and Jay Mac then joined him in defacing the Raven Boot Boys logos, before adding their own. From the entrance to their present location, whilst maintaining a watchful eye for enemy troops, they had been marking every available space with their Crown Boot Boys emblem and this joint effort was intended to be their masterpiece.

Jay Mac though diligently performing his assignment, was also observing Macca (G) and his dealings with the Ravens Boot Boy, who was wearing a similar three-quarter length leather coat. The earlier light rain gave them the appearance of shiny-backed insects, caught under the orange glow of the one functioning street lamp that had only recently blinked into life on top of its tall, precast concrete post, announcing the falling dusk.

The shoebox was handed over, opened and the goods examined. Clearly they were of sufficient quality Jay Mac thought, as he watched the purchaser pass a thick bundle of notes secured with a broad rubber band, to Macca (G) in exchange. After a quick but careful count, the Heron leader replaced the rubber band and put the bundle safely inside his leather coat. Without a word to his companions he turned and ran as fast as he could manage through the gap that he had previously entered by. The proud new owner of the shoebox casually walked away, counting out loud as he did.

"10... 9... 8... 7" he enumerated steadily like a talking countdown clock.

"Weaver, fuckin' leg it now!" Jay Mac shouted in warning.

"3... 2... 1" Countdown completed and securely carrying his valuable package, the spiky-haired Ravens Boot Boy stood still and shouted "Weaver's 'ere, we've got 'im, come on!" Even before his warning words had finished echoing around the concrete canyons, five eager Ravens players ran up behind Jay Mac and Weaver, blocking the escape route that Macca (G) had taken.

Using the most convenient weapon to hand Jay Mac sprayed the nearest boot boy fully in the face, sweeping directly across his eyes and temporarily blinding him. Weaver preferred a more direct approach and smashed his metal spray can hard into his potential captor's nose and mouth. A gap opened to their immediate right and both Crown players dashed though it.

"Weaver's here, we've got Weaver!" the exultant shout rang out prematurely from all sides. Others now joined in the chase.

Sprinting as fast as the winding litter-strewn terrain would allow, they both knew they had no notion of where an alternative escape route may be found. Running and keeping ahead of the pack was uppermost in their minds for the moment.

"Jay Mac, try here come on." Weaver suggested randomly with no obvious indicator that this may be successful. They now ran diagonally to their left, leaping over an upturned, wheel-less pram and tried to avoid slipping on sodden items of discarded clothing that were scattered everywhere about. Suddenly a wide brick lined alley appeared just off to their right ahead. Even as they raced into its mouth their pursuers had all cleared the pram obstacle and were closing on them rapidly.

"Fuck! It's a dead end!" Jay Mac shouted initially fearing the worst but as they neared the end of the alley, he was relieved to see they were in fact entering a broad open rectangular space that contained four burned out garages.

No streetlights illuminated this area only a pale partially risen half moon cast a weak glow into the evening's gloom before them. The furthest garage shell directly diagonal to their left, had one of its double wooden doors detached and wedged at a raking 60°angle against the asphalt covered roof.

"We're away mate, come 'ed, we can easily sprint up that door and over that roof." an elated Jay Mac shouted.

One of the surprised occupants of the stinking garage had other ideas. An excited male in his early twenties was being frantically masturbated by a young captive female and the sound of raucous laughter, clink of beer bottles and the red pinpoint glow of cigarettes, revealed there were other users also waiting for relief.

"Where the fuck d'yer think you're goin'?" he shouted stepping forward without bothering to put his angry member away.

Jay Mac answered his question by running towards him then leaping up and forward with his two feet, thrusting them into his enemy's stomach. Both males fell to the floor but the Crown player was up first and stamped hard several times onto the face of the other. Their three remaining original pursuers, who were leading a pack not far behind, now entered the arena.

Jay Mac was already running up the slanted door 'ramp' when he heard Weaver shout, "I'm Weaver, I did this to yer! I'm Weaver!"

Turning round he saw to his horror the crazed psychopath was dispatching their would-be captors, armed with his deadly steel toffee hammer in his right hand and his other weapon of choice, a glistening Stanley knife, in the left. Instantly he knew Weaver was giving him his chance to escape, he would buy Jay Mac the vital time to clear the garage roof and find an alternative exit from the walled estate.

Standing on the tattered asphalt sheet covering of the derelict building's roof, he looked for the best possible route to safety. Even as his elevated vantage point helped him decide, he cursed himself, self-confessed coward as he was, he could not abandon the hammer-wielding maniac to be overcome. In the garage chamber below his feet four more Ravens Boot Boys had stirred and were about to surround the wildly thrashing Weaver, as he vanquished all comers who ventured into the neck of the brick built alley.

Not carrying any form of weapon because of his recent court sentence for a similar offence, Jay Mac knew the key to survival here was improvisation. His knowledge of military history and guerrilla warfare came to the fore, as he searched for anything that could be used or fashioned into an instrument of war.

Still shouting his eponymous battle cry, Weaver was finally brought down by sheer weight of numbers and became a human football, while the Raven Boot Boys unleashed their anger upon him. The heavy gauge milk crate that Jay Mac smashed violently into their backs, took them totally by surprise. As they turned towards their attacker they were struck by the three foot length of timber, replete with an assortment of rusty nails at one end that he had picked up and was wielding with the devastating stroke of a major league baseball player. Noses and teeth were broken and flesh gashed as each new face obligingly moved within range. With the frenzy of years of pent up rage driving him on, Jay Mac had become an avenging mad man himself.

Slashed and bleeding some of the casualties staggered into the alley, only to succeed in blocking the path of any new arrivals. A bloodied Weaver had regained his feet and although he too was injured, he wanted to rejoin the fight.

"Gerrup that fuckin' door, now!" Jay Mac shouted without even considering the possibility of his team mate refusing. For once, whether it was due to the shock of being spoken to in this manner, or just common sense finally taking hold, Weaver sprinted up the battered wooden door and onto the garage roof. A blood spattered Jay Mac followed within moments.

"Stay behind me when we hit the deck, right? I know the way." he instructed once more, Weaver complied without saying a word.

When they had dropped into the street below they followed a zigzag route, running at full speed until they reached the only other exit from the walled estate, some six-hundred yards to the south of their original entry point. They burst out through the brick lined opening like divers coming up for air after a long ascent.

Making their way carefully past the rows of terraced houses, facing Ravens Hall, they looked for signs of enemy patrols knowing full well they were far from safety as yet. Even before they reached the tower blocks which were opposite the cemetery and marked the northern boundary of Ravens Boot Boys territory, they could see the familiar blue flashing lights.

"Ambulances, Jay Mac," Weaver observed unnecessarily.

"What's happened 'ere then?" Jay Mac asked in reply, glancing across the dual carriageway at the emergency vehicles and the numerous police officers also present.

"Keep in Weaver, we don't wanna get pulled." he advised, equally unnecessarily.

A short time later they had climbed into the damp, misty cemetery and began the final leg of their journey back to the Crown Estate and the Heron pub as previously arranged. There were no obvious signs of a major struggle having taken place within the eerily silent grounds and both youths concluded that something major must have prevented this. They did not know then, that two Raven boot boys who had been in a group pursuing Macca (G) intent on recovering their cash, had been struck by speeding outbound vehicles and were critically injured.

Within an hour Jay Mac and Weaver were seated in the Heron lounge bar with two pints of Double Diamond and two whiskey chasers in front of them, courtesy of a grateful but unapologetic Macca (G).

"I told yer I wasn't gonna stop for anyone. So what's *your* problem?" he asked, smiling slyly and addressing his question primarily to Jay Mac.

"Why didn't yer give us a shout and why was that cunt countin' down, before he started shoutin' his head off?" Jay Mac pressed on.

"Look, I ran past yer, ok? That should've given yer a clue to gerroff. An how would I know why some fucker was countin' maybe it was his idea of a joke." Macca (G) lied knowing full well that he had 'sold' Weaver to the Ravens Team, to sweeten the deal.

"Do me a favour, don't ever ask me to do anythin' like that again, ok?" Jay Mac said, before downing his whiskey in one gulp.

"Are y'sure about that JayMac, lad? Yer did good, Weaver tells me y'held y'nerve." Macca (G) began, then took the bundle of notes from his inside pocket and peeled off two lower denomination bills. "Before yer make up yer mind, here's y'wages." he said smiling as he passed him two £5 notes.

Jay Mac took the cash without hesitation but understood that he had just agreed a contract that could only end one way. Nearly two weeks of his usual wage had been earned in one evening. Jay Mac did not ask again what was in the shoebox but the images of the overdosed Crown team senior, Gaz, lying amidst the stinking refuse, continually played over in his mind. He knew the two were connected, though his moral dilemma was alleviated by the lure of easy money.

A disconsolate Weaver was more concerned with the loss of his recently acquired headgear and bemoaned his misfortune.

Chapter 4

Why Can't We Live Together?

Monday 9th April 1973

It was a warm, pleasant spring day with an almost cloudless, pale blue sky stretching over the city centre. Jay Mac had been delivering bills of lading and shipping notices for the company were he was employed, to several other forwarding agents and his planned route ended near St John's Gardens. Old Stan, the ex-Royal Artillery B.S.M and Jay Mac's immediate boss, had reluctantly agreed that he could commence his lunch hour as soon as he had completed his delivery round. As a consequence all of his office communiqués were handed out at each location in the shortest possible time.

Standing in front of Tony Harris menswear store on Lime Street, Jay Mac was admiring some of the latest essential fashion prerequisites for the young male, when he heard a familiar if affected voice behind him.

"Hi there Jay Mac my man, doin' some window shoppin', yeah?" Floyd asked in his best soul singer's drawl.

The Crown team player turned to see the ever cool, good looking, six foot two, apprentice chef standing with two tall black youths who worked with him and were his closest friends. All three were sporting medium sized afro hairstyles including Floyd and were similarly dressed in well-cut leather coats of varying lengths, patchwork jumpers, wide flared trousers and platform shoes.

"What's happenin' people?" Jay Mac asked affecting his own version of Floyd's contrived American accent.

"We're just cruisin' around town checkin' out the snatch." Floyd answered for them all, then added, "Listen we're goin' for a few drinks over in the Moonstone, come with us man, it'll give us a chance to catch up."

"Why not, I've got a bit of extra time today." Jay Mac replied then crossed over the main road with Floyd, Kenny (D) and Frenchy, heading towards St John's shopping precinct and the Moonstone bar.

A few minutes later all four were seated in the relatively comfortable, trendy leather furniture and dimly lit surroundings of this popular, modern subterranean drinking establishment.

Elton John's *Benny and the Jets* was playing on the jukebox and it was clearly not to Floyd's taste.

"I'm not into this shit. Frenchy put somethin' decent on man, when this ends." Floyd asked, with his usual ingratiating smile.

"Fuck man how did yer know I don't happen to be a big Elton John fan?" Frenchy replied with a grin as he rose from his seat to check the available selection.

While they sat drinking their bottled lager beers from tall glasses, Jay Mac listened to Floyd explaining how his 'business' was prospering. He quickly began to find his former associate's comments irritating.

"See what get's me Floyd is this, I'm glad yer doin' well an I've got no problem with yer sellin' knock-off but this shite yer movin' on the estate now, it's not right man." Jay Mac announced.

"Supply and demand my man" Floyd began, "where there's a demand, I supply, simple as that."

"Yeah, that's cool Floyd but it's a bit chicken and egg situation, y'know what I mean?" Jay Mac replied. "Which came first, the demand or your friggin' supply?"

"We'll never know, Jay Mac, we'll never know." Floyd said with a smile but added coldly "One thing's for sure, while I'm makin' big money, nothing is gonna get in my way, *nothing*."

"I'll tell that to Gaz next time I see him, now that he's back out of hospital." Jay Mac said sarcastically intending to end the conversation.

Floyd momentarily dropped his usual charming demeanour, "Gaz is a fuckin' tit, yeah? He mixes pills with grass and then drops a half bottle of J.D. I can't help that. So leave it there, I don't need a fuckin' sermon."

Almost instantly he reverted back to his former character. "Anyway, when y'ready, there's plenty of cash waitin for yer, no need to window shop anymore, just say the word." Floyd then turned toward Kenny (D), the skilful Martial Arts exponent. "Kenny yer gonna have to start takin' lessons from my main man here. He's gettin' a bit of a rep for fuckin' people up and savin' the day."

They all laughed including Frenchy, who had returned from the jukebox and the bar with another round of drinks.

Jay Mac was uncomfortable with any talk of him being a capable fighter, or worse being considered a hero. He knew Weaver had told Macca (G) what had happened in their Ravens Hall skirmish but believed the story had gone no further.

Quickly changing the subject, he too addressed Kenny (D) "What's happenin' with your Karate, Kenny where about are y'now?" he asked.

"It's goin' good man, am takin' my black soon, so I'm gonna step up my trainin'." Kenny replied.

"I wish I knew some of that Martial Arts shit", Jay Mac began "a guy on the estate, Jimmy McCoy, showed me some blocks and strikes and I've definitely been on the receivin' end of some bad kicks, so I'd like to deliver a few of them meself."

"If y'serious man, come up on Sunday mornin', I'm trainin' at the club, doin' some Kumite and Kata." Kenny (D) offered generously. "Wear some loose gear an I'll give yer a few tips, I'll ask my Sensei, he'll be cool."

Under the influence of alcohol, Jay Mac felt this seemed like a good idea and accepted the invitation. After obtaining the directions to Kenny (D)'s club, he went to the bar and got another round of beers, conscious of the time, though acting blasé about it.

"Yeah, that sounds good to me Kenny. I'm lookin' forward to it." he said then relaxed back into his seat and enjoyed his drink, listening to Frenchy's selection on the jukebox as Marvin Gaye's outstanding *Inner City Blues (Makes Me Wanna Holler)* began to play.

Ten minutes later two young office women entered the bar wearing blouses and short skirts, revealing their slim figures in silhouette. In the gloom it was practically impossible to make out their facial features and yet before they had reached the bottom stair, Floyd was already waiting at the bar.

"Hi ladies, what are you having?" he began, flashing his trademark charismatic smile. "It's my birthday and I'm sure that you would like to help me celebrate."

Both females laughed and joined him at the bar. Jay Mac knew it was time to depart and return to work leaving Floyd to his.

Sunday 15th April 1973

On a grey Sunday morning with a cool breeze blowing, a week after receiving Kenny (D)'s offer, the bleary eyed Jay Mac arrived shortly before ten o'clock outside an old Victorian mission hall, now home to the 'South City Karate Club'. In the cold light of a typically bleak English spring Sunday morning, he was wondering why he had accepted his friend's proposal. Living on the Kings Estate at the furthermost northern edge of the city and without personal transport, his journey across to its opposite side had taken nearly two hours travelling on the unreliable Sunday municipal bus service. Even though he had curtailed his drinking on the previous evening, he was not feeling in top condition or ready for major physical exertion.

Leaning against the grimy, aged, formerly red sandstone brick wall, dressed in his black Harrington-style jacket, twenty-two inch parallel Flemings jeans and cherry-red Airwair, he was acutely aware that he was a long way from home in an area that he had never visited before and which was totally unfamiliar to him.

Two excessively tall black youths were casually strolling towards him, dressed in long soft leather coats of brown and camel colour, wide bell-bottom flared jeans and high platform shoes, their large loose afro hairstyles were waving about in the strengthening breeze, as they sauntered up to where he was standing. The taller of the two, the camel-coloured leather wearer, positioned himself directly in front of Jay Mac; he had a dark moustache and goatee beard with thick sideburns down to his jaw-line.

"Am I trippin' or somethin' Kyle?" he began, quizzically glancing at his friend then back to the Crown team player. "Is this a skinny white boy just standin' in front of our club like he owns it?"

Kyle cupped his chin with his right hand and said "I think this is one cheeky mother-fucker, just strollin' in here lookin' for trouble with his big red booties."

"Am waitin' for me mate lads, I don't want any trouble, thanks." Jay Mac said, as calmly as he could manage.

Kyle was not happy with this response, "Listen to this white boy, Marcus, tellin' us he don't want trouble but eyeballin' us like *he's* the man."

Marcus leaned in close to Jay Mac and prodded him in the chest with the index finger of his right hand, "Hear what I'm sayin' to you, you skinny little spook, you ain't got no friends round here, right?" When he had finished speaking he stepped away a few paces and squatted into a low stance, preparing to deliver a powerful thrust kick.

"What the fuck is goin' on here?" Kenny (D) shouted as he came sprinting towards the trio.

"That's what we've been askin' Kenny, now we're gonna fuck this whitey up good." Marcus replied, misunderstanding Kenny's irate question.

Instantly placing himself between Jay Mac and the two youths, Kenny spoke to them in a clear, strong voice. "This is my friend Jay Mac, I invited him here. You make one move against him an I will drop you both now."

There was a brief, tense pause while Kenny's words were fully absorbed. Kyle was the first to speak.

"Fuck! Kenny, man we were just jokin' with him, y'know. I mean, he looks like one of those South Klan dickheads, no offence man."

"Yeah, how are we to know 'whitey' is friends with a brother?" Marcus asked.

Kenny snapped "Shut the fuck up! Tits like you two make me puke. 'Whitey'! What's that supposed to mean?" he paused and stared angrily at them both. "My woman's white and the last time I saw her, your mother was white too Marcus, so are you sayin' y'gonna fuck them up too?"

Neither youth replied but looked away. Just then a small, stocky white male in his early fifties, with grizzled features arrived wearing a black bomber jacket, blue jeans and an old pair of Converse All Stars basketball boots.

"If anyone's gettin' fucked up round 'ere it'll be by me, either in this club or outside, ok?" he paused and looked at all four youths. "Don't ever let me hear anyone talkin' shit, or they'll be in a fuckin' world of pain."

The three club members responded as one. "Yes Sensei."

With that the older male unlocked the door and led the way up the well-worn, creaking stairs.

"Thanks Kenny." Jay Mac said as they reached the top, before they all bowed silently as a mark of respect to the spirit of the Dojo.

"Don't mention it Jay Mac, you're a mate, that's it. 'Ere catch these, yer can't train in those fuckin' jeans." He laughed as he threw the youth a pair of white Karate bottoms from his kit bag.

"Fuckin' great, these look just like me bakers kecks," Jay Mac replied, smiling.

Two hours later after completing hundreds of wrist strengthening two-knuckle press-ups; gut shredding sit-ups and ball bursting leg stretches, plus attempting dozens of focused dynamic punches and kicks, an exhausted Jay Mac took his place kneeling at the edge of the polished wooden floor drenched in sweat with aching muscles, waiting for a display of free-style fighting or Kumite by the 'seniors'.

When Kenny (D) entered the human-enclosed arena, there was a palpable sense of expectancy from the assembled students or karateka. Five opponents from the third Kyu (brown belts and above) were selected by the Sensei and entered the 'ring' one after the other, without a moments respite in between for the black belt candidate, Kenny (D). Despite impressive displays of technical ability, power and channelled aggression, the first three contenders were dispatched effortlessly by the serenely calm Shotokan warrior. Kyle and Marcus were invited to make a joint attack and threw themselves into their task with a determined ferocity. Spinning jumping kicks, sweeps, blocks combined with powerful punches, elbow and edge of hand strikes dazzled the spectators, as the three combatants engaged in the contest without reservation or thought of personal injury.

The grim Sensei made no attempt to call time or halt the proceedings and stood watching impassively as it raged on, despite blood having been drawn by all three. Eventually Kyle, who was clearly tiring, made a momentary lapse of concentration receiving an unbalancing ankle sweep, instantly followed by a devastating thrust kick to his abdomen as a reward for his error. Marcus tried to seize the advantage as his partner dropped to the floor but the lightning fast Kenny (D) sidestepped his lunging punch, deflected it with his forearm and immediately struck him in the face with a ferocious back-fist whilst simultaneously delivering a stomach-churning groin kick.

The contest was decided and the Sensei bowed slightly in acknowledgement of his star pupil's prowess. A few moments later after all the students and Jay Mac had also made a formal bow to the spirit of the Dojo, the session ended. When Kenny (D) and Jay Mac had changed from their training clothes and were about to leave after thanking the Sensei, the grim instructor spoke directly to Jay Mac.

"You did a little bit of trainin' today and then you watched. That was a one off favour to Kenny; no one comes here to watch. If you've got the balls to come back you take part and you fight. If that's not for you, don't come here again."

Jay Mac understood perfectly the Sensei's admonishment and left in silence with the triumphant, yet ever humble Kenny (D). He thanked his friend again then departed on the first stage of his journey back to the Kings Estate.

By the time the tired youth was seated downstairs at the rear of his second bus, it had begun to rain heavily. After ten minutes of travelling along on a grey, wet Sunday afternoon with his limited vision through the grimy window, obscured further by an additional covering of dirty rain rivulets and the seeping warmth of the engine soothing his aching back, he began to drift into a semi-consciousness where though not quite asleep, he was no longer aware of his immediate surroundings.

Whilst contemplating the events of the morning, particularly those preceding his entrance to the club, he adopted a philosophical interpretation of Marcus and Kyle's actions. Similar to the way he had explained to Blue that the Billy Boys and 1690's Skins were not really motivated by genuine sectarian issues, so too he felt their anger was directed at him not because of deeply embedded racial prejudice but mainly because he was different. Skin colour was as much a pretext as religious denomination, all that mattered was he was not one of their group, therefore he was a potential enemy and target. Living out on the northern extremities of the city in a vast, almost exclusively white, blue-collar, proletarian ghetto, he wondered how any of the Kings or Crown team players would react if Marcus and Kyle suddenly arrived unannounced, or worse still a decent, honourable character like Kenny (D). As he finally drifted into a deep sleep, he hoped that he would never have the occasion to find out.

Monday 16th April 1973

The dismal, grey Sunday slipped into a dull, wet Monday morning, announcing the start of another working week for the masses, including the still tired Jay Mac. Arriving just past his 8.30am start time, as he ran into the small reception and mail office after bounding up the two flights of stairs leading from the front entrance, he was greeted by the stern figure of his immediate boss 'Old Stan'. At seventy-one years of age the six foot two, eighteen stone ex-battery sergeant major, Stanley Atkins, was still very much an imposing figure. Standing immediately inside the doorway of the dingy room with its peeling paintwork and cracked plaster, unusually wearing his full uniform including cap but still incongruously clutching his old briar pipe, Stan stopped Jay Mac from proceeding any further.

"Don't bother coming in or taking your coat off" he began.

"C'mon Stan, don't arse about. I'm sorry that I'm half a second late, the friggin' bus broke down on London Road." Jay Mac offered honestly by way of an explanation.

"Aye, you've always got an excuse 'aven't you? Not like in my day, in the Army, we couldn't just give an excuse to hordes of mad Nazis trying to invade our country..." Stan stopped himself before launching into one of his many lengthy tirades about the lack of moral fibre of today's youth.

"Anyway, don't get me started on bloody kids. One of the senior partners wants to see you, sharpish, so move y'arse and get along to Mr Roache's office, now." Stan instructed then took a huge satisfying draw on his glowing pipe.

"Yes sir, three bags full, sir!" Jay Mac replied, clicking his heels together while saluting the old soldier, then turned and marched briskly along the narrow, glazed-tile lined corridor with the sound of his footsteps echoing in advance.

Mr Roache was in his office but his secretary told Jay Mac that he was otherwise engaged and instructed him to wait in the adjoining boardroom. Jay Mac was more than happy to comply as this was his favourite room in the Victorian chambers where his employment was located. Unlike the drab, utilitarian front office where he and Timothy Murphy, his fellow office junior worked with Old Stan, this grand chamber had been designed to entertain and impress shipping line owning prospective customers in the great days of sail. A huge highly-polished Peruvian mahogany table dominated the space, with its fourteen matching richly carved chairs; set all about the walls were portraits both of the fastest Clippers of the day and of serious men of business with magnificent moustaches and, or, substantial sideburns .

One of Jay Mac's underling tasks had been to lay out the company's silverware under the watchful, ever-critical eye of the aged ex-B.S.M in preparation for major board meetings of all the senior partners. It was a rare, satisfying chore, the only aspect of his lowly position that he actually enjoyed, setting the places; fine writing implements; drinking vessels; port and sherry decanters and precisely positioning the glorious centre-piece of a sliver plated three masted sailing ship heroically crashing through tempestuous waves.

"Ah, young Master Mack," Mr Roache the balding, portly, double-breasted suit wearer, announced in his public schoolboy manner on entering the room from his adjoining office.

"Good morning Mr Roache," Jay Mac replied politely.

"Yes indeed good morning, although some of us were here a lot earlier than others." He paused and casually strolled towards an exquisite walnut veneered bureau, which stood against the far wall and opened the ebony wood humidor on its top, then extracted a large, thick, dark-leaved cigar. Taking a few moments to light this sizeable smoke he spoke to Jay Mac in short staccato bursts.

"At a dinner party the other night... great bunch of fellows... and their charming ladies of course... One chap, magistrate... surprised to see one of our people up before him, twice." He finished lighting his cigar and enjoyed a few satisfying puffs before continuing.

Jay Mac began to fear the worst but said "Listen Mr Roache if this is about the promotion I was promised last year, I'm happy to accept."

The senior partner scowled "Yes, bloody funny, you are a wit aren't you?" He did not wait for a reply to his rhetorical question. "Anyway, the thing is, we can't have 'Edwin Roach, Symes and Butterworth' associated with a common thief, a hoodlum, it just won't do."

Jay Mac now knew exactly the direction this conversation was taking.

"I see and what do you propose to do about this, change the name perhaps to something less snooty?"

Mr Roache the great, great, grandson of the company founder Sir Edwin Roache, who initially made lavish profits from his lucrative dealings in the slave trade, was aghast, almost apoplectic. "How dare you speak to one of your betters in such a manner! We made a grave error of judgement employing one of your sort in the first place. So I won't waste any more time on this unpleasant matter. You're finished here; no need to work out your notice, there will be two weeks wages in lieu waiting for you at the petty cash. Off you go." He tapped the grey ash from his expensive cigar into a silver plated ash tray that he had just taken from the top of the bureau and turned to exit the room.

"Is that it? After nearly two years of fillin' bloody envelopes, openin' mail, runnin' errands and makin' coffee all day for Old Stan and his mates for a fuckin' pittance. I'm out of a job because some rich cunt mentions my name to you at a dinner party for twats?" Jay Mac shouted angrily at the senior partner.

"No you're not out because of that, it's because of what you are. Now, collect your money and leave these premises at once." Mr Roache replied calmly.

"Fuck you! Mind if I don't tug me forelock on the way out Master" Jay Mac snapped before leaving the boardroom for the final time and slamming the heavy wooden door behind him.

A few moments later, after collecting his two weeks' severance pay, he marched back along to the front office to say goodbye to Timothy his fellow junior, however, when he made to enter the small office Stan barred his way.

"Got rid of you then, finally?" he asked smiling. "Good riddance I say, y'no good, you'll come a cropper soon enough, mark my words."

Jay Mac drew himself up to his full five foot ten height, stood to attention and saluted the old veteran sharply. "Permission to live my life sir?" then as he turned to walk away, he echoed Stan's usual morning request for a hot beverage "Stan, you fuckoffee!" and leapt down the two flights of stairs into the cool morning air outside and freedom.

Saturday 28th April 1973

Almost two weeks had passed since Jay Mac's dismissal from his Office Junior position. Sitting at a table in the Eagle with his team mates on a warm spring evening repeatedly counting his small change, he began to fully comprehend the meaning of the adage 'freedom isn't free.' With his resources rapidly diminishing and little hope of any additional funds in the near future, having been refused unemployment benefit for six weeks because his former employer had stated he had been 'sacked' due to gross misconduct, Jay Mac knew his prospects were bleak.

"Short of cash, mate?" the ever-chirpy Blue asked, sitting on Jay Mac's right with the sullen Irish next to him. "I'll get yer ale in, don't worry about it." he added.

"Nah, I'm ok Blue. Just waitin' for some dole cunt to pay up, y'know what they're like." Jay Mac replied, recalling the pleasure with which the benefits clerk had denied his claim, having continuously sneered throughout his lengthy interview particularly at the youth's lack of qualifications.

"I'm just gonna finish this pint, then I'm off anyway." Jay Mac advised. He knew the one cardinal rule that his uncle had drummed into him was to never accept a drink, if he could not buy one in return.

Irish was engaging in his usual pastime of attempting to blow a sequence of smoke rings, in between taking regular drinks from his pint, he leaned forward and spoke, "Hard times eh, without yer little job?" he began. "I bet that went down well with yer aunt and uncle, gettin' the boot from work?"

"They were fine with it Irish, seein' as yer askin'." Jay Mac lied not wishing to remember the furious argument, accompanying profanities and threats that had followed his announcement of his dismissal to his guardians.

"Yeah, thee said it was time I moved on anyway."

Irish laughed at this unlikely statement, "Maybe y'could ask yer mate Macca (G) for a bit of spare cash?"

Jay Mac was becoming tired of his team mate's questioning and tone, "You don't need to worry about what I do, yeah? I'm thinkin' of going down to the Irish Centre to see if they'll give me a loan. I'll tell them I know you and they'll be bound to help."

Before anything further was said, the distinctive sound of loud air-horns blasting outside the main entrance could be heard even above the general clamour and Argent's *God Gave Rock and Roll to You* which was currently playing on the old jukebox.

"That's me ladies, I'm off." Jay Mac announced then swigged the last of his pint and made a hasty departure.

Outside sitting on his ultra-cool Lambretta SX200 with its dazzling array of mirrors, gleaming silver side panels, chromed Florida bars and black Perspex fly-screen bearing two silver stars, was Floyd wearing a white peaked Centurion helmet, black sunglasses, a dark brown leather jacket, grey checked wide flared trousers and platform shoes.

"There's a spare lid on the backrest, jump on and let's gerroff, we've got people to see man." Floyd called to Jay Mac smiling with his usual easy manner.

The youth fastened the helmet and secured the white plastic chin cup, then sat behind Floyd ready to take a journey that would change more than his fortune.

Speeding along the apparently random, confused route that Floyd had deliberately chosen to ensure Jay Mac would be unable to retrace it; except for a few brief exchanges when stopped at traffic lights, the incongruous pair were silent. Dressed in his black Harrington style jacket, blue twenty two inch parallel Flemings jeans and cherry red Airwair, Jay Mac represented a youth cult that was disappearing and in the process of metamorphosing into its next cycle, Floyd had already made the transition and was the face of things to come.

With dusk falling and an orange red sky rapidly losing its under-lighting as the sun sank into the west, exiting along the River Mersey out to the Irish Sea, the Crown players finally arrived at their destination. Floyd turned the scooter into a dimly lit side street then mounted the pavement before eventually bringing his vehicle to a halt outside a small, shabby, old Victorian public house at the end of a row of shops with boarded fronts that appeared derelict. An antique, heavily weathered, painted wooden sign hung on two small rings above the entrance, depicting a salty old sea dog and a barely decipherable name 'The Seafarer.' On the opposite side of the narrow rubble and litter strewn street was a bookmaker which was closed and secured with heavy steel shutters, covered in graffiti and, a grimy looking fish and chip shop. Bathed in its yellow fluorescent light, five males in their early twenties were leaning against the chip shop's single pane window, eating their fish suppers. All but one was black and wore large Afro hairstyles, flared jeans and capped-sleeved t-shirts; even in silhouette it was obvious that they trained regularly with heavy weights.

Floyd dismounted then called over to them "What's happenin'? Usual rate, yeah?"

One of the stocky crew casually strolled over to Floyd, "You know the deal, depends on how long you is stayin' man." Then he shook hands with the Crown player receiving a folded five pound note as he did. "Later Floyd." he said with a smile then returned to his colleagues.

It appeared the noisy scooter's arrival had clearly been heard from within the small alehouse, when its swing door was opened by a huge, muscular, bald-headed black male, although the blaring din of *Simmer Down* by The Wailers loudly playing within, effectively drowning out all other sound suggested it was more likely that the doorman had been expecting them.

"Evenin' Floyd my man." he said slapping the former's right palm with his open hand. He did not speak to Jay Mac but scrutinised the youth intently as he passed by.

There were two adjoining ground floor rooms in this tiny drinking establishment; they had entered the bare-boarded smoky bar where the jukebox was situated. Two groups of older black males were seated at the small circular tables playing cards and smoking either cigars or cigarettes, they ignored the new arrivals. A surly barman dressed in his shirtsleeves nodded in their direction, "Go right on through Floyd." he said, gesturing towards a small parlour.

Jay Mac was now not sure that this was a wise venture, realising that he was once again in a totally unfamiliar environment, a long way from his own area. Stepping into the small parlour he was relieved to see some familiar faces. Already seated around the room were Frenchy, Kelvin, Delroy and to Jay Mac's surprise, Kenny (D). Two other males, one of similar age to Jay Mac and Floyd and the other in his early sixties were also present.

"What's happenin' brothers?" Floyd asked as he and Jay Mac pulled over two stools and sat in front of the six-strong group. The older male was heavy set with a tight greying Afro, a grey moustache and goatee beard and wore a colourful floral print open-necked shirt with several gold medallions on display; he was studying Jay Mac carefully as he sat before him.

"My name is Sherman, ok?" he began, "you know why they call me that boy?" Jay Mac shook his head then Sherman replied with a broad smile "Cos I am a tank and if you fuck wi' me I will roll right over you and crush you into de ground."

"Right, I'll make sure I remember that." Jay Mac managed to reply trying to appear calm.

They all laughed and then without being summoned the barman appeared with a tray of beers for the whole party.

"Nice one Sherman, I think you've put the shits up my friend good style, so let's get down to business, yeah?" Floyd said, suddenly taking control of the situation.

He briefly but concisely outlined what the 'arrangements' would be and where Jay Mac fitted in. "So most of you already know this guy and I'm makin' sure tonight we're all clear, he is the only one you ever hand a 'drop' to, no other fucker white or black." Then he turned towards the youth whom Jay Mac did not recognise at first. "This young man is Samuel, been livin' here a few years now from Ghana, if I'm right?"

"Yeah Floyd you is right." Samuel replied smiling, revealing his impressive teeth. "I know Jay Mac, I have met him before at de club."

Jay Mac looked at him more closely and the small tribal scars cut deeply into his prominent cheeks.

"Yeah, I remember you now, yer a yellow belt, I was partnered with yer for some kicks and blocks, I think."

"Good." said Floyd, "I don't want any fuck ups. I've worked with Jay Mac in the past and when he came to me a couple of days ago lookin' to earn some bread, I knew it was gonna be a good set up for everyone."

Floyd once again explained precisely how Jay Mac would meet any one of the group at different previously agreed locations in the city centre shopping district. The 'package' would be delivered to Floyd when and where he specified and Jay Mac would receive details of his next assignment and payment at that time. Once everyone was familiarised and happy with their role they began to relax, especially as more beers had been arriving continuously.

Jay Mac sat back listening to the sounds of The Upsetters and *Return of Django* playing on the jukebox in the bar. However, no amount of alcohol could drown the nausea he felt at the contract he had just agreed to, he knew his recent arrangements with Macca (G) were nothing in comparison and paled in the significance of possible consequences. Attempting to reassure himself he tried to consider his new delivery job as work of some form; he could still see his uncle's enraged face screaming at him "Find some work, any fucking work, or you're out."

"I didn't think you'd come on board Jay Mac" Kenny (D) said, raising a curious eyebrow.

"Everyone needs some cash Kenny and if yer can't get it one way, y'gonna have to find another." Jay Mac replied trying to convey his dilemma in a few lines. "Anyway, no offence mate but I definitely wasn't expecting to find you in on this game."

Floyd laughed and interrupted them both, "See that Kenny, Jay Mac thinks you're too much of a decent guy to be involved with the likes of us." He paused and took a lengthy drag of his dark cigarillo then continued "Yer see Kenny's into this Bushido shit, he's an honourable warrior but he also likes puttin' it about a bit and that can end up costin' a brother some heavy coin. Am I right Kenny?"

The skilled martial arts exponent accepted Floyd's comments apparently without resentment and explained "Yeah, y'know its true Floyd. I've got a kid that I'm payin' out for and my woman's gonna drop one in a couple of weeks, so I am truly fucked up man."

They all laughed at Kenny's honest assessment of his situation and carried on with their drinking.

Jay Mac left the room to use the toilet facilities, which in this case meant urinating against a crumbling, lime washed brick wall in the yard outside. The actual lavatory had long ceased to function, though from the powerful, pungent aroma escaping from the free-standing, doorless, privy not all customers regarded this as any reason not to use it.

When he re-entered the small parlour his new business associates raised their glasses to him and welcomed him to the venture "Y'need to go into the bar and upstairs Jay Mac," Floyd began cryptically. "It's upstairs, first door on y'right, in fact it's the only door that opens. I've left it there for yer. So could yer get it for me?"

Jay Mac was totally bemused by Floyd's request but took this to be part of a test or initiation rite and said he would get the item for his 'boss'.

"Off y'go then," Floyd said with an unusually serious expression on his face.

Jay Mac left the parlour once again and passed through the small adjoining bar before climbing a narrow, steep, creaking staircase. At the top of the stairs immediately facing him was a battered wooden door without a handle but instead was padlocked with a heavy chain through a metal hasp. Turning to his right he saw an equally aged door but this one had a handle of crazed off-white porcelain. Without knocking he turned this, opened the heavy door and stepped into the room to retrieve Floyd's 'mystery' item.

"That's ok sugar, no need to knock, I've been expectin' you." said an attractive brown skinned woman in her early thirties, reclining on a large bed with a plain dark wooden headboard.

"Sorry, er... I think, er... I'm in the wrong room." Jay Mac stammered, genuinely believing he had made a mistake.

"That depends on what y'want, sugar, if you want some good lovin' you *is* in the *right* room." She smiled sweetly, changing her posture slightly, causing her large breasts to move against each other, barely contained as they were within the black satin basque that emphasised her curvaceous figure.

Jay Mac stood at the foot of the bed which dominated the small room and, except for a dressing table topped with a triptych mirror, was the only item of furniture within the confined space. His gaze darted from her shapely nylon stocking clad legs to her voluptuous, deep cleavaged bosom, then fixed on the dark thatched mound clearly visible through her tiny, black transparent panties, at the top of her thighs, framed by her taught suspenders. His nervousness was subsiding as rapidly as his desire began to rise of its own accord.

"What's the matter sugar, have y'never seen a full-grown woman before?" she asked curiously. "I can tell you like what y'see," she added, genuinely.

Jay Mac's mind flooded with a thousand sensible thoughts all of which were entirely redundant. He threw his jacket to one side, pulled off his patchwork jumper and bent down to untie his boots, before removing his jeans; all was done awkwardly in the utmost haste.

"My name's Sally, everyone calls me 'Sweet Sally' you ain't got to rush with me, just take your time and let it come natural." Sally advised kindly, watching the youth's rapid divestment of clothing.

He stepped round to the side of the bed with his straining underwear barely containing his throbbing erection and his lithe, athletic form primed for vigorous action.

"Condoms are on the dressin' table in the glass bowl. Put one on or you ain't puttin' it in." Sally instructed calmly.

Jay Mac grabbed a prophylactic from its 'dispenser' and tore open the wrapper. His intended paramour looked on as he rolled the rubber sheath down the length of his member and then signalled her formal agreement that proceedings may commence.

"You really are pleased to see me, climb on sugar, don't let it go cold," she called opening her arms and legs to him in one welcoming movement.

Her more than ample bosom was soon released from the faint pretence of a restraint, which her struggling satin underwear had feigned. Jay Mac gave each well-rounded breast his full attention before attempting to remove the gossamer-thin triangle of material that barely covered her desire.

"They're tied at the sides." Sally breathed softly into his ear with her perfume engulfing him.

Deftly tugging the loosely tied bows at each side of her panties, he drew the tiny garment from her and she accommodatingly raised her large, rounded bottom to assist. Even as the discarded panties fluttered onto the nearby dressing table, where they had been flung, Jay Mac entered the expectant female, who instantly clamped her legs around his waist.

He rode her with determination increasing his pace then holding back before resuming again, he wanted to stay the course and not be spent before reaching the final furlong. Sally squeezed and pulled him to her with her experienced thighs, she perfectly matched his every thrust with her own undulations. For his part, Jay Mac knew that downstairs in the parlour his business associates would be awaiting a detailed post-race report from him and no doubt at some point from his skilled partner.

Sally suddenly released him and shifted her position, bringing her ankles to either side of his face. She pushed hard against his deeply embedded member with her most private part and drew him in further than he thought possible, squeezing him tightly as she did. Both parties were now glistening with sweat and he gazed at her magnificent, tanned breasts whilst pummelling her harder and faster with each stroke. Sally increased her pace again to match his and began moaning softly. Jay Mac knew he could not hold on much longer. Even as this exciting thought passed through his mind, he could hear the gruff voice of his brutal school PE teacher urging him on to win another gruelling cross-country race 'Come on Mack you little turd, you Nancy boy, you're letting everyone down, stay the bloody course and step it up.' He pushed on arching his back, riding for his life then exploded in an overwhelming climax.

"I've won, I fuckin' did it!" he shouted.

"You certainly did sugar, you did it." Sally acknowledged, herself breathing erratically and drenched in their sweat.

A few moments later the exhausted but smiling Jay Mac rejoined the expectant crew in the parlour below. He was greeted by a chorus of cheers as he entered the small, smoky room; *I Can See Clearly Now* by Johnny Nash was playing on the jukebox.

"Had a good time Jay Mac?" Floyd shouted. "Welcome to the *'Firm'*."

Another round of drinks appeared and Jay Mac swallowed his refreshing pint in a series of rapid gulps, much to the amusement of his peers. After Floyd had downed his drink the pair stood up to leave. Sally appeared in the doorway dressed in a long blue silk Chinese print dressing gown. She squeezed into position and sat on Sherman's lap.

"How did the white boy do Sally?" he asked with a broad smile.

"That boy has got a lot of anger believe me." she announced and the crew all laughed.

Floyd turned to Jay Mac as they stepped out from the bar into the cool night air, "Take that as a compliment my man, you done well."

Chapter 5

John Barleycorn Must Die

Sunday 17th June and Thursday 21st June 1973

During the seven weeks since his warm welcome to the firm of 'Floyd & Co.' Jay Mac, the courier had accepted five 'packages' from his contacts and delivered them all safely. His 'employer' was pleased with the service he was providing and had paid him well for his efforts. With his unemployment benefit having commenced also, the usually financially challenged youth was beginning to feel relatively affluent. As an added bonus he had 'earned' further emoluments for accompanying Macca (G) and Weaver on two more 'shoebox' ventures to the Meadow Green housing estate that bounded their own territory to the immediate south. These excursions, unlike that to Ravens Hall passed without incident and Jay Mac received a similar fee for each trip adding further to his coffers.

On this warm summer's evening, after a hot June day, Jay Mac attired almost entirely in new apparel, including an expensive ox blood leather jacket and the latest checked parallel trousers, known locally as 'Ruperts,' was strolling through the Crown Estate with his unlikely friend the hammer-wielding psychopath, Weaver. In recent weeks the unstable Crown player had attached himself increasingly to the slightly perturbed youth and a friendship of sorts had developed.

"Should be a good do Jay Mac." Weaver stated as they approached their intended destination, the Unicorn Public House.

"Yeah mate, it'll definitely be interestin' to see who shows up tonight." Jay Mac replied, then added "An if y'main man is there, he's always fuckin' entertainin'."

Even as they turned into the lane where the pub was located they could see numerous other team players approaching the entrance. Shortly both youths joined the throng and made their way inside to one of the three bars in this huge, extended, former eighteenth century coaching house.

The Unicorn was by far the most opulent drinking establishment and thereby in stark contrast to any other on the

Crown, Kings or, nearby estates. As a consequence their prices were somewhat higher and as they tried to enforce a limited dress-code, their clientele were usually older than the youths that frequented the Eagle and Heron, also they were not attired in an obvious gang members' style. However, even with these restrictions meaning essentially that all denim jeans and white Baker's trousers were banned, as they failed to include footwear, the appearance of highly polished Airwair boots on dozens of individuals was a clear indication that on this occasion the crews were present in large numbers.

Standing at the crowded bar waiting to be served Jay Mac was casually engaging in his usual pastime of trying to identify the different players.

"Fuckin' hell Weaver, they're all here tonight, aren't thee?" he asked rhetorically glancing about the heaving press.

"Yeah, there's some of our lads from the Heron and the Eagle over there and a crew from the Hounds with a few Bear players." Weaver replied, also studying the assembly for his own purposes.

Jay Mac had been surprised not to see Irish or Blue with Johno and the rest of the Eagle contingent but when his attention was drawn to the Bear crew, he was even more surprised to find his two friends amongst them.

Once they had obtained their pints, Jay Mac and Weaver followed the surge of drinkers towards the main lounge at the rear of the building. This was a spacious wide rectangle of a room with two of its sides considerably longer than the other two. After they had entered through the glazed panel swing doors, they managed to squeeze into position with some of their own team already seated around one of the many circular tables. Just visible to them sitting in the centre of the long back wall, like a lord at a banqueting table in a medieval tapestry, was the object of tonight's celebration, the recently released from prison Sean Devlin or Devo (S) as he was known to them all.

Jay Mac like most of the crew had not seen this founder member of their team since the spring of 1971. Shortly after that Devo, Tommy (S) and Terry (H) were unwisely attacked by a group of Kings Team Skins, who were their main rivals at that time. As all three of the Crown players happened to be ranked amongst the very best of their fighters, they soon dispatched their enemies leaving one partially blinded, another with serious head injuries and a third stabbed in the chest, resulting in a collapsed lung. Devo (S) had been identified as the knife-wielding Skin and he received the maximum sentence of three years imprisonment when the youths stood trial for the affray. Having just been released after serving only two thirds of his term a few days earlier, the former leader of what had been a dangerous gang of Skinheads, was back and ready to resume command.

"He looks totally fuckin' different, don't yer think?" Jay Mac asked Weaver and his Eagle crew team mates.

"Yeah, he's not exactly a fuckin' big Skin now is he? He just looks like anyone of us." Johno the farm labourer observed genuinely.

"That's cos you haven't looked at him properly," said Weaver "he is yer original nutter." he concluded.

"Fuck! That's good comin' from you Weaver, y'mad cunt." Jay Mac said, ensuring that he smiled as he did so.

Everyone laughed, even Weaver and then before there were any further exchanges a tall stocky crew member seated on the left of their returned leader at the back of the room, rose to his feet and, lifting his pint into the air, proposed a toast.

"Everyone raise yer glasses to Devo, back with us and ready to roll!" he said in one unchanging droll tone.

The whole assembly responded enthusiastically and the stone-faced leader nodded his acceptance of their felicitations. Some wit in the crowd had selected Gary Glitter's *I'm the Leader of the Gang* on the jukebox and as this began to play it was greeted by a series of ribald cheers. When Terry (H) entered the room with two of the Eagle crew old guard, before he could join their table, he was summoned to join Devo and his party by the toast master.

"I'll get a round in lads, same again is it?" Jay Mac asked feeling generous due to his improved financial circumstances.

He made his way to the bar and nodded to Irish, who was sitting at a table with a group of youths that he did not immediately recognise. Pushing his way through the massed ranks of dedicated drinkers at the bar and managing to attract the attention of one of the staff, he was about to be served when he heard a familiar voice alongside him.

"Alright Jay Mac?" the ever-chirpy Blue shouted above the din. "Haven't seen you for a bit, mate. We're up here with the Bear crew tonight, goin' to a party afterwards, they're supposed to have some top birds who hang around with them, so one of them might get lucky."

'Just like that' Jay Mac thought the garrulous Blue had revealed who they were with and their plans for the evening without thinking of any possible consequences.

"Top birds, 'ey? I might just tag along meself and bring Weaver, he's always good for a few laughs." Jay Mac replied in jest.

"No... no... er... you couldn't come and Weaver is defo out." Blue replied nervously instantly regretting his unguarded comments.

"Am jokin' Blue, don't sweat." Jay Mac began then changed the subject swiftly "Anyway I don't know any of the Bear crew, I know thee were mates with Yad an I think their leader's called J.K. if am right, bit of an albino or somethin' like that?" Jay Mac was being entirely genuine and honest about his limited knowledge of this particular crew. Blue decided some clarification was required.

"They're a top crew Jay Mac and their main man is Jerry Keane or J.K. like yer say. Yer must 'ave heard what a fuckin' nutter he is?"

Jay Mac's order of drinks was being handed to him on a small round metal tray and he was also listening half-heartedly to a record that he happened to like, *Brother Louie* by Hot Chocolate, which was currently playing on the jukebox, consequently his casual reply which followed, though innocuous was not well received.

"Yeah, like I said Blue, I've never really 'eard of them, or 'im. How many more nutters do we need anyway? Good luck to yer all the same, I'll see yer again." With that he walked away from the bar firmly holding his tray of pints filled with amber and golden hued ales.

"Y'wanna watch what yer sayin' Jay Mac," Blue called after him but his warning was totally lost in the clamour of the bustling bar.

Jay Mac had not long resumed his seat and distributed the drinks when he too received a surprising summons from the ominously dressed toast master in his black Crombie, dark parallel trousers and black Airwair "You, the one called Jay Mac," the tall, stocky, bald male announced having crossed the floor to their table. Without waiting for a reply, he placed a heavy hand on the youth's shoulder "Right, gerrup move yer arse, Devo wants a word."

The rest of his drinking companions looked away, even Weaver, Jay Mac was on his own. If he had somehow antagonised the recently released knifeman, that was *his* problem, who were they to get involved? Jay Mac rose to his feet, left his pint on the table and wove his way through the maze of seated drinkers, growing more anxious with each careful step.

"You, move!" said his escort to an older ex-Skinhead who was occupying a chair close to where the team leader was ensconced. The male complied without argument and Jay Mac was given his seat, then moved directly in front of Devo (S) for his audience to begin.

For a few moments nothing was said and both interviewer and interviewee scrutinised each other. At this close proximity Jay Mac, who had met Devo previously in his Skinhead days, could clearly see the changes that prison life had brought about. Although he had shoulder length, corkscrew curled hair and was dressed in a dark blue, wide lapelled velvet jacket, over a long pennyround-collared white silk shirt, making him look more like a Jacobean prince than a late twentieth century thug, his battered, scarred countenance with deep set eyes under a badly damaged prominent brow ridge and crushed right orbital socket, testified to his actual violent character. When he had begun his sentence Sean Devlin had been a scrawny seventeen year old youth but after two years of dedicated daily weight training with the addition of certain illegal supplements, he had bulked up considerably and his neck had become thickened with pronounced arterial veins, appearing like a vascular relief map.

"Jay Mac is it?" Devo began, "What's yer actual name?"

"John Mack." the nervous youth replied unable to transfer his gaze from the grim visage before him.

"That's interestin' to me." He paused and swigged a tumbler of dark rum in one swallow. "Not bad, I prefer '*Woods Original*' meself but this'll do for now. I've heard good things about you from people who count." Again he paused and looked first to his left where Terry (H) was sitting and then to his right, where a thin, sickly looking male with thick dark hair and large sideburns was seated. Jay Mac realised to his horror, as he followed the direction of Devo's nod that he was looking at their courageous former leader, Tommy (S). Moved to pity on seeing his terribly weakened state he spoke without waiting for official sanction.

"Tommy, it's good to see yer, how are yer? Yer lookin' alright." he lied.

"I'm sound Jay Mac, thanks for askin'." Tommy (S) replied then began a bout of violent coughing.

"Here y'are Tommy 'ave a drink of yer pint." said a girl with long dark hair and hard features sitting next to him.

Once again Jay Mac was surprised upon recognising Joan (M), Tommy (S)'s formidable partner, leader of her own notorious girls' crew from the Hounds Public House and awesome scrapper. He was quickly brought back to the moment as Devo snapped his fingers and spoke again.

"You do a bit of business for Franny Lloyd don't yer?"

Jay Mac tried to conceal his astonishment having believed that no one else on the estate other than Floyd, knew of their arrangement.

"Er... yeah... I've done a few bits an pieces for him, only now and then, like." he replied, hoping to appear sincere.

"That stops from tonight." Devo instructed firmly.

"Yeah, of course, whatever you say Devo, I'll speak to Floyd and let him know." Jay Mac offered by way of a response.

The leader drew back in his seat and a scowl settled over his craggy face, "Are you takin' the piss?" he asked angrily "Maybe you didn't understand what I said. *You* won't be sayin' anythin' to Floyd, I'll be talkin' to him that's all *you* need to know." He paused and began drinking his pint of Guinness, having ensured that he had completely drained his glass of rum. "Have yer ever met 'Fritz' before?" he began cryptically, at the same time reaching inside his velvet jacket.

"Er, no... I don't think so." Jay Mac replied trying not to stammer and wishing that his audience would end.

"Put your hands on this fuckin' table in front of me, palms facin' up," he ordered then after a moment's hesitation added, "Thee better be clean."

Jay Mac complied with Devo's instructions and placed his hands, palms upward on the beer stained table. As if revealing an object of religious significance, the crazed team leader reverently produced a dark steel knife with a five inch blade that incorporated a four-socket knuckle duster in its brass and darker steel handle. He placed it carefully onto Jay Mac's palms. The youth could not help but notice it was heavily stained with a dark brown patina.

"There y'go meet 'Fritz', he's a beaut isn't he?" He paused and looked directly at Jay Mac waiting for a response.

"Yeah, oh definitely, yeah." was all he could manage in reply.

"Me arl fella got it from his arl fella, an he gorrit off a Kraut in the First World War, top quality German workmanship." He took a long draught from his pint then added, "The blood of every fucker that I've ever cut, slashed or stabbed is on that blade. Don't let me have to add yours." He finished speaking and replaced the precious family heirloom inside his jacket then took another drink.

Jay Mac was not certain about the dubious provenance of the combat item. He liked military knives and would have collected them if he'd had the funds when he was younger, particularly Wehrmacht, Kriegsmarine, Luftwaffe and Waffen SS items and had some basic knowledge of them. Looking at this piece he felt that if it came from a German soldier he in turn must have taken it from an American GI, as it had the appearance of a US made M-1918 Trench Knife, although it lacked its original crimped metal sheath. He wisely decided not to challenge the unbalanced leader about its origin and sat quietly waiting for his next instruction, which followed momentarily.

"Go 'ed then, fuck off." Devo said casually then returned to his conversation with Tommy (S) and Terry (H).

Jay Mac stood up and made his way as steadily as he could back to his waiting friends, including the brooding Crusher who had arrived late.

"Weaver, I take it all back. You were right *he* is the real fuckin' nutter." he announced just before he picked up his pint of ale and began rapidly swallowing it. Nobody laughed, they could all see by his drained colour and expression that he was deadly serious.

A short time later Devo rose to his feet and gestured to his monotone assistant, who in turn closed the lounge doors, then positioned himself in front of them on guard. The room began to fall silent with the assembly gradually realising that something significant was about to happen.

"Quiet everybody. Devo is gonna speak now." the menacing announcer ordered without altering his intonation at any point.

"Right, I've waited long enough for yer all to get 'ere, so I'll get straight to it. What I'm gonna say to yer tonight yer keep to y'selves, y'tell no one." He paused while he surveyed the room to ensure everybody was listening. "We all know that Tommy 'ere has led this team on his own for the past two years and he's never backed down once." He stopped again to allow the spontaneous cheers in favour of their injured leader.

"But since he's been out of action after takin' on the top boys from the Kings Team, some cheeky cunts are beginning to say we are gettin' soft, that the Crown Team is nothin' to worry about anymore. Next thing we're gonna find is little no-mark crews comin' right into our area and takin' the piss."

There were a number of angry shouts at this point and Jay Mac noted that the orator momentarily appeared pleased. Devo restored order then continued.

"That's right be pissed off, you know what I'm sayin' is true. So I'll tell yer what we're gonna do about it. This week on Wednesday night a crew of us are gonna give a reminder of who the fuck we are, the Crown Team, yeah?"

This time the crowd cheered spontaneously even though they had been given no indication of what action they were going to be involved in, or who they may be facing.

"Ok, listen now, me and these two lads 'ere have been talkin' together and we've agreed on what's gonna happen and whose gonna be doin' it. So my mate at the door there 'Morgo the man' will be comin' round to each of yer an if he gives yer a tap on the shoulder, yer in. If he doesn't, tough, don't start cryin' about it. One more thing, those who are picked, yer come in full kit and tooled up."

As soon as the speaker had resumed his chair, Morgan 'Morgo' Jones commenced his selection round. Those who were chosen felt as if their prowess and loyalty had been formally acknowledged, those who were not tried to mask their public disappointment but privately asked themselves why they were found wanting. At Jay Mac's table only the monocular Brain was omitted and although he feigned dismay, in reality he was relieved, having lost an eye in their epic battle with the Kings team the previous Halloween.

Jay Mac looked across to Irish's table and saw that one of the Bear crew was bypassed as was Blue; the latter he knew would be delighted.

Sometime later after the consumption of a considerable amount of alcohol, the evening began to draw to a close, the chosen men, forty in total, were all told to muster outside their present hostelry at 8.00pm on the Wednesday of that week. Jay Mac, Weaver and Crusher made their way from the lounge to the bar exit. They were about to step into the cool air of the clear summer night, when a few yards in front of them, standing on the loose gravel of the empty pub forecourt, starkly lit by the yellow beams of two small wall mounted flood lights, were a group of around a dozen youths.

"You in the middle, Jay Mac, you're gonna get a fuckin' good kickin' now." shouted a tall albino youth who bore an incongruous thick black continuous eyebrow. "I'm J.K from the Bear and you've been mouthin' off about us bein' a shit crew, aven't yer, y'cheeky twat?

Jay Mac looked just to the right of this angry gathering and could see Irish and Blue standing nearby, he knew instantly where the irate J.K had obtained his information.

"Listen mate, you've got it all wrong," Jay Mac began, "it's a misunderstandin' so no disrespect intended, let's leave it at that, right?" he asked trying to ameliorate the situation.

"Move the fuck out of our way, or there's gonna be a lot of pain happenin'." Weaver shouted angrily though effectively sabotaging any hopes of a diplomatic settlement.

"This has got nothin' to do with you Weaver, we've got no problem with you. Just let that big mouth cunt step over 'ere." the Bear crew leader responded. "He's a fuckin' Kings rat anyway, he shouldn't even be here tonight, he'll probably run back and tell them all what's been said."

Jay Mac now became angry and his alcohol-fuelled bravery overrode his natural cowardice. "Alright Keane, that's enough out of you. I don't want any trouble but y'wont fuckin' listen, let's have it, me and you, come 'ed." Jay Mac stepped out onto the gravel and removed his leather jacket which he passed back to Crusher who was standing immediately behind him; Weaver was nowhere to be seen.

"Look at that, even y'mate Weaver's fucked off and left yer." J.K said with a sneer. "Dickhead, steppin' out on yer own, get 'im lads and bring 'im over to me." With that the crew ran forward and surrounded Jay Mac.

"You'd better stop right where you fuckin' are boys." a firm voice commanded. Everyone froze in their places as Devo (S) stepped into the doorway. "Keane, whatever problem you've got with my friend Jay Mac means you've got a problem with me. So have yer got a problem with me?"

Transfixed by the ice cold stare of the crazed knifeman, J.K crumbled instantly. "No... er... sorry Devo... there's been a mistake,

I've got no problem... sorry." he stammered then recalled his troops.

"That's good cos I don't really want to hurt yer, I'm gonna need yer for Wednesday, now piss off." Devo said calmly before turning to a smiling Weaver who was standing next to him. "Lucky yer got me when y'did Weaver, I might 'ave had to get 'Fritz' out a few days early."

The Heron leader laughed though he had no idea what his fellow psychopath was talking about. Jay Mac attempted to thank Devo but he had already returned to the lounge. A few moments later the relieved youth, Weaver and the silent Crusher strolled out into the lane where the pub was located. Irish and Blue were still standing amongst the disconsolate Bear crew.

"Y'got lucky again!" Irish shouted across to the trio.

"Yeah, must be 'the luck of the Irish'!" Jay Mac shouted back in reply.

Thursday 21st June 1973

A pale sun was still fully visible sharing the clear blue sky with a bright moon and away to the north a twinkling star hung like a brilliant pendant, as Jay Mac walked across the lower edge of the Crown estate, lost in his thoughts. In the three days since the team meeting at the Unicorn, he had only visited the area once briefly to enquire if there had been any last minute changes to the scheduled rendezvous. On that occasion he did not approach the Eagle but spoke to Weaver in the Heron to confirm what had been agreed, he wanted to avoid Floyd at all costs.

Now as he approached the tenement block where the Heron co-leader lived, on this stifling evening without the slightest breeze following a scorching day, he was in turmoil. Jay Mac knew he could not just abandon his business associate without a word and he also knew that Floyd's reaction was likely to be less than amicable. However, with Devo's dire warning hanging over him, he wanted to ensure that any meeting with Floyd was as clandestine as possible. For the moment he was deliberately procrastinating while he searched for the safest solution.

Despite the warmth of the evening he was wearing his Levi's denim jacket with bleached collar and pocket flaps over a plain white tee-shirt. He had learned from bitter experience that when the Stanley knives began to slash, a couple of layers at least offered some degree of protection. His Flemings twenty-two inch parallel jeans were well scrubbed and had been ironed to pristine perfection without a single crease to their wide fronts by his old soldier uncle and as usual his cherry red Airwair were at their gleaming best. The only new addition to his kit was a wide patch of outstretched scarlet wings, edged in gold and bearing a proud Liver bird standing in a white roundel at their centre, with the letters L.F.C in gold underneath its feet. This had been sewn also by his uncle across the shoulders at the rear of his jacket, just below the collar and effectively obscured his old hand-written black ink Crown Skins emblem. He had intended to add the new Crown Boot Boys chevron but decided to leave this until another time, as he felt that his guardians may not appreciate its inclusion and ask difficult questions as to its meaning.

On reaching Weaver's block, he entered by the door opposite the stinking bin cupboards and ascended the three flights of stone stairs to the top floor landing where he lived. Jay Mac laughed to himself at the ridiculous amount of graffiti that covered the walls to such an extent as to make any of it virtually unreadable. Giant phalli replete with hugely inflated testicles vied for position with over-ripe breasts sporting extended nipples that could have suckled an entire army of toddlers and unlikely female genitalia surrounded by the densest forests of wildly exaggerated pubic hair. Struggling vainly across these murals of marvellous anatomy, were the names and legends of various team players both past and present, usually accompanied by a forceful sexual instruction.

Jay Mac stepped out of the stairwell and onto Weaver's landing, narrowly avoiding the pile of faeces and pool of urine of undetermined origin, positioned immediately in front of the stair door as a snare for the unwary. Finally he arrived at the flat that Weaver shared with his mother, father and three brothers. After knocking on the battered wooden door and then calling through the broken letterbox, he eventually heard his team mate coming along the lobby to meet him.

"Alright, what's all the fuckin' knockin' and shoutin' about? I was just enjoyin' a good shite." Weaver declared angrily.

"Well don't let me stop yer, I hope you've wiped yer arse, y'smelly fuck. Go back and take yer time if yer want. I'll tell Devo you were too busy squeezin' a few out to come tonight, yeah?" Jay Mac responded with a grin.

"Nah, the mood's gone now; I'll have to hold it in." Weaver advised, then as he pulled on his denim jacket he changed the topic to his heightened anticipation of the coming action and his particular preparation ritual. "I'm really lookin' forward to this fuckin' kick-off," he began. "I 'avent had a toss since we got told about tonight."

"Thanks Weaver that's really more information than I wanted." Jay Mac replied. "I think y'might be gettin' a bit confused, whoever we're goin' after tonight we're gonna be fightin' not fuckin' them."

"Same difference," Weaver replied disturbingly.

"What the fuck are you talkin' about? Are you sayin' sex and violence are the same thing?" Jay Mac asked, intrigued with a morbid curiosity.

Weaver looked directly at him and replied "Yeah, that's right. Different sides of the same coin, not much between them."

Jay Mac stared blankly at his Crown team mate trying to decide if he was revealing his genuine philosophy of life, or just trying to reinforce his psychopath reputation. "So love and hate is that it, are they just on either side of this fuckin' coin as well?"

"I've just told yer 'avent I, one always turns into the other. Now shurrup or I'll show yer the other side of me bein' friendly." Weaver laughed grimly then disappeared back into the flat.

When he reappeared moments later he passed Jay Mac a heavy metal item of equipment, "There y'go, this'll come in useful tonight, seein' as how yer too shitty to carry a proper weapon."

Jay Mac looked at the solid brass knuckle-duster that Weaver had just given to him. It was virtually identical to the one Yad had used in their fatal fight the previous November. He had to admit it was a lot more lethal looking than his three sharpened darts, with their odd coloured plastic flights.

"Where did y'get this from, it looks just like the one Yad belted me with?" he asked curiously.

"It is the same, he had one and he gave me and Macca one each as well. Yad always said his arl feller got the three of them as a job-lot for him and his brother but their Dayo never bothered with his, so he had two goin' spare." Weaver replied.

"Fair enough, seems a bit of a harsh Christmas present though, I wonder what he got his missus that year, a fuckin' sawn-off shot gun?" Jay Mac responded wryly.

Weaver finished lacing his black Airwair boots which contrasted starkly with his white parallel Baker's trousers. "Come 'ed let's gerroff and pick up the big man," he said pulling the door of the flat shut behind him.

A few moments later after leaving Weaver's tenement block they arrived at a similar drab building where Crusher lived with his family. Sitting on the low wall outside his residence and dressed identically to Jay Mac, with denim jacket, jeans and the ubiquitous standard red Airwair, he looked even more morose than usual.

"Alright Crusher mate, lookin' ready for action there," Jay Mac said trying to cheer his fellow L.F.C supporter who he normally attended 'home' games with.

"Am lookin' ready to hurt some fucker, if that's what yer mean Jay Mac." Crusher replied calmly.

"Should be a fuckin' good night then, cos am well up for it." a smiling Weaver concurred. "Let's gerrup there."

The three Crown team mates strolled up through the estate, along the main central road that bi-sected the western and eastern halves. Their route took them past Glynn's terraced residence and as they approached, they could see that the former Eagle crew member was standing outside talking with his Bristolian uncle. Glynn observed them at the same moment and unwisely stepped into their path.

"You really are scrapin' the bottom of the barrel now Jay Mac, hangin' round with this rapist cunt." he shouted angrily.

"Don't be callin' Crusher a rapist, yer cheeky twat," Weaver replied quickly with a cruel grin.

"You know who am talkin' to yer fuck..." he began, before Jay Mac interjected.

"Ok Glynn, good to see yer again, take it easy then mate, we'll have t'get off." He placed himself fully between his friend and the bristling Weaver.

The incensed Heron co-leader moved forward "Listen tit, I'm gonna give yer a break tonight cos am goin' somewhere, you ever speak to me again or look in my direction, an I'll open yer fuckin' head right up." Weaver spat onto the floor at Glynn's feet, narrowly missing Jay Mac's gleaming Airwair, then turned away. Crusher and Jay Mac followed close behind.

A short time later they collected Johno; Tank; the 'Ants' and the dour Irish from the Eagle, then continued their trek to the Unicorn on the southern boundary of their estate.

"Yer slimy mate Floyd was in the Eagle lookin' for yer before." Irish said casually as the eight-strong group were nearing the lane where the public house rendezvous was located. "He said he wants a word and he didn't look too happy." he added with a smug grin.

"Thanks for that." Jay Mac replied trying to appear unconcerned by this information.

All thoughts of Floyd and his possible reaction to Jay Mac's inevitable conversation where he must respectfully offer his resignation were instantly banished when they arrived at the loose-gravel forecourt of the Unicorn. Not for some time since their earlier massed conflicts with the Kings Team, had the disparate crews that comprised the Crown Team been assembled in such a manner. Bear; Eagle; Heron; Hounds and Unicorn public houses were all represented in the forty chosen men contingent, under the leadership of the sinister Devo (S) and his second-in-command for the operation, Terry (H).

Although the latter was visible in the midst of the troops having arrived earlier in advance of his actual crew affiliation, the Eagle party, Devo was nowhere to be seen. Eventually with the final stragglers' appearance, Terry (H) called them all to order and carried out a cursory 'head-count' to satisfy himself that there were no absentees. Jay Mac had wondered if an individual's presence would be noticed but he knew their absence would be noted and did not wish to even consider the consequences; clearly neither did anyone else as the roll call was complete.

At this point Devo emerged from the same doorway that Jay Mac had occupied when he received J.K's challenge on the previous Sunday night. The 'No Workwear' ruling did not appear to apply to him Jay Mac thought, or perhaps the bar staff were less diligent in the middle of the week he surmised, generously allowing them the benefit of the doubt.

He was dressed in a close copy of Jay Mac's 'uniform' with bleached collar and pocket flaps on his Levi's denim jacket but in addition he had bleached the half-inch wide turn-ups on his blue twenty-two inch parallel Flemings jeans. His gleaming cherry red Airwair even equalled the Eagle crew member's for depth of shine. Though Devo's kit matched most of the group who were almost universally dressed in full denim, with the odd exception of a blue or black Harrington jacket, or white Bakers trousers, that was where the similarity ended. He had greased and tied back his long dark, corkscrew hair making his distinctive, damaged features even more prominent. Jay Mac looked at their leader standing calmly ready to give them their orders, yet appearing like a sole survivor of a lost Neolithic tribe that had only recently been discovered in some remote wilderness, there was not the slightest trace of fear about him, nor pity in his eyes.

"I wouldn't want that mad fucker comin' after me." Weaver announced, causing Jay Mac to return to the moment.

"I think that's what most people say about you." he replied with a grin trying to mask his apprehension.

"Right quiet the lot of yers." Devo began; the whole assembly quickly falling silent. "Now I know we're all lookin' forward to a good night but we've gorra go over a few things first. I told yer all to come tooled up, so let's have a quick weapons check."

A wide variety of coshes of varying length, an assortment of blades, including a pen knife and the ubiquitous Stanley knives, several knuckle-dusters including Jay Mac's loaned item and Weaver's sole solid steel, toffee hammer were proudly displayed; there was also a solitary six inch long wood chisel.

Devo's gaze fell upon this item and then the pen knife, "What the fuck is that? We're not gonna carve them to death and *you*... did I say this was a Boy Scout's meetin'?" Both team players were suitably ashamed and wisely accepted their admonishment without response. Jay Mac was thankful that Weaver had lent him the heavy brass knuckle-duster, as he was certain that his own three pitiful darts may have drawn even worse derision.

"Oh well, it's too fuckin' late now. When it all kicks off at least pick up a brick or bottle and make y'selves look respectable." Devo concluded before finally revealing their all-important operational objective for the evening. He stepped into their midst and the anticipatory throng formed a loose circle around him.

"Okay, we wanna get rid of any doubts about the Crown Team's reputation don't we?" he began forthrightly, although Jay Mac thought curiously to himself that he had not been aware of any such concerns.

"So let's fuckin' blow that reputation right up, yeah? Let's do the top team, the oldest team, the hardest team, am talkin' about the Barley Boys." Devo waited for a few moments as the content and enormity of his words settled upon them like a devastating pestilence, arriving without warning from nowhere.

Everyone knew them; the John Barleycorn Team, now the Barley Boot Boys but formerly the Barley Skins, before that the Barleycorn Mod Men and they in turn preceded by the Barley Teddy Boys. There had probably been a team in that locale going back to Tudor England and the original alehouse; there had always been a tavern on their present site. They were a massive gang with powerful allies close by, including the huge Breck Team and nobody wanted to cross them. Being a long established firm with a distinguished reputation and an extensive portfolio of violence, they were currently concentrating on expanding their market beyond the domestic, wrecking football specials and battering rival supporters with their travelling mob, becoming one of the first officially recognised teams of 'football hooligans'. Their hall of fame boardroom, the lounge bar of their eponymous public house headquarters, was reputedly bedecked with a colourful array of the scarves of first and second division clubs from across the country. They no longer sought trouble in their immediate area and Jay Mac personally had not heard of any local incident involving them in the last twelve months, the moral he felt was: best to leave them alone and let sleeping, extremely vicious, dogs lie.

"I bet yer've all seen yer arses now that I've told yer 'avent yer?" Devo asked, smiling wickedly. "Good, that's what's needed, fear it'll drive yer on. Fear can be very useful if yer handle it right." he advised.

Everyone was completely silent with many internally questioning the wisdom of this proposed attack but they were all young males in the company of their peers and no one wished to lose face by publicly raising an objection. Devo surveyed the group as if probing their minds, whatever he gleaned from this and from scrutinising their body language he pressed on regardless.

"Fuckin' hell where's all y'balls gone?" he began. "Look if any shit-house wants to walk away now, then do it." he offered, appearing reasonably magnanimous for him, until he added, "but don't ever let me see yer yeller arse round 'ere again. Yer out the Crown Team and y'might as well lash yer kit and boots, cos yer ain't a fuckin' Skin or a Boot Boy no more."

The silence became deafening until Weaver broke it, "We're all in Devo, everyone's with yer."

Immediately a spontaneous outburst of similar sentiment was expressed by the different crew members and for once Devo actually smiled. Satisfied with their response he went on to outline his plan of attack and allocate specific objectives, reserving the primary target for himself.

"So like I said there's three ways in; one to the lounge; one to the bar and the outside gate into the beer garden at the back. I'm goin' in through the lounge doors with my crew, I'll be givin' yer their names in a minute and Terry (H) is goin' in through the bar with a crew he's havin' but I need someone to lead a small crew into that garden."

Even as he said his final words Weaver shouted "That's me then, I'll do that!"

Devo appeared delighted "Good lad Weaver, yer a nutter with balls." He paused for a moment allowing the Heron co-leader to bask in the glow of formal recognition by their commanding officer.

"Right, when me and Terry have picked our fifteen players each, you'll be gettin' the other nine for your side." He laughed amused by the similarities of selection for the first and second teams in school football and added like an encouraging, benign coach, "Now you lads goin' in with Weaver, do yer best, you've got the hardest job, so do us proud."

Again the different crew members responded positively to this praise some even changing their minds and hoping to be 'selected' for Weaver's crew. A few moments later the choices were called out. Jay Mac found he was with Devo's group and that Johno and Tank would be alongside him. Irish was in Terry (H)'s selection, accompanied by the 'Ants.' Crusher, the powerhouse would smash into the beer garden-bowling green area at the side and rear of the pub, with Weaver and eight others.

"Ok, we're all happy with what's gonna happen, there's just a few other things to get clear. Y'might not know but running the Barleys now are the Morrison brothers. The older one's about twenty and the other's eighteen, they're a pair of nasty, vicious cunts, and I'll be droppin' them both. So unless I'm down you leave them two fuckers to me." He paused and unsurprisingly received no objections. "At the back of their alehouse on a fuckin' big white pole is their flag, thee say they've had it for years and they'll kill anyone who even touches it. I want that fuckin' flag! I don't care who gets it, or what yer have to do but someone from this team is gonna do the business tonight." Once more he paused and again there was only muted response. "Before we get off remember this, we're not playin' John Wayne, there's no rules and no help, if yer go down yer on yer own, if y'get gripped by the bizzies, keep yer mouth shut."

A popular member of their team from the Hounds crew incongruously nick-named Felix because his facial features bore an uncanny feline resemblance, asked a pertinent question, "I know y'said before we're gettin' down there on the bus but when it's all over, how are we gettin' back?"

Devo stared at the youth who unfortunately always wore a permanent grin, causing his former teachers to constantly tell him to 'wipe that stupid smile of your face."

"I don't know what's amusin' you, cat boy but I hope yer not tryin' to take the piss? Listen, all of yer, unless we get split up no one runs until I say, right?" He paused and waited for their universal agreement. "Then once we've done the job, you get back any way you can, jump on a bus, or in a taxi, or use yer own two legs. Whatever yer do, go home, don't meet up in the alehouses, the bizzies are bound to start off there."

Just as he finished speaking two young bar staff arrived with a metal tray each, on which there were sufficient shot glasses filled with a measure of whiskey for the entire cohort and one of dark rum reserved for their leader.

"Drop these lads and we're off. Good luck to yer." he shouted raising his glass then downing his drink in one.

The whole crew responded in like manner.

Irish who was standing not far from Jay Mac looked across and said "Slainte" before swallowing his whiskey in a single gulp, his friend repeated the gesture.

Within half an hour they had all crammed onto the first green Atlantean bus unfortunate enough to arrive at their local stop, just as they did. Devo (S) had led the way acting like a caricature of a deranged teacher on a school outing, chaperoning his charges.

"Everyone jump on and get a seat, move down the bus there's loads of room." he shouted springing onto the platform and glaring at the driver, who wisely chose not to request even the customary ten pence fair. The middle-aged male was almost physically overcome by the sheer volume of raw testosterone, considering seriously the attractions of early retirement while praying that the crew would depart from his vehicle as soon as possible, without incident.

While they travelled the two miles plus to their target destination, Devo explained how a disgruntled mole from within the Barleys whom he had shared a cell with in Walton Jail before his early release, had told him about a regular Thursday evening high-stakes poker game that the Team leaders always attended, with only a handful of other select players present. He had also given the precise location of this game at the rear of the lounge, close to the outdoor bowling green.

They all listened intently as Devo reiterated several times his plan of attack, how the three-pronged pincer movement would work with the two outer arms forcing their prey into the central killing zone and then combining for an all-out slaughter. Not one of them even suspected that their information was outdated and incorrect in a number of vital respects. It would not be long before they found that accurate intelligence was critical in any campaign, battle or skirmish and faulty intelligence was worse than none at all.

With the bus rapidly nearing the stop where they would alight, the witty banter began to fade at a similar pace. Jay Mac was lost in the *'Boy's Own'* world that his immature, juvenile brain often inhabited. Here he was, the paradoxical coward who lived for the rush, the excitement, the buzz of being involved in the most risky actions, with the odds of success stacked against him. His stomach was beginning to churn and the adrenalin starting to flow and he thought about one of his favourite group of heroes, the US Airborne units of World War Two; The 82nd and The 101st, who followed their courageous pathfinders, sharing the honour of being the first allied troops to set foot in Hitler's Fortress Europe, commencing the action that would liberate an entire continent, D-Day 6th June, 1944. Whenever he reflected on their totally altruistic heroism and his own embarrassing apprehension before these childish events, his respect for the former increased exponentially.

"Here we go, get ready!" Devo shouted along the bus as they reached the jump off point.

The vehicle stopped and one-by-one they rapidly filed out between its folding doors, much to the relief of the sweating driver and the few other nervous passengers.

The bus stop was no more than three hundred yards from their target but they had to negotiate a busy dual carriage, four-way junction before they had covered the first fifty of those yards. After darting between the speeding vehicles in small groups or individually, they reassembled and formed ranks ready to advance once they had all reached the side of the road where their objective lay.

Two hundred yards – "Start movin'." Devo ordered.

Now all was silent for Jay Mac except for the sound of his own breathing and of his rapidly increasing heartbeat.

One hundred yards – "Pick up the pace." Devo shouted.

The ranks had morphed into a phalanx with Jay Mac keeping in the van, driven on by his own internal monologue which told him to stay near the leader; the leader always survives.

Fifty yards – "Sprint, come on." Devo exhorted.

There it was, the chipped varnished, wooden double door of the lounge bar of the John Barleycorn.

Devo charged forward, closed the last ten yards, then jumped at the doors with one powerful flying kick, crashing them violently back against the interior.

"CROWN TEAM!" he bellowed with his mutilated face and distorted neck imbued with a purple rage.

The silence of Jay Mac's thoughts was instantly shattered as a cacophony of noise exploded all around him, following close behind their wild leader. No time for further reflection, now frenzy and mayhem must be unleashed.

In the adjoining bar Terry (H) had also made a similar spectacular entrance and the sound of heavy wooden tables crashing to the ground after being overturned, mixed with that of glass shattering as upset pints and bottles, plus an expensive wall mounted mirror, were reduced to glittering fragments. Everywhere was filled with urgent shouts of panic, anger and delight, above all were the cries of pain with anyone in the path of the torrent being struck or slashed.

Outside things were not exactly going to plan. The old wooden door that led to the beer garden and bowling green, had recently been replaced with a wrought iron item faced with sheet metal, to deter unauthorised access. Try as he might, the powerful Crusher was unable to force it open much to the annoyance of the unsympathetic Weaver.

"What's wrong with yer? Smash it in, y'supposed to be fuckin' strong." he shouted angrily.

Providence then chose to smile on them if not the Barleycorn regulars, as a shrieking female unbolted the door from the inside and dashed out hoping to escape the carnage within the main building. Weaver's toffee hammer struck her in the middle of the forehead causing her to stagger forward a few paces, then drop to her knees with the blood from the wound streaming into her eyes. Her boyfriend, following almost immediately behind, tried to draw his Stanley knife but the angry Crusher's meaty right fist smashed him so hard in the face that he collapsed, pole-axed momentarily in the doorway before being lifted bodily by the strongman and thrown into the path of the other prospective escapees, who were converging on the open portal.

Weaver leapt into the exposed beer garden with Crusher and the rest of his eight-man team, proceeding to attack anyone who came in range and those who cowered attempting to hide on the sidelines. A trail of battered, bleeding faces lay in their wake as they moved across from the drinking area with its upturned picnic tables to the bowling green and on towards their objective, the double French doors which led to the lounge, where they hoped the real blood-letting would commence. A light breeze had accompanied their arrival and was beginning to stiffen causing the treasured flag on top of its tall white pole to flutter, allowing John Barleycorn to look down upon the devastation below.

In the small bar room the master plan was beginning to unravel. The space was in reality, too restricted for a sixteen-strong group to be fully effective; they were all inside but were unable to make forward progress. Added to the spatial difficulties, some of the more mature drinkers who were not happy with this invasion of their local, having their drinking disturbed or worse still their pints spilt, were putting up a ferocious resistance. Irish and the two Ants were exchanging blows with a couple of middle-aged males who were less than impressed by the youths' combined efforts.

The wood carver and the Boy Scout were engaged in a struggle with a stocky barman who was trying to throttle the latter whilst dragging him across the beer-soaked counter. It took the intervention of the former and the use of his previously ridiculed wood chisel, which he plunged into the purple-faced barman's left brawny forearm, carving a deep inch-wide, bevelled edged gouge spurting blood freely, to resolve the encounter.

Terry (H) had by far the most difficult task. His adversary was a hardened drinker and experienced bruiser in his early thirties and a former Barley Teddy Boy. With the fingers of his heavy fists adorned with a variety of rings, each of his accurate punches left their mark. Only the Crown player's years of brutal tutelage at the hands of his unlicensed boxing champion father saved him from being overcome, he could absorb tremendous punishment and also give it out.

"Go down, y'fucker, go down!" he shouted as he threw punch after vicious punch into the face and body of his opponent. Finally the ex-Teddy Boy was defeated by the constant pummelling and slipped on the wet floor falling back against the interconnecting lounge door with its frosted glass half panel. Terry (H) leapt onto him in an instant, driving his head into the glazed section of the door, smashing it into razor sharp shards as he did. With blood pouring from a dozen head wounds turning his heavily Brylcreamed, D.A. style hair from jet black to deep scarlet, the battered male slid to the floor. The blockage had been removed and Terry (H)'s bar raiders could now force their way into the lounge to join their colleagues, closing the pincers.

"Where's the Morrisons, where the fuck are thee?" Devo was bellowing across the wreck of a room with its upturned tables, broken glasses, bottles and bar optics. Their intelligence was completely flawed in respect of this plush saloon, there was no card school situated anywhere within its confines and instead of being almost empty, it was filled with a dozen couples enjoying an evening's drinking.

When Terry (H)'s party broke through they found both males and females in casual 'civilian' dress, with no obvious signs of being Team players. They were all bloodied with face and head wounds and most of the younger women were reduced to tears. The barman here, who happened to be the landlord, had also tried to resist and as he had been reaching for a large wooden baton that he kept beneath the counter, Jay Mac had launched a well-aimed pint glass which struck him full in the face peppering his skin with dozens of glass splinters. With a sodden bar towel draped over his head, hanging down across his wounds he was in considerable pain, though this drew no mercy from the crazed leader.

"Tell me where these fuckin' Morrisons are?" Devo demanded, holding the agonised male by the throat with his left hand and pressing the blade of 'Fritz' against his blood stained face with his right. While the interrogation continued, Jay Mac and

Johno stepped through to the extension of the lounge where Weaver's party were entering through the open French doors.

All the while that the assault had been proceeding the jukebox had faithfully continued with its last selection of records, although no one was listening. With a temporary hiatus in the action and a momentary silence of sorts except for the sobbing females, Terry Dactyl and the Dinosaurs' *Seaside Shuffle* began to play. Unfortunately for Jay Mac who was standing nearest to a narrow door marked 'Private,' opening inwardly and leading to the landlord's quarters above, his attention was diverted for a fleeting second by the sudden start of the popular song, which was a Crown Team favourite.

"Fuck off twat!" was all that he heard in warning as a devastating flying head-butt struck him violently on the right side of his face, just above the ear. As the youth was sent crashing into Johno, the older Morrison brother Gary, known as Gazmo, burst into the room followed by his marginally younger sibling Tony, or Motone as he styled himself. With half a dozen of their top players immediately behind, the dramatic arrival of this eight-man crew changed the dynamics of the struggle.

Armed with a foot long, cast iron poker which bore an ornate fleur-de-lys style tip, Gazmo immediately set about the nearest enemy player, who in this case was the unfortunate J.K. from the Hounds crew.

"Lets 'ave it, come 'ed Barleys." their leader shouted as his impromptu weapon repeatedly struck the skull of his victim, cracking the bone beneath the bloodied flesh.

His brother and their senior players were inspired by this spectacular reprisal and threw themselves into the fray with ferocious enthusiasm. Split pool cues reversed with their actual handles being used as the striking points, were slammed onto the heads, shoulders or backs of any Crown raider within range. Their efforts had a similar encouraging impact on their wounded 'civilian' colleagues who, roused from their torpor, also joined in the melee. The ripple of resistance spread as far as the walking wounded outside in the beer garden and bowling green. Gathering together, this band of alfresco drinkers forced their way into the rear of the lounge, through the open French doors and attacked Weaver's contingent from behind.

Any unfortunate Crown player to pass near the perimeter tables where the couples had been seated fell victim to the formerly weeping young women, who had transformed into terrifying harridans, employing either broken bottles, glass ashtrays or their own lengthy scarlet claws. Soon it appeared as though the Crown Team were about to snatch a stunning defeat out of the jaws of certain victory, caught between the Scylla of the furious Barley males and the Charybdis of their screaming females.

Devo the commander could see the way the tide of battle was turning and exhorted his troops to make a determined effort.

"Come on Crown Team, these are no-marks! Their fuckin' slag bitches 'ave gorra do their scrappin' for them." Then he changed the direction of his offensive, "Gazmo! Yer fuckin' shitbag come to me if yer've got any balls, let's have it outside."

There was no reply, the violence swept on impelled by a mixture of self-preservation and outrage. Heads, noses and teeth were being broken, lips split, ears flattened and eyes closed, ribs were cracked and testicles crushed. Gradually the fear of being trapped in their enemy's stronghold overtook the Crown Team and this proved sufficient motivation to make them begin to turn the tide back in their favour.

One by one badly injured Barley players retired from the fight and abandoned the struggle, more concerned with their individual wounds than the potential shame of an ignominious defeat for the team. Standing amidst the carnage in the wreck of the lounge another brief hiatus occurred with the two bloodied, exhausted opposing sides facing each other panting and drenched in sweat.

The Barleys literally had their backs to the wall, which in this case happened to be the one that displayed their famed collection of F.A. flags, pennants and rosettes. A now redundant, silent jukebox was positioned under this work of art in the corner adjacent to the French doors, leaving the only audible sound that of heavy breathing and the crunch of broken glass under the boots of individuals as they shifted their weight, assuming new attack positions, ready for the final clash.

"Save yer fuckin' team Gazmo, one last chance. You an' me now, what d'yer say lad?" Devo called to his opposite number, appearing genuine in his offer.

Bleeding from a number of facial cuts the Barley's co-leader straightened up to his full six foot one height and considered his enemy's proposal. He glanced about at his wounded team mates, including the 'civilian' auxiliaries of both sexes and at the utter chaos that had been wrought in the previously plush lounge bar.

"Alright Devo, just you and me, yeah?" he replied. "But, here's my conditions; if I lose, you walk out of 'ere with yer team and leave everyone else alone. If you lose, I let your team go and they can take what's left of yer with them, ok?"

Devo smiled slyly, "Yeah that sounds fair. When I win, I'm not gonna be arsed about your team. I won't be losin' so what happens to my boys doesn't come into it."

Jay Mac looked at their crazed commander, then across to Gazmo considering their different styles of leadership. Of the two he knew which one cared for his players, reminding him of the courageous Tommy (S) and which one was most likely to abandon his troops without a second thought.

No further discussion was required, Devo crouched low and began swaying from side to side, weaving an undulating pattern through the air with 'Fritz' clamped securely to his right hand. Gazmo also leaned forward passing his improvised foot-long weapon from hand to hand. Everyone else moved away to the edges of the 'arena,' nobody noticed a sole member of the Barleys slip out of the open French doors, into the deserted bowling green area.

Gazmo struck like lighting and drew first new blood bringing the pronged poker sharply down onto his rival's left shoulder, a dark stain soon appeared in that area of Devo's denim jacket. A diagonal slash across the front of his short-sleeved, checked Ben Sherman shirt was Gazmo's reward for this daring blow. The original Skinhead, who had adopted the aggressive fashion shortly after its creation by London's working class youth in 1969, had remained true to its style and ethos. He still looked the part, with a number one crop and he never backed down.

The new and the old faced each other once more making slight adjustments, looking for a tell-tale sign then pounced simultaneously. As Gazmo's dark iron poker cracked Devo's already damaged brow ridge *his* brass encased fist smashed up under the former's jaw dislocating it as it did. In a repeat down stroke, even as he withdrew, 'Fritz' cut a parallel gash across the front of Gazmo's torn shirt, this time drawing a line of blood.

They separated momentarily, gauged their positions and options in a split second then laid into each other again. Gazmo passed the poker into his left hand and swept it across Devo's right arm above the elbow, hoping to make his opponent drop his weapon, or at least slow his assault. Devo laughed as if, once again, employing his telepathic powers and using a curving back stroke caught Gazmo on his right cheek cutting him from ear to chin.

The heavily bleeding, wounded Barley leader snatched his grinning opponent by his tied back, long greased hair then pulled him down to his knees while repeatedly striking him across the head and face with his reddened poker. Still wearing a sinister smile, Devo looked up directly into the eyes of his dominant foe almost imploring him to strike again. The Barley crowd sensed victory was close at hand, watching their leader triumphantly beating Devo's scarlet mush of a face beyond recognition.

Devo's left hand reached out as if to plea for mercy then grabbed hold of Gazmo's right buttock, pulling the Barley leader to him forcefully and plunging 'Fritz' into his unprotected groin with all the strength that he could muster. It was Gazmo's turn to fall to his knees and as he did the blood-soaked Devo slowly rose from his. He coughed, cleared his throat then spat a clot of bloodied phlegm onto his defeated rival.

"What d'yer want?" he muttered leaning over Gazmo, placing his left hand behind his cropped head. "Eye, or ear?"

"It was only a matter of time... I knew thee'd send you." he mouthed cryptically in reply, then added, "...ear."

Devo stared at him almost sympathetically for a fleeting second and said, "Yer should've took the fuckin' warnin'." then he changed his grip, snatching hold of Gazmo's right ear and sliced it off with the scarlet 'Fritz'.

"Strike it Danny, save J.B!" the valiant, disfigured leader shouted, as loudly as he could manage.

Devo looked in the direction that Gazmo had been facing when he cried out, Jay Mac followed his gaze. Outside in the far corner of the bowling green a young Barley player, who had already lowered the Barley Corn flag was releasing it from its rope fixings and preparing for flight, leaving only the empty flagpole up-lit by a single floodlight at its base.

The Crown Team commander glared back at Jay Mac, "You're the runner aren't yer? Fuckin run, get that flag!"

Jay Mac did not require any incentive to be free of that place, he had been sickened by Devo's action and wanted to put as much distance as he could between him and that sight. As if back in the starting blocks in his school athletics' days with the pistol just fired, he was off in an instant. Danny 'the flag bearer' and fastest runner of the Barleys, being a cross-country champion and track star, had already sprinted across the manicured lawn of the bowling green, negotiated the upturned picnic tables of the beer garden and darted through the opening past the sheet-metal covered door. His running rival, Jay Mac, leapt over the battle debris in the lounge and out of the confines of the wrecked room in hot pursuit, behind him he heard yet another cry of anguish from within.

Even as Devo was placing his grizzly trophy into his denim jacket inside pocket, Motone was trying to staunch the flow of blood from his brother's horrific wound with a beer soaked bar towel.

"You fuckin' cunt," he shouted at the dispassionate Crown team leader who was calmly preparing to leave.

"What's the matter with you boy?" Devo asked. "He got what was comin' to 'im, anyway he'll live." he laughed as he spoke which proved too much for Gazmo's younger sibling.

Reaching down to the floor he snatched up the blood-stained iron poker then in one blur of a move, jumped up and forced its barbed tip into Devo's right shoulder, tearing through the denim and shirt beneath. It was a brave but futile gesture; the weapon only punctured the flesh by less than an inch. Still smiling the crazed Devo withdrew it with his left hand, staring all the while at Motone.

"Now why did yer go and do a thing like that?" he asked rhetorically before raising his right arm sharply despite his injury and slashing the youth diagonally from under his right eye down across his lips to the left side of his chin. "'Ere, get y'Ma to stitch that and see if she can sew yer brother up, while she's at it." he laughed loudly at this then turned to his composite team. "I think we're done here, let's gerroff."

The members of the assault party filed out through the open French doors or the shattered lounge entrance by which some of them had arrived, none of them spoke and none of them were in good spirits, apart from Weaver.

In the warm night outside a cool breeze was blowing, improving the running conditions appreciably. A red sun had finally departed from the solstice sky, leaving a deep blue velvet canopy for a brilliant moon to dominate. Away to the west beyond the dark brown turgid River Mersey and Wirral peninsular, angry thunder clouds rumbled passing over the Welsh mountains, a storm was coming.

Danny the Barley's running ace, was delivering the race of his life but to no avail, even with a head start he was now firmly fixed in Jay Mac's sights with the Crown sprinter gaining ground on every stride. This was *his* event and for once he was supremely confident not through arrogance or conceit but purely from practical experience. He recognised that he was at best a mediocre scrapper; he knew he was acknowledged as a peerless runner.

Tearing along the central reservation, having dodged between the speeding vehicles, Jay Mac was totally in his Zen state, legs and lungs working automatically, independent of the brain, divorced from the body's other demands ignoring pain, the pursuit was all that mattered. For a supposed experienced runner Danny revealed a novice error, he turned his head and looked over his shoulder to see where the running machine was. Jay Mac registered his mistake knowing that slight movement had altered his rival's balance, aerodynamics and crucially, pace. Too many narrow escapes of his childhood had taught him what to do and what never to do.

Twenty yards now separated them, the Crown player's meditation was only disturbed by the encouraging sound of his Barley opponent's heavy breathing, he knew he was tiring. With his own lungs bursting, abdominal and leg muscles demanding oxygen, Jay Mac increased his pace, driven on by an eclectic mental montage of his favourite running images; Champion the Wonder Horse; The Lone Ranger on Silver; the great Phidipides; Athenian Hoplites at Marathon; Henry Fonda outrunning the Huron natives in *'Drums Along the Mohawk'* and Tom Courtney's stunning performance in *'The Loneliness of the Long Distance Runner.'*

With only a five yard gap remaining, he became an NFL running back closing on an opposing team player who was about to score a game-winning touchdown. He leapt forward tackling Danny around the waist, sending him crashing to the ground, just short of the 'end-zone,' the contest was over. With his heavy brass knuckle-duster fixed to his left fist, Jay Mac repeatedly smashed the exhausted youth in the left side of his face, then caught him by his 'feather-cut' hair and began pounding his head onto the hard concrete paving that demarked the crossing area. Danny lay in his own blood, barely conscious while Jay Mac stripped him of the prized flag which he had tied around his waist.

"Y'done well lad, I enjoyed it but don't try to get up, or I'll finish yer." Jay Mac said triumphantly holding onto the blood-spattered image of a smiling orange face, framed with hair and beard of golden ears of barleycorn, on a field of emerald green.

"Yer fuckin' bastard, yer've done young Danny." shouted an angry voice as Jay Mac was struck from behind with a sharp Stanley knife. Twice more he was cut before he fell to the ground, only to receive a vicious boot to the right side of his face by a second Barley player who had arrived just after his team mate.

"He's done Danny, the shitbag." his friend advised, unnecessarily stating the obvious with the battered youth lying just in front of the kneeling Jay Mac.

"Do the cunt." the new arrival instructed and then they set about their task enthusiastically.

Quickly assuming the survival position, Jay Mac tucked himself into a tight ball with his knees drawn up and his chin embedded in his chest, he knew what was coming next. Suddenly they noticed their treasured standard, which he had quickly tried to conceal inside his denim jacket.

"Give us J.B. now or we'll fuckin' kill yer!" Jay Mac heard one of them shout before a second round of wild kicking began.

"Give it up yer bastard." demanded another irate voice as he booted the Crown player's head as hard as he could. Jay Mac held on to the flag and rolled back and forth with the tremendous impact of each new blow.

"Crown Team!" Johno shouted sprinting to his beleaguered friend's aid, closely followed by Irish, Terry (H) and the two 'Ants' leading the rest of their team in an extend line of anger. Weaver, Crusher and the delighted Devo were bringing up the rear, joining the mob just as the three Barley Boys including the unconscious Danny were being kicked and stamped by everyone who could manage to reach them. The latest arrivals were keen to join the 'fun'.

"Gerrout the way." Devo demanded using his leader's prerogative to deliver a number of bone-cracking blows of his own.

Weaver had to go one better and insisted each of the three battered figures were sat up, so that he could mark them all with his prize toffee hammer. Commencing his work with a vicious delight he smashed their bleeding facial features one by one, concentrating on noses and teeth as he did.

All around they could hear the shouts of angry Barley Team members of varying ages who, unknown to the Crown raiders, had been alerted by the lowering of the flag, which had been deliberately set on high so as to be seen as widely as possible. It had become an established tradition across the area that if the John Barleycorn flag was not visible then a disaster had befallen the public house and everyone should muster there without delay. The dark, rumbling thunder clouds had crossed the Mersey and were about to break upon friend and foe alike.

"You've got somethin' that belongs to me, let's have it." Devo demanded standing close by a distracted Jay Mac, who was beginning to feel sorry that he had tackled the young Barley runner, as he watched Weaver repeatedly striking the unconscious Danny's blood drenched skull.

"Yeah, yeah... sure... 'ere y'are," he said, passing Devo the folded rectangle of material.

"Good work Jay Mac, y'done good, I won't forget this." the leader responded taking the precious item and unfolding it, then wiping his own bloodied countenance noisily with it.

The wild cries of the gathering Barley mob could be heard coming from every direction and groups of dark silhouetted figures were becoming increasingly visible as they raced toward the Crown Team's current location, having initially rallied at their wrecked public house. A chill ran through almost the entire assault group, on realising their dangerous position.

Devo appeared unconcerned and unmoved by the possible dire fate that may befall his team.

"I told yer from the start it'd be every man for 'imself, so get back any way y'can, I'm off." he paused then shouted, "Weaver, leave them fuckers they're finished, dive out into the road and stop a taxi with our name on it."

Weaver put his beloved toffee hammer away safely and darted out into the busy thoroughfare holding his hands up in the air, as if surrendering to the vehicles. Within minutes he had managed to attract a black cab driver's attention, who surprisingly chose to stop for him. The heavily built, grey haired cabbie seemed remarkably unconcerned about pulling across the road to their forty-plus group. Jay Mac would have been fascinated to talk to this individual under any other circumstances, if he had known that he was another heroic veteran of World War Two. He too had landed on those same Normandy beaches at 'Sword' with the First South Lancashire Regiment on that fateful June morning twenty nine years previous.

"I don't give a shit about some daft kids." he often remarked genuinely to his colleagues. When he had been a young man of twenty-two he had raced across deadly sands, facing German machine-gun positions. It was impossible for him to be afraid of a motley gang of youths.

"Hurry up, jump in lads if yer gettin' in." the driver shouted.

Devo led the way opening the right hand passenger door, "Terry (H), Weaver, you're with me. J.K., you look fucked, yer better join us as well and Crusher y'miserable bastard, I don't think a two mile run's for you, so get in there. Nice one driver, Crown Estate when y'ready. Don't 'ang around 'ere lads for too long, it could get nasty." With that brief warning he was gone.

They were abandoned, leaderless in enemy territory. As the Barleys closed upon them leaving only one possible escape route, there was a sudden blinding flash of sheet lightning immediately followed by a terrific crack of thunder. Accompanying blobs of heavy rain announced the arrival of a tremendous downpour.

For some reason unknown to himself, Jay Mac assumed command. "Right come 'ed, let's form up and start runnin'. Johno you take the lead, Irish keep in the centre and I'll look after any stragglers at the rear, we can piss this off if we all stay together."

Instantly there was dissent. "Fuck you, who are yer?" shouted one of the Unicorn crew, followed by a member of the Bear party, "Yeah, I don't know yer, am not takin' orders from a fuckin' Eagle player."

Others quickly followed suit causing a rift in the ranks.

"What are y'gonna do now, 'General Jay Mac,' Sir?" Irish asked with a sly smile.

"Well one thing I know is I'm not stayin' here." Jay Mac replied then shouted "Ey fuck you too, I'm off, this is a joke run for me. If any cunt wants to join me, do it now." Then he darted out amongst the speeding traffic, heading to the main road that led off to the right from the dual carriageway.

Two separate groups quickly formed: one behind Jay Mac comprised of Eagle and Heron players with some undecided Hounds, lost without J.K. their leader and a second containing the whole Unicorn and Bear contingent with the residue of the Hounds. When they reached the main road the original Unicorn dissenter remembered that he had an aunt who lived somewhere nearby and he was certain by taking a backstreet route, which led past her house, it would prove to be a safe shortcut. The two groups branched away from each other at a 30° angle splitting into two fast running 'hares' for the relentlessly pursuing Barleymen to course.

The pouring rain drenched them as they ran and they were glad of it, gaining some revitalising refreshment and much needed energy. Jay Mac's original suggested grouping, with Johno in the lead, had organically formed without word or question, with Jay Mac reducing his pace and falling back to the rear. A large number of their pursuers had chosen to break off and follow the divergent Unicorn led runners, smiling with an informed confidence as they did.

Screaming for their blood, shouting derision and howling curses, some of the mixed assortment of Barleymen introduced a new element, artillery. Catapults of varying size and strength including the bait throwing type were now brought into action.

"Fuckin' shit what's that?" one of the leaderless Hounds shouted as he was struck in the back with a small gauge steel ball bearing.

Similar items of shot and pieces of stone peppered those at the tail of the running column, including Jay Mac.

"Thee must have catties but at least thee'll have to slow down to use them." he said reassuringly though assuming incorrectly.

Like the Scythian archers of the ancient world, these pursuers could also 'ride' and shoot at the same time, with only a minimal change of pace.

Out of the driving rain across the main road to their left, two green Atlantean buses could be heard, their heavy tyres splashing through the surface water almost aquaplaning as they did. Johno instinctively led the way altering his direction and running diagonally at a narrow angle on his mentally plotted course, designed to intercept those vehicles at the nearest stop, everyone followed his lead.

Even as both buses came to a halt two hundred yards further on, Johno ran around the front of the first then leapt through the open doors onto the platform, hampering those passengers who wished to alight. Ensuring his group where all on board he leaned out of the doorway and exhorted Irish to bring up the middle and rear.

"Come on Irish, get them on!"

The driver was not happy with the delay but waited a few more vital seconds, allowing Irish to get most of his party on safely. As that bus pulled away from the stop, Irish stepped off and ran back to the second vehicle.

"Keep those fuckin' doors open, right!" he shouted at the driver who was also becoming angry, concerned about potentially missing part of his break at the municipal bus depot.

"Come on Jay Mac, come on man!" he shouted holding onto the hard rubber encased edge of the nearest door, watching his friend desperately trying to encourage the weakest runners who were in danger of missing their one chance of escape.

"Get the fuck on, come 'ed, pile on," Jay Mac bellowed, though his lungs were on fire.

He pushed the last of his group through the opening, reached out to Irish with his right hand as the driver released the break and began to move away from the stop.

"Hold on y'cunt!" Irish shouted desperately to the livid driver.

Jay Mac was alongside trying to reach his friend's outstretched hand then, just as he had almost made contact, a well-aimed large gauge solid steel ball bearing found its target. Struck violently between the shoulder blades, what little air he had left departed from his exhausted lungs and he stumbled forward a few paces then fell to the ground.

Even as he went down he could hear the hiss of the hydraulics and the snap of the doors closing. A wild ecstatic cheer erupted from the Barley horde.

"I told yer, I'm not waitin' any longer, so fuck the lot of yer." the driver snarled at Irish, ignoring his remonstrations.

Quickly Irish forced his way to the back seat of the lower deck and peered through the rain-streaked filthy rear window. He watched as Jay Mac staggered to his feet, stretched himself then began a final desperate run with the lead Barleys almost upon him.

Tank and a number of Hound's players joined Irish and the former spoke. "He's fucked, he's got no chance there's too many of them, he can't outrun them all."

Irish turned towards him with a grim smile, remembering their days in the hell of The Cardinal's School for Catholic Boys, escaping from sadists and sexual perverts.

"I'll give yer odds on that, Jay Mac's gotten outa' tighter scrapes than this."

The bus sped on into the dark, rainy night. Irish stared out of that same window fixed on the diminishing image of his friend running for his life, with the howling mob in close pursuit.

For Jay Mac, here he was once more, in the fantasy world of his running heroes, both two and four legged.

'Who would win really in a proper race, Superman or the Flash?' he asked himself, knowing the issue had been hotly debated by comic fans like him for years. 'What about Captain America-versus-Batman, over, say two hundred yards' he speculated, considering the athletic capabilities of his two favourite characters. He turned under a tall railway viaduct and smiled momentarily on observing a huge Barley Boot Boys chevron, painted roughly across the red faced engineering bricks that lined the support walls.

'Fuck, how big is their territory?' he asked himself.

Random shots of smaller ball bearings and stones stung him every so often or whizzed past his head, just to remind him they were still there, he never made the mistake of looking back.

Calls of "We've got yer, y'fuckin' cunt!" and "Give it up, yer shitbag, we're on yer!" also assailed him, drawing more wry smiles in response.

One thing that he knew for certain was that if they were fully upon him, they would not need to advertise the fact; he would already be a bloody pulp at their feet.

'Good, let them waste some air shoutin' their stupid boasts.' he thought as he crossed a double roundabout, darting recklessly between numerous vehicles containing irate drivers. The lead Barley's footsteps could no longer be clearly heard; being more cautious they had stopped at each circular road feature, then negotiated their path carefully.

Once past the second of these obstacles Jay Mac knew he was spent, he needed a brief respite to gain his second wind, if he wished to maintain his current pace. Confident that he had shaken off his lead pursuers for the moment, he took a calculated risk and in a 'Fosbury Flop' high jump manoeuvre, threw himself over a tall, soaking hedge of a nearby front garden of one of the neatly painted, well-presented town houses that lined the main road in this area.

The torrential rain had stopped and only a light drizzle was falling, he crouched behind this evergreen battlement breathing deeply, filling his lungs with life-giving air. Discordant two-note police sirens could be heard coming from several directions.

"Quick you'd better come in," a soft female voice called from behind him. Jay Mac turned sharply like a cornered beast, cursing himself for stopping and for not even registering the door being opened.

There was no light on in the hall or doorway but something about the beguiling silhouette seemed familiar to him, without a second thought and abandoning all caution, he scrambled forward into the house.

On entering inside he realised there was more than one female present, as he heard two other voices calling from above at the top of a darkened stairwell.

"Are you mad... bringing him in here... they could come back at any minute." one whispering voice warned, followed by a slightly younger sounding girl, "Tell him to go... there'll be murder if they find him here.

The original hostess appeared to be unconcerned for the moment, "You'd better go into the kitchen, there's a back door that leads outside, just in case." she said calmly.

Once he entered this room and she had followed, the light was turned on finally he saw her, recognising instantly who his benefactor was, the stunning 'girl of his dreams' whom he had been searching for since their 'cancelled' date the previous December. Standing in the light in this small but well equipped kitchen, which included a gleaming white refrigerator and a washing machine, she looked even more captivating than he had remembered.

"It's you... I can't believe it, I've looked everywhere for yer, all over town... by the bus stop... everywhere," he began, now feeling genuine anxiety, far more than facing any number of enemies. There she was, tall, elegant, with long dark hair framing a beautiful face, flawless skin and perfect features.

"Well this *is* a surprise, what a small world", she said with a curious smile, causing Jay Mac to completely lose his usual casual style.

"Yeah, I can explain about that night... why I couldn't make it..." he began.

"Don't bother, you didn't show, that's it, you had your chance and blew it. If you step out of line, you lose your place." she replied dispassionately.

"No, y'see the bizzies had me, they pulled me in the night before, there was nothin' I could do." he tried to offer in desperation.

"Like I said, forget it, I know I have. I moved on, the next day as a matter of fact. You're only in here now because me and my cousins were watching through one of the bedroom windows upstairs, to see what all the commotion was about outside and you looked like you were hurt or in trouble." She explained how she had been visiting her cousins that evening when news of an attack on the John Barleycorn pub had spread by 'bush telegraph.'

The recent harsh calls of the police sirens had roused their curiosity further and they had put out the lights in order to see without being seen. Throughout her explanation Jay Mac had been staring, transfixed by her radiant beauty, admiring her slender figure revealed even in her casual attire of tight fitting t-shirt and jeans with platform shoes.

"You are one of the Barleys, aren't you?" she asked, suddenly changing her expression.

"Yeah, I'm definitely a team player."

She laughed at his response, "I'm only joking, I don't bother with all that rubbish, it's only for kids and I'm not interested in kids.

The stunning female walked over to the sink, ran some water onto a clean flannel then returned to where he was standing, dirty, bedraggled and still bloodied despite the rain.

"Here y'go." she said with a smile and came close to him, wiping his face with the wet cloth, "You look almost human now," she laughed.

In that instant her tender, kind action towards a wounded, hunted animal confirmed in Jay Mac's heart what he knew from the beginning, she was the woman for him.

Unable to frame a suitable response he said, "They've got a few bob these cousins of yours by the look of it."

"Yes, y'right my uncle's on the docks and so are his two sons, yeah, they do alright, the Morrisons, they've even got a colour TV that's not rented." She finished speaking and looked at Jay Mac curiously, noticing how pale he had become.

"Are you alright, you don't look too good?" she asked genuinely concerned.

Jay Mac was still reeling from the impact of realising she was related to the Morrison brothers.

"Are Gary and Tony your cousins then?" he asked, trying to appear casual.

"No, no. I know who you mean, they lead the Barleys so I've heard but like I said, I don't bother with all that. These cousins are related just by their dad being married to my mum's sister." she answered honestly, allowing Jay Mac some partial relief.

"Maybe we could still go out some time?" he now felt bold enough to ask.

She looked him up and down, then opened the door to the hall, took a pen and paper from a small table and wrote down her name and telephone number. As she passed it to him she said, "This is my number maybe in a few years, when you've grown up and know what you really want, you can give me a ring. Who knows if I'm still there I might even pick up the phone."

Jay Mac gratefully accepted the precious paper note then turned sharply on hearing the front door open.

"They've done our Gary and Tony, those Crown bastards," an angry male voice shouted, followed quickly by another of similar mood, "We've been chasin' one of their shitbags all over the place but we've lost 'im."

Jay Mac was already at the back door when they closed the front one behind them and turned on the hall light. Quickly leaning forward he followed the old adage that fortune favours the brave and kissed the stunning female lightly on her soft lips.

"You're a cheeky one aren't you?" she said with a smile.

"So they tell me," he replied, then stepped into the rain-soaked back garden. "See yer Dream Girl," he said in a whisper.

"See yer Crown boy" she replied softly.

After vaulting over the low wooden fence he sprinted towards the railway line that passed behind these houses on its northern route out of the city, heading eventually towards Manchester. Once he had carefully crossed the metal rails, he ran as fast as he could manage. Following the line finally out of Barley territory past the Meadow Green shopping district, he ran across, onto the main road that led to the Crown estate and safety. All the while he kept one pleasing image at the forefront of his mind managing to suppress the earlier horrors of that evening, at least for the moment.

Even while Jay Mac had been enjoying his brief encounter with the beautiful female, not far away to the east of the Barleys' territory, the Crown players who had chosen to follow the Unicorn dissenter's path, were receiving the definitive lesson in the value of reliable intelligence. Memory had played a cruel trick on their leader, his childhood recollection of where his aunt's house lay, was correct but during the intervening years since, the city councillors in their infinite wisdom had allowed kindly developers to build on the former 'green-field site' to the rear of his relative's property, purely for philanthropic purposes of course. As a consequence the guaranteed escape route over open meadows had become a certain trap; the through-road was now a cul-de-sac, a dead-end.

Those who had put their faith in the Unicorn prophet to lead them to the path of salvation were betrayed. When the eighteen-man mixed crew ran into the road of no return, they soon realised their error, there was no way out. Their only hope lay in unity and they quickly formed into a tight throng, even as the Barley mob descended upon them. The avenging fury of that night, the righteous anger of the Barley men, could now be fully unleashed.

Punched, kicked, slashed and struck with every available weapon from broom handle to iron bar, they were mercilessly attacked as a group then dragged apart for the individual assaults and tortures to begin. Their cries of pain could be heard all around but no one interfered, curtains twitched but remained closed, with all doors and windows firmly shut. John Barleycorn may have been bloodied beset as he was by his heraldic enemies: The Bear, The Eagle and The Unicorn on that stifling solstice evening and even brought to the ground but the torrent that followed ensured that he did not die and would rise up again. Felix the ever-smiling feline-featured member of the Hounds crew was less fortunate, the group that relentlessly battered him were becoming increasingly enraged as their determined efforts failed to remove that 'stupid grin' from his face. It would cost him almost all of his nine lives to survive that night.

Chapter 6

Dazed and Confused

Saturday 23rd and Wednesday 27th June 1973

At 10.00am on a hot Saturday morning less than a full forty-eight hours since the storming of the John Barleycorn, Jay Mac was sitting stretched out with his feet up, eating a bowl of cornflakes floating in a sea of tepid milk.

"I tell y'what mate if I ever get any money, I'm gonna get the biggest friggin' fridge in the world." he said out loud, addressing Patch the ancient recumbent hound, who as usual was also lying at full stretch on the faux fur rug in front of the electric fire, convincing herself that heat was still coming from the dull grey parallel element bars of the unplugged appliance.

Jay Mac's aunt and uncle had gone away for the weekend on a coach trip with some other aged relatives and as a consequence he had full run of the small, cramped council flat. The door to the tiny outside balcony, which was an additional feature of each alternative group of four flats within the long two storey high tenement block, was wide open and already the humid air from outside had filled the living room.

Trying to listen to the '*Ed 'Stewpot' Stewart Show*' on the small transistor radio, which he had brought from the kitchen and placed on the dark brown utility sideboard, Jay Mac was conscious of the traffic noise from the busy road below. The accompanying leaded petrol exhaust fumes hung heavily in the room's permanently nicotine scented atmosphere, making him feel drowsy and considering whether to get up from his couch bed or try to fall asleep again.

Ever since the events of the previous Thursday, Jay Mac's sleep pattern had been more disturbed and erratic than usual and he was constantly awakening with a start, drenched in sweat, throughout the sticky nights after his disturbed mind had been flooded with a kaleidoscope of horrific images. Usually accompanying these visions were the ever-present huge, menacing, dark statues, who maintained a constant vigil observing and scrutinising his every move, waiting, it seemed, for the right moment to strike. During the previous night's visitation one of the more amorphous statuary giants reached out for him with an open hand, at which point the fearful youth sat bolt upright shouting loudly, causing the sleeping hound on the floor nearby to begin barking angrily.

As Fleetwood Mac's *Albatross* began to play on the radio a tired Jay Mac returned to reading the same, small, page two article in the Friday evening edition of the local broadsheet, *'The Liverpool Echo'* about a vicious assault upon an old established popular public house; the extent of the damage and a list of casualties with graphic details of their injuries. Police were apparently pursuing a number of lines of enquiry and although they were confident of making early arrests, having obtained several eye-witness statements, they were appealing for anyone with any knowledge of the incident to contact them without delay.

"What d'you think mate, shall I get in touch?" he began, addressing his canine companion once more. "I suppose it would be the right thing to do as a decent citizen. Yep, I think I'll mosey on down to the sheriff's office and tell him where t'find those pesky varmints what done what they done. Why, I'll most like get a reeward, Goddamn." The distinctive sound of twin air-horns blasting outside could be heard above the general din, rousing him from his ramblings.

Standing on the balcony he looked down to the lay-by immediately below, where there were a number of parked cars and one gleaming Lambretta scooter.

"Any chance of you openin' the door my man?" Floyd shouted, removing his Centurion helmet as he did.

Jay Mac froze for a moment knowing what must inevitably be about to follow, then replied, "I'll be right down man, bump y'scooter up on the pavement and we'll put it in the bin cupboards for safety.

Not long after, when they had securely parked the prized vehicle in the corridor next to where the tenant's refuse bins were stored, Jay Mac admitted Floyd to his aunt and uncle's flat. Immaculately dressed as ever in a tan leather jacket with wide lapels, cream Levi's sweatshirt and blue jeans, with crisp white Converse basketball boots, Floyd relaxed in one of the old comfortable armchairs still wearing his aviator's sunglasses.

"Nice place Jay Mac, sort of vintage ugly meets modern tat." he observed with a smile.

"Yeah, thanks Floyd it's taken me a few years but if y'know the right people, y'can always pick up some shite, I'm tryin' for the 'nothing matches' look." Jay Mac replied smiling.

"You've pulled it off my man," Floyd acknowledged.

Jay Mac rose to his feet as if to end their conversation, "Anyway, thanks for stoppin' by to look the place over, sorry it's not for you." he said, miming the action of showing Floyd the door.

His lugubrious business associate laughed then proceeded to light a slender cigar without bothering to enquire if that would be allowed. Jay Mac passed him a small circular ashtray then resumed his seat.

"What was it that y'wanted mate?" he asked trying to appear as if everything was perfectly normal.

Floyd looked Jay Mac up and down studying his clothing, which on this occasion happened to be a plain white tee shirt, blue twenty inch parallel Wrangler jeans and a brand new pair of white Converse basketball boots that matched Floyd's in spotless condition.

"Nice keds my man, lookin' sharp." Floyd began. "Expensive but worth it, quality always costs. Then again the bread you've had from me lately you could probably afford two pair, am I right?" He displayed his usual ingratiating smile all the while that he spoke, though Jay Mac knew exactly where this conversation was heading. Floyd continued, "I've been lookin' for you Jay Mac but you ain't been around. I tried the Eagle last night and all I'm hearin' is about a big kick-off against the Barleys and that you done well, got a lorra people out of there." He paused to take a lengthy drag of his cigarillo.

"Don't believe all y'hear Floyd, it was every man for himself." Jay Mac responded.

"Maybe it was and maybe some people had their own reasons for attackin' the number one team's alehouse. All I'm sayin' is you are becomin' a bit of a legend, yeah?" Floyd watched Jay Mac for any change in expression, to see if he fully understood what had been said.

"I don't know anything about anyone's reasons; I was told it was for the name of the team. As for a legend... that's all me arse, I'm just glad I'm still here in one piece and not fucked up like some of the lads." he answered honestly.

"Yeah it's a pity; I hear some of the Unicorn boys took a bad kickin' and Felix the Cat's finished, just about hangin' on in hospital with fuckin' tubes and wires all over him." Floyd advised.

Jay Mac was genuinely sorry to hear about Felix, like most members of the Crown team he enjoyed his witty banter whenever they met in the Eagle or one of their other regular watering holes.

"That's shit; Felix is a good lad I hope he pulls through." Jay Mac replied.

"Yeah, it is sad; I'd hate to see *you* in that state... that would be a real shame." Floyd responded still smiling, and then moved on to the real reason for his visit. "Anyway we've got business to talk about haven't we?" He did not wait for a reply, "Yeah, I'm expectin' a really important package next week and you're gonna be collectin' it for me, right?"

Jay Mac knew if he was ever going to tell Floyd he wished to 'resign' this was probably his best opportunity, on home ground with no weapons immediately to hand.

"Yeah, the thing is Floyd, I can't do this no more. I got a real serious warnin' off Devo (S) and after seein' him in action in the Barleycorn, I don't really wanna cross 'im."

Floyd stopped smiling, removed his cigar from his lips and tapped some ash into the small tray. "Do you really wanna cross me then?" He paused but Jay Mac did not reply. "Or maybe you think Sherman's a pussy, cos if yer do yer makin' a mistake. He makes Devo (S) look like Mary fuckin' Poppins and the people who supply 'im, they like usin' fuckin' big machetes to make sure y'get the message."

Jay Mac listened in silence then after a brief pause replied, "So I'm fucked either way, is that what yer sayin'... its get sliced by Devo the nutter if I carry on with you, or get sliced by Sherman's nutters if I don't."

Floyd smiled once more, "Yeah, that's about the size of it."

Jay Mac felt ill; a terrible nausea overtook him as he searched for a reply that would extricate him from his dire predicament. "Listen Floyd, I'll make a deal with yer cos I really can't do this anymore. Like I said, I've seen Devo in action, I know he *will* find me on the estate or even here and start cuttin' but I don't wanna let you down or, have Sherman's boys on my case, so I'll do this one last pick up for yer and then I'm out, how's that?"

Floyd sat smoking his cigar for a few moments then gave his judgement, "Alright Jay Mac me and you have always got on and y'straight, I know I can trust yer. You do this one last job for me for free. I'll speak to Sherman, that's the best I can offer... deal?" He reached out with his open right palm.

Jay Mac slapped his open hand with his in return, then Floyd repeated the movement this time placing his hand over Jay Mac's waiting open right palm. As he concluded their contract he spoke, "Just remember Jay Mac, never speak to anyone about this and don't even consider lettin' me down. You think you know me but yer don't. Ask Devo sometime about a few of those scars he's got, we go way back. Things aren't always the way they look."

When he had finished speaking he leaned down and stroked the old mongrel, who lazily wagged her brush of a tail. "Fuck me, I thought that thing was dead, just shows yer, looks can be deceiving."

Ten minutes later Floyd was riding out of the Kings estate on his ultra-cool Lambretta SX200, having given Jay Mac precise details of his final assignment. As he watched his former 'employer' and Crown team mate ride away, leaning over the balcony rail he knew that he had less than a week to find a way out. One thing he was certain of was that he had no intention of making that collection.

Later, on the evening of that same day, after Jay Mac had fed and watered the hound, then ensured that a light was left on to deter burglars, with the television also playing as an additional deterrent and as company for the appreciative canine, he set off for the Crown estate. Having spent most of that scorching day with his brain in turmoil, he finally felt as if he had a solution that may resolve his dilemma, at least for the present.

Seated on the bus, travelling the short distance between the two estates, Jay Mac reflected on his conversation with Floyd and his earlier one the previous Sunday with Devo. There was obviously bad blood between the two rival Crown players and he was considering how he could best exploit this to his advantage. He was unsure whether he would be able to deal with Floyd on his own but he was certain that any conflict with Devo would be suicidal and concluded that he must try to manipulate one to remove the threat of the other, he would set a thief to catch a thief.

Deciding to take a calculated risk, once he had collected Weaver from his tenement block, he began to test the water as they made their way to the Heron.

"Listen mate I wanna ask yer some stuff, cos I need a bit of advice about a problem I've got, so let's dive in 'ere before the crew turn up." he began cryptically.

"If you've gorra dose of V.D. or crabs, Jay Mac, I can't help yer, y'need to see a doctor," Weaver responded laughing unsympathetically.

"Yeah I wish it was that simple." Jay Mac replied as they entered the pub and sauntered up to the bar.

Once they had been served, with the saloon being reasonably empty for an early Saturday evening, Jay Mac sat at a small table with Weaver and outlined his dilemma, providing vague details of his business relationship with Floyd. While they were talking the first of Jay Mac's selection of records from the jukebox Jimmy Hendrix's *Voodoo Child* began to play, conveniently obscuring their conversation from any eve's droppers, however unintentional.

"Alright, the way I see it is yer fucked." Weaver gave his considered judgement after listening to all the evidence, "but there is a way out if y'can get Devo on board and I think *you* can. Yeah, Devo fuckin' hates Floyd, not just doesn't like him and it goes back a long way." Weaver paused and took a drink of his pint of Sköl lager which he was trying instead of his usual bitter. "I think I could get into this." he said before returning to the matter in hand. "When we was in school, they were in the year above me and what a fuckin' year that was; yer had Tommy (S); Quirky; Devo and Floyd. Anyway, everyone knew Tommy (S) was the cock, he had been since the fuckin' infants, he probably would've burst kids in the nursery, if he'd gone to a nursery." He paused again to take another lengthy drink. "When thee were at the end of the fourth year, thee just decided to see who was second cock, so Quirky, Devo and Floyd were gonna 'ave a go but that never happened. Floyd and Devo had a fuckin' brilliant scrap, we all went over to the field to watch and Quirky was gonna take on the winner. After about twenty minutes Devo started gettin' the better of Floyd and he tried to give up but Devo wouldn't stop and it looked like he was gonna boot him to death. Next thing y'know Floyd grabs his leg and whips him up, then he picks up a half brick and twatted Devo right in the face, then *he* wouldn't stop. Quirky and Tommy (S) had to drag 'im off. Everyone thought Devo was dead, his fuckin' head was totally bashed in." Weaver stopped once more and finished his pint holding the empty glass towards Jay Mac.

"Alright, I can take a hint, its thirsty work, tellin' y'story, I'll get another round in."

When Jay Mac returned from the bar with their drinks, Weaver explained how the proposed fight with the insane Quirky and the winner of the first bout, Floyd, never took place and how he left the school shortly after to become an apprentice chef.

"Devo was missin' for a bit then when he came back he said how Floyd had cheated using a weapon and from then on he always carried a blade. Not long after he left as well to start off as a butcher's apprentice. The two of them love knives 'an thee both know how to use them." When he had concluded his brief history of the origin of Devo and Floyd's mutual hatred, he added "If yer tell Devo what yer've told me, he'll definitely back yer up and take care of Floyd, for good."

"Who'll take care of Floyd for good?" a smiling Macca (G) asked as he emerged from behind the bar.

"What the fuck are you doin' there?" asked Weaver.

"A bit of business with Sid, the landlord, he knows a good opportunity when he sees one," Macca (G) replied mysteriously, without adding any further detail. "So what are you two ladies plottin'... people will start talkin' if thee keep seein' the both of yer out like this whisperin' together." He displayed his usual sly smile while he spoke and Jay Mac was worried how much he had actually overheard.

For the moment he chose to change the subject from Floyd to Macca (G)'s 'business' activities, "Talkin' of deals, is there any more shoebox deliveries goin'?" he asked.

"Not now but I'm expectin' somethin' big mid-week, so I'll probably need yer then." Macca (G) replied as he joined them at the table holding three shot glasses of whiskey, which he had helped himself to whilst behind the bar. "Drink up lads, I'm in a top mood, business is lookin' good." he said before they each downed their measures of whiskey in one swallow. "Now tell me what's all this about takin' care of Floyd?" he enquired insistently.

Both Weaver and Jay Mac paused for a few moments then the Eagle player replied, "No, what we were talkin' about was who'd win in a scrap between Devo (S) and Floyd and Weaver was tellin' me about the go they had in school." He stopped for a moment trying to gather his thoughts then continued, "I said, I was surprised that Floyd won but Weaver said, if there was a re-match, Devo would definitely take care of Floyd for good."

Jay Mac's explanation seemed to satisfy the curious Heron co-leader for the present. He then began to discuss his plans for the evening with them. "Listen, am just gonna slip out the back for a bit. I've got a couple of young birds waitin' there, y'know what I mean? You'd be surprised what they'll do for a bit of puff or a few tabs." He paused and let them consider his words, whilst he mentally conjured images of the vile acts he was about to commit. "If y'fancy joinin' in there's two of them, so we could give them a real hard time, what d'yer say?"

Jay Mac looked across at Weaver whom he could tell found his co-leader's generous offer very tempting but replied, "Nah, sounds great Macca but I think I've got a bit of a dose or somethin' me cock's been killin' me, so I'll jib it tonight, we're gonna have a stroll round the estate to see if any fucker needs a smack, am just in the mood for it."

Jay Mac appreciated the crazed psychopath's gesture and followed suit, "Another time thanks Macca, decent of yer to offer, enjoy y'self anyway."

"Oh, I will, believe me, I will. These two are gonna be learnin' about real pain tonight." he salivated as he spoke.

Jay Mac and Weaver stood up and left the sexual sadist to his fantasising in preparation for his evening's pleasure. They sauntered out of the Heron and headed up the central road in the direction of the Unicorn, hoping for an audience with Devo (S).

Within half an hour the two Crown team mates turned into the lane at the southern-most boundary of the estate, where the Unicorn public house was located. Fortunately they were both reasonably attired in casual clothing that did not include denim jeans or jackets. Jay Mac was wearing a black Harrington style jacket over a plain white short-sleeved Ben Sherman shirt, with Prince of Wales checked twenty inch parallel trousers and his cherry red Airwair and Weaver wore a grubby yellow and green patchwork jumper; blue-green two-tone twenty inch parallel trousers and his black variety of the popular footwear.

As they were about to enter this more salubrious drinking establishment, Weaver turned to Jay Mac once more and reminded him of the favour he had done for him that evening, as he had several times during their walk to the pub.

"Don't forget Jay Mac, you owe me big time. I've just given up a fuckin' good session with two dirty skanks. I'm only doin' this cos I never liked Floyd, he's a flash cunt."

"Yeah, thanks Weaver, you've made yer point, about a dozen times so far." Jay Mac replied. "I'll make it up to yer, alright? When we get back, I'll give one of Molly Brown's girls ten pence so you can 'ave a wank at least."

Weaver was less than impressed, "What? A ten pence toss, yer must be jokin' mate. We'll be goin' into town when I decide and bangin' the arses off a couple of smart birds, not bleedin' dogs, right?"

Jay Mac looked at Weaver in surprise, he had not realised that he might have any ambitions beyond life on the estate. Although he thought it was highly unlikely that they would find two sophisticated females, who may be prepared to consider a sexual encounter, he decided to humour the dangerous psychopath.

"Yeah, that sounds great; I'll be lookin' forward to a night in town with yerself on the pull."

Once inside, they pushed through the crowd of Saturday night drinkers and took their place at the bar. Fortunately there was several staff on duty ensuring that they had their pints without much delay. Carefully negotiating the tables surrounded by seated revellers, while securely holding their beverages, they made their way to the rear lounge, the court of 'lord' Devo. Their luck held and positioned exactly where they had seen him the previous Sunday, surrounded by his loyal retainers, dispensing wisdom and favours as he saw fit, was the sinister leader.

Thinking they would have to take a seat near the door and then wait for an opportunity to seek an audience, they found the nearest convenient table just inside the room. Even before the two youths had sat down they received an official summons.

"You two, Devo wants t'see yer both now, move yerselves," Morgo 'the Man' advised, then led them through to the senior crew seated along the back wall, with Devo at their centre.

"Well, well, if it isn't Weaver and Jay Mac." he began. "Pull up a stool lads and tell me what brings two of my favourite Crown players all the way up here to The Unicorn; my alehouse."

Devo was not far from the truth when he spoke. In fact his presence ensured no other teams or even foolhardy individuals risked approaching *his* public house. His senior bodyguard always accompanied him when he was in residence, acting as unofficial bouncers throughout the hostelry effectively dealing with any potential trouble usually before it erupted, or ruthlessly quelling any isolated outbreaks that did. For the cost of providing a few rounds of 'free' drinks, the landlord had inadvertently hired a highly effective security team and he appreciated this symbiotic relationship, at least he did at the beginning, until it changed to one of master and servant.

For a few moments neither Jay Mac nor Weaver spoke. The former appeared transfixed by the incongruous image of their leader calmly sitting dressed in his Levi's denim jacket, unchallenged by the management, his deep purple paisley shirt and with his dark, unkempt, corkscrew hair loosely framing his even more battered countenance. Yet a starkly contrasting picture of the blood-soaked maniac holding his rival's severed ear covered in shiny, fresh, sticky, scarlet fluid kept appearing before his eyes. Weaver just seemed to be in awe of his hero, the role model that he aspired to.

Before either of them could frame the question of how Devo may be of help with Jay Mac's problem, he decided to speak.

"I dunno what's wrong with you two. I'll ask yer again in a minute and then I wanna hear an answer." He rose to his feet and without requiring Morgo, his master of ceremonies to quieten the crowd, his own physical presence appeared sufficient and within moments the room was silent except for the sound of David Bowie's *Drive in Saturday* playing on the nearby jukebox.

Once he was certain that he had their attention he began, "Last Wednesday night we got a major result for the Crown team." Everyone cheered at this.

"These two lads 'ere, they really played their part. Now, most of yer probably know Weaver, some of yer might even 'ave gone t'school with him like me and you'll know he's a bit of a nutter but the other night he stepped up, put himself forward and led a crew right into the Barley's alehouse."

Again there was more spontaneous cheering. Devo turned his attention towards Jay Mac, "What can yer say about this lad? Some of yer probably don't even know his name, well yer fuckin' should. Jay Mac 'ere comes off the Kings Estate, takes a chance on them grippin' him, fights for our team and then does us proud against the Barleys." There was a slightly more muted response this time, leading Devo to add further weight to his original praise. "I'm not sure if yer heard what I just said, so I'll make it crystal for yer. The Barleys sent their fastest runner off with their flag t'save it, yeah?

He had a head start and was really movin'; this lad 'ere went after him, took him down, had their flag away and then took a good kickin' off two of their boys while he was on the deck. Would he give them their flag back? No he fuckin' wouldn't! When we got there it was their turn to take a few digs and we had their bleedin' flag off."

Devo paused before building to the climax of his brief eulogy. "And where's that flag now then?" His grim visage contorted into an evil smile, making him appear like a grotesque pantomime villain and he roused his audience accordingly. "I can't hear yer, where's their flag now then?" he repeated causing some brave souls to participate in his act. "It's behind yer!" they shouted.

Devo beamed with delight and turned around slowly to reveal the very item, the blood-stained standard of the John Barleycorn folded and sewn across the back panel of his Levi's denim jacket, below the shoulders. He had played to the house and now the appreciative crowd responded in like manner, stamping, cheering and calling out wildly "Devo!" or "Crown Team!"

Standing completely still after turning to face his team, Devo stretched out his hands toward them in a further theatrical gesture, Jay Mac looked at him half expecting a bow to follow. He considered how a bizarre cocktail comprised of a large measure of fear, laced with a dash of misplaced admiration and finished with a splash of perverse charisma, could intoxicate a crowd of young males to such a state of frenzy that they would surrender their will to that of the orator. On reflection he knew that history was littered with dozens of examples of such deranged demagogues.

Devo had one final question to put before them, "Yer all know I am a reasonable feller, don't yer?" No one was foolish enough to reply to this rhetorical question. "So all I'm sayin' to the Barleys is, if yer want yer little flag back, just come 'ere to me, ask me nicely and then... yer can kiss my hairy arse!" Thunderous applause greeted this final twist of sarcasm and Devo resumed his seat, while the noisy ovation still resounded around the stifling smoky room, with its ornate patterned red and gold flock wallpaper and skilfully plastered lattice-covered high ceiling.

He stared directly at Weaver and Jay Mac "I bet yer wonderin' what I did with Gazmo's ear. I was gonna fry it up with a bit of onion and 'ave it on some bread."

Jay Mac looked suitably aghast, Weaver sufficiently impressed.

"Nah, I'm only jokin' I'm not Jack the fuckin' Ripper. I threw it in a jar of pickles at the back of the fridge, me ma will get a shock if she finds it. Anyway I'll probably send it back to 'im when he gets out of hospital."

His expression changed instantly "Right, what the fuck do you two want, let's have it?" Devo asked without the faintest trace of his previous warmth or sinister smile remaining.

"It's Jay Mac, he's havin' a problem with that flash cunt, Floyd." Weaver began, having summoned up the courage to speak.

"Really? Now that is interestin' you've come to the right person. Give me all the details Jay Mac and I'll be happy to help yer." Devo responded, smiling slyly once more.

Jay Mac outlined his working arrangement with Floyd, how and where the collection was made and how he subsequently passed the package onto him at the Eagle. He emphasised that he had never had a problem before with Floyd but now that he wished to resign, following Devo's instruction, Floyd had threatened him with dire consequences if he did.

Devo appeared to be delighted "Alright Jay Mac, you've done the right thing, I'll take care of this. Yer don't need to worry about Floyd anymore, he's the one who should be worryin' it's been comin' to him for a long time and now he's really gonna pay."

He paused and snapped his fingers at one of the bar staff who was collecting glasses from a table nearby. "Over 'ere!" he said on catching the young man's attention.

"What are you's drinkin'?" Devo asked.

"Lager for me." said Weaver, with Jay Mac adding, "Guinness thanks."

Devo looked at both of them, "Surprised at you Weaver, I took you for a traditional bitter man, Jay Mac's a lad after me own heart, on the Guinness, I'll have the same. We'll have two whiskey chasers and a rum as well, unless one of yer wants t'join me for a proper drink?"

Weaver did not respond, still reeling from what he perceived as a stinging criticism from his 'hero'.

Jay Mac decided to accept the offer, "Yeah, why not, I'll give it a go." he replied.

"That's more like it, a man of taste,'ey? Yer won't bother with the whiskey once yer've had this. The landlord's got me own special supply in, 'Woods 100', it's a fuckin' belter." He turned suddenly to the waiting barman, "Yeah, what are yer still standin' there for? Go 'ed then, yer've heard the round, off yer go, chop chop."

The evening was progressing well for Weaver who had been mentioned in dispatches and particularly for Jay Mac who had received a commendation from their commanding officer and he began to finally relax believing that his problem with Floyd would soon be over.

While the whole crew were enjoying their drinking and storytelling, a tall, well built male in his mid-thirties, entered the room. He was dressed in a grey Gabardine Macintosh over a grubby white Bri-nylon shirt with an open dirty collar and a large garish patterned kipper tie, fastened with a loose Windsor knot hung at half-mast. His dark blue flared trousers had become shiny in patches with wear and strained desperately to hold back his substantial beer belly, with the assistance of a black plastic belt which matched his wet-look, scuffed Chelsea boots. With an ambling gait he made his way directly to where Jay Mac and Weaver were sitting facing their leader Devo.

"What the fuck is that smell?" Devo began then held his nose, "Has someone stepped in bad dog shit, or is that your guts droppin' Morgo?" he asked wafting the air in front of him. "Oh sorry D.C Banks, I didn't smell yer there, I mean see yer there."

"Evenin' Devlin, y'little prick." D.C Banks replied staring down at the smiling team leader. "Only out a couple of weeks and y'causing trouble already, looks like it's back to nick for you, only this time they won't be letting you off early for 'good behaviour'."

"I'm not sure what you mean officer. Has something happened? Have I been named? Have you got a reliable witness? Or, is it just you flappin' yer gums, pickin' on me, the soft target cos yer don't know what else to do?" Devo replied with a smile.

"Gerrup Devlin and turn your fuckin' pockets out now!" D.C Banks snapped.

The team leader slowly rose to his feet then one by one emptied each pocket and displayed their lining. Apart from some small change, an open packet of Wrigley's spearmint gum and a brown leather wallet, there were no other items; much to the annoyance of the overweight detective.

"No knife on you tonight Devlin? I'm surprised you've even come out the house, you little shitbag, usually y'start crying if yer haven't got a blade with yer, in case one of the big boys hits yer."

This remark seemed to anger the violent youth and he replied coldly "Are you arrestin' me or chargin' me with somethin'?"

The detective looked directly at him, "I'm just asking you a few friendly questions, I only want you to talk to me."

Devo picked up his wallet then said, "Hang on, I've got somethin' in 'ere yer can have... it's me solicitors business card, he'll be happy to speak to yer. Give him a ring, cos I will be."

Detective Banks leaned forward over Jay Mac who had remained seated with his back turned at an angle towards the questioner. He could smell the officer's overpowering halitosis mixed with his pungent body odour and glancing up he instantly recognised him as one of the detectives who had interrogated him the previous December, noticing particularly the deep scar running from his left nostril up to the outer corner of his eye.

"What the fuck are you lookin' at?" the sweating heavyweight asked angrily, catching Jay Mac's furtive glance.

"That's the question we would all like an answer to officer." Jay Mac replied, causing a few laughs from the nearest crew members.

"I know you, you little tit, you'll be joining him in a minute outside." He turned his gaze back towards the smiling Devo. "Right, outside you, and you two might as well come with him, seeing as how y'both sittin' right in front of the knobhead, you were probably there with him.

Devo stood up and said, "After you officer." then followed, pushing Weaver and Jay Mac in front of him.

Once they had reached the usually vacant loose gravel-chip covered forecourt, they were surprised to find two police panda cars parked immediately in front of the main entrance. The breathless detective caught hold of Devo by the forearm and pulled him towards the lead vehicle, where a young male was seated in the rear behind the driver.

"Stand still you." Detective Constable Banks ordered, then shouted, "Is this him, do you recognise this one, did he cut you and your brother?" he asked insistently trying to encourage the passenger to make a positive identification. The youth came closer to the door and stared through its window at Devo. Even where they were standing Jay Mac and Weaver could clearly see the ugly, disfiguring scar that ran down his face diagonally across his lips from his cheek to his chin, with its zip of multiple fresh stitches.

A few tense moments passed when no one spoke before the detective shouted angrily "Come on lad, this is the one isn't it, just say, nod yer head or point at him." The silent passenger shook his head and refused to identify the one who had attacked him and his brother. Devo pulled his arm loose from D.C Banks' grip and stepped away still facing forward, all the time keeping his back out of sight. Weaver and Jay Mac were brought to the vehicle next and again although the youth stared at the hammer-wielding psychopath for a few moments, there was no positive identification, even with the detective's active encouragement.

"Go 'ed, the three of yer, piss off." the exasperated detective shouted to the Crown players. Before they did and even as D.C Banks was getting into the second vehicle, Devo called to him, "See yer Banks, I'll tell me arl feller y'called round, he'll be sorry he missed yer, this time."

Raising two fingers in victory salute, the detective wedged himself into his seat then closed the door. Driving away he recalled the hot summer's night fifteen years earlier when he had been a young constable patrolling his beat and was summoned to a disturbance at the Bear Public House. While he struggled desperately with the main culprit, one of the crowd drew a distinctive knife which incorporated a knuckle-duster handle and cut him deeply under his right eye down to his nose, leaving a deep permanent scar.

Michael Devlin or Micky (D) of the Crown Teddy Boys was never charged, having fled the scene and subsequently providing a convincing alibi which placed him nowhere near the location of the incident. Despite his repeated exaggerated boasts over the years, particularly to his hero-worshipping son, Sean, Michael Devlin remained out of the reach of the long arm of the law. D.C Banks was determined that one day he would bring him and his son within its grasp.

Laughing and joking about the incident the three Crown team mates strolled back into the lounge of the Unicorn. While they downed several more rounds of beer and spirits, Devo gave Jay Mac precise details of what he must do on the day of the collection and insisted that he must act exactly as if everything was normal. Before they left later that night an intoxicated Jay Mac was now fully reassured that his problem would soon be over.

"Yer won't be seein' Floyd anymore after Wednesday, don't you worry, yer can be sure of that." were Devo's final chilling words.

Wednesday 27th June 1973

Jay Mac arrived a full hour before his five o'clock pick up appointment, on that hot, sticky Wednesday afternoon. He stood across the road from his arranged collection point; outside Dolcis shoe shop and Chelsea Girl, surveying the scene. None of the usual couriers had arrived as yet and there were no obvious signs of a contingent from Devo (S) being present either. He passed a quarter of an hour looking in all directions from his vantage point, casually following the movements of some of the attractive females, as they floated by in their revealing light summer dresses displaying their wares, oblivious to his lustful gaze, unaware of his dark dilemma.

In the days since his reassuring meeting with the Crown Team leader, he had once again resumed his mental turmoil. He had no wish to betray Floyd, they had always enjoyed a reasonably amicable working relationship but he knew that he would never really allow him to depart from the firm. Jay Mac recalled a specific part of their conversation on the night of his 'initiation', where Floyd had said "...course I could never let yer leave the business, yer know too much, I'd have t'kill yer." Floyd may have been smiling at the time but Jay Mac had no doubt his words were genuine.

He strolled away from the area intent on repeating his circuit approximately every quarter of an hour to reassess the position. Floyd always picked busy sections of the shopping district and random times when they were likely to be most crowded, usually lunch hour or at the end of the working day. Now approaching rush hour this current collection location was becoming increasingly busy. Finally on his third return trip Jay Mac could just make out the tall figures of Kenny (D) and Frenchy. He failed to notice the actual courier, Samuel, who was standing apart from them in the open entrance of the female fashion store, admiring what was on offer inside, hoping to catch an exciting glimpse of the unwary shoppers as the doors to the communal changing rooms swung open.

Jay Mac was wearing his Levi's denim jacket with bleached collar and pocket flaps, which also bore his recently added scarlet

LFC wings on the back and even more recent Stanley knife gashes below. Devo had told him to wear this after asking if he had something distinctive, that would identify him when the action began. Just before five o'clock with the crowd becoming ever denser, Jay Mac crossed the busy road and began his approach towards the waiting Kenny (D) and Frenchy. He hoped that whatever happened they would not be harmed in any way.

Even as Jay Mac looked directly at the martial arts exponent, he spotted the Crown player. They both smiled in exchange and the youth pushed through the bustling throng towards his friend. With Jay Mac just feet from Kenny (D) he saw his expression change to one of anger and realised that someone or some group must be following behind him. Kenny looked away and did not even acknowledge his presence, then suddenly without warning began attacking his partner, Frenchy. A violent struggle developed with female shoppers screaming and commotion all around. Jay Mac understood in an instant what Kenny was trying to do, pushing past him without a second glance.

"Alright, break it up you two!" shouted a firm angry voice from behind. On reaching a safe distance Jay Mac quickly looked over his shoulder to see what was happening. His honourable friend had noticed the two plain clothes policemen closely following Jay Mac and realised something was wrong; without a second thought for himself, he created a diversion which allowed both Jay Mac and Samuel to slip away into the crowd. Kenny the Bushido warrior offered such fierce resistance as to require uniformed reinforcements to be called for, until finally when he was certain that the Crown player and the courier had escaped, he allowed himself to be taken, although the truncheon strikes continued long after; Frenchy was arrested also, for good measure.

After turning into one of the nearby side streets, Jay Mac removed his identifying jacket, folded it and began a rapid march in the direction of the Pier Head bus and ferry terminal. He was overcome with nausea and guilt as he thought of the brave Kenny (D)'s altruistic sacrifice, which had allowed him to escape. Jay Mac knew that the brutal treatment he, a white working class youth had received, on two separate occasions the previous year at the hands of the police, would be nothing in comparison to that which the two black working class youths would endure, particularly Kenny (D) for his furious resistance of arrest.

On reaching the Pier Head the paranoid Jay Mac checked to see if there were any police following or waiting for him. Satisfied that he was safe he boarded the first bus that was due to leave for the Crown estate and quickly made his way to the back seat on the lower deck. Travelling along through the still hot early evening on the humid vehicle, which had rapidly become filled to capacity, he was lost in the torment of his thoughts.

As he analysed and cross-examined the facts over and over, it became increasingly clear to him that the only way the police would have been present, was if someone had alerted them to the transaction that was supposed to have taken place. No matter how he approached the problem the solution was always the same, the most likely candidate, the informer, had to be Devo (S).

Jay Mac convinced himself that his deduction was correct and that for some reason known only to him, Devo was trying to close Floyd's operation down. He felt that he now understood what the crazed leader had meant when he said *he* would not be seeing Floyd again; Devo was going to allow Jay Mac to be arrested with the incriminating package and in the company of the other couriers. The more he considered the evidence and sequence of events, the more persuasive his theory became. Something about Gazmo's comments to Devo after their fight at the close of the Crown assault on the Barleycorn, also kept playing over in his mind. He knew there was far more behind these events than appeared on the surface.

Forty minutes later he leapt off the green Atlantean bus at the terminus stop on the lower edge of the Crown Estate, facing Weaver's tenement block. Jay Mac raced over to his unlikely friend's residence and banged on his front door.

"Alright, fuckin' hell, who's that? The rent's not due till Friday," Mr Weaver senior shouted angrily on having his evening meal disturbed; fortunately his son, the Heron co-leader sprang up to answer the door.

"It's alright Da, I'll gerrit, it's probably for me anyway." he said adjusting his black half inch braces as he left the table."

"What's your fuckin' problem Jay Mac?" he asked angrily upon opening the battered front door.

Jay Mac quickly provided a garbled explanation which included his suspicions concerning Devo (S).

Weaver was not happy, "Listen you, say what yer want about any other cunt but I'm tellin' yer, don't ever call Devo a grass."

Sufficiently chastised Jay Mac decided not to pursue the matter further for the moment but instead continued "Look Weaver yer can see I'm in a shit situation. I've gorra meet Floyd at seven o'clock in the Eagle with his package, which I haven't got." He paused hoping his team mate may respond positively but instead Weaver just looked at him impassively saying, "So what the fuck's that gorra do with me?"

Jay Mac felt isolated and trapped, there was no point in hiding from his fate, he knew one way or another he had to face Floyd at the Eagle, or risk him arriving unannounced outside his aunt and uncle's flat.

"I've got the knuckle duster you leant me but I need another weapon, what 'ave yer got?" he asked desperately.

"Hang on 'ere." Weaver replied before disappearing into the flat. A few moments later he reappeared and handed Jay Mac a supplementary weapon from his own family arsenal; a black leather cosh filled with lead shot.

"Here, take this for tonight and don't fuckin' lose it, it's me arl fellers. He was a bit of a lad himself once but he doesn't use it now, not much anyway." he said smiling slyly.

"Thanks mate, I'll gerroff." Jay Mac replied gratefully.

"Hold on y'fucker, I'll get me denim and come with yer. If it kicks off, I'll jump in, I hate that flash cunt anyway."

Considerably relieved, Jay Mac accepted Weaver's generous offer without hesitation and the two set off for the Eagle.

Their route up the main central road took them once again past Glynn's small terraced residence and on this warm evening he too was again outside with his uncle painting the window frames. Glynn looked up from his task glancing at Jay Mac and the hated Weaver as they walked by. Fortunately for all parties on this occasion he chose not to make any comment, merely following them with his eyes while a murderous rage burned in his heart and an all-consuming desire for vengeance tormented his soul. As they passed beyond his line of sight he knew without doubt that ultimately his day of reckoning with Weaver would dawn.

Perched on the continuous semi-circular concrete sill of the library were: Irish, Blue, Johno, Tank and Brain discussing recent events, particularly the legend of the night John Barleycorn was cut down, almost one week earlier.

"Alright Jay Mac, y'made it then?" Tank observed casually as their Eagle crew mate arrived with Weaver alongside.

Never a Dull Moment 1973 ▪ 159

"Yeah, turned out alright after all." Jay Mac replied nonchalantly as if his desperate run was a routine occurrence.

"Told yer Tank, I should've took that bet." Irish said with a wry grin. "Up to the Unicorn are yer, t'see yer new friends?" he asked addressing his comments to Jay Mac.

"Nah, I'm goin' over to the Eagle to meet an old one." Jay Mac responded.

Before anything else was said two girls ran over from the direction of the eponymous alehouse dressed in an eclectic mix of the now almost obsolete ridiculously short mini-skirt, combined with short-sleeved checked Ben Sherman shirts and the latest incongruous high platform shoes, they were this seasons version of Molly 'Skank' Brown's business associates. One of them happened to be the youngest sister of the deadly cut-throat razor carrying mad man, Quirky, who fortunately for the moment was residing at Her Majesty's pleasure.

"'Ey lads come over to the Eagle, see what we've got there." she shouted grinning broadly.

"Yeah, come on." her friend began, "We've gorra talkin' monkey and he's askin' for Jay Mac."

In an instant Jay Mac darted across the road and leapt over the small brick wall which surrounded the ever-empty car park of the pub. He was closely followed by his Eagle companions and Weaver, the Heron co-leader. Running to the side of the building, he could see a large crowd of mostly young males with a scattering of females, gathered around something or someone on the floor near the rear wall, which marked the boundary of the building and barren field behind.

"Let me 'ave a go, come 'ed, don't be fuckin' sly." shouted one of the excited youths.

"Come on darkie, try sayin' somethin' in English." another fair haired boy was demanding whilst kicking violently in the direction of his instruction.

"Please... I just want to find Jay Mac." the crouching figure called out.

Whatever instincts normally motivated him, whether cowardice or self-preservation, in this instance on hearing Samuel's pleading voice, Jay Mac's mind snapped. No thoughts passed through his logical brain, no rapid calculations taking into account the odds, the probability of success or failure, the risk of personal injury, only uncontrollable blind rage possessed him. Slipping the heavy brass knuckle-duster onto his left hand and drawing the leather covered cosh with his right, he ploughed into the mob like an avenging fury unleashed. He punched faces, backs and ribs while cracking heads, deadening shoulders and arms with wild strikes.

"Fucking leave him!" he bellowed, his face purple and his neck thickened as the blood coursed through his engorged veins.

Irish and Johno assisted in flinging dazed, wounded youths to one side, both following in the wake of their maddened team mate, cutting a bloody swathe through the previously ecstatic mob. When he reached the battered, bleeding Samuel, Jay Mac stood over him trying to raise him to his feet; the young Ghanaian looked up recognising his friend and smiled warmly revealing his magnificent teeth.

Not everyone was pleased with Jay Mac's action. One of the leading youths who had been struck by him was the sadistic younger brother of the lugubrious Tank and although he was indifferent to his sibling's part in the vile attack, he was outraged at Jay Mac's assault upon him.

"Hey you, yer fuckin' cunt, don't you touch our Stevie," he shouted before booting Jay Mac in the back.

Other members of the mob augmented by recent arrivals also began verbally remonstrating before physically attacking the trio of rescuers. Beleaguered as they were Irish and Johno stayed close to Jay Mac, all three acting as a human shelter for the kneeling, dazed Samuel.

"Gerrout the fuckin' way!" Floyd commanded mounting the kerb then driving through the gap in the low walls, directly into the angry throng on his Lambretta SX200.

Casualties fell to either side while the speeding vehicle struck any in its path without prejudice. On reaching the 'human shield' Floyd came to a halt, keeping the engine running all the while, then shouted. "Get 'im on here now!"

With the assistance of his two friends, Jay Mac raised Samuel to his feet and placed him onto the vehicles seat behind Floyd. The driver wheeled the gleaming scooter around and ploughed out between the mob, creating a trail of injury as he did. Once he was safely on the road again he looked back towards Jay Mac and called "This is down to you Jay Mac, down to you, now you're gonna pay!" With that he was gone racing along the central road, southbound, intent on escaping the Crown Estate, taking Samuel to safety.

Standing with their backs to the wall, now the three rescuers were in need of rescue as the hostile mob turned their anger and frustration towards them.

"Fuckin' twats, what did yer think yer were doin'?" shouted one of the younger males, covering a head wound with one of his hands.

The main thrust of their recrimination was focused on the 'foreigner' in their midst, Jay Mac.

"You don't even belong here y'cunt, get back to yer own estate, where y'came from!" Stevie Turner or Ste (T) as he styled himself, the younger brother of the long-time Eagle crew member, Tank, shouted.

He in turn looked to the only ranking officer present, Weaver co-leader of the Heron, "You saw them Weaver, turnin' on their own kind to help a darkie, fuckin' hell it makes me sick." Tank spat onto the floor to emphasise his disgust.

Weaver had remained almost entirely motionless throughout the incident, standing just inside the low walls with his arms folded, watching impassively. He stared directly at Tank and said, "I did see what happened and I liked it, three lads with balls takin' on a crew of shitbags and bitches." He paused allowing them to absorb what he had said.

Their angry faces no longer wore masks of mindless hate and slowly their features assumed a calmer disposition.

Weaver continued, "I've got me hammer 'ere in me pocket, I haven't had the chance to use it for nearly a week. If any fucker wants to give me the excuse that I'm waitin' for then raise yer hand against these three... *please*."

Faced with this ultimatum the righteous anger of the mob suddenly dissipated and their wrath was sheathed. Their numbers diminished as they shuffled out of the dark grey tarmaced car park, leaving only a handful of exasperated youths led by Tank, facing Irish, Johno and Jay Mac with a glowering Weaver at the rear.

"Make yer move Tank, it's down to you," Jay Mac called to his fellow Eagle member.

A cold silence created a void in the warm evening air while Tank's fevered brain scrambled to find a face-saving solution. In the end pragmatism won over any desire for elevation within the ranks by risking a clash with Weaver and he replied simply. "Nah, it'll keep, we're all on the same team 'ere."

A few moments later and the ever-empty car park returned to its usual state. The Eagle crew members and Weaver decided drinks all round was the best option and took their places in the semi-circular seating arrangement at the rear of the lounge, Wizard's *See My Baby Jive* was playing on the jukebox in the corner as they sat down.

Even as the argument had been raging in the Eagle car park and Weaver had been providing his judgement, Floyd was racing past the eastern edge of the municipal cemetery, close to Ravenshall territory. If he had not been so distracted by his furious anger, he may have noticed the dark saloon car that had been following him since he sped away from the alehouse and was closing on him rapidly, choosing this moment to accelerate.

On hearing the roar of the vehicle's engine behind him, Floyd finally glanced at his array of mirrors, momentarily gaining a fly's compound eye, multi-faceted, simultaneous burst of images. It was too late and of no avail with the speeding car pulling alongside the uber-cool scooter, before smashing into it, forcing a violent skid which separated riders and vehicle, throwing them in different directions. Without the protection of a helmet Samuel suffered worst from the intentional collision, striking his bare head against the kerb as he landed, fracturing his skull leaving him drifting between consciousness and oblivion. Lying in the road with blood streaming from his serious head-wound, his eyes strained to catch glimpses of what was occurring around him.

The dark saloon car had parked nearby and three of its passengers approached the stricken pair. Samuel tried to form the words to ask for assistance as he watched two males, one of them totally bald, carrying Floyd in through the cemetery opening; the other man stood over him and began dragging the injured youth's purple bomber jacket and colourful shirt open.

"Where is it lad? C'mon, I don't wanna hurt yer." Devo asked, calmly at first. "Where's the fuckin' package."

"I don't... know... what..." Samuel began, then received a vicious kick to the ribs.

"Don't fuck me about, where's the package, did yer give it to Jay Mac, is that it?" Devo demanded becoming increasingly angry.

"No... he was too late... one of de boys... dey was hurtin' me... dey took it." Samuel replied, finally abandoning his struggle with the conscious world and slipping into a deep coma.

"Fuckin' shit I think this cunt's gone." Devo snapped then booted the limp youth once more to confirm his diagnosis.

Burning with frustration the Crown team leader joined his two companions who had already removed Floyd's Centurion helmet and opened his clothing to check for the illusive contraband.

"He's clean; he's got nothin' on him but this knuckle-duster and some thin cigars, no fuckin' package." Morgo advised in his monotone voice.

Devo transferred his kicking skills to Floyd's broken body probing for his most damaged, painful region.

"Oh, that's it, got a good response there." he observed smiling slyly. "Y'need to take care of those ribs on y'left side, yer heart's only nearby and from the blood comin' outa y'mouth I think yer've punctured a lung. What's that? Y'want a second opinion; of course whatever y'say." Devo stepped back then instructed Morgo, "Give'im a good kickin' Morgo will yer an..., er..., concentrate on that left side, the patient's been complainin' of some pain there."

Morgo did as ordered working methodically from Floyd's right ribs, both sides of his head and then finishing on his left.

Floyd cried out in agony much to Devo's delight. Morgo looked at his boss and said "I think yer right Devo, every time I boot that left side, look how much more blood he spews out."

"Well then me old mate Floyd, it's gonna have to be a case of lovin' yer and leavin' yer." He glanced around as he spoke, looking for a specific item. "Yer've always been a good lookin' lad, Franny, ever since we was kids. The fuckin' birds loved yer, didn't thee? Mind you remember what thee was like for me, everyone said we were the top skirt chasers, until you did this to me." He paused and told Morgo to look for a suitable object.

"Crack one of them arl grave stones if yer have to."

Again Morgo followed his orders to the letter and returned momentarily with a broken piece of funery headstone, which he passed to the waiting Devo.

"This'll 'ave to do Franny, sorry I couldn't find a half-brick," he knelt down and leaned over the stricken super-cool Crown player, immaculately dressed as ever, then asked, "Any last words before I begin?"

Floyd was struggling to breathe with blood gurgling from his mouth but gasping as he was he managed to spit a wad of blood and phlegm up into Devo's smiling face, "Fuck you!" were the final words he uttered from his previously unmarked, handsome face before Devo began his reconstruction work with a true artist's passion.

Samuel had lied, mainly to protect Jay Mac who during their brief 'business' association had become a close friend. During conversations they had shared he told Jay Mac of his childhood in Ghana and how he had come to England with his family to make a better life, unfortunately the only 'employment' he had found was with Floyd's 'company'. Jay Mac had responded with tall tales of his infant world growing up in late 50s, early 60s Liverpool, exaggerating for good measure wherever he saw fit about Lewis's, Blackler's and T.J. Hughes' Christmas Grottos and trips to New Brighton and cockling in Moreton.

Having never seen the Crown estate or the legendary Eagle public house but believing Jay Mac's comical descriptions, he decided that when their scheduled meeting had been aborted earlier that day, he would make his way there and find his friend. He too had boarded a bus destined for the Crown Estate and alighted at the stop nearest to the Eagle but he did not find his friend, or any of the warm welcome he had expected. Kneeling in the forlorn car park, battered and bleeding he knew one thing only was true; he must give his delivery to Jay Mac and no one else. He had made sure that he carried out that instruction despite everything.

Shortly after midnight Jay Mac's aunt finally stubbed out her last cigarette of the day and closed one of her beloved, well-thumbed Agatha Christie murder mysteries, having reached the exiting dénouement were all was revealed, exactly as it had been on dozens of previous readings.

"Am off t'bed and you look like you could do with some sleep y'self. Don't forget first thing in the morning you're out looking for work, you're not sitting around here all day like a lazy bum. What would the neighbours say, the shame of it, a young lad sponging off his relatives and not even bothering trying to get a job." She stood up and made her way to the living room door, which led into the tiny hall beyond.

Jay Mac, who had returned to the small council flat an hour earlier having curtailed his usual drinking session, thought that his lecture had ended, believing it was safe to remove his denim jacket, which he had worn all evening despite the uncomfortable warmth.

Just as he was about to slip the damaged garment off his shoulders and remove the package which he had hidden behind his back, secured beneath his half-inch red elasticated braces, his aunt stopped in her path. "When you're ready you can explain how you got those cuts all across the back of your coat and whatever it is you've been hidin' all night, I hope it's not one of those dirty magazines with pictures of nude women in it."

Jay Mac looked at her in surprise then considered that perhaps all those years of studying lurid crime thrillers had not been in vain; his guardian had developed some detective skills of her own.

"Me denim got caught on a wire fence I was leanin' against, alright, that's all. I tell y'what though if yer've got a few of those magazines, I wouldn't mind borrowin' them off yer for a bit." he replied with a smile.

His aunt shook her head in dismay, "Just like y'father a liar and a deadbeat." With these cheery observations she finally left the room, closing the door behind her.

After allowing a quarter of an hour for her to attend to her ablutions, particularly the nightly ritual of removing her false teeth and running them under the tap, before placing them in their plastic beaker filled with *Steradent* solution to allow them to soak, Jay Mac laid the much sought after package in front of him on his knees where he sat on the couch.

"What d'yer reckon mate?" he began as usual addressing the ancient hound who now seemed to find it an effort to even raise one of her whiskery white eyebrows, in acknowledgement of being addressed. Without waiting for any sign of agreement from his canine companion, Jay Mac broke his own rule of never opening the package and began carefully cutting through its layers of shiny brown tape, with a pair of scissors from the kitchen.

Whilst he removed each layer of wrapping he continued his mental reflections on the events of the evening, particularly the shocking behaviour of his team mates towards Samuel which he felt exposed a much darker, uglier side of their nature. He tried to apply the same philosophical logic that he had when he experienced the unreasoned prejudice of Kyle and Marcus earlier that year but he knew whatever excuse he allowed, relations between him and those members of the crew who had taken part in the incident, were soured, never able to return to their former naïveté.

Once he had exposed the inner core of the package he examined its selection of clear plastic bags, which were filled to capacity with small orange tablets that were either star or heart shaped; tiny phials of clear liquid and strips of postage stamp sized squares of blotting paper, printed with cartoon character images.

Though Jay Mac had no experience of drugs in any form, believing that they were damaging to both body and mind, he surmised that what he was holding represented a considerable amount of lucrative narcotics. Knowing that Floyd only ever dealt in what he referred to as 'pills' and 'grass' and initially finding nothing unexpected in this package, he began to wonder why so much urgent anticipation was attached to this particular delivery. He did not know then that he was holding a small fortune in Lysergic Acid Diethylamide or LSD, in three of its varied forms.

If the sight of a dozen rectangular see-through bags tightly packed together, filled with a selection of pills, phials and blotting paper squares, failed to significantly surprise, when he carefully released them from their clear tape binding, what they were surrounding almost sent him apoplectic. He knew the package was heavier than usual when the kneeling Samuel had insisted on surreptitiously passing it to him in the car park and when he had quickly secured it behind his back beneath his braces but now he fully grasped why Floyd was determined to receive this unique parcel.

Jay Mac the obsessive Americana fan instantly recognised the magnificent gleaming metal item that he was holding in his excited hands; a .357 Colt Python with a four inch barrel finished in highly polished, ultimate stainless steel. Another small bag containing six bullets was taped to its handle. He stared at the perfectly crafted lethal weapon in awe, handling it similarly to Devo (S) and his knife familiar, 'Fritz,' in a reverential manner. Carefully he passed it from one hand to the other feeling its smooth coldness, gauging its finely balanced reassuring weight.

For a youth who had played countless wild games of Cowboys and Indians, racing around the old Victorian cobblestone streets and back alleys of his childhood inner city neighbourhood, this was perhaps the ultimate prize and could only have been bettered if it were a genuine Single Action Army Peacemaker from the Old West. It had an intrinsic value and an aesthetic beauty that belied its deadly capacity, yet to Jay Mac's fevered brain even thoughts of that potential could not have diminished his sheer pleasure as he grasped the handle of the prized piece, directing the weapon of choice around the room with an outstretched straight arm.

He rose to his feet slowly and stared at his reflection in the three panelled Art Deco mirror, the gleaming gun held diagonally before his face with its barrel pointing to the ceiling, "Whose got the biggest fuckin' tool now then 'ey?" he asked his evil, grinning twin looking directly into his glowing eyes. The balance of power had just changed dramatically. He possessed the ultimate equaliser, Floyd and, for that matter, the insane Devo could both now kiss *his* arse.

After several minutes of admiring himself holding the awesome piece imagining the terrible retribution he would deliver to his enemies, he returned to the present and more prosaic concerns such as where to hide the item, its bullets and the drugs. Eventually he decided on the ideal place and when he had wrapped everything securely inside a plain, white tee shirt, he stealthily approached the hall cupboard where an old battered suitcase containing his comic collection was stored, together with other items no longer in everyday use. Once he had carefully opened the case he placed the precious items within and snapped its locks shut.

Returning to the living room, he stretched out as best as he could on the couch that served as his bed and pulled a coarse blanket over himself. When he eventually drifted away it was the best night's sleep he had experienced in a long time.

Chapter 7

Take a Walk on the Wild Side

Thursday 5th July and Saturday 28th July 1973

Speculation and wild rumour circulated the Crown estate and beyond following the events of that fateful Wednesday evening in late June, particularly after a dog walker had found the unconscious Samuel on the roadside, with the barely alive Floyd lying in the nearby cemetery. Once again the police issued a less than convincing statement concerning two youths, one black the other white, who had been the victims of a road traffic accident. They appealed for witnesses who may have seen the now damaged beyond repair Lambretta SX200, at any time up to its collision with an unidentified vehicle, which from the paint residue found on the right silver side panel of the scooter, suggested it was black in colour.

Jay Mac initially felt relieved when he heard about Floyd's 'accident' and his condition but on reading subsequent newspaper reports regarding the young anonymous black youth who remained in a coma, with doctors expressing grave concerns, his temporary alleviation was submerged in a wave of guilt. Added to this, for several days, Devo the unhinged Crown leader had been conducting enquiries of his own, trying to trace the elusive package; eventually these led him back to his original suspicions and Jay Mac.

Fortunately for the Eagle player when he was summoned to the Unicorn for an 'interview,' despite Devo's best efforts, including intimidation, coercion and reverse psychology, Jay Mac held firm, ultimately convincing the leader that he may be telling the truth.

"I like you Jay Mac, you've got balls. Let's say yer are tellin' me a pack of fuckin' lies, so what? What good would it do yer, if yer did happen to have Floyd's gear, cos if yer tried to shift it on the Estate, 'Fritz' would cut those fucking big balls of yours right off and I'd make yer swaller them till yer choked." Devo had stated when he concluded their convivial chat on the Sunday evening following the scooter accident.

Weaver who had also been present listening to the discussion was impressed by Jay Mac's cool responses, mentioning it as they strolled back down to the Eagle later that night.

"Fuck me Jay Mac, are you on somethin'?" he began. "I think yer've got Floyd's stash an yer've been dippin' into it, the way yer fuckin' brass-necked it there with Devo in yer face."

Jay Mac smiled knowingly, "Yeah, it's like the man said I've got balls, six of them."

Weaver looked at him quizzically waiting for more information but Jay Mac said nothing and walked on smiling. His new found confidence was not through clean living or divine intervention but was based on the cold, hard steel reality of a .357 Colt Python and six bullets carefully concealed in a suitcase full of 1960s American Superhero comics.

By the time they reached the Eagle, Weaver had reminded Jay Mac repeatedly of the debt he owed him, that he now wished to collect, "So like I told yer I missed a fuckin' good night bangin' those two dirty skanks, accordin' to Macca (G)." he advised for the sixth time. "Next Thursday's me birthday right? Me and you are goin' into town and shaggin' anythin' that moves and twattin' any fucker that gets in the way."

It was now Jay Mac's turn to look at Weaver curiously "You do surprise me Weaver."

"Why's that, can't imagine me after the birds? Yer cheeky cunt."

"No it's not that, I just can't imagine yer havin' a fuckin' birthday." Jay Mac replied with a smile as they entered the lounge of the eponymous alehouse.

Thursday 5th July 1973

"Business still boomin'?" Jay Mac asked the sullen Macca (G), who was sitting on the low wall close to Mr Li's Golden Diner, eating his fish and chip supper.

"What do you think? Course it's not fuckin' boomin'." the Heron co-leader replied angrily, spitting small pieces of steaming white cod from his over-stuffed mouth as he spoke.

Jay Mac and Weaver stood close by staring down at him whilst he ate. Both were well scrubbed and turned out for the evening, with Weaver having polished his black Airwair to an acceptable shine. Wearing his dark brown leather jacket, open necked white

Ben Sherman shirt and checked 'Rupert' parallel trousers, he looked presentable, almost normal; almost. In the pockets of his jacket he was carrying a selection of weaponry supplementing his beloved solid steel toffee hammer. He was intent upon making it a memorable evening one way or another. His small triangular eyes glinted as he surveyed the landscape even while talking to his fellow crew leader; he was always on the lookout for potential trouble, usually of his making.

"You fuckin' owe me Jay Mac." Macca (G) began, pushing a final handful of greasy, heavily salt and vinegar dowsed chips into his cruel mouth. "Yeah, you had to fuck things up didn't yer?"

"Macca, I don't know what yer talkin' about but don't start blamin' me for your fuckin mess." Jay Mac replied, becoming angry also.

Dressed in his ox blood leather jacket, extensively patterned deep collared shirt, twenty-two inch cream parallels and gleaming red Airwair, he was ready and prepared for an entertaining night in town with his psychopath team mate, however reluctant he had been when the evening was first proposed.

"Yer couldn't leave things as thee were could yer? Now everyone's fucked." Macca (G) continued before rising to his feet and throwing the rolled up wrappings from his fish and chips directly at Jay Mac.

"Fuck you dickhead!" the livid Eagle player shouted as he leapt forward striking Macca (G) in the chest with his open palm, thrusting him backwards.

He in turn made to grab hold of Jay Mac's lapels intent on grappling him to the ground. "Step in any time yer like Weaver, yer saw what that cheeky cunt did to me!" he shouted enraged.

Weaver did as instructed but not as his co-leader expected. Instead of attacking Jay Mac he laid his hands on them both, separating them forcefully.

"Listen yer pair of squabblin' bitches, it's me birthday tonight and I'm gonna have a fuckin' good one. You two better not try to frig it up."

Jay Mac and Macca (G) glared at each other just an arm's length apart.

"It'll keep to another time." the Heron player said smiling slyly.

"Yeah, leave it, there's no rush." Jay Mac responded without altering his angry expression.

A few minutes later, having walked away from the still grinning Macca (G), Weaver and Jay Mac boarded a city bound bus waiting at the terminus, situated on the lower edge of the estate. While they set about covering every available surface at the rear of the upper deck with fresh graffiti, Weaver warned his travelling companion about his fellow Heron leader.

"Don't take 'im for granted Jay Mac, I've seen Macca scrap. He's fast, slippery and dirty, he'll always go for yer bollocks if he can, he'll try and rag them off."

"Thanks for the warnin' I don't want any trouble with 'im but I'm passed takin' any shit from 'im either. So if it comes on I'll do me best to put 'im away, permanently." Jay Mac replied, casually reading some of the existing messages and slogans as he spoke. He was surprised to note that listed amongst an extensive work by the Hound's crew were the names of Irish and Blue. Things were changing all round, he thought, twelve months earlier he would never have contemplated this evening's trip with the volatile, toffee hammer-wielding Weaver.

During the remainder of the forty minute journey through the warm, pale blue summer's evening, Jay Mac considered Macca (G)'s words and gradually began to understand what had been occurring between him and Floyd. He realised that all the while he had been delivering packages to Floyd, he in turn was redistributing their contents across the estate and beyond, with the aid of Macca (G).

The 'shoebox' missions that Jay Mac and Weaver had accompanied the Heron co-leader on all relied on that original link between the Eagle player and Floyd, with that broken Macca (G) was out of business.

Although Jay Mac was glad to no longer be involved in a trade which he found morally repugnant, part of him still contemplated how he could best exploit the situation. As Floyd had told him "Where there's a demand, I make sure I'm the supply," now there was an established demand that source of supply had been terminated but Jay Mac still held the goods. For the moment he decided to keep his own counsel and say nothing to anyone, including the crazed 'birthday boy,' Weaver.

When they finally reach the city centre they alighted as usual near the Empire Theatre, across from the spectacular Saint George's Hall and began making their way along Lime Street. If Jay Mac had thought Weaver may have been a different animal once he was away from the Crown estate, relocated into the thriving metropolis, he was about to be sorely disappointed, the Heron player was now an even wilder animal escaped from the confines of his grey concrete cage and loose amongst the unsuspecting citizens.

The heat of the day had barely dissipated by any appreciable degree, despite a light southerly breeze that had recently begun to blow. In the darkening blue sky the sun had commenced its downward, arcing trajectory heading towards the Irish Sea, out to the Atlantic Ocean before disappearing below the edge of the western horizon. Floating just above the silhouettes of the tall office buildings away to their right, were thin fingers of cloud under-lit with a warm, red glow holding the promise of another pleasant day to follow.

Everyone was dressed in their summer evening finery and, although the male revellers were all but invisible to the two excited Crown youths, their female counterparts were providing an alluring display. Even though the bottom revealing micro-mini skirt had virtually disappeared, with its bottom-hugging hot pants co-conspirator sentenced to the pages of the fashion history books for crimes against male concentration, there were still plenty of pleasing sights to behold, as the warm weather encouraged the flirtatious, fashion conscious women and girls to wear their most revealing outfits, much to the appreciation of the opposite sex. Whilst Jay Mac kept his mildly erotic fantasising to himself, Weaver tended to be more vociferous; within moments of their arrival he began bellowing comments and requests at the top of his voice towards almost every passing female, without regard to the presence of their disgruntled male companions.

Starting with the observational and pleading "Alright darlin' you've got nice legs, d'yer fancy wrappin' them round me?" Or, "Hey love you've got a great arse, d'yer wanna come and sit on me face?" moving on to the demanding and instructive, "Get yer tit's out for the lads," or simply "Get yer kit off." All were accompanied with appropriate gestures of one arm being bent forcefully up across the other at the elbow, or one index finger being rapidly inserted into an obliging circle formed by the thumb and forefinger of the other hand. His face displayed a permanent grotesque grin with wide open mouth and extended tongue vigorously being lapped up and down.

For Jay Mac it was like being in the company of a dozen randy construction workers all morphed into one lewd mouthpiece, constantly calling out obscenities.

'Yeah, it's gonna be one long night.' Jay Mac concluded. 'Come back Irish, Blue and Glynn, all is forgiven.'

He looked at his wild companion as his gaze swept the landscape, no longer looking for potential trouble, registering only female forms and said, "You have actually seen women before haven't yer Weaver?"

His companion made no reply having moved on to the second stage of his assault, from the verbal to the physical, as he began touching and pinching any feminine bottom that came into range with his right hand, whilst simultaneously projecting his left elbow like a rigid isosceles triangle of flesh and bone, into the breasts of unwary oncoming female traffic.

"Hello, earth to Weaver, are you receiving me? Can you slow down before we both get burned, they do *have* women on the estate y'know?" Jay Mac tried to reason with the leering lecher.

"Not like these thee don't. Now leave me alone while am enjoyin' meself." Weaver finally replied with his right hand constantly reaching out before him.

Jay Mac knew it would only be a matter of time before his groping companion's luck would run out and they would both have to face the consequences. When they reached the busy corner junction, where the Punch and Judy cafe faced the Crown Hotel Public House across Skelhorne Street and had to stop to wait for the passing traffic to be halted by a red light from the nearby control beacon, that moment arrived with a bang.

Three women in their mid to late thirties, stopped suddenly directly in front of them. They were wearing loose fitting dresses of thin material just above knee length, which clung to their voluptuous figures in all the right places. These were not the emaciated waifs promoted and promulgated by the fashionistas as the only acceptable shape for women of the Twiggy generation, they had the curves of full-grown women, the type that make grateful men cry and fantasizing young boys yearn to be older. Jay Mac joined his Crown team mate in admiring these ladies, he drank in their intoxicating, expensive perfume, savoured their shapely legs encased in American Tan, fully fashioned nylon stockings, with Cuban or pointed heels, even if they were somewhat incongruous with their tall modern platform shoes. With the glamorous look of the 1940s and '50s Hollywood starlets, at least from the rear, they were 'on the town,' confident that they were top of the food chain, outshining any younger competition.

Even in the brief moments while they waited for the traffic lights to change, Weaver struck. Thrusting his predatory right hand under the hem and up the dress of the central female in front of him, he grabbed hold of as much well rounded bottom as he could grasp.

"You dirty little fuckers!" said the offended 'lady' as she turned sharply and delivered a powerful straight right with her jewellery encrusted fist into Weaver's grinning mouth, splitting his lip on contact.

Her two friends also turned and joined in the righteous reprisals, which Jay Mac the voyeur felt were unwarranted in his case, as he had only been guilty of mentally groping them.

The three harridans may have had magnificent bodies but they possessed the terrifying facial features of enraged gorgons with high cheek bones, angular jaws, thin cruel lips and flashing eyes. While the trio set about extracting vengeance for their affronted member, slapping and punching both Weaver the culprit and Jay Mac the innocent, passing motorists and pedestrians laughed loudly pointing at the ridiculous spectacle.

For a few seconds Jay Mac was back in his early childhood being unjustly slapped by his older cousin, the dreaded Teresa, for bringing back the wrong amount of cash from his errand of purchasing her cigarette order from the corner shop, where the boy had been deliberately short-changed. Teresa and her female siblings, the sisters of the 'Gerard Boys' had been battering the skulls of unwary sailors from all nations with their stilettos, once lured outside the Lacarno Dance Hall with the promise of easy sex, since she had barely reached her teens. If they had been facing her apart from receiving punches and slaps, she would have robbed them of every penny they had for good measure.

"Let that be a lesson to yer, yer dirty little toe-rags." their lead assailant called back to them as all three women made for the entrance of the Crown Hotel. "We're meetin' our fellers in 'ere, so you'd better hope we don't bump into yer later on, or they will kick the fuckin' shite outta' yer."

Jay Mac stared at Weaver who was still beaming. "Yer know yer asked me a few days ago if I was on somethin', I think you're fuckin permanently on somethin' yer maniac."

Weaver laughed, "Now that's my sort of woman."

"What sorts that, any bird with a decent arse and a fuckin' rock hard fist?" Jay Mac asked rubbing the side of his jaw.

"Come 'ed, let's get sniffin' there's yards of pussy out there an we're missin' out." Weaver replied, still highly amused by the incident.

They continued their stroll along Lime Street, past the States Bar, which Jay Mac often frequented with his friends. Tonight, however, was not the right occasion for 'drunk-watching' they both accepted that any women dotted amongst the serried ranks of dedicated drinkers in that establishment, were likely to be lost too deep in the canyons of the mind, oblivious to all approaches, seeking only oblivion. Instead they chose to try their luck in the more salubrious Orchard Public House, or 'Mansion' as it was colloquially known.

"Listen Weaver, when we go in 'ere let's get a couple of pints down us *before* we get thrown out, ok?" Jay Mac asked as they entered the doorway.

"Yeah, alright, so long as no one starts anythin'." Weaver replied smiling slyly.

Once they had been served they stood by the bar with their drinks which included a dark rum for Jay Mac and a whiskey for Weaver, along with their pints.

"Got a bit of a taste for that stuff 'ave yer?" Weaver asked curiously.

"Sort of, thee haven't got that Woods 100 in 'ere but this Lambs Navy hits the spot." Jay Mac replied studying the bar room where they were presently standing and the lounge on the opposite side, which was connected by a narrow passage.

"Anyway, cheers yer mad fucker, happy birthday!" he said raising his tumbler of rum, with Weaver responding ready to down his whiskey.

"What are yer talkin' about, what fuckin' birthday?"

Jay Mac decided not to even bother questioning his drinking companion about the apparent misunderstanding, taking it to be yet another quirky aspect of Weaver's psychopath character.

A couple of rounds later, Weaver began to become more vocal about their present surroundings, "What sort of place is this anyway? There's no birds in 'ere, yer haven't brought me to a fuckin' queers bar have yer?"

Other male drinkers nearby could hear what the Crown player was saying despite the general din and the jukebox which was playing *Good Vibrations* by the Beach Boys at that moment. They were clearly becoming irritated with this loud-mouthed youth; staring angrily in the direction of him and Jay Mac

"Keep it down will yer mate? Anyway there are birds in 'ere but most of them are with their fellers." Jay Mac advised while still desperately searching the crowd for unattached females.

Whether by divine providence or fate, a few minutes later he spied two young women in their early twenties, trying to get served in the adjoining lounge. They did not stand out as ravishing beauties, or were dressed in an outrageous provocative manner, their looks were passable if not particularly pretty and as a consequence in a world of vicious social Darwinism were only the strong, loud, handsome or beautiful survived, they were being totally ignored by the bar staff, as well as most of the male clientele.

"Listen Weaver there's two birds over there. I'm gonna get in before some other cunt does and I'll try and bring them over. You've got to promise me yer not gonna start rapin' them or somethin' if I do get them here, ok?" Jay Mac asked genuinely.

"Go 'ed, gerrin there, as if am gonna do that. What d'yer think I am, a fuckin' animal or somethin'?" Weaver replied.

Jay Mac did not respond but quickly darted through the corridor and round to the bar facing where he had previously been positioned. Time was of the essence though not so vital as it may have been under different circumstances. For Jay Mac and all other males of the 'baby boom generation' the post war decade had indeed produced an exponential growth in the number of babies being born. Unfortunately for them the gender ratio appeared to be 5:1, meaning there were always five males competing for every one female. Whether this was correct or not, in this case perception was reality. Jay Mac had his own personal sliding scale which increased this ratio from its disadvantageous starting point, depending on the looks and other qualities of the particular female. He felt in some cases this could rise to more than double, triple or even quadruple; in rare examples the odds could become 100:1 although there would be only a finite number of these specimens.

For Jay Mac, however, totally smitten and enamoured as he was of his beautiful 'dream girl' whom he had enjoyed only the briefest conversation with, the odds surrounding her were incalculable and entirely unique. Even given the present factors he knew he had to act fast, two unattached females, though only to be considered in the lower echelons of his defining criteria, would soon be snapped up by the predatory males who also understood the secret, unspoken arithmetic equation and did not want to end their evening alone.

"Alright ladies, Jay Mac's me name... nice t'meet yer... hard t'get served in this place... mind if I squeeze in there?" he began, smiling ingratiatingly. "Here y'are, I'll get the drinks in if that's ok? Yer might like to join me and me mate over in the parlour, it's a bit more pleasant there, what d'yer say?"

Both girls appeared quite shy, Jay Mac began to feel guilty about approaching them and potentially exposing the pair to the lustful Weaver's advances. It was too late for second thoughts as they responded positively, introduced themselves and accepted Jay Mac's offer. He quickly caught the attention of one of the bar staff, ordered their drinks and then escorted them through to the parlour where Weaver had secured one of the small, cosy booths. 'Like lambs to the slaughter,' Jay Mac told himself, determining that if Weaver did employ his usual brutal seduction technique, he would intervene at once.

"This is Janet and Pauline," Jay Mac said by way of a formal introduction, then sat on the outside left of the girls with them sandwiched between him and Weaver to their right.

"You're a bit younger than the lads we usually go out with." Janet advised with a smile, though looking at Weaver's grim countenance framed by his wild hair and extensive side-burns and Jay Mac's off-centre broken nose surrounded by numerous small scars from various scrapes, they did not exactly appear angelic or particularly youthful.

"We prefer the more mature ladies; anyway yer can't be more than twenty-one if that." Jay Mac replied flatteringly.

"We're a bit older than that but compliment accepted." said Pauline, smiling.

Weaver seemed lost, not sure how to engage in normal conversation and merely said, "Yeah, a bit older than that," while he sat staring at their faces, surveying their forms and admiring their legs.

Several rounds later everyone appeared relaxed and in good spirits, both Weaver and Jay Mac where sitting close to their respective partners with their arms around the girls' shoulders, enjoying the warmth of their soft skin and breathing in their pleasant perfume.

Never a Dull Moment 1973 ▪ 178

Everything was going according to plan, Weaver had taken things slow as requested by his team mate, matters were proceeding towards their inevitable conclusion until Janet said, "Anyway, we'll have to be going now."

Jay Mac tensed as he saw Weaver's expression change in an instant.

"Who's goin' where?" he asked angrily.

"Yeah, we like to go clubbin' and to be honest you two are a bit too young. They probably wouldn't let yer in." Pauline advised with her friend adding...

"...not with those big, daft boots on either," she laughed as she passed her seemingly innocuous comment.

Weaver snapped, in an instant he clamped his teeth onto the left side of Janet's neck biting hard, whilst thrusting his right hand under her thin, knee-length dress, forcing her thighs apart and firmly groping her most private parts.

Both girls screamed, chaos erupted in a split second; the pleasant calm was shattered, their table overturned and remaining drinks spilled as glasses fell shattering to the floor.

"Weaver! What the fuck are yer doin' let her go man!" Jay Mac shouted leaning across Pauline, grasping hold of the mad man's offending forearm.

"Please, get him off me, he's trying to rip my knickers off!" Janet cried out desperately.

Other punters were now protesting with some approaching intent on rescue, accompanied by two members of the bar staff. Weaver carried on with his assault only pausing from biting the girls bleeding neck to warn Jay Mac, "Take yer fuckin' hand off me or I will cut yer."

Janet struggled wildly; her friend was slapping Weaver about the head and Jay Mac persisted despite the genuine threat, in trying to pull his crazed companion's arm from between the legs of the screaming girl.

Weaver was intent on his prize and tore through the flimsy material until he finally ripped her undergarment from her.

Barmen, customers and Jay Mac overcame him, dragging him and his 'trophy' onto the floor freeing the weeping girl, desperately trying to cover her embarrassment.

"Get the police someone, hurry up. Y'pair of dirty bastards!" one of the barmen shouted urgently to his colleague in the adjoining room, where the phone was located. On hearing this and realising that he had wrongly been incriminated in Weaver's attack, Jay Mac went insane, punching, kicking, lashing out everywhere in all directions, he was not going to be arrested again.

Weaver having stuffed his prize into his pocket to enjoy later also flew into a frenzied rage, fortunately for the crowd attempting to restrain him, without resorting to the use of any of his weaponry.

Yard by yard the desperate duo struggled and scuffled their way forward until they eventually tumbled into the bar room, where other drinkers inadvertently assisted them thinking they were being ejected and joined the mêlée.

"Get them fuckin' kids out of 'ere, ruining everyone's night!" they shouted kicking Jay Mac and Weaver in the backside as they flung them out of the boiling pub into the warm night air, onto the hard pavement.

Realising their good fortune both youths were up and running in an instant, racing away past the Adelphi Hotel up the rise of Mount Pleasant and eventually hiding in the doorway of the Y.M.C.A. building.

Jay Mac turned to Weaver who was still catching his breath and said, "That's it, yer a fuckin' wild animal, I'm off. I said I'd come into town with yer and I've done my part but you need to be on a fuckin' lead."

Weaver was bent double and he looked up at Jay Mac with a sly smile, "Piss off Jay Mac, yer just like me, never mind all yer nice talkin' to the birds, yer wanna jump them nothin' else, so drop the act."

Jay Mac was stunned by Weaver's comments but accepted their partial truth. "Maybe I do fancy birds for the same reason as you but I'm tellin' yer there's ways and means and you're out of fuckin' control."

Weaver straightened himself up fully and stared at Jay Mac. Without warning he dug into the right pocket of his dark brown leather jacket then pulled out the torn panties, which he proceeded to hold over his face, breathing in deeply.

"Ahh that's better," he said, grinning broadly. "Reminds me of the night we done Glynn's Ma. Macca (G)'s still got her knickers; we all had a good sniff of them that night."

Standing facing the beaming psychopath Jay Mac felt ill, he knew the hell that his friend Glynn had gone through since the horrific incident.

"Do me a real favour Weaver, don't ever mention that in front of me again." he said with a deadly seriousness.

Weaver studied him for a few seconds then replied, "Alright, calm yerself down, don't get yer knickers in a twist." He laughed at his own joke. "Let's make a deal, we'll have a few more bevvies, no more messin' with the birds, then we'll get a couple of pies down the Pier before we get off, after all it is me fuckin' birthday."

Jay Mac reluctantly agreed and they set off on a drinking circuit of the city centre, stopping at numerous alehouses on their way.

Weaver was as good as his word until they reached the final hostelry for the night, located just off Castle Street, not far from the magnificent Georgian Town Hall, The Barrister. If, when they had arrived at this particular alehouse they had not been so intoxicated, they may have responded in like manner to the aggressive bouncer who initially barred their way while he studied their dishevelled appearance; focusing particularly on their distinctive footwear.

"Listen you two, I don't know what yer supposed to be but I've clocked yer, right? I run this joint, fuck about in 'ere an yer'll have me t'deal with." he advised before finally allowing them to enter.

Instead of rounding on the stocky, bald headed, moustache wearing, mid-forties male, they were, at this point, in an alcohol and spirits induced euphoric state, choosing to greet his remarks with a polite response.

"Thanks for that doorman, most kind of you to mention it." Jay Mac said grinning broadly as he and his equally amused carousing companion, stepped into the semi-darkness of the recently refurbished interior of this small, single-roomed public house, which was in reality no more than a bar. Now reduced from a formally quaint, atmospheric, late Georgian alehouse to a contemporary soulless, utilitarian shell, its only remaining attractions to them were that it reportedly possessed a particularly good jukebox with a varied selection of singles to choose from and it was one of the few establishments that stocked Newcastle Brown Ale in its distinctive bottles.

Funds were running low but they still managed to purchase a round each, which they ordered at the same moment to avoid wasting any valuable drinking time. The bar was not filled to capacity partly due to its location at the business end of town, which was always quieter than the city centre and because of the recent updating to fixtures and fittings, leading some prospective customers to believe they had not yet re-opened. Weaver and Jay Mac collected their four bottles of ale and two accompanying pint glasses, plus a selection of salted snacks, then made their way to the farthest end of the long rectangular room.

"I've got a bit of spare change, so I'll go and bang on a couple of decent tunes, you're gettin' the pies in down the Pier, remember." Jay Mac said to his grinning friend.

They were both at the stage of drunkenness where everything appeared pleasant and all was right with the world, the crushing depression and violent rage phases that often followed, either sequentially or sometimes simultaneously, had yet to arrive.

As they sat drinking their clear, golden brown ale, listening to the first of Jay Mac's selection *Stuck in the Middle with You* by Steeler's Wheel, Weaver frequently removed his trophy from his pocket and draped the tattered, pink garment over his face breathing in deeply then blowing out forcefully, watching the flimsy item flutter down onto the table in front of him. They both laughed at his amusing antics, no longer caring about the brutal way in which he had secured his prize.

"Giz a go." Jay Mac asked slightly slurring his words.

"No, fuck off, get yer own." Weaver replied in a similar manner.

"I will do mate, I will do, oh yes you can be sure of that, don't you even doubt it." Jay Mac rambled, before adding, "I'm dyin' for a 'Geoff Hurst', I've gorra find the Gents. Yer better not start anythin' while I'm gone." He rose to his unsteady feet standing not quite still for a few moments, trying to get his bearings until he spotted a sign stating 'Toilets'.

Weaver called after him "Do one for me while yer there, yer fucker." then began laughing uncontrollably.

A few moments later when the much relieved Jay Mac returned, everything had changed, the dynamic was completely altered. The four young males who had been occupying the black leather upholstered semi-circular seating arrangement, directly facing their small round table had departed. In their place two flabby, overweight men in their early forties had arrived and were sitting on each side of their much younger-looking female partners.

Weaver's expression and disposition had also completely altered, as he sat staring across at the considerable amount of bosom and deep cleavage displayed by one of the females, whose revealing open blouse of finest, virtually transparent synthetic material, made it obvious that her well-rounded breasts were without artificial support, or restraint.

"Hey, Weaver, wake up mate, don't fuckin' start again." Jay Mac requested urgently.

Weaver was not entirely to blame. In mitigation it had to be accepted by his team mate that the attractive blonde, who was clearly bored with her corpulent partner, was partially complicit by furtively returning the leering youth's stare and provocatively circling her ruby red lips with her pink tongue. Lou Reed's *Walk on the Wild Side* was now playing and the flirtatious pair continued their less than discrete game. Weaver then produced his trump card, cancelling all bets, sealing all their fates, he draped his pink 'handkerchief' over his eyes and nose then began sticking out his tongue to its physical limit, lapping it up and down vigorously.

"What d'you think you're doin' lookin' at me wife's tits?" the furious, heavyweight, male demanded, leaning over Weaver with clenched fists pressing down on their table.

Weaver laughed at the ridiculous closed-ended nature of the question, which invited only one possible reply. He slowly removed his trophy, placed it back in his pocket, whilst taking one of his two Stanley knives from the other, which he casually passed under the table to his team mate, then replied "Fuckin' enjoyin' meself, what d'you think fat arse?"

"Gerrup, gerrup yer cheeky twat, we're goin' outside and I'm gonna teach you a fuckin' lesson!" the outraged, sweating older man shouted.

"Leave it mate, he can't help 'imself, yer really don't wanna do this." Jay Mac tried to plea.

"You can shut yer fuckin' mouth or I'll do you as well." He turned his gaze towards Jay Mac as he spoke, making the fatal mistake of taking his eyes off his intended target.

The empty, clear glass Newcastle Brown bottle that Weaver had snatched by the neck from the table as he sprang up, smashed against the left side of the man's head, even before he had finished speaking.

Once again all Hell let loose. With David Bowie's *Jean Genie* now playing loudly on the jukebox almost drowning some of the piercing screams from the females and angry shouts of the men, the familiar game began. The injured male was of no further concern to either youth, tiny splinters of glass had entered his left eye causing him to stagger about clasping his streaming wound with his hand, crying out in terrible agony. His friend jumped forward from his seated position and to their surprise produced a flick knife in a shiny black and silver casing. Even as he thrust it towards Weaver, his shaking hand revealed his novice status; he was out of his depth facing these two experienced veterans of street combat. With a lightning fast downward slash of 'his' Stanley knife Jay Mac struck the wrist of the man's knife-holding right hand, causing him to drop his weapon instantly.

Having already slipped the heavy brass knuckle-duster onto his left hand, Weaver's companion sprang into his victim delivering a devastating straight metal encased left as he did.

Their only concern was the stocky bouncer, who fortunately for them, had been standing outside smoking a cigarette and admiring the few females that passed in front of this off the beaten track establishment. He now came at them through the maze of tables like a raging bull, trying to grapple them both. If he had received even the slightest assistance from any other drinker or even the newly hired barman, who occupied himself with vigorously cleaning his counter surface as if oblivious to the action, he may have proved successful. As it was with Jay Mac's left assisted fist pounding into one side of his face and body, whilst Weaver skilfully employed both his toffee hammer and family heirloom cosh, he was hopelessly out-gunned.

Gamely he tried to hold on to them even after he had been downed but they were desperate animals seeing the ever widening escape portal of the front door, coming closer with each determined step.

Finally after receiving a vicious kicking from both youths he collapsed just inside the entrance. Whether he was inspired by his workmate's bravery or shamed by his own lack of action, the young barman nervously struck out with a foot long solid wooden baton, which had been secured under his extremely well-polished counter. He caught Jay Mac with a glancing, harmless blow across the shoulders causing him to falter and momentarily stumble as he fell out into the street. Weaver was infuriated, unable to accept the indignity of this unwarranted, sneak attack as he saw it, from a declared non-combatant. The Heron co-leader leapt towards the bar, caught hold of the terrified young man by his mop of hair and repeatedly struck him across the forehead and nose with his weapon of choice, his solid steel toffee hammer. Even here, as they were intent on escape and entirely unscathed, he could not resist the

Never a Dull Moment 1973 ▪ 184

opportunity to announce his usual triumphal acclamation, "I'm Weaver, I done this to yer, I'm Weaver!"

Moments later he joined the waiting Jay Mac and they raced along Castle Street, down Brunswick Street before choosing to hide in Drury Lane. There they surveyed the landscape, crouching behind the functioning modern art installation which comprised steel tubes and buckets constantly pouring water entitled 'The Fountain'; the scene of Jay Mac's first arrest eighteen months previous.

"Fuck me that *really* is it, never again." Jay Mac began, as he leaned against the concrete slab wall of the modern office building, behind the water feature, which housed the City Planning Office.

Weaver also raised himself from his crouched position after he too had recovered his breath, "Stop fuckin' moanin'. I don't know what yer goin' on about; I think it's been sound so far."

Jay Mac was about to argue the case but was rendered unable to speak as suddenly the nausea, that he had been experiencing for the past few minutes overtook him and he spewed a torrent of stinking vomit onto the floor in front of him.

Weaver was highly amused and shouted "Can't hold yer ale, yer a fuckin' lightweight." His vicarious pleasure was short lived, the concoction of lager, whiskey and brown ale, assorted salted snacks combined with running as fast as his inebriated body could manage through the streets, exacted its revenge upon him also. Holding his aching stomach with both hands whilst bent double, he too let forth a hot, multi-coloured, stream of his own. The eye-watering acrid smell from their combined liquid display caused them both to perform a noisy encore, until their stomachs were satisfied that they were entirely vacated.

"I don't remember eatin' those carrots," Jay Mac said with a weak smile, wincing as he delivered the old cliché.

"Come on yer've got to admit yer've had a few laughs, yer miserable cunt." Weaver responded, walking toward the low perimeter wall then leaning on its ledge for support while he surveyed the landscape of Strand Road below.

"Oh yeah, it's been fuckin' ace, thank God it's ended." Jay Mac replied sarcastically before Weaver interrupted him, "Wait a minute, what's that I spy across the road by the Liver Buildings? The night's not over yet, come 'ed." With that he dashed down the stone stairs from their elevated position and darted between the traffic which passed both ways along this key arterial road. Jay

Mac reluctantly followed, curious to see what new attraction had roused his companion to such an excited state.

When he too had woven his way through both streams of vehicles, he arrived next to his grinning team mate on the corner of the site that housed the world famous, iconic building. Sitting on the cold, hard pavement with her knees drawn up and her hands clasped together around them, was a girl of roughly their age. She looked up in Weaver's direction but stared past not at him, out beyond the reaches of the deep blue night sky.

"Well, well, this is a bit of luck, what 'ave we got 'ere then?" he said smirking lasciviously.

Jay Mac was studying her unkempt, dishevelled appearance. She had dark brown curly hair of shoulder length, though this was bedraggled, with some loose strands blowing across her pale elven features. Her black mascara had run onto her cheeks as if she had been crying for some time; her deep red lipstick was smudged and smeared about the lower part of her face. What caught Jay Mac's attention was a large, blue outlined star filled with shiny silver make-up, which spanned her forehead from hairline to eyebrow.

"Hello girl, are you alright? What's yer name?" he asked without receiving any response.

Suddenly she rose to her feet and both Crown players noticed that she was without any shoes. She stood staring up at them from her full five foot two height, searching their faces, then she tried to smooth her short smock-style dress, which was black in background but covered in dozens of bright flowers; her dark tights were badly laddered and torn. Jay Mac was uncomfortable with this situation and as he studied her bare arms he noticed they were covered in bruises.

"Fuck this, she's had somethin' bad done to her by some cunts, she needs help Weaver."

"Don't be too hasty there, let's have a think about it before we..., er... decide what to do... yeah?" Weaver replied with a sly smile lighting his face as he too let his gaze travel over the distressed, petite girl.

If they had arrived half an hour earlier they would have seen the filthy Volkswagen camper van as it stopped just long enough to dump the well-used girl, after its gang of peaceful, philosophising, intellectual sounding, bull-shit spouting, hippie occupants had each enjoyed some 'free love' at her expense.

Jay Mac looked down into her vacant eyes and spoke calmly to her "Listen 'Star child' there's a police station down there on the front by the river, we're gonna walk part of the way with yer, t'see yer get there all right."

"Whoa, hold on mate, are you fuckin' mental? We go anywhere near those pigs and we're the ones who'll need help." Weaver advised.

Transferring her dead gaze from one to the other of the Crown players, the girl interrupted them speaking in a sad, wistful tone. "My friends will be coming back for me soon. They wouldn't leave me here."

"Where are yer friends, are thee nearby so we can call them?" Jay Mac asked.

"They live up there, they're watching us now." the girl replied once more looking beyond them with her doleful eyes.

"What? Thee live up in the Liver Buildings?" Weaver asked curiously glancing to the upper floors of the building behind them.

"No, yer tit, she means up in the friggin' sky. She's totally away with the fairies." Jay Mac responded. Having decided that their presence was of no further use he was about to walk away, fearing the arrival of the local police. "Alright 'Star child' nice one, say hello to the other space cadets when yer get back home to your own planet."

Weaver had been studying the iron railings around the base of the building and noticed an unlocked gate, which led to a staircase that descended below ground level. With a leering grin he spoke to Jay Mac, "Listen it won't do her no harm if I have a little go. Fuck, she won't even know. So I'll take her down there and give 'er a good seein' to, then you can have a turn, yeah?"

Jay Mac was horrified and shouted at his team mate, "Are you totally fuckin' sick? Yer can see she's had a bad time, if we can't help at least don't make it any worse, just leave her alone."

Weaver laughed loudly at this suggestion, leading Jay Mac to try another approach with a health warning.

"Yer'll be pickin' the crabs out of yer pubes for weeks after if yer do this..."

Again Weaver found this highly amusing and replied, "I'll take that chance, anyway if I do get a few extra thee can mix with mine and keep them company."

Weaver caught hold of her small, grimy hand with his large, blood-stained paw and led her away to her fate with Jay Mac calling after him, "Don't do this man, she's off 'er 'ead, she doesn't even know where she is."

Weaver replied coldly, "Just keep Dixie for me. I'll give yer a shout when I've finished, then you can have go."

Unfortunately their loud, shouted conversation attracted the attention of another nearby listener, who instantly became an interested party.

A middle-aged tramp whose life had been turned upside-down when his wife acquired a new lover and he was forcibly evicted from his own comfortable home, at least that was the case according to his often recounted tale, was enjoying a well-deserved respite from his arduous daily routine of begging for two pence donations at the Pier Head bus and ferry terminal. Intrigued by their conversation, he sat upright on the hard wooden bench that served as his bed and stretched his stiffened joints. With arms raised above his head in an attempt to stimulate his circulation, he watched and listened to the unfolding drama occurring below, across the road from his elevated vantage point, close to the edge of the aged stone wall, topped with its dark iron railings that enclosed the well-maintained, formal gardens of the church.

Fifteen minutes later Weaver emerged from his subterranean love-den pulling up the zip of his trousers, wearing a beaming smile.

"Fuckin' hell I needed that. She was a bit wooden at first but once I'd got it in, she wasn't a bad ride."

"Shit! That's fuckin' low man; spare me the details, yer sick bastard." Jay Mac shouted in disgust.

"Ah grow up Jay Mac, yer sound like a fruit, yer wanna bang her just the same. Anyway I've left her waitin' for yer with her knickers and tights down, so get in there." Weaver replied smiling.

"No. I told yer that's where I draw the line, it's not gonna happen." He paused, "I'm surprised yer left 'er with 'er knickers. I thought you'd have them away for another reminder of a shit night."

Weaver laughed, "Nah, I was thinkin' about it but thee was too fuckin' smelly even for me. Come 'ed let's get some pies down us, I'm bleedin' starvin'."

Their conversation trailed off as they entered the glass cloisters of the bus depot and made their way to the 'pigeon pie' shop for their evening's repast.

Over in St Nicholas' gardens, perched on high, another suitor was preparing for a passionate sexual encounter with the unsuspecting 'Star child'. Her anxiously waiting next prospective paramour could hardly contain his ardour. He rose to his feet looking down at his cracked, split, filthy shoes with his threadbare socks emerging from each gap and their flapping fronts as he did. After removing his battered trilby, which he had literally acquired by windfall when it was blown away from a busy city gent one particularly blustery day, he spat heavily into his blackened, rough hands, rubbed them together then patted his strings of matted, greasy dark hair back away from his face.

Once he had replaced his headgear he quickly scrutinised his fingers, particularly their grime embedded broken nails; they also received a cursory saliva wash. Satisfied that all was as it should be for his 'special date' he ran his hands over the front of his crusty, heavily stained, dark grey, double-breasted suit, attempting vainly to straighten out the dozens of deep furrowed creases, whilst also removing any of the less sticky mixed detritus debris. As if to propel him forward on his quest he forced a loud protracted fart, before setting off.

"She's waitin' there for yer... with her knickers and tights down, ready." The enticing words that he had heard one of the youths call out played over and over in his mind.

"Well, if she's all ready and waiting, expecting a bit of cock, it would be rude not to." he told himself walking as quickly as he could down the well-worn steps and out under the Gothic revival arch onto the road below.

At about the same time the two Crown players were salivating over their steaming mixed meat pies, he too was drooling over the stupefied girl. As they greedily tucked into their food with relish, he forced himself into her with all the vigour his worn frame could muster. Not long after while he grunted and groaned his way through the deed, his none responsive, silent partner suddenly looked directly into his bloodshot eyes, reality hit like a bolt of lightning and she was instantly back in the horrifying here and now.

Whether it was his fetid breath escaping from the gaps between his few remaining rotten teeth; invasive tongue or overpowering, nauseating stench of filthy clothing, unwashed body and unwiped rear; the agonised girl was now fully cognisant of what was happening. She let out a chilling, piercing scream matching those of the seagulls perched nearby in intensity, attracting just as little attention. Star child may have longed for her home in the heavens but for the present, despite her pitiful cries, she remained trapped in hell on earth.

Saturday 28th July 1973

During the days and weeks that followed Jay Mac and Weaver's night on the town, while the Eagle crew member agonised over some of the events of that 'adventure' his Heron counterpart enjoyed telling and re-telling the tale of their exploits. Adding details or omitting them as he saw fit, exaggerating wildly to enhance particularly lurid aspects, Weaver the toffee hammer wielding psychopath became Weaver the 'Storyteller', creating the legend of the 'Knicker-thief and the Saint'.

After entertaining his own Heron crew mates, giving theatrical performances worthy of the Victorian stage to packed houses, Weaver took his 'show' on the road appearing at each and every drinking establishment across the Crown Estate. So it was that on a warm Saturday night at the close of July, the star turn was in full flow regaling the assembled Eagle crew in their eponymous alehouse, much to Jay Mac's embarrassment.

"I'm tellin' yer the truth, not a word of a lie, honest an yer all know me, I wouldn't say it if it didn't happen." Weaver prefaced his routine then, when he was satisfied that he had everyone's attention, he began. Act One consisted of the performer describing the female cast in precise anatomical detail to whet the appetite of his audience. This was followed by a graphic mime depicting the grasping of a mature female's large, rounded bottom, which had everyone laughing preparing them for the second act and the appearance of the celebrated knicker thief himself. As this part of the tale unfolded there was some audience participation.

"So are you sayin' right there in the middle of the packed alehouse, you just ragged this bird's fuckin' knickers right off?" asked an incredulous Tank.

"Too right I did, straight up her dress, had a good feel first of course then ripped the fuckers right off." Once again everyone was highly amused, some turned toward Jay Mac who had become the straight man, the foil, the patsy for Weaver's comic act.

"Did you see all this Jay Mac? Is this cunt havin' us on or what?" a sceptical Johno asked.

"No he's not lyin' I was there, worse luck, watchin' him roll about tryin' to have this poor girl's knickers away." he replied regretfully.

With Jay Mac's affirmation still fresh in their minds, Weaver produced his tattered flimsy pink trophy with a flourish and draped it once more across his face, drawing a rapturous response from the appreciative crowd. After moving on to a vigorous description of their desperate fight in the Barrister's Bar, where multiple assailants were dispatched, including one of the toughest bouncers in the city, according to the storyteller, he began to build the expectation toward his graphically detailed finale.

"I tell yer what; I was just in the right mood for it as well. Once I got her down those stairs I had her knickers round her ankles and was right up her, no messin'. Then I banged the fuckin' arse off her an she loved it." Weaver declared, drawing admiration from one and all, except for Jay Mac who was becoming increasingly bored by the Heron player's exaggerated tale.

"How did yer know she was lovin' it? What did she do fuckin' blink it to yer in Morse code, or did yer just read her mind? Cos she was too spaced out to 'ave told yer." Jay Mac pointed out critically, deflating the crowd's mood.

"Hey dickhead, don't be ruinin' my story." Weaver snapped angrily, "I'll tell yer how I knew, she didn't have to say anythin' because she was comin' like fuck, ok?"

Jay Mac did not reply but sat shaking his head, drawing a further angry response from Weaver.

"Listen to this lad will yer, he was too fuckin' scared to go down the stairs an give her a seein' to, even though I'd left her shagged out with her kit down and her legs wide open."

This statement drew derision from most of the crowd which was directed towards Jay Mac.

"Say what yer like Weaver, the girl was in a bad state and from the look of her she'd had a good few dicks up there already that evenin'. Anyway how are yer crabs these days?" he responded calmly, forgetting who he was dealing with.

"What's that? Are you lookin' for a good kickin', don't even think of takin' the piss out of me, yer cheeky cunt." said a furious Weaver.

For a few tense moments it appeared their fragile, amicable relationship was about to come to a sudden violent end. Jay Mac's rescue came from an unlikely source, the permanently scheming Macca (G).

"Forget about that tit Weaver, tell us that bit again where yer ripped that bird's knickers off, I really liked that part." he said with a sly smile.

As if a switch had been flicked off in his disturbed mind, Weaver instantly reverted to the comedy actor once more and began his routine again. With Mungo Jerry's *Alright Alright Alright*, playing on the jukebox, the team soon resumed their high spirits drifting into their own conversations, paying no more attention to the two Heron leaders now savouring each juicy detail of the psychopath's lurid tale.

"Sounds like an interestin' night." said Irish, who was sitting to the right of Jay Mac with Blue next to him.

"Yeah, that's one way of lookin' at it." Jay Mac began, "Yer know the expression holdin' a tiger by its tail, well this was like tryin' to hold onto a fuckin' sex-crazed gorilla armed with a toffee hammer."

Irish and Blue both laughed at this comparison.

Then Jay Mac's former school friend revealed their plans for the evening. "Me and Blue will be gettin' off in a minute, we're meetin' some of the Hounds crew, we're gonna fuck up a couple of Ravens boys." He paused to swallow the last of his pint then continued, "Yeah they've been sellin' drugs up by the cemetery comin' into our estate. Devo's not happy about it, he's set them up tonight so we can get into them good-style. Thee won't be comin' back with their shite onto the Crown after this."

Jay Mac raised a curious eyebrow on hearing his friend's intentions and who had organised the evening's 'lesson'.

"He's a decent lad, old Devo, isn't he? Always thinkin' about the good of the Crown Estate, makin' sure no cunt messes with us and givin' out these warnin's, especially if sellin' drugs is involved."

"Have you got somethin' on yer mind Jay Mac, cos if yer have, leave it there." Irish warned.

"Nah, it's nothin' forget it," Jay Mac began "but y'must have noticed he wanted to send a message to the Barleys, he wanted Floyd stoppin' and now he's gonna step in and close down a couple of dealers from Ravens Hall. Yer know what, he'd be better off in the bizzies, he's doin' their job for them, or is he shuttin' everyone else out for some other reason, funny don't yer think?"

Jay Mac finished what he had to say and took a lengthy drink from his pint, while Irish threw back his whiskey chaser in one gulp.

"Jay Mac, like I just said to yer, here's some good advice you can have for free, any thoughts you've got about what Devo's doin' or is up to, keep them to yerself, fuck with him and there'll only be one winner." He paused to light another cigarette then leaned in close to Jay Mac and in a low voice said, "I saw what the black lad handed to yer, I don't know what was in that package but I do know that slimy cunt Floyd. Whatever it was, don't you bring it onto this estate there's enough problems 'ere already." With that he rose to his feet and strolled out of the lounge bar with Blue close behind.

Several hours later after yet another re-telling of Weaver's legendary tale with additional embellishments, last orders had been called and Jay Mac was making his way to the bus stop at the lower end of the estate in the company of Macca (G), the sexual sadist and Weaver the psychopath. It was a warm, late summer's night; the sky was filled with pale grey clouds, each competing for a space in the tightly packed heavens.

"I wish I'd been there when yer done that bird down at the Pier Head, I'd have given her some pain alright." Macca (G) said with an evil smile, his mind racing with vile images.

Weaver somehow interpreted this as a slight and replied angrily, "Hey, let me tell you she was in pain, alright, don't you doubt it lad. When a bird's been done by Weaver, she fuckin' knows about it."

Jay Mac was about to interject but decided on this occasion, wisely, to hold his tongue.

Despite Macca (G) trying to ameliorate the situation, all attempts to placate his co-leader failed. "Alright mate, don't take it the wrong way, yer blowin' up for nothin' remember we're the Heron boys, we stick together."

Weaver was unreceptive to any appeal, "Piss off Macca, am gettin' a bit sick of you and this crew, fuck-all goes on down 'ere now, even the Kings Team don't come over anymore. I think I'll start hangin' around with the Bear, or the Hounds, or Devo's Unicorn Boot Boys." He turned and walked away to his tenement block nearby without another word.

Macca (G) strolled on with Jay Mac, still smiling. "Fuck 'im, the lunatic, I couldn't give a shit what he does, he's becomin' too cracked to be any more use."

Jay Mac stopped walking as he was directly opposite his stop and could easily run across the road if he saw a bus approaching. "Is that it with you Macca, everyone's got a price, if they're no use, you fuck them off?"

"That's right Jay Mac, don't act shocked you play the same game yerself. Yer a bit stuck now without Floyd, aren't yer, no spare cash anymore?" Macca (G) said accurately.

"How d'you know about any business me and Floyd had?" Jay Mac asked.

"I thought you were quicker than that lad, who do you think supplied me? No Floyd, no more shoe box deliveries, the problem is I've got me regular customers, and I don't wanna lose them. Maybe you could help me?" Macca (G) asked, watching Jay Mac's face all the while for any change of expression.

"I don't know what yer talkin' about Macca, how can I help yer? Floyd's gone out of it, so no more packages comin' this way." he replied.

"Oh yeah, I know that there's no more comin' not that way anyhow. And Devo's gonna put this whole estate on lockdown so that he can flood it with *his* gear." He paused allowing Jay Mac to appreciate fully what he had revealed. "Anyway before he does that we can still make a bit of cash; cos we both know, you've got Floyd's last big delivery, don't we?"

Jay Mac tried to protest, though he knew the smiling Macca (G) found his words amusing and argument transparent.

"I had me suspicions with Devo searchin' everywhere for that fuckin' package, an when he couldn't find it, I knew you had to 'ave it. And tonight, when yer mate Irish was whisperin' his little warnin' to yer, I was listenin' to every word. Anyway, 'ave a think about it, I'll do a good deal with yer but don't leave it too late...'ere's yer bus, see yer."

As he turned away, Jay Mac sprinted across to the stop with his mind in turmoil, racing even faster. He knew the decision was his but he did not fully comprehend the enormous consequences that would follow, if he accepted the scheming Macca (G)'s offer.

Chapter 8

Something in the Air

Saturday 8th September 1973

Despite wild exhortations from the assembled congregation of Anfield faithful, particularly those who gathered for their worship on the steep, stone terraces of the Kop, that afternoon's lack lustre match in early September failed to satisfy either side's expectations. Having clinched the first division title, three points clear of their Southern rivals, Arsenal, at the end of the previous season and also winning their first major piece of European silverware, albeit by the narrowest of margins when a two-nil defeat by Borussia Monchengladbach at their Bokel Bergstadion had followed a three-nil victory at home, giving the mighty Reds a three-two win on aggregate, the loyal fans of Liverpool FC felt this was their time, the legend was beginning. With the greatest inspirational manager that the game ever produced, Bill Shankly, at the helm who could blame them?

Unfortunately the euphoria of the previous season's triumphs began to dissipate after the first three games of this current one, against Stoke, Coventry and Leicester produced a total of two goals only in the Red's favour and the record of one win, one loss and one draw.

Jay Mac and the rest of the Crown Team's LFC supporters had been cheered, though, by the previous week's match where Liverpool had defeated Derby County by two unanswered goals and they were looking forward to a similar result today against Chelsea.

Individual shouts of "Do them Cockney cunts!" and "Come on you Reds" erupted spontaneously throughout the game accompanied equally randomly by communal anthems, particularly the highly charged emotive *You'll Never Walk Alone*. Directly opposite in the Anfield Road end of the ground, the massed Blue ranks of Chelsea's travelling supporters, answered with jeers and derogatory comments about Scouse poverty, offering to kindly purchase rows of houses with their Southern cash, or even an entire new team, such was their wealth. Core to their insults was the comic character created and perpetuated by the BBC television programme *'Till Death Us Do Part,'* which featured the archetypal, loveable, workshy, Liverpool rogue, or 'theivin' Scouse git.'

For ninety minutes plus, the Chelsea fans displaying a conspicuous lack of imagination, constantly referred to this 'scallywag.'

"Fuckin' have them, they're only a bunch of Scarse gits." And "You wot, you wot, you wot, d'you want some, you Scarse gits?" challenges floated across the mid-field only to be drowned by the deafening stamping of boots and rafter raising, guttural, communal chanting of the Red beast in full voice.

Despite all the rhetoric, vocal aggression and ferocious amounts of testosterone produced by this verbal clash of Northern and Southern English working class males, Kevin Keegan's thirty-five minute winning goal proved to be the only real highlight on the pitch that day. The action outside the hallowed ground would prove to be an entirely different affair.

"Alright, we can't get these Cockney blurts here, so some of us will have a go while the bizzies lead them down to Lime Street Station, everyone else get on ahead and be waitin' round by Saint George's Hall in the gardens behind." Mickey Savage or 'Savvy' one of the original leaders of the Kings Skinheads commanded as his combined force of LFC Boot Boys from both estates gathered around him. In the absence of their usual leaders, Tommy (S), Dayo (G) and the insane Quirky, either through serious injury or imprisonment, old rivalries had been temporarily forgotten and the Crown Boot Boys were prepared to be directed by one of their former enemy's star players.

Jay Mac with Johno, Crusher, Tank, both Ants and the recently returned, now upgraded Merchant Seaman, James 'Treky' McCoy were in the crew who pushed on towards their city centre rendezvous with several dozen of the Kings combined team.

"This is what yer miss when yer away," said Treky, the salty sea-dog, who always had new tall tales to recount on his sporadic returns. "Yeah, in the States it's fuckin' ace, don't get me wrong but yer can't beat a Saturday afternoon after the match layin' into some Cockney twats."

As usual they all played the game of drawing comical observations from their team mate. "So would yer rather be kickin' the fuck out of yer Cockney, yer Brummie or yer Geordie?" Johno asked, beginning the sport.

"That's a good question Johno... I think yer best puttin' them in order of who yer'd wanna do first." He paused to gather his thoughts, "Obviously yer Brummie and yer Geordie are decent lads when it comes down to it, so the answer's gotta be, yer Cockney gets it first."

Jay Mac decided to risk the obvious "What about if yer had all of them three and a Manc, who are yer gonna go for there?"

Treky tried to compose himself, as if he had been struck a physical blow, "Jay Mac, I don't know what's been goin' on while I've been away but you must 'ave been twatted on the head or somethin'. It wouldn't matter if yer worst enemy was standin' right in front of yer, if there was a stinkin' Manc doin' nothin' even to wind yer up, you'd have to give 'im the best kickin' he'd ever had, it'd be yer duty."

All the disparate crew members within earshot laughed at the sheer vehemence of Treky's impassioned response.

Enjoying his fifteen minutes of fame, the comic 'sailor' continued his routine for the remainder of their rapid march towards the city centre, regaling them with exaggerated tales of unlikely ambitious sexual liaisons with exotic maidens from around the globe, despite the fact that his present route took him from Southampton to New York only.

Moving from the general to the more specific, Treky finished his fascinating assessment of females of the world focusing his closing observations on the ladies of Manhattan.

"Course, when I'm in New York City, I'm spoilt for choice, yer've got them all there: Irish, Italian, Polish, Chinese and my favourite yer Puerto Rican birds, fuckin' gorgeous."

Of all his listeners Jay Mac was the most envious, always eagerly absorbing new positive material to add to his mental catalogue of the advantages of life in America.

When they arrived at their specified destination this combined crew of Kings and Crown team players assembled in Saint John's Gardens, facing the rear of the neo-classical Saint George's Hall, with the imposing cluster of other architectural masterpieces including the Walker Art Gallery and the Liverpool Museum on their left and the drab modern Saint John's shopping precinct to their right. Other teams from across the city where also mustering in this key strategic location.

"Fuckin' hell, reminds me of the night we came into town to see Clockwork Orange" Jay Mac said to Johno and Crusher who had not been present that evening.

"There's some big teams 'ere alright." Johno acknowledged.

"Here thee come!" a lookout positioned just a few yards ahead of them shouted.

Snaking all the way from Commutation Row back across Hunter Street, down to Byrom Street and out along Scotland Road, the angry, disappointed royal blue column came into view, with their inflammatory chants preceding them. Even as they crossed the Row which contained a number of small shops and businesses, including one of the Skin's favourite fashion stores, Eric's and moved into Lime Street at its junction with London Road, they were pelted on their left flank with a hail of glass missiles, including pint glasses, beer bottles and ashtrays. Anything else that could be thrown was then launched, with additional volleys of stones and sod's of earth being brought to bear on their right flank also.

Despite the presence of both mounted police and numerous constables on foot, the beleaguered Chelsea fans erupted in a burst of righteous rage, breaking out from the confines of their unwanted escort, charging directly towards their howling enemies, determined to give a good account of themselves.

"Let's 'ave these Scarse cants." "Give'em a fackin' slap." their leaders shouted as they tore into the Red mob that raced out from their municipal gardens assembly area, with similar violent intent.

For their part the Chelsea Boot Boys contingent within their football team's loyal travelling supporters, could not be happier. They did not need a police escort, or to be herded and chaperoned from Liverpool Football Club's ground to Lime Street Station, for them this was a result, a welcome chance to smash a few Scouse faces and crack some ribs. 'Fack what 'appened at the match' they thought, this action would be remembered and sang about in the alehouses long after the present season had been decided and forgotten.

Jay Mac, Crusher, Johno and Treky had moved as one with the mob and were caught in the centre of the mêlée; punches, head-butts and close range kicks were the order of the day, artificially assisted where possible by the use of knuckle-dusters and coshes. Staying upright and not losing their footing was as vitally important here as on the terraces, those who went down were not getting back up.

With the police regrouping and forcing their way into the brawling mass the inevitable splintering into smaller clusters occurred. Jay Mac and the farm-labouring Johno suddenly found they were with a small band of LFC Boot Boys, who were outnumbered by a crew of furious Chelsea Seniors.

"Fuck this," Jay Mac announced breaking free for a moment, bleeding from several facial wounds, "come 'ed Johno, let's fall back into the park, there's more of our boys there."

Both Crown youths darted through the entrance in the aged sandstone walls, intent on joining Savvy and his team of Boot Boys, who had rallied near the cenotaph memorial to the heroic King's Liverpool Regiment.

"Get them two Scarse shitbags!" a burley male shouted, beginning a chase by six original London Skins, determined to deliver a severe beating to the two fleeing Crown players.

Under any other circumstances Jay Mac would have been fascinated to have talked to these individuals who, all in their late teens or early twenties, where there at the birth of the legendary Skinhead lifestyle. Today, however, was an occasion for avoiding their seasoned, gleaming, cherry red, high-leg, Cockney Airwair, not for swapping polishing tips, favourite Ska and Reggae bands or anecdotal tales of similar violent encounters.

"Run darn that cunt wiv those shitty red wings on his back!" the leader of the half-dozen pursuers ordered.

'Why me for fuck's sake?' thought Jay Mac, whose usual blistering running pace was hampered by other combatants engaged in desperate duels, obstructing his path. In a similar move to that which he had brought down the Barley's runner, he too was wrestled to the ground, though in his case, Jay Mac tried to regain his feet, even while receiving his own personal close-up view of his assailant's boots as they struck him from all sides.

Johno had taken his main assailant to the floor with him and both grappled each other determined to gain the upper hand. The Eagle crew strongman was experiencing a similar kicking to Jay Mac, even if some of the excited Chelsea 'originals' blows struck friend as well as foe.

As Jay Mac finally righted himself, he was seized by the lapels of his denim jacket followed instantly by a tremendous head-butt which cracked his already broken nose, opening his old wound once more. Dazed and bleeding as he was, he still managed to smash his attacker in the right side of his face, with his left fist encased in the heavy brass knuckle-duster that he had on permanent loan from Weaver.

Forceful though his blow had been, it appeared to have little impact on this experienced, veteran Chelsea Skins brawler.

"Not so fackin' tough nar, are yer, when yer ain't frowin' bricks and bottles at old men and young boys?" the grinning male asked drawing his head back, preparing for another strike. He never managed to land his intended coup de gras.

"On the deck you Cockney bastard!" Savvy of the Kings Team ordered while cracking him hard across the skull, with the heavy cosh that was his weapon of choice.

Overcome by sheer weight of numbers, the half-dozen pursuers of Jay Mac and Johno were now the victims of the combined LFC Boot Boy crews, rolling around on the floor of the ornamental gardens, becoming footballs themselves. Their torment did not last for long as the officially sanctioned, uniformed, boot boys of the Liverpool police truncheoned their way into the action, having once again regrouped and this time supplemented their numbers with hastily recalled reinforcements grateful for this 'overtime' opportunity.

Every one of the varied team players knew the routine and understood the primary rule, self-preservation mattered above all else, it was every man for himself; escape by any means or route. In all directions both Red and Blue former adversaries scattered, each scrambling for personal safety.

The bloodied Jay Mac had lost sight of Johno, becoming separated from any of his Crown team mates. Running as fast as he could manage he darted through Saint John's Shopping precinct out onto Elliot Street, down past Owen Owen's store until finally he felt safe to merge with the bustling civilian crowds, on this warm, early Saturday evening.

Standing not far from the spot of his last failed collection for Floyd, admiring some of the pretty shop girls as they finished their work for the day and were hurrying home for their big night out, he took his red and white LFC scarf from where it was draped, folded in two equal lengths over the metal snap-fastening of his half inch red elasticated braces. Casually he wiped his blood-stained face then returned his scarf carefully back to where it hung, like the colourful favours a medieval knight would have worn in a tourney or joust. Jay Mac had several examples of these football souvenirs, though he preferred to think of those from other clubs that he had acquired by force as 'scalps', usually displaying the rival teams captured prize on the day of their next fixture with Liverpool FC.

He had been hoping to acquire a royal blue and white Chelsea 'scalp' that day but had found that acquisition more dangerous than he had anticipated, similar to the dire warning issued to the French herald in the only Shakespearean play that Jay Mac knew well *'Henry V'*:

> *"The man that once did sell the lions skin*
> *While the beast lived, was killed with hunting him."*

The angry Chelsea lion had almost done for him that day.

Strolling slowly down towards the Pier Head bus and ferry terminus considering different London teams and evaluating their crews, he amused himself with these thoughts. He imagined in one fanciful instance what it would be like to encounter the legendary 'Joe Hawkins' the fictional, archetypal Skinhead from Richard Allen's highly successful paperback novels about the exploits of this member of West Ham's firm. 'Thank fuck Millwall are in the second division.' he concluded. 'Imagine tryin' to take on their crew of nutters.'

"Alright Jay Mac, hang on for me." he suddenly heard being called after him, as he was about to cross the two-way main arterial road with the imposing Cunard Building in front of him.

Instantly drawn back from his mental speculations he turned to see the stocky, solid figure of the Crown Team's champion strongman, Crusher.

"Alright Crusher, lad, what's happenin' with you mate?" he asked smiling.

"I got separated from Johno and the others; I think some of the lads got pulled by the bizzies." the six-foot, fifteen stone, dark haired apprentice dray man advised, then added "I'm friggin' starvin' d'yer fancy gettin' a few pies in an a brew down at the shop?"

"Crusher mate, that's where I'm headin' meself, what sort of match day would it be without a couple of pies down yer neck? Come 'ed." Jay Mac replied eagerly.

A short time later having each purchased two mixed meat pies from the illustrious Pier Head venue and a mug of dark brown stewed tea, they made their way to the side of the Second World War merchant seaman's monument and greedily tore into their food.

"Am not sure Crusher but I think this first one's mostly seagull, it's got a real salty sea taste about it but I haven't found the beak yet as proof." Jay Mac noted, spitting fragments of gristle and hard crust from his mouth as he spoke.

His powerful team mate did not reply having consumed his first pie entirely, including the more indigestible elements; he was now part way through his second. Finally he spoke, "Yeah definitely a lot more seagull than usual." he said continuing the long-running joke that they all enjoyed perpetuating, suggesting that the unscrupulous owner of the eatery captured local wild fowl for his fare to reduce his costs.

They both laughed and while Jay Mac continued eating his final pie, they leaned on the iron railings staring out across the dark brown River Mersey, towards Birkenhead and the now silent slipways of the world-renowned ship builders Cammel Lairds on the opposite bank. A cold, early autumn breeze was blowing with a sky filled with wispy grey strands of low lying cloud, obscuring their vision of the majestic Welsh mountains beyond.

"You're a decent lad, Jay Mac, you're one of the only characters that yer can talk to on that fuckin' estate and know that yer'll keep it to yerself." Crusher began, resting his heavy frame on his powerful forearms reaching across the railings, with hands clasped tightly together.

"Have yer got somethin' on yer mind mate? Y'can tell me, if y'want. Yer know what thee say, a problem shared is a problem halved." Jay Mac responded generously though uncomfortable with finding himself in a position that most males regard as excruciatingly awkward, sharing a concern with another man.

"Yeah, I've got a major problem." Crusher paused before revealing his dilemma. "It's me kid yer see."

Jay Mac interrupted, "What fuckin' kid? I've never heard that yer had a kid. I mean, I know yer never say much but that's usually the sort of thing yer might happen t'mention."

"Nah, it's a bit more tricky than that. Yer see he's mine an Molly's kid." Crusher replied without taking his gaze from the fast flowing river below.

"Fuck me!" Jay Mac blurted out, "You are jokin' aren't yer, you and fuckin' skank... I mean Molly Brown, no way. How the fuck d'yer know it's yours, every arsehole on the estate has jumped her from the arl fellers to the juniors...?" He stopped quickly as his team mate turned and glowered at him.

"I know he's mine alright, and I wanna do the right thing by him."

"Crusher man, I don't mean any disrespect but think it through. The last time I saw her she was tryin' to get cash off Macca (G). Him and Weaver and Yad all had a few goes there mate. The kid could as easily be one of theirs." Jay Mac tried to reason with his team mate.

"No Jay Mac, the boy's mine, right? Remember when I joined the Heron crew and Yad set Molly up to be gang-banged and I went first?" he asked rhetorically, "Well I was supposed to pull it out before I shot but I didn't so I know I'm the one."

Jay Mac still sought to persuade the agonised Crusher, "Fuckin' hell, don't let that convince yer; probably most of them came their load without pullin' out. I'm tellin' yer this kid could be anyone's".

Crusher remained unmoved, "Listen, I might as well tell yer the lot." He paused then revealed all, "She was my first, I'd never done it until that night with Molly, I fuckin' love that girl." He broke off from speaking and spat forcefully into the river below. Jay Mac was considering what response to make now that he had received all the details of his friend's sorry plight.

"Two pence lads, just two pence." the dishevelled forty-something, trilby wearing, tramp called, having shuffled unheard towards the pensive pair, lost in their own thoughts.

Jay Mac turned sharply, "Fuck off mate, we're not interested."

The tramp unwisely pressed on, "Just two pence lads, me wife's thrun me out, gorra new feller, the fuckin' bitch, just two pence." His overpowering body odour and physical stench seemed to envelop them, even in the presence of the prevailing breeze.

Crusher also turned towards him, "Did yer hear what he just said? We're talkin' here, so fuck off."

The disconsolate tramp shuffled away a few feet then stopped, deciding to remonstrate with them, "I only asked yer for two fuckin' pence, yer pair of tight bastards go an fuck yerselves."

His last words barely escaped from his reeking mouth as Crusher leapt forward, seized him with one hand by his scrawny throat and lifted his shaking body above head height at full arm's length. The Crown strongman walked forward a few paces and slammed the terrified, dangling tramp into the circular stone wall with its brass plaques that surrounded the outside of the memorial.

Jimmy 'Two pence' as his fellow 'business' associates had named him, gasped out a plea for mercy in much the same way that the wretched 'Star child' had done, while he violated her several weeks earlier. His windfall trilby slipped from his greasy head, floating on the breeze until it settled for few moments on the turgid waters below.

Jay Mac caught hold of Crusher's brawny forearm with his right hand, "Put him down mate, he fuckin' stinks, he's scarin' the seagulls with his screamin'." Other passers-by were also watching the performance and Jay Mac was worried that they may contact the police at the nearby station.

"He's goin' in there for a fuckin' wash." Crusher announced passing sentence, preparing to act as executioner as well. He swung the raggedy man over the railings and dangled him out above the equally stinking waters below.

"Fuck, Crusher, don't do it, there's enough shite in this river and it doesn't need any more pollution from this smelly cunt. Think of the Mersey fish, even they'll choke on this fucker." Jay Mac was desperately trying to save the tramp from his fate and them from possible arrest.

After a few tense seconds where only the shrill screams of the passing gulls could be heard, in one swift movement Crusher returned his prisoner over the railings and threw him to the ground some distance further from them.

"Come 'ed let's gerroff before I change me mind and do somethin' nasty." Crusher said calmly.

The floored Jimmy 'Two pence' sat where he was and wisely said no more. Both youths walked away towards their bus stop without a backward glance. A few moments later when he had regained his composure and his feet, after adjusting his crusty attire, the tramp shuffled forward towards the iron railings. As he looked down to the swiftly flowing river, he was just in time to see his filthy headgear sink below the surface.

"It's a pity that, I really liked that hat." Then he turned and began his familiar litany once again, "Two pence, just two pence that's all."

When they arrived at the Crown Estate the permanently hungry Crusher decided that his growling stomach was in urgent need of additional sustenance, leading both youths directly to Mr Li's Golden Diner. A quarter of an hour later they emerged from the favoured eatery each with a large fish supper plus extra chips, topped with two spring rolls as a nod to the healthy option. While they sat perched on the low wall immediately outside the shop attacking their food like ravenous animals, Crusher reaffirmed his feelings towards Molly Brown, in between stuffing handfuls combined of heavily salted and vinegar drenched golden battered, steaming, white cod and thick cut soggy chips into his considerable capacity mouth.

Pausing momentarily for breath, Jay Mac asked, "So 'ave yer ever told Molly any of this shit?"

Similarly during vital breathing spells Crusher replied, "Yeah, I've told her how I feel about her and that I wanna help her with our kid but she just laughs and won't have it. I think she's got a bit of a thing for Macca (G)."

Jay Mac though sympathetic, gave his considered response, "This is fucked up, why not just forget about it and walk away before it gets any worse?"

Crusher did not reply and began tearing through the crispy outer layers of his spring rolls, staring ahead into the distance.

"Giz some chips lads, an yer can 'ave a feel." called one of the young female camp followers, who seemed to permanently loiter near the shops and Heron public house.

Jay Mac looked at the girl standing close by dressed provocatively in a thin blouse, a micro-mini skirt and high platform shoes, wearing a theatrical amount of make-up. He flicked a solitary chip in her direction, "Here yer are 'ave this, yer can keep the feel t'yerself."

The girl caught the greasy chip and swallowed it like a small bird with a worm, "Eee! Dirty bastard, listen to him tellin' me to feel meself."

"Fuck off, 'Little Jane', go home or I'll tell your Molly when I see her." Crusher said sternly.

"You keep away from our Molly, yer fat git, yer've already told her enough lies, sayin' our baby Gary's yours. Eee, the thought of it." said Little Jane, the younger sister of Crusher's forlorn love interest.

Jay Mac had been unaware that Molly Brown even had a sister. This revelation and her cruel comments towards his team mate made him appreciate his plight further. He knew that if this rumour was to reach the ears of the sexual sadist Macca (G), he would do his best to wring out the cruellest twist possible from the agonised Crusher.

"Listen mate, I'll just give yer one bit of advice 'ere, don't let this story go any further, keep a lid on it. If the wrong cunts hear about it, things could end badly all round, yeah?"

Crusher made no response and Jay Mac immediately changed the topic. "Anyway, come 'ed let's get up to the Eagle for a few pints, we can 'ave a laugh with the crew about the match and the scrap in town, not to mention you gonna drown that smelly tramp down the Pier."

Crusher rose to his feet, rolled up his fish and chips paper wrappings into a tight ball before striking them underhand, volleyball service style out into the road. "Nah, I'm off home. See yer around Jay Mac."

The Eagle player watched as his powerful friend lumbered away towards his dilapidated tenement block, with his head bowed looking like he was carrying the weight of the world on his broad shoulders.

'Little Jane' was standing outside the newspaper and tobacconist shop trying to barter a cigarette from any of the older male customers.

Jay Mac turned and called to her "'Ere yer are girl, finish these chips."

She came close to him enveloping him with the scent of her cheap perfume, dowsed as heavily as the vinegar on the greasy chips. Quickly she snatched the food remnants out of his hand then drew back.

"What d'yer want for these, yer dirty git?" she asked as she began to stuff the chips into her garishly red lipsticked mouth.

"Nothin' girl, I've just lost me appetite." he replied then turned away from her and began walking up the main, central road.

Passing Glynn's house enroute, he found his former team mate once again working with his uncle, redecorating the tired front wall.

"Alright Glynn!" he called.

His friend walked over to him, paintbrush in his right hand dripping with magnolia coloured distemper as he did.

"Alright Jay Mac. Where's yer fuckin' dirty rapist mates tonight?" he asked.

"Don't start Glynn will yer, there's enough shit goin' on on this estate as it is. Anyway they're not me mates I can tell yer that for certain." He paused then looking his friend up and down, dressed in his paint spattered bib and brace overalls, he said, "What the fuck is goin' on anyway, yer look like a proper person out here with yer uncle doin' the place up? Why are yer doin' the Corpy's job for them?"

Glynn smiled, "I am a proper person Jay Mac, if you drop all this gang shite before yer get stuck down, or it kills yer, yer never know, you might grow up too." He paused then turned in the direction of his mother's small, mid-terraced property.

"Me mum's applied for this 'right to buy' thing that the Council's got on the go now. So we're doin' the place up, cos once it's agreed she's gonna sell up and get as far away from this shithole as possible." He looked back at Jay Mac whose face still bore the stains and marks of the day's events. "I see yer nose has been banged in again. Look at yer standin' there in yer fuckin' boot boy kit, yer denim jacket, Flemings jeans and Airwair." He laughed then added, "Do yerself a favour, put all that gear in the bin where it belongs. See yer Jay Mac, I *have* got something to do." Glynn walked back to his uncle and they continued their redecorating.

Jay Mac strolled on toward the Eagle hoping for a better reception there.

On entering the lounge bar letting the swing door with its upper frosted glass panel close behind him, the youth could quickly tell that the atmosphere was also muted. Even with Nazareth's *Bad Bad Boy* playing on the jukebox and the usual cheery sounds of glasses and bottles clinking together as brown ales or dark stouts, poured into pints already half filled with bitter or mild, his team mates' despondent faces revealed their gloomy mood. After collecting two bottles of Guinness and a pint glass, Jay Mac strolled over to his crew in the midst of the less crowded than usual, early evening assortment of drinkers.

"Alright lads, what's happenin'?" Jay Mac asked wedging himself into the centre between Johno on his left and Terry (H) on his right with Brain and Treky occupying flanking positions respectively, at either side of those two.

Never a Dull Moment 1973 ▪ 207

"Good result against Chelsea, even if it was only the one goal." he observed, looking from left to right, waiting for acknowledgement from the other Eagle players.

"Yeah, good result for the Reds but a bit shitty after." Johno stated.

"That kick-off with the Chelsea boys cost us three of our crew." Terry (H) advised, having personally been with some of the old guard in the thick of the action.

Johno picked up the story, "Tank was takin' a fuckin' good kickin' from yer Cockney twats then the two Ants got stuck in throwin' punches like fuck." He paused to take a lengthy drink of his pint, then continued, "Next thing, those bastard bizzies waded in with their truncheons, crackin' heads everywhere. Bobby Anton went down so their kid, Liam, went fuckin' mental, course the pigs weren't havin' that, all I saw next was Liam gettin' pounded by three of them fat arse cunts, until finally thee got him down too." Terry (H) concluded the sorry tale, "We've heard Tank's in the cells but both the Ants are in Walton Hospital with bad head injuries." He paused and threw back his whiskey chaser in a single movement. "So, one-nil on the pitch to the Reds but three-nil in extra time to the fuckin' bizzies."

Treky, the merchant seaman and part time unlicensed boxer, who as usual, appeared distracted and unmoved, finished his pint then said dismissively "Thee was unlucky but there y'go. Everyone knows the score, gerrout the way or get fucked, if yer gripped by the bizzies don't cry about it, yer luck ran out that's all." He turned towards Jay Mac, "Anyway mate tell us how you got back, and for fuck's sake throw in a few laughs, before all these start cryin' in their ale."

Jay Mac looked again from left to right, took a lengthy drink of his Guinness then began his own tale, "Funny y'should say that Treky lad, wait till I tell yer what happened to me and the big feller, Crusher."

A few moments later just as Jay Mac was concluding his graphic account of his escape from the Chelsea Boot Boys and those of the Liverpool police and Crusher's dramatic response to Jimmy 'Two pence's' irritating entreaties, which amused all of his listeners, particularly Johno, the Crown Team's other strongman, Irish entered the lounge with Blue. Terry (H) announced that he was meeting a female in the city centre and when he vacated his seat to leave, Jay Mac's other former school friend, Irish, took his place between him and Treky. After Blue arrived from the bar with their pints he drew up a stool and sat directly in front of them.

"What's happenin' Irish? What 'ave you and this feller been up to?" Treky asked genuinely, having not been at home on the estate for some time.

Irish appeared to be more angry than usual as he replied "That's a good question Treky, I don't know what the fuck's happenin' on this estate anymore." He paused to light a cigarette and take a drink of his brown bitter. "Some fucker is sellin' drugs to the kids all over the place and it's startin' to be a real bastard of a problem for everyone who *lives* here."

Blue interjected excitedly "Yeah, we had two lads off the Raven Hall Estate by the cemetery an we give them a real good beatin'. Thee said thee'd never come back but next thing yer know some other cunt's selling the gear, Devo's really pissed off with it."

"Is he now, why's that then?" Jay Mac asked curiously.

Irish had just completed blowing two perfect smoke rings when he turned sharply towards him, "Why's that then, what's that supposed to mean? He might be a mad fucker but he really cares about this estate, he doesn't wanna see it flooded with poison ruinin' all the kids that are comin' up."

Jay Mac laughed, "No, not unless it's his gear and he's the one supplyin' it."

Irish was not happy with this remark, "Before yer start slaggin' off Devo, just answer me this." He paused and looked directly at Jay Mac, "Are y'sure you're not involved in movin' this shite?"

Jay Mac put down his pint and returned Irish's angry stare "Watch where y'goin' there Irish. I'll tell yer straight, I'm not sellin' any drugs to any kids on this estate or anywhere else. So fuckin' drop it."

Irish would not let the matter lie, "What about yer mate Macca (G), what d'yer have to say about him?"

"I'll tell yer what I say about him, walk up to him and fuckin' ask him yerself and see where that gets yer. But do me a favour, don't you ever put that question to me again." Jay Mac replied angrily.

Blue interrupted once more, "Anyone fancy some crisps, or peanuts an a round of shorts?"

"That's more like it Blue, yer a good man. Fuckin' hell after listenin' to these sad characters in 'ere tonight, I think I'll be gettin' back t'sea, soon as I can." Treky announced.

The moment passed and gradually the mood changed as the alcohol and spirits flowed, supplemented by copious amounts of salted snacks. Jay Mac was encouraged to re-tell the tale of his and Crusher's encounter with Jimmy 'Two pence' which even amused the dower Irish.

"Funny thing, Irish, somethin' about this tramp cunt was familiar. He reminded me of that smelly twat who was followin' us around last year, when we saw those dwarves havin' a go at that bird an her feller."

Irish laughed as he recalled that night the previous February, which now seemed a lifetime ago.

Shortly before last orders were called, Jay Mac, who had been drinking heavily, decided to depart and make his way down across the estate to his bus stop. Leaving the crew singing loudly, joining in the chorus of *Alright Now* by Free, he walked awkwardly through the doorway of the cigarette-smoke filled lounge out into the cold, early September night air. Instantly he was revived, becoming aware of his chill surroundings and removed his red and white Liverpool FC scarf from his braces then wrapped it around his neck.

Strolling past the library with his bleached white collar turned up and his hands dug deeply into the pockets of his denim jacket, he was aware he was being followed.

A few yards farther on with the heavy brass knuckle duster firmly in place on his left hand, Jay Mac stopped suddenly and turned sharply ready to lash out, "What the fuck d'you want, sneakin' up like that yer tit?" he shouted as he was about to deliver a devastating punch to his stalker.

"Sorry Jay Mac, mate, I just needed to talk to yer about somethin'." Brain said nervously."

Jay Mac looked at his team mate standing hunched over, trembling, shuffling his feet and curbed his angry tone.

"Alright Brain, lad, chill out will yer, no need to be flappin'. What did yer actually want?" Jay Mac smiled as he spoke calming the monocular youth, whose right eye had been burst by an airgun pellet fired by their once bitter rivals, the Kings Team, during their final epic battle the previous Halloween.

"It's just... I've always got bad pains in me 'ed from me eye, an I used to get some gear off Floyd that stopped the pain." Brain began cautiously.

"Yeah, ok, so now yer can't get any shit off Floyd try askin' yer doctor. Thee must have all kinds of friggin' pain killers yer can take." Jay Mac offered in reply.

Brain began shuffling nervously once more, appearing as if he desperately needed to use the toilet. "I've tried them all Jay Mac an they're no fuckin' use. I just need a bit of grass, or a few of those pills, yer know what I mean. I'll pay yer whatever yer want for them..."

"What are you sayin' yer cheeky cunt?" D'you think am some sort of dealer? I'll fuckin' twat yer right here now, if yer tryin' t'say that about me." the self-righteous Jay Mac snapped angrily.

"No, no, please Jay Mac... I'm sorry, no offence mate... it was just with Irish sayin' all that in the Eagle... am in fuckin' pain man... I can't take it." He cowered as he spoke and the cold night air conspired with his nervous energy to make him shake involuntarily.

Jay Mac once more felt a wave of sympathy pass over him and again he softened his tone as he spoke, "Ok, calm yerself right down, yeah? Right, am gonna trust yer now so don't fuck me over. I can't help yer but I have heard that Macca (G) sometimes has a bit of gear he's sellin'. I'm walkin down that way, so yer can come with me an if yer lucky he might be in the Heron."

Jay Mac paused then caught hold of his fellow Eagle player by the shoulders and looked into his watery, bloodshot eye, "He might be able to sort yer out but I'm not gettin' involved. Just be careful if yer dealin' with him, he's a fuckin' sneaky bastard. One other thing Brain, yer an Eagle Boot Boy just like me, don't think that'll save yer if yer tell any cunt about this, right? Yer don't wanna lose yer other eye do yer?"

"Thanks Jay Mac, thanks. I won't tell anyone mate, I knew you'd help me." Brain replied gratefully.

They set off down the main central road in the direction of the Heron public house, walking briskly through the sharp, cold night air. Not long after, they arrived by the bottom row of shops, now closed and firmly secured with their graffiti covered steel shutters. The two Eagle players stopped by the low wall outside the Heron where the stiffening, cold breeze had blown a disparate selection of chip paper wrappings and a couple of pages from the local broadsheet newspaper, the *Liverpool Echo*. If Jay Mac had looked more closely at these crumpled items he would have noticed that the latter contained a detailed report of Liverpool's match with Chelsea and the violence that had followed.

"In yer go Brain and watch what yer say in there, yer not in the Eagle now." Jay Mac warned tapping his nervous companion on the shoulder as a signal to move off.

Brain kept his head lowered and his hands dug into the pockets of his denim jacket, with its Eagle Boot Boys chevron across the shoulders, while he walked through the gap in the low walls, across the permanently empty car park and up the stone steps into the entrance of their Crown Team rival's alehouse.

Two young girls were perched farther along on the wall, casually engaged in kicking the paper litter about with their dangling feet; they were watching Jay Mac even as he was watching to see that Brain actually entered the pub. They wolf-whistled at the Eagle player to attract his attention.

Jay Mac looked at them both, recognising one of the shivering girls as 'Little Jane.' "You two look freezin' haven't yer got any coats?" he asked genuinely.

"Why? Are you offerin' to warm us up?" Little Jane shouted much to the amusement of her cackling friend who advised, "She fancies you Jay Mac."

To which the mortified Little Jane responded immediately with a high pitched scream, which preceded her vehement denial, "Eeee! No, I don't. Fuckin' shurrup you!"

Two drunken, dishevelled mid-forties males with massive competing ale guts suddenly appeared in the doorway of the Heron, their badly, distorted over-indulged silhouettes illuminated from behind by its amber entrance light. The clear 'winner' of the bloated stomach contest called to Little Jane and her friend.

"Here y'are girls, we've got yer a couple of bottles of beer and some ciggies. Shall we go round the back and have a bit of fun?"

"Alright but we want the beer an ciggies first, before yer get started, yer pair of dirty gits." Little Jane answered.

"Yer gettin' the beer only before, an, yer can have the ciggies when we've *both* finished with yer. Now get yer little arses over 'ere," the 'winner' called back, rubbing his excited crotch with his left hand as he spoke.

Negotiations were completed and terms agreed, the goods were about to be exchanged. Both girls walked over to their smiling, eager partners, with a comical, exaggerated cat-walk style.

Jay Mac strolled away towards his bus stop; he did not bother to look back.

It was well after midnight when Jay Mac was finally convinced that his aunt was asleep, after she had lingered even longer than usual in the small living room, until she had completed re-reading a vital chapter of one of her murder mysteries and finished her final cigarette of the day before going to bed.

Feeling that he was relatively safe on hearing the combined efforts of his elderly guardians as they strove to outdo each other in a thunderous snoring chorus, he carefully opened the hall cupboard filled with obsolete items and removed the old battered suitcase that contained his collection of American Superhero comics.

Back in the main room, having laid the case on the mustard coloured, stretch fabric covered sofa, he unlocked its two snap fastenings with a small rusty key that he always kept safely secured inside his brown leather wallet. Jay Mac placed the contents of the special delivery that Floyd never received across the cushions and studied the content once more, partially diminished as it now was. Irish and Brain had both been correct in their assumptions that Jay Mac was responsible for selling narcotics on the estate and conversely he felt that he was entirely right in denying this. As far as the youth was concerned he was only a wholesaler who provided a product to one specific client, Macca (G). What that purchaser did subsequently with the goods he, Jay Mac, had managed to disingenuously convince himself was of no concern of his. He had effectively absolved himself of any responsibility, denying any duty of care.

Placing a selection of colourful blotting paper squares and orange tablets into some smaller plastic bags, sufficient to placate the demands of his eager business associate, he continued to reconcile his action momentarily lapsing into his usual rhetorical questioning of his canine companion.

"What d'you say mate? Am not doin' any harm am I? We're both survivors us two..." He broke off mid-sentence and looked across to where the ancient hound always lay on the faux fur rug in front of the two-bar electric fire. Now there was only an empty space, a few remaining persistent long white hairs and a phantom presence of his one real friend, lying recumbent in the recently deceased dog's place. Fourteen years was a good age for any animal Jay Mac told himself prosaically, though the pain of that day two weeks previous, when he and his uncle had taken the dying animal to be mercifully euthanized by the veterinary surgeon, would always stay with him.

He replaced his remaining supply into the case then removed the gleaming Colt Python .357 to admire it once more briefly, before returning his stash to its hiding place. 'Imagine takin' this to the match' he thought, amusing himself with mental images of waving the deadly firearm about, challenging all comers, 'That's right I'm the fuckin' boss now... what's that you wanna argue about it, are yer sure? Bang! Argument over!' While he was enjoying his lurid fantasising Jay Mac casually looked at the late edition *Liverpool Echo* and its complementary *Sporting Pink* issue:

"Liverpool's one-nil victory over Chelsea resulting from Kevin Keegan's first half goal was marred by ugly scenes post match. For a full report and pictures turn to page 6."

Quickly turning to the appropriate page of the colourful broadsheet, he glanced briefly at those photographs which contained match action then studied in detail those which displayed the after full-time entertainment. Grainy images further obscured but somehow paradoxically enhanced by the colour of the actual paper fascinated his eye. Bloodied faces of rival supporters and injured policemen with graphic accounts of sickening violence stimulated his immature fevered brain. He congratulated himself and his comrades on being present at such a notable action and read on to the end of the column. The writer had concluded by asking the inevitable question of why this violence was occurring; including a dire warning that matters could only get worse in his opinion. For further comments the reader was advised to turn to the editorial column. Jay Mac thumbed through the pages until he found this article also. Once again though this time written with the seniority and gravitas of the Editor-in-Chief, a hyperbolic analysis was attempted of why this dreadful outbreak of organised mayhem had grown and spread like a contagion. The usual solutions were offered; bring back the birch; reinstate National Service; even capital punishment, without any real understanding of the problem and its root causes. They were all too close to the events too myopic to be able to obtain an unbiased, objective view and place what was happening in a sociological, geopolitical perspective.

It was a peculiarly English malaise, a very popular domestic brand that would soon be exported across Europe. The dad and lad of the 1950s-60s crowd who attended every game dressed in their bobble hats and scarves carrying their wooden rattles and sportingly clapped good play from either side, were being replaced, ousted from the terraces by a new generation, a new breed of violent organised thugs. Their interest in the result on the pitch often paled in comparison to their obsession with settling the score long after full-time.

The national game had become a mirror which reflected the dire state of the nation with fuel shortages; power cuts; three-day weeks; wild-cat strikes and rising unemployment. A country being held to ransom by those who produced in abundance the one natural resource that it was sadly deficient in, oil, black gold.

Jay Mac and his contemporaries were equally unable to comprehend the bigger social and global issues. What they were concerned with was the *realpolitik* of the here and now. As the youth prepared his next supply of mind-bending drugs for the sadistic Heron co-leader, his only thoughts were based on his perception of reality, his individual survival. Jay Mac's next choice of actions would be catalystic, threatening the existence of others close to him, unleashing a chain reaction that could not be stopped until it had run its deadly course.

Chapter 9

Broken Wings

Saturday 6th October and Saturday 13th October

For almost a month after the Crown players' involvement in the Liverpool-v-Chelsea post match incident, life had been fairly quiet on the bleak housing estate. Jay Mac had made several carefully measured sales of his much sought after merchandise to his best and only customer Macca (G). So far his special arrangement with the Heron co-leader had remained secret, with the Eagle youth never questioning what happened to the goods once he had sold them. However, signs of the damaging effects this trade was already having and portents of a doomed future for a generation of young addicts were becoming more visible with each passing day.

Jay Mac observed the creeping sickness and convinced himself that his small supply of poison could not be responsible, absolving his guilty conscience and burying his head in the shifting sands. Macca (G) had reached the same conclusion, though lacked any pangs of guilt, with a simple trial balance calculation, he knew exactly the amount he had sold, who it was sold to and how much money he had made, after deducting his overheads. Someone else was clearly expanding their distribution at an exponential rate, soon his captive market would be completely saturated, his product obsolete and his lucrative business forced into closure. When Macca (G) had told Jay Mac that they were both very much alike, apart from being intelligent deviants, he was correct in one other vital aspect, they were also pragmatists. Now faced with the imminent closure of his hugely profitable enterprise, he decided that he must obtain the entire remainder of Jay Mac's supply and flood the streets in pursuit of his toxic revenue, before it was too late.

Sitting very comfortably in his Unicorn base of operations like an all-seeing spider at the centre of his web, the sinister Devo (S) was waiting poised ready to pounce as soon as the slightest twitch of the thinnest strand, revealed the presence of even the tiniest threat to the drugs distribution empire he was spinning in ever increasing circles. The Crown Team overlord had his suspicions regarding Jay Mac and Macca (G); he watched them through other's eyes from afar and listened to a thousand conversations reported by his ever-present ears, for just that one act of confirmation, then they would both come to understand real pain.

Saturday 6th October 1973

Standing in the heaving, smoke-filled bar of the George public house on the corner of Breck Road, with his LFC supporting Crown team mates and the tightly packed throng of other post-match revellers, Jay Mac was blissfully unaware of any of the machinations occurring at team leader level back on the grey concrete estate.

"Yeah, come on now that's the way to take a fuckin' pen, y'know what I mean," Johno observed, referring to Alec Lindsay's eighty-sixth minute penalty, which had secured a pleasing victory for the home side after Irving Nattrass's goal for Newcastle had threatened a disappointing draw, when it nullified Peter Cormack's earlier first half scoring strike in the twentieth minute. It had been an entertaining game acting as a salve to an unconvincing nil-nil result against the hated Manchester United the previous week. Everyone was in good spirits and in agreement with Treky, their merchant seaman colleague, who had now returned to sea, having previously observed 'yer Geordie's a good lad.' They all had declined the kind invitation of a large contingent of LFC Boot Boys drawn from several teams to join them in ambushing a tiding of 'Magpies' for some amusement.

"I tell yer what, that fuckin' Super Mac's some player don't yer think?" Terry (H), the senior Crown team member present that day observed.

Jay Mac was pleased to note that his friend the Heron crew strong man, Crusher, appeared in better spirits joining in the conversation also.

"Yeah Terry, MacDonald's a fuckin' rock. Him and Tommy Smith are a pair."

This sparked a heated debate concerning who was the hardest player of the two sides, which then expanded into considering all of the most likely candidates from the entire First Division. As the drinks poured and their intoxication grew, time lost all meaning until finally that strange phenomenon of urgently needing to consume some form of fried, battered, greasy sustenance became dominant, leading them from the stifling alehouse out into the cold, grey early October evening in search of their prey.

A short time later armed with their fish suppers and sausage dinners, the four youths left the pleasant warmth of a crowded local chip shop with its distinctive aroma combined of sizzling oil, salt, vinegar and hot comfort food trailing after them almost until they had reached the nearby bus stop. They took their places at the end of the lengthy queue, mostly comprised of older members of LFC supporters who had also been enjoying celebrating post-match.

While they waited patiently for their bus to the Crown Estate, they devoured their food as if several days had passed since they were last fed. Dusk had fallen and the grey, sombre day when the sun forgot to rise, lapsed into a darker grey evening bringing a chill breeze with it. Autumn may be the season of 'mellow mists' in the leafy suburbs of the Home Counties but in the grim industrial north, it heralded the arrival of head colds, sore throats and outbreaks of flu. The chill breeze stiffened calling for its partner a drenching downpour of ice cold rain; when their bus finally arrived a steaming crowd forced their way forward through its folding doors as keenly as they had passed through the turnstiles of the hallowed ground of Anfield.

With the lower deck being full to capacity, the Crown players pushed on up the metal stairs, finally finding four vacant seats near the rear of the vehicle, which they immediately seized. Jay Mac and Johno sat together on the right hand side of the bus, with Crusher literally squashing a regular-sized passenger two places behind them on their left and Terry (H) occupying the central position of the back row seating arrangement. The youths finished the last morsels of their meals then tossed their newspaper wrappings onto the floor, to join the assortment of litter that already cluttered the central isle.

The general feeling of elation had transferred from the alehouse to the bus with some passengers dissecting every element of the day's game, punctuating their observations with appropriate swearing for emphasis, some swapping wildly exaggerated tales of ancient physical encounters, either of a violent or sexual nature, or in some cases both, while others, feeling the mood was right, began the communal singing.

"Walk on, walk on, with 'ope in yer hearts." the elderly toothless choirmaster led, with his male voice ensemble enthusiastically joining in as the bus stopped at the traffic lights of the busy four-way junction, now outside of the Breck Road territory.

The first few bricks of the hail of missiles that followed smashed and thudded against the windows and metal sides of the green Atlantean vehicle, as the well-planned ambush enveloped them.

"What the fuck is happenin'," shouted a disgruntled male in his early fifties, almost dropping his Capstan full-strength cigarette from his lips as he spoke.

Jay Mac and his three Crown team mates knew exactly what was taking place. Their own speciality, that they reserved for attacking the coaches of rival supporters as they exited the city by its most northerly route, a stone and glass artillery barrage fired from all sides, trying to cause the maximum damage, was being used against them.

"Barleys! Barleys!" they all heard as their assailants changed tactics moving from long range to the immediate vicinity, surrounding the beleaguered immobile bus, preventing it from moving on by sheer weight of numbers. The traffic signals changed then changed again, though wisely angry motorists erred on the side of caution not wishing to attract the mob's attention, curbing their usual vocal protestations, hoping to slip past without incident.

"Barleys, Barleys, let's have them!" the urgent command rang out signalling a lead group to force a breach in the vehicles left side, kicking in its folding doors.

The Crown players now recognised where they were located, immediately opposite the John Barleycorn public house and they knew what was coming next. Looking out of the toughened glass windows, which, though crazed in some cases had still held, they could see a huge mob of denim jacket-wearing boot boys completely surrounding their stationary vehicle, armed with poles, sticks, chains, bricks and a selection of spray paint cans.

"It doesn't look good mate," Johno said, turning from his vantage point of the cracked window next to him, towards Jay Mac.

Coming from downstairs they heard the vain protestations of their driver, followed instantly by the distinctive slapping sound of hard fists smashing into flesh covered bone as the man's head was repeatedly punched. No one on the lower deck intervened, the boarders seemed to be intent on storming the upper tier; why should they bother to protest and risk a painful reprisal? For a few pregnant seconds an eerie silence occupied the metal stairwell, only to be abruptly shattered by the sound of heavy boots delivering the news of the lead Barley Boys' imminent arrival.

"Crown twats!" bellowed the six foot berserker on appearing at the top of the stairs, with his long greasy black hair matted to his hard angular face. He ran the full length of the upper deck flailing a heavy, rusty bicycle gear-chain about him, striking passengers on all sides as he did. A second, third and fourth Barley player arrived in rapid succession and they too began lashing out in every direction, dividing their forces fore and aft.

Momentarily frozen while each of their individual brains struggled to make sense of what was happening around them, the four Crown team players studied their wild enemies forming a considered response, in the micro-seconds of real time in which the attack was occurring. The brief period for reflection was over for Jay Mac as the second of the Barley Boot Boys arrived alongside him, armed with a three foot shiny black pole, which the Crown youth initially took to be an iron bar. Turning his body so that only his back and left shoulder where angled towards his furious assailant, he received four violent blows swiftly delivered with as much force as could be generated in the close confines of the upper deck. The fourth hit was sufficient to convince Jay Mac that the 'bar' was made of wood not metal and that it was the final unanswered blow he would be accepting.

Quickly closing the fingers of his left hand around the end of the gloss black painted pole nearest to him, he leapt from his seat to face his surprised foe. Looking directly at the Barley boot boy holding the improvised weapon at its other end, Jay Mac was presented with almost a mirror image of himself, a youth of similar height and build dressed virtually in the same uniform, except for the distinctive bleaching of pockct flaps and collar of that of the Crown player.

"Let it go yer Crown shitbag!" the Barley boy ordered kicking out at Jay Mac's legs as he did.

"Fuck you, yer Barley tit." he replied, successfully wrenching the half length of wooden broom handle from his opponents grasp.

In one lightning fast movement he brought the three foot baton up diagonally across his own right shoulder, then immediately returned it violently in the opposite arcing trajectory, into his enemy's face, cracking his nose as he did. A straight right jab to the same spot followed by a powerful thrust kick to the lower abdomen effectively dispatched this Barley Boot Boy, removing him from the struggle.

At the rear of the bus the chain wielding mad man was engaged in a desperate struggle with the senior Crown player of the day, Terry (H). Although the Barley youth had enjoyed some initial success striking all around with his rusty metal flail, when he attacked this highly capable scrapper the tables were soon turned. Dodging expertly to one side receiving only a glancing blow to the left temple, Terry (H) caught his assailant's right wrist in a vice-like grip with his left hand, delivering a gut-wrenching punch into his exposed groin at the same moment. Bent double directly in front of the Crown Boot Boy his unprotected face became the target for a flurry of hard accurate punches, whilst he clutched at his own aching genitals with both hands.

Similarly near the front and mid-section of the upper deck, the third and fourth Barleys who had also lashed out with their weapons of choice, respectively a short heavy shank metal dog lead and an ornately carved old, dark wooden chair leg, were now finding their immediate superiority of surprise of no further value. Seeing his comrade, Barley boy number two, effectively dispatched, the dog lead exponent wrapped the solid steel linked item around his right fist cestus style, pushing past the former intent on smashing Jay Mac in the face with his devastating metal clad mitt.

"Watch out mate!" Crusher shouted leaping from his seat and thrusting himself between his Crown team mate and the oncoming attacker, taking the full force of the blow himself.

"Come 'ere you, yer fucker." the strong man ordered after absorbing the impact of the hit to the right side of his face as if it were nothing more than the slightest tap, even though it opened a nasty scarlet gash above his eye. Grabbing hold of the Barley Boot Boy's denim jacket by the open front, he lifted the startled youth a foot off the floor, slamming the top of his skull into the graffiti covered metal ceiling above.

A heavily built older male in his late fifties seated at the front of the vehicle, had just about come to the end of his patience with these 'children' delaying his return home, for a night's drinking in his local. Even as the screaming Barley boy, the fourth of the quartet of attackers struck him across the back of his grey haired head, with the wooden chair leg, with its ball and claw foot, almost dislodging his greasy old, cloth flat cap, the man was already about to rise to his feet.

"Give me that stick y'little tit," he demanded, seizing hold of the youth by both arms rendering him incapable of further movement. The hard labouring stevedore squeezed his captive's upper arms with the iron fingers of his huge hands that bore a black swallow tattoo on the left, between finger and thumb and another of the Royal Marines proud crest on his right in the same position, causing the agonised boy to drop his weapon to the floor. The tremendous head butt that followed rendered this Barley player virtually unconscious.

Almost at the same moment that Crusher was rapidly approaching the opening at the top of the stairs carrying his prey, so to was the World War Two ex-commando with his. They smiled as they slammed both of the denim-clad 'rag dolls' together banging their heads violently as they did, before flinging them down the metal stairs to join their comrades below.

Barley Boot Boys numbers one and two soon followed equally unceremoniously, assisted by Jay Mac, Terry (H) and Johno and some of the other older LFC supporters, whose righteous indignation had been awoken. A red leatherette covered, detachable double seat was removed from its grey, metal frame and flung over the aluminium rail at the top of the stairwell, effectively sealing off this point of ingress from any further Barleys foolhardy enough to risk another assault.

Outside the wailing two-note discordant sirens and flashing blue lights announced the timely arrival of the constabulary, as the action was almost at an end. The mob disappeared as quickly as it had assembled with youths scattering in all directions. After a brief word with the injured driver who gamely would not leave his vehicle, insisting on staying at the wheel, the police moved the bus on, anxious to ensure that their main priority, the smooth flow of traffic on these arterial roads was resumed without further delay.

"Well, they were a bunch of Jessies weren't thee?" announced one of the older male travellers, delivering his disparaging assessment of the four Barleys' efforts.

"In my day, when lads were 'ard, we could've battered a whole tram load, if we'd 'ave felt like it." added another aged LFC fan, before taking a long draw on his old briar pipe.

For the remainder of the journey to the Crown Estate, the passengers of the upper deck reflected on the relative merits and strengths of the youths of their own particular generations, exaggerating their fighting potential as they saw fit to ridiculous levels. The four Crown players laughed as they sat listening to fantastic tales of the hooligans and toughs of yesteryear.

Finally when they reached the bleak estate Terry (H) and Johno left the bus at their stop, which was located close to the Eagle public house, with Jay Mac and Crusher continuing on to the terminus at the lower edge of the drab utilitarian housing development. They had all agreed to meet at the eponymous alehouse later to regale their team mates with the latest legend, based on the events of the day. Jay Mac was intending to catch another bus onwards to his own estate and return that night, when Crusher spoke:

"Listen mate, instead of gettin' off, yer can come back to ours, 'ave somethin' to eat an get a wash before goin' up to the Eagle. I've got somethin' I wanna show yer anyway, just t'see what yer think."

Happy to accept, Jay Mac strolled off with his powerful friend in the direction of his dilapidated tenement block. Once inside the metal double doors at the front ground level, they climbed the three flights of stone stairs to the top landing. Attempting to read the varied layers of graffiti, Jay Mac amused himself by successfully deciphering a number of the older more imaginative sexual suggestions that were often accompanied by early 'cave' drawings of fabulous biological specimens.

"It's only me, Ma. 'Ave got one of me mates with me, ok." Crusher shouted as they entered the small lobby of the council flat.

"That's good lad, am glad yer back, come in 'ere a minute will yer?" Mrs Tierney, Crusher's mother called from the living room.

Both boys carefully stepped over a selection of toys that were scattered along the length of the lobby, from the front door to the main room.

"Come in lads" a grotesquely overweight female in her mid-forties invited as she lay stretched across a heavily stained old couch, with her fleshy head propped up on one of her huge, flabby arms. Her painfully swollen legs were bare except for their dark hairy covering of several weeks' growth and her shoeless feet were desperately in need of a wash. Jay Mac quickly scanned the stuffy, grimy room, which had an overpowering smell of soiled nappies urgently in need of changing filling it to capacity, even dominating the odour of sweat and stale nicotine its principal competitors. Apart from the exhausted couch, there were two chairs of similar condition, a small table cluttered with cups and other items of crockery still displaying the remains of their no longer digestible contents and in the corner directly facing the recumbent woman, a black and white television blaring out some inane variety show.

Three small children ranging from eighteen months to six years of age were scrambling about amidst the collection of chocolate bar wrappers on the linoleum covered floor amusing themselves with a wide variety of 'toys', both of a genuine and improvised nature. Mrs Tierney looked away momentarily from the flickering television screen, glancing towards her son and his companion.

"Can yer 'elp me out Morris? I 'avent got anythin' in me purse an I've run out of fags."

Crusher looked affectionately at his lazy, obese mother and replied, "Of course Ma, just give us a couple of minutes and then me an Jay Mac will nip down to the shops for yer."

The indolent female casually looked across at the Eagle player, "He's a good lad, bit of a daft lump but he looks after 'is Ma. The ciggies is me only pleasure now yer see, since 'is Da left me."

Staring at her huge bloated body, Jay Mac said to himself 'Yeah and two dozen Mars Bars a day, y'fat fuck' but replied politely "Recent was it, yer husband gettin' off?" He gestured naïvely towards the squabbling children as they disputed the ownership of a cardboard cereal box.

"Oh them, no lad, they're not from Morris's Da." she laughed opening her mouth wide, revealing her spectacular collection of rotted teeth, "No, that bastard cleared out not long after soft lad was born, these three are from different fellers who've been very kind to me, if yer know what I mean. After all I am only a young woman in me prime, an I do 'ave me needs." She broke off their conversation as a performing dog wearing a clown's conical hat and a dress was being made to 'dance' on its hind legs, as part of the enthralling entertainment currently playing on the television.

Jay Mac appreciated this timely interruption, desperately trying to jettison his masochistic mind's cruelly conjured, grotesque, Technicolor images from his internal cinemascope, silver screen, of Mrs Tierney engaged in the carnal act with a series of clearly mentally disturbed lovers.

"D'yer fancy a sarnie or some toast mate?" Crusher enquired.

"Nah, d'yer know what, am still full up from the chippy, so I'll jib it thanks mate." Jay Mac replied, diplomatically.

"Right yer are then, I just wanna show yer somethin' before we go down to the shops." He paused then called to his mother

"Alright Ma, we'll be off in a minute, I'm just gonna show Jay Mac me room."

Without turning or moving in any way, the swollen female replied, "Ok son, don't forget I like Consulate, king size, menthol filter tips, they're good for me chest yer see." then added, "A pack of twenty or two tens would see me through until tomorrer, if yer can. Yer a good lad t'yer Ma."

After walking the short distance along the narrow hall to Crusher's room, the youths stepped into the small square box that seemed barely capable of admitting one, let alone two teenage males even of average size. Dominating the floor space literally was a tired-looking old single mattress, covered with a couple of crumpled, threadbare, dark brown, coarse army blankets. A rickety wooden chair wedged into one corner served as a dressing table-cum-wardrobe, with the majority of the heavyweight male's clothing folded into neat piles, spread across the remaining bare wooden floor area; a single shadeless bulb illuminated the room, there was no window.

Jay Mac recognised the sparse conditions and empathised with his team mate without saying a single word. Crusher reached into the inside pocket of his Crombie which was draped unceremoniously over the back of his all-purpose piece of bedroom furniture.

"Have a look at this Jay Mac, tell us what yer think." he said, passing his friend a small box covered in black felt. Already beginning to have a sinking feeling in his stomach, when Jay Mac opened the tiny presentation box and saw the simple, thin ring with its centrally positioned solitary faux diamond, he knew instantly things could only end badly for his naïve team mate.

"Crusher lad, I don't wanna piss on yer parade but tell me this is an early Christmas present for yer Ma, or some bird I've never met who doesn't happen to live on this shit-hole of an estate."

His team mate was crestfallen, he closed the little box and placed it into the inside pocket of his denim jacket then led them from his 'cell' along the lobby to the front door. As they stepped out from the dingy flat into the illuminated chamber of the landing, Crusher spoke once more, "I thought you'd understand Jay Mac but yer don't. Do me a favour, don't fuckin' mention this to anyone. I'm gonna speak to Molly next time I see 'er and tell 'er I'll stand by 'er, no matter what happened in the past, or who the father is."

Looking directly at his friend, Jay Mac could see that his mind was made up and that any argument would be futile. They walked down the three flights of stone stairs in silence, then made their way from the tenement block towards the bottom row of shops. A small group of Juniors where gathered outside the Heron public house looking in the direction of the bus terminus and chattering excitedly.

"I'll get me Ma's fags an see yer in a minute." Crusher announced lumbering into the newspaper and tobacconist's shop.

"What's happenin' youngsters?" Jay Mac asked on approaching the lively group of prospective members of the Heron crew.

"Haven't yer seen the bus Jay Mac?" an anonymous boy with a crusty, snotty nose asked, pointing towards the immobile green Atlantean, that still had not moved from where Jay Mac and Crusher had alighted a short time earlier.

"Fuck me!" said the Eagle player on arriving alongside the stricken vehicle, having strolled across from where the youths were gathered.

An inspector and a maintenance man from the municipal bus depot were also standing in front of the formerly all green Atlantean, having just completed their joint inspection.

"Well, it can't go out looking like this, we'll have to get your boys onto it straight away Ronnie." the officious inspector announced holding on firmly to his prized clipboard as a badge of his authority.

"Oh no we won't brother." Ronnie replied, "not unless you wanna be payin' time and a half, this is Saturday night yer know? 'Course if yer really want it doin' my lads will oblige tomorrer but that's gonna cost yer double time, brother." the smug union shop steward replied with his arms folded firmly across his puffed up chest.

Across the entire length of each side of the bus and its front and rear, was a continuous warning sprayed in bold black letters, which read, "BARLEY – NO GO FOR DEVO'S DRUGS – FUCK DEVO THE DRUGGIE SHITHOUSE." For added emphasis the Barleycorn sign writers had also included several versions of their chevron logo on every available space.

Jay Mac realised that while the Crown players had been engaged in their scuffle on the upper deck of the immobilised bus, the real action and actual purpose of the ambush had been occurring downstairs, outside the vehicle. It was blatantly obvious to the youth, who was the focus of the Barleys' anger and he smiled with a certain perverse satisfaction, pleased to see that far from having learned their lesson, this major team had risen phoenix-like from the ashes of defeat and were sending a clear message of defiance to the crazed leader of the Crown players.

"Cheeky bastards, wait till Devo hears about this, they're fucked." Weaver shouted angrily as he arrived next to Jay Mac with his sinister Heron co-leader, Macca (G). Both were dressed in three-quarter length leather coats, Fleming's jeans and their Airwair boots, Weaver favouring the black as opposed to the usual red. Jay Mac made no comment other than to acknowledge their presence then made to walk away.

"What's the fuckin' rush Jay Mac? Don't yer wanna talk to us or somethin'?" Macca (G) asked, grinning slyly.

"Alright Macca, don't start gettin' yerself upset, it's not that time of the month is it?" Jay Mac replied smiling equally disingenuously.

"You wanna watch that mouth Jay Mac, remember we're business partners and speakin' of that, I've been wantin' to catch yer for a quick word anyway."

Jay Mac began walking back toward the shops where Crusher had just exited from the tobacconists. Macca (G) followed with Weaver close by.

"'Ey, I haven't finished yet... don't walk off when I'm fuckin' talkin' to yer." Macca (G) called after him.

Weaver had remained silent up to this point but now decided to interject and caught hold of Jay Mac by his right arm. "You 'eard him Jay Mac, listen to what he's got to say, stop actin' like a prick."

Crusher was watching as he stood outside the shop waiting for his friend to return. "What's the problem Weaver," he asked calmly.

"You what? 'Ave you lost yer fuckin' mind fat boy? Don't ever question me, cunt!" Weaver snapped angrily.

Both Jay Mac and Macca (G) quickly intervened, the former not wishing to see his team mate take a possible frenzied beating from the toffee hammer wielding psychopath, the latter because such a beating did not suit his plans, as yet.

"Ok lads, chill the fuck out will yer, we'er all on the same team 'ere." Jay Mac offered.

"Yeah, listen to him the pair of yer. Lookin' at that fuckin' bus, there's gonna be plenty of action for everyone soon enough, when Devo hears about it." Macca (G) advised, smiling.

The tense situation gradually calmed with only a cool atmosphere separating the two potential protagonists.

"I'll just drop off me Ma's fags Jay Mac and then come up to the Eagle with yer, I'll catch yer up." Crusher announced before ambling away towards his block with his mother's vital supplies.

"Goin' the Eagle mate? Me an Weaver might just come with yer; be a change from the Heron." Macca (G) said with a grin, adding, "It'll give us a chance t'talk on the way up there, Jay Mac."

The Eagle player did not reply as all three crossed over from the shops, to join the main central road that bisected the estate into its eastern and western halves. Macca (G) wasted no time and immediately began pressurising his business associate for his remaining supply.

"Come on Jay Mac, y'can see the signs all round yer. Look at that friggin' bus, even the Barleys are on to it. Devo's pushin' his gear all over, if we don't unload our stash now it's gonna be too fuckin' late."

"Macca, I don't wanna talk about this in the fuckin' street, so just leave it an I'll think it over." Jay Mac replied becoming increasingly irritated.

Just as they arrived at the corner of the road where Glynn lived with his mother and uncle, the two Heron leaders stopped walking, with Macca (G) determined to make Jay Mac comply. Crusher was coming up towards them moving more rapidly than his usual ponderous pace. The reason for his animation was also about to arrive from the opposite direction at this accidental rendezvous. Molly 'Skank' Brown, proudly pushing her young progeny, Gary Junior in his small pram at a rapid pace, having seen the object of her desire, Macca (G) standing with the two other Crown players, was almost upon them. She was equally determined to confront the person that she believed was the actual father of her child and make him acknowledge his responsibility.

"Stop fuckin' about Jay Mac, just sell 'im the stuff." Weaver advised, adding his weight to the argument.

"No disrespect Weaver but this has got fuck all to do with you, so leave it will yer." Jay Mac said as calmly as he could, not wishing to unintentionally anger his unpredictable team mate.

"D'yer want me to have a quiet word with Devo? Cos if yer not gonna let me have yer gear, I might as well let him ask yer for it." Macca (G) said with his usual sly smile.

Without thinking of the consequences Jay Mac caught hold of the grinning Heron co-leader by the lapels of his leather coat, shouting "You sneaky cunt, yer really are a piece of shit!"

Macca (G) grasped Jay Mac's wrists with his hands firmly and laughed loudly, "Grow up little boy, there's fuckin' big money t'be made here an you're throwin' it away."

Just then with Crusher and Molly Brown also arrived at the scene, Glynn came out of his house and walked the short distance to where they were standing, intending to remonstrate with them all.

"Hey, keep it down will yer, me mum's tryin' to relax in there." He paused as they turned as one, to look in his direction. "There's decent people livin' round here as well as the likes of you, so move on, take yer noise somewhere else."

Weaver sprang forward, reaching for his toffee hammer as he did. Jay Mac broke away from Macca (G) and quickly stepped in front of Weaver, shouting, "Fuck off Glynn, go back into yer house, now!"

Whilst speaking and acting as a shield for his former team mate, he inadvertently placed his hands upon Weaver. A spontaneous, powerful head butt from the unstable Heron player, cracked the bridge of his nose, releasing a steady flow of scarlet fluid within seconds of the blow landing.

"I've warned yer, never put yer fuckin' hands on me!" Weaver shouted angrily.

Jay Mac placed his right hand over his wounded nose, trying to keep his balance while feeling queasy and unstable. Glynn wisely retired to his house and stood watching for developments in the relative safety of his front doorway.

Before anything further occurred between the angry males, an agitated Molly interrupted, "Gary, why d'yer keep avoidin' me? Look at yer son, why don't yer wanna know yer own child?" she cried desperately.

Macca (G) looked down at the infant whose mop of dark hair was clearly visible, even though partially obscured by his knitted woollen hat, "Looks more like you Crusher." he said, knowingly, being well aware of his Heron crew mate's feelings for the unfortunate female and her offspring. "Yeah, am sure this fuckin' kid's yours mate. We'll soon know if he starts liftin' his friggin' pram over his head, wont we?" he laughed at his own cruel jest, though nobody else appeared to be amused. "C'mon skank, give Crusher a big sloppy kiss, yer know y'want to." the Heron co-leader added, still laughing.

"Eee, no, fuck off will yer Gary, I hate him, y'know I love you, no one else." Molly replied genuinely, without even considering the heavyweight youth's feelings.

Crusher stood rooted to the floor staring down at it, as if the solution to his dilemma was to be found carved into the concrete paving slabs.

"I need some money Gary, babies aren't cheap, they've gorra have stuff an it all costs. Please Gary help us out will yer, please?"

Macca (G) stared once more at the child seated in his small pram, then looked across at the devastated Crusher, "What d'yer think 'Daddy' does your little fella need some cash? Should I help them out?" Then without warning he coughed up a huge globule of phlegm and spat it onto the infant's face, "There y'go, there's a gold watch in there for yer."

As the baby began to cry uncontrollably, Crusher crossed the short distance between him and Macca (G) in an instant, lifted him bodily into the air and ran towards the edge of the kerb with the struggling youth. Nobody intervened, impeded his progress, or assisted the terrified sexual sadist as he now screamed desperately for help. In one powerful movement he launched Macca (G) into the road, directly in the path of the speeding green Atlantean bus that had not long left the municipal depot.

The frantic driver performed his best ever emergency stop bringing the vehicle to a halt in the shortest distance possible but not before the broken body of Macca (G) had passed beneath its heavy wheels. Molly let out such a scream as if her heart had been pierced; Weaver fled the scene immediately, running as fast as he could; Jay Mac tried unsuccessfully to drag Crusher, the leadened hulk, from where he stood as if welded to the ground. Finally, realising the futility of his endeavour, he too ran from the ugly, pathetic tableau, glancing over his shoulder only once to witness the distraught girl violently lashing out at the unmoving, silent strongman.

Glynn finally closed his neatly painted front door and entered the comfortable, well-decorated living room, where his mother lay on the couch, her long winceyette dressing gown pulled tightly around her. She casually glanced away from the rented colour television as the 'clapometer' was registering the audience's response to the final act of the night, a musical muscle man and asked disinterestedly, "What's all the noise outside Daniel, there's nothing wrong is there?" A broadly smiling Glynn replied, "Nothing's wrong mum, *everything's* alright." then added quietly and with grim satisfaction, "Two down, one to go."

Later when Morris 'Crusher' Tierney had been formally arrested and charged with attempted murder, the meagre contents of his pockets were placed into an envelope which was then sealed. Apart from some loose change and his front door keys, the only other item was a small, square, black felt-covered box containing the single stone ring that he had worked hard to buy for the girl whose subsequent, passionate testimony would convince a jury that he was a brutal animal and the only possible verdict could be unanimously... guilty.

Saturday 13th October 1973

On a cold, rainy Saturday night exactly one week since the arrest of the unfortunate Crusher, Jay Mac was sitting in the lounge of the Eagle with a number of the usual crew, including Johno and Brain.

"Looks like you're the strongest player in the Crown Team now, Johno." the partially sighted Brain said tactlessly.

"I don't know about that mate." Johno replied honestly, "but even if it was right, it's still shit on Crusher. Pity he didn't kill that bastard, Macca (G), though."

Jay Mac was only partly listening to their conversation; he too was considering his team mate's fate and whether or not to contact the police to provide a statement which may help to explain the youth's actions. He knew it was against all the rules and established traditions to voluntarily assist the police in their enquiries. When he had broached the subject even tentatively with Weaver earlier that week, his predictable reaction had been explosive.

"Don't you go near those fuckin' bizzies, Jay Mac and don't let me hear anythin' about yer mentionin' my name, or yer dead. I wasn't there an I know fuck all about it, get that straight." Weaver had warned.

Never a Dull Moment 1973 ▪ 231

"I'll get the ale in." Johno announced bringing Jay Mac back to the present then added generously, "Whiskey chasers all round as well, ok lads? I've 'ad a bit of win on the nags, so am feelin' flush."

Jay Mac quickly checked the remaining loose change that he had in the pockets of his oxblood leather jacket then called to his friend, the powerful farm labourer, "Just a bottle of Guinness for me, Johno lad." His funds were almost depleted and despite genuinely making a determined effort to find legitimate employment, daily walking around the huge industrial area that enclosed the Kings Estate on three sides, asking for any menial position, he was without success. The realisation that his situation was becoming increasingly desperate led him to contemplate selling his remaining supply of goods directly himself.

"Brain, I've been meanin' to ask yer somethin'." Jay Mac began, with an ingratiating smile, "Yer know you was gettin' yer gear off Macca (G) and he's out the game now... so, er if yer like... I could probably help yer out."

The lugubrious, visually challenged youth looked at Jay Mac with his one functioning eye and replied, "Nah, yer alright *mate*. I was fuckin' desperate when I asked yer but yer didn't wanna know, did yer?" He took a lengthy drink of his pint making his anxious team mate wait for his concluding words. "Yeah, I don't need Macca (G) or you anymore. I've got meself a regular supplier now an I don't think any fucker's gonna be puttin' him out of business, yer know what I mean?"

Jay Mac said nothing further; he knew exactly where he stood there was no point in pursuing the matter.

Sometime later after finishing his Guinness and whiskey, not possessing sufficient funds to buy another round for his team mates, the youth left them to their drinking and departed from the noisy alehouse. He stepped out into the cold night, the heavy rain of the earlier evening had ceased and the temperature had dropped considerably. Jay Mac turned up the collar of his coat and dug his hands into its pockets.

"Hey I wanna word with you, hold on a minute." a familiar voice ordered angrily.

"What's yer problem Irish, am not in the mood for any shit off you." Jay Mac replied sharply.

Suddenly he was surrounded by Irish, Blue and four members of the Hounds crew.

"It's been you all the fuckin' time, 'asn't it? Yer lyin' cunt." Irish shouted positioning himself directly in front of Jay Mac.

"I don't know what yer talkin' about but yer better get yer ugly face out of my fuckin' way." he said coldly

"Don't act soft I've known yer too long Jay Mac. You're the one who's been sellin' yer poisonous shite all over the estate, with yer partner Macca (G). What are yer gonna do now 'ey with him out the game, start dealin' yerself?" Irish almost spat out his words and Jay Mac knew that there could be no reasoning with his livid team mate in this mood. He was also aware that someone had revealed his business arrangement with the now critically injured, part-paralysed former Heron co-leader. Jay Mac's first thoughts were that it must be a vindictive Brain, though he had no time for further conjecture, as Irish put his right hand on his chest and pushed him backwards.

"Patrick don't do this lad." Jay Mac began but his former school friend was beyond considering any rational argument.

"In the car park now you. I've got me two younger sisters and our Sean to think about, you're not gonna be dealin' to them, so let's have it." Irish was already removing his old, heavily stained Crombie as he spoke, handing it to Blue who was acting as his second.

The word quickly spread back to the noisy, drunken revellers in the dingy pub and they rapidly filed out, some carrying their ale, clutching their pints tightly for fear of spillage and soon formed the obligatory human ring around the potential protagonists.

"'Ere yer are Jay Mac, I'll take yer coat." Johno offered, automatically assuming the second's duties for his Eagle crew mate. Jay Mac passed the now unchallenged Crown Team strong man his leather jacket, then pulled back the yellow sleeves of his blue jumper with the two white stars positioned diagonally on its front.

"Alright Patrick if this is what yer really want, let's do it."

Both youths raised their fists, crouched over and began circling each other watching for the first move and the vital opening that it would reveal; their rapid breathing could be measured by the condensing vapour rising from them both in short sharp bursts.

"Smash his fuckin' face in Irish." Blue shouted from the encircling crowd, causing Jay Mac to make the novice's error of momentarily looking away from his keen-eyed opponent.

A tremendous straight left thudding into his right eye rocked the stunned youth's head backwards as his reward. Two more unanswered blows to the face had him reeling and the disappointed spectators fearing this would be only a brief contest.

"Fuck that Kings twat." the partially sighted Brain called out enjoying this one-sided bout.

Irish required little encouragement, he was enraged yet totally in control of the fight in its opening stages. Grasping hold of the hair on the top of Jay Mac's head, he dragged his face down to meet his rising right knee several times in rapid succession, then keeping him at arm's length but within kicking range, began booting his Eagle crew mate's bloodied countenance from side to side.

Jay Mac was reduced to his knees, barely able to see with rivulets of blood running from several facial wounds. Irish stepped back to admire his work breathing heavily as he wiped his sweat-soaked, bedraggled hair away from his eyes.

"You're fucked Jay Mac and yer know it." he said with a satisfied smile.

Crouching low to the ground trying to get his bearings and clear his spinning head, Jay Mac was far from spent. Leaping like a tightly coiled spring that had suddenly been released, he delivered a powerful thrust kick directly into the unprotected stomach of the over-confident Irish. The impact of the blow expelled the air from his body forcing him to bend forward, just in time to receive a vicious right upper-cut that lifted his jaw violently, snapping his head back. Now it was Jay Mac's turn to unload a flurry of combination punches to his opponent's face and body. The crowd's mood changed accordingly, believing that this could turn out to be an entertaining affair after all, sporting bets were being placed; wagers concluded.

"Go 'ed Jay Mac 'ave that fucker," Johno shouted, closely followed by several others with financial and liquid incentives in mind.

Standing toe-to-toe both combatants exchanged hard blows, grunting and panting as they did. Irish threw a wild head butt intending it to be a coup de gras, hoping to re-open Jay Mac's long-standing nasal injury, so recently the target of Weaver's attack but, in his tired bleary-eyed state he struck the youth on the right cheek bone instead. Jay Mac caught his wavering foe by his unkempt sweat-soaked hair, pulling him towards him in one sharp movement, bringing his own head to bear successfully onto the bridge of Irish's nose. The resounding crack as the cartilage gave way discharging its stream of snot and blood heartened the appreciative crowd; Irish's accurate left cross to Jay Mac's mouth in response spurred them on further.

"That's it lads, yer both doin' great, there's plenty of fight left in the two of yer yet." one of the neutral older males advised before taking a hefty draught of his dark stout.

His assessment, though viewed as a credit to the sparring team mates was incorrect; they were almost exhausted and soon would digress to the less enthralling grappling stage. As Irish threw his arms about Jay Mac hoping to squeeze the remaining air from his burning lungs in a powerful bear hug, the ensnared youth threw a head lock around his neck and began crushing his windpipe with all the strength he could still muster. For several indecisive minutes they staggered about in a spastic dance, dark silhouettes caught sporadically under the yellow beam of one of the few remaining street lamps not yet vandalised.

"Give it up yer fucker." Irish demanded gasping for air, with his blood stained face turning purple as Jay Mac tightened his python's strangle hold upon him, even while he was attempting the same around his enemy's waist.

"Fuck you cunt, am gonna snap yer neck." Jay Mac offered breathlessly in reply. Neither could achieve dominance, both were equally worn and equally determined to continue.

"Right that's enough, break it up." Terry (H) their former school friend and Crown Team senior ordered sensibly, calling for assistance from one of the old guard.

Johno and Blue, the rival 'seconds' also intervened and together all four managed to separate the drained, though still raging, pair. Again the formidable scrapper, Terry (H) brought his wisdom to the fore, pronouncing his judgement which seemed to concur with that of the appreciative spectators.

"You've both 'ad a good go, we'll call it a draw an leave it at that for tonight." He paused, then on sensing the reluctance of both parties to acquiesce, added "Listen to me the pair of yer, shake hands for now an if yer wanna carry on another time, I'll be happy to set it up."

Jay Mac offered his hand to Irish and after a brief moment of hesitation he returned the gesture, shaking hands firmly to signal the formal cessation of hostilities. With the floorshow ended the crowd rapidly dispersed in search of liquid refreshment and salted sustenance; the two adversaries were of similar mind.

In the way that male animals often resolve their differences by resorting to a physical confrontation and then are reconciled almost instantly, so too were the former combatants on this occasion.

"It wasn't a bad go, y'done ok, I almost felt some of yer punches." Irish acknowledged magnanimously.

"That's decent of yer, thanks. Yer didn't do too bad yerself, considerin' yer condition." Jay Mac replied with a grin.

"Listen d'yer both fancy a bit of scran from Mr Li's, cos I'm fuckin' starvin'?" Blue offered generously, trying to redeem himself, conscious of his less than impartial support during the bout.

"Blue, just tell me when aren't yer starvin'? Yer fat fuck." Jay Mac asked cruelly, adding "Anyway if you're payin' am defo loadin' up until I'm fuckin' burstin'."

"Me too." Irish concurred, "A large sausage dinner with extra chips and gravy will be goin' down my neck quick-style, so let's get movin'."

Less than half an hour later, all three were seated on the low wall outside the Golden Diner with Johno and Terry (H); the Hound's crew members having departed as soon as the fight had ended. They were all casually discussing the relative merits of their own choice of meal from Mr Li's popular establishment, in between offering philosophical observations about life in general and particularly that on the estate.

"Yeah, I don't know what the fuck's goin' on with all this drugs shit but if it carries on the way it has been lately, no one's gonna be able to live round 'ere soon." Terry (H) the senior Crown player observed.

Jay Mac was unsure if this comment was directed at him or not and chose to remain silent until Irish stated, "That's what I was talkin' about, we don't need any fucker comin' in 'ere an makin' life worse than it already is, just so they can line their own pockets."

This time Jay Mac felt a slight had been aimed at him and responded, "Irish, look, let's not get started again, yeah? Yer right, I was out of order, I should never have passed on Floyd's gear to Macca (G) but that's all over now. Nothin' else will be comin' here from me, ok?"

"Am not talkin' about you and you're shitty little dealin's right?" Irish paused to light his post-meal cigarette continuing "I mean the big supplier, we all know who I'm goin' on about, he's the fucker who needs to be stopped."

Terry (H) stood up to leave having ensured he had finished every last morsel of his deep fried meal, "Good luck with that one Irish but let me give yer a bit of advice there..." He gestured to Irish to pass him a cigarette which he then proceeded to light from the donor's own glowing smoke, "...keep the fuck away from that mad cunt. I know him better than anyone else, except Tommy (S) and am tellin' yer straight, you cross him and some fucker will end up dead." He strolled away toward the nearby bus terminus, calling back to them with an accompanying hand gesture, "I'm off to see this bird I've been knobbin', so you wankers enjoy yer evenin'.

The boot boy sage had only been gone a few minutes when Little Jane and one of her associates arrived by the shops, opening for their business as all the legitimate vendors, except for Mr Li, had closed for that day.

"Giz some chips lads, go'ed." the leading sales negotiator began.

"Piss off girl, yer too late, we've all finished," Irish replied curtly.

"Giz a ciggie then," she persisted.

"'Ey you, did yer 'ear what he said? Frig off yer little grass." Jay Mac added angrily.

"Eee, I fuckin' hate you Jay Mac. Am made up I told Macca about yer fat arse mate sayin' he was our baby Gary's dad."

Jay Mac looked at the girl dressed in her usual ridiculous outfit, teetering on her tall platform shoes and replied "D'you know what, you are disgustin'. Because of your fuckin' mouth a good lad's gonna get stuck down for a long time."

"Yeah, well I hope so, thee 'orrible fat bastard, our Molly's gonna go to court and make sure he's gonna go down for good." Little Jane responded angrily.

"Piss off yer little bitch!" Jay Mac shouted.

While the brief conversation had been passing between the Eagle players and the young camp follower, Johno and Blue had been studying Little Jane and her friend talking amongst themselves as they did.

"Hold on a minute there Jay Mac." Johno began then addressed the coquettish, giggling girls, "What's on offer tonight?"

"That depends on you and what yer've got." Little Jane replied formally opening the bargaining.

"'Ey girl, don't worry about us, we'ere both broosted an I've just had a little win on the gee-gees, so when yer ready let's have a bit of fun." Johno advised smiling broadly as he did.

"Let's see some cash then?" Little Jane asked pragmatically.

Blue and Johno quickly each drew out a handful of mixed coin and notes from their respective pockets in support of their claim.

Little Jane's eyes lit up and she too smiled, "We're all your's boys, let's go round the back of the shops, come on."

With negotiations completed, the two excited Eagle players strolled away with their arms around Little Jane and her equally provocative colleague. A light drizzle began to fall but appeared unlikely to be sufficient to dampen their ardour.

"D'yer fancy a pint back in the Eagle, Jay Mac?" Irish enquired, rising from his seated position on the low stone wall.

"Nah mate I'm out of cash to be honest, so am gonna get off." Jay Mac announced as he too rose to his feet. "I'll see yer." he added before walking away from the battered, graffiti covered shops to the rear of which a sordid encounter was taking place in its reeking alley.

As Irish crossed the road, turning up the collar of his Crombie against the cold, light rain, a speeding black saloon car coming from the direction of the Eagle pub, screeched to a halt mounting the kerb immediately in front of him. Two males leapt out from the doors on the passenger side of the vehicle both front and back, one of them being the bald headed, dour, monotone Morgo, henchman of the sinister Devo (S). They quickly seized hold of the stunned Irish and bundled him into the rear of the car.

"What the fuck are yer doin?" Jay Mac shouted as he jumped onto the back of Morgo, after running to the scene on hearing the commotion behind him.

Devo's wild captain threw the ill-matched Eagle player from him with ease then proceeded to stamp on his chest as he lay supine on the wet pavement. Reaching inside his black Crombie he deftly withdrew a gleaming meat cleaver from a concealed pocket, that he had attached to the lining and raised it above his head preparing to deliver a vicious blow.

"No Morgo! Leave it!" Devo commanded, stepping out of the black Ford Cortina. "Not now, just give 'im a kickin'."

Morgo, though clearly disappointed, returned his weapon of choice to its special sleeve then set about his task with relish; his heavyweight colleague in the abduction, known as 'Fat Joey,' could not resist joining in and after receiving a nod of approval from Devo, he too enthusiastically took part in the fun.

"You stop now, leave boy alone." Mr Li ordered calmly, though with a deadly seriousness.

Both males ceased as suddenly as they had started and stepped away from their bloodied victim as if stunned by the sheer audacity of this cold, firm instruction.

"D'you want somethin' mate? Can I help yer with a problem yer've got?" Devo shouted across the road to the unmoving, impassive Chinese warrior standing in the doorway of his shop, wearing his white apron and holding his own gleaming cleaver in the firm grip of his strong right hand. Though no further words passed from his lips an unseen resonance seemed to emanate from the enigmatic aura that surrounded him, conveying the clearest, unequivocal message to Devo and his cronies.

Morgo and his assistant kicker, Fat Joey, lowered themselves back into their seats within the vehicle, Devo leaned on its rain-spattered shiny roof, looking down at Jay Mac who had risen to a seated position on the floor and addressed his comments to him.

"I've been lookin' for you, yer lyin' little toe-rag." Devo began. "I 'eard yer had a lover's tiff with yer mate 'ere but yer all happy again now, is that right?"

"We're mates Devo, we had a bit of a disagreement but we're still mates." Jay Mac replied honestly.

"That's good lad, very good. I might be wrong but from what people 'ave told me, you two 'ave known each other since school and you know his family well, is that true?" Devo asked smiling slyly. Jay Mac nodded in reply. "Great stuff, cos unless you really want 'is Ma to start gettin' bits of 'im through the fuckin' post, you're gonna turn up at the Unicorn tomorrer night with *everythin'* that was in that last package you never delivered to Floyd." He stopped momentarily then spat onto the seated youth. "You tried to fuck me over, nobody does that to me, nobody. So get this straight, you bring the goods to me or I send slices of yer mate to his family, until there's nothin' left of 'im. Remember, I was a butcher's apprentice, I know how to cut meat an I'll make his pain last a long time." He lowered himself back into the vehicle, wound down the window and shouted, "Twenty-four hours from now, I'll be seein' yer!" The driver spun the dark car in a sharp noisy u-turn then raced up the main central road, away in the direction of the Unicorn.

Jay Mac rose to his feet watching as the speeding black Cortina disappeared from view. The rain had increased in intensity but he was unaware of it. Across the road in the Golden Diner, Mr Li had vacated his sentry position in the doorway that was bathed in the fluorescent tube lighting from within. Apart from a small crew of Juniors who were sheltering in the entrance of the Heron public house, no one else was aware of what had transpired.

"What's been happenin'?" a smiling Blue asked, zipping up his jeans as he emerged from the reeking alley, where Johno 'the big spender' was still being entertained by both girls, "What's all the fuckin' noise about?"

Jay Mac strolled over to him and replied, "Nothin', nothin' at all, just a bit of unfinished business that I've got t'take care of." then he walked away into the dark, rainy night lost in his own thoughts.

Chapter 10

Silver Machine 'the other side of the sky'

Saturday 13th and Sunday 14th October 1973

"It was all Jay Mac's fault, he took Floyd's gear for himself and forced Macca to sell them, even though he wanted to stop when he heard what you said about no drugs on the estate," Molly Brown, the willing messenger of the devious Heron co-leader advised her enthralled listener, Devo (S) during that fateful Saturday afternoon several hours before the kidnap of Irish.

"Go on girl tell me exactly what Macca told yer to say." Devo asked calmly, successfully masking for the moment his growing rage. "Don't miss out anything, yer've no need to be afraid."

"Well he was always sayin' that you were too stupid to catch 'im and that he was gonna get more stuff from where Floyd gorrit, then put you out of business." Molly paused and assumed her well-rehearsed, innocent, naïve young female character, forcing the bitter tears to come forth, then sobbed, "Macca loves me and our baby Gary, an he just wants t'take care of us but that greedy Jay Mac's ruined everythin'. I dunno what we're gonna do for money now." The girl's shoulders rose and fell as she wept, the salty tears staining the front of her thin transparent, white blouse, which already fully revealed her tiny, inadequate black bra beneath. Standing in front of the Crown team leader in her usual ridiculously short skirt, laddered tights and tall platform shoes, she had delivered Macca (G)'s words almost as if she were auditioning for the part of a destitute waif, who had been forced to sell her virtue in order to feed her starving baby, now that her honourable man had been robbed of his ability to support them.

It was exactly what the sexual sadist had planned when, on regaining consciousness almost a week after his near fatal encounter with the speeding bus, he had found the devoted girl sitting by his hospital bedside continuing her constant vigil. With a shattered spine, crushed pelvis and both legs broken, he was almost totally paralysed but still able to communicate his damning lies, ensuring that his first waking thought, the desire for vengeance on Jay Mac, would be fulfilled. Molly had followed his instructions to the letter and after leaving the hospital made her way to the Unicorn public house seeking the crazed Devo. Whilst waiting for his judgement she wrung her hands together in front of her, just at the hem height of her micro-mini skirt.

Devo studied her for a few moments then said "Ok Molly, yer've done well, next time y'see Macca tell him he's got nothin' to worry about, I can see from what yer've told me it was all down to that lyin' cunt Jay Mac, I'll be dealin' with 'im later." He paused and drank his dark rum raising the glass tumbler from the old desk in front of him, seated as he was in the landlord's private office at the rear of the alehouse. "You're not a bad lookin' girl Molly, nice legs, good tits, no need for you to be short of a few bob, yer know what I mean?"

In truth she was not unattractive with her pretty face, shapely legs and trim figure, in another life with some parental guidance or even interest, matters may have been very different but these were not the cards Molly had been dealt, she made the best of those she held.

Molly raised her previously bowed head and looked directly at his grim, scarred countenance, fluttering her heavily mascara laden eyelashes at him and replied with a sweet smile, "Oh yeah, thanks Devo, did yer wanna go yerself? I mean I had to have a few stitches when I had the baby but everything's workin' alright. Or, I could give yer a blow job if yer wanted, or just a toss... whatever yer fancy."

Devo held up his hand signalling for the obliging girl to stop talking, "No thanks Molly, its very kind of yer, I wasn't thinkin' of meself but more the lads in my Unicorn crew, there's a few of them who could do with a good regular servicin'. Yeah, I don't see why we can't do a bit of business *and* pleasure." He paused once more and finished his drink then concluded their deal. "I'll sort yer out with a few bob, so yer'll be ok for a bit of dosh, an if servicin' the whole crew is too much for yer, y'can bring in a couple of yer mates to help out, how's that sound?"

Molly beamed with delight, "Thanks Devo, yer so kind, that'll be great, I won't let yer down. Are yer sure yer don't wanna freebie before I go, I could just suck yer off if yer like?"

Devo looked her up and down once more and replied, "Go on, why not, it'll close the deal better than a hand shake," he said smiling as he casually unzipped his jeans.

Long after midnight, well into the early hours of the next morning, Jay Mac wrestled with his terrible dilemma. Pacing round the small room, sitting on the old couch, or standing completely still in front of the Art Deco mirror, he could find no equitable solution, no peace of mind. Here he was, the coward by nature faced with an unnatural choice; submit to his self-preservation instincts follow the craven path and leave his friend to his fate; or take the diametrically opposed way, act entirely out of character, defy the odds, disregard the danger, be the hero.

In the absence of his usual muse and confident, the now deceased ancient hound, stopping once more in front of the decorative mirror he sought advice from his own enigmatic reflection.

"What d'yer think, forget about Irish, let him suffer, or dive in there, take them all out and go down in a blaze of glory?" He hoped that his evil alter-ego may grin back at him agreeing the gung-ho option but all he saw was a pathetic, indecisive teenager who just wanted to hide away and pretend everything would be alright. Eventually he drifted into a disturbed sleep where even his usual tormenting demons, a race of menacing statues, paled in significance retreating shamefaced from the shadowy, undulating landscape of his fevered brain. The constant driving rain hammered on the large, single pane window throughout the long night.

Sunday 14th October 1973

Sunday morning arrived early with a loud disturbance. His aunt and uncle were already up and about clattering their breakfast bowls and cups in the tiny kitchen, running the noisy tap, allowing the kettle to whistle to its heart's content long after boiling, with the old soldier singing a rude parody above the din, of an antique show tune blaring out from the small transistor radio. They were intending to visit their daughter Margaret and her family, who lived on the opposite side of the city at its southernmost boundary and would be gone all day, not returning until late evening. Their plans and inconsiderate noisy preparations, though untimely waking the exhausted youth from his much needed sleep, suited Jay Mac's own intentions perfectly. He would have the flat entirely to himself, what needed to be done in readiness for his ultimate decision, to face Devo and his crew in order to save his friend, would be carried out without his guardians' knowledge, or interference.

"Roust mach schnell! C'mon lazy arse, gerrup!" his uncle ordered who, having been a prisoner of war and spent a lot of his time in the Black Forest region or Upper Silesia, often lapsed into snippets of the basic German he had acquired during his lengthy captivity. "Yer couldn't lie in bed all day like that if you were in the army, you'd be on a charge thrown in the fuckin' glass house, it's nearly eight o'clock, yer've lost half the day already." he concluded.

"Why, is there only sixteen hours in a day now?" Jay Mac asked, straining a smile.

"No lad there isn't, we haven't been forced into the Common Market yet and had to surrender our national rights to Europe but that'll be comin' if the fuckin Tories get their way." the paradoxical King and Country – socialist advised. "Anyway, the paper's in the kitchen if yer can drag yerself out of yer pit and have some breakfast." He paused, listening to the sound of the lavatory being flushed, "That's it we'll be goin'... now she's got the weight off her chest. I think I'll give it a few minutes before I risk it. We'll be back later tonight, so behave yerself, don't wreck the place, or do anythin' stupid."

A quarter of an hour later his elderly relatives had departed on the first stage of their lengthy bus journey, leaving the youth to his own devices.

The cold grey day passed and by the late afternoon, having carefully considered all his options once again and having dismissed almost all of them but one, Jay Mac began the ritual preparations for the fateful encounter to come. None of his mental speculations had included even the slightest notion of contacting the police, the youth having a deep distrust of this particular agency, both from an inherent working-class, ill-disposed perception and through recent personal experience.

Violent, decisive action was the order of the day; no outside intervention was expected or required. He knew that he had unintentionally brought about the present situation by his own choice of deed and if he ever hoped to become a man, he must resolve it.

Jay Mac studied the mixed contents of the remaining clear plastic bags for one final time, before packing them carefully into his old army surplus bag that he had not used since leaving school and placed it to one side on the seat of the shabby armchair in the corner by the electric fire. Once he had selected his kit, which included his twenty-four inch parallel jeans for a specific reason, he began to get dressed. Switching on the radio and tuning it to the Radio One frequency he turned the volume up to its maximum capacity and was pleased to hear one of his older favourites playing at that moment. With no sound other than The Rolling Stones' *Sympathy for the Devil* filling the small room, once he had completed polishing his gleaming cherry red Airwair to a parade ground finish, he slipped on his damaged Levi's denim jacket with its bleached collar and pocket flaps then stood in front of the mirror suspended over the fireplace. After applying a generous amount of his uncle's sticky white Brylcream paste, he combed his long, dark feather-cut hair away from his forehead and back behind his ears, similar to the older D.A style of the infamous Teddy Boys.

Satisfied with his appearance he sat down onto the couch and armed himself for the inevitable fight. He placed the heavy brass knuckle-duster into one of the inside pockets of his coat, with his Stanley knife in the other, both were intended as red herrings, the youth anticipating that he would be searched at some point. Jay Mac's primary weapon that he hoped would tip the scales in his favour and be the deciding factor in the coming encounter, the fabled Colt Python .357, felt just right in his hand with its reassuring perfectly balanced weight as he slipped back the sliding catch, allowing the six-cylinder chamber to fall open. Carefully he placed a bullet in each precisely bored space then with a quick wrist action, which he had secretly practiced many times since acquiring the piece, he snapped the chamber shut. He rolled up his left trouser leg and using a length of his uncle's adhesive, grey, all-purpose tape, bound the loaded firearm to the inside of his left calf, midway between his knee and boot top, the extra-wide parallel heavy canvas jeans easily accommodated the weapon, totally obscuring it from view. It was a deadly gamble that he would be able to bring it into Devo's presence undetected but it was one that he must take.

Jay Mac checked his overall appearance once more then switched off the radio, replacing its noise with that of the supposed burglar deterrent, the chattering television, left on the light and departed from the small, first floor council flat. Either way he knew there was no turning back now, the die was cast, once he had 'crossed the Rubicon' into Devo's realm, his fate would be sealed.

Having strolled over the road to the remaining wreck of the pre-cast concrete-slab bus shelter, Jay Mac decided he might just as well wait outside rather than within the windowless shell for all the protection it now afforded from the elements. It was a typical mid-October Sunday, late afternoon, with the gloomy, leaden sky painted in English autumn grey as far as the eye could see. The weather was turning colder, everywhere pools of dirty rainwater from the night's torrential downpour lay static, liquid mirrors reflecting the dark, foreboding heavens above.

Suddenly the lazy silence that spanned that certain time between expectant morning and disillusioned evening, with none in too great a hurry to greet the new working week, was rudely shattered by a terrified boy of about thirteen years running for his life, turning the corner nearest to the chip shop. Closely followed by Danny (H) and six of his Anvil crew in hot pursuit, the youth looked as if he would escape unscathed, widening the gap with each stride. Danny (H) was not sprinting at his usual pace Jay Mac noted and as if tiring of the chase in a chilling, prescient portent of what was to come, he raised his right arm in order to fire the air-gun that he was carrying as his new weapon of choice. The solid steel ball-bearing found its target within a split second, cracking painfully into the back of the boy's skull, immediately opening a scarlet flesh wound, crucially causing him to stumble. For a speeding runner that unbalancing assault was fatal, his step faltered betraying him as one foot slipped on a pile of sodden, mixed litter of chip wrappings, newspaper and discarded greasy fare.

Begging for their non-existent mercy, he was quickly surrounded before being dragged back into the convenient opening between the chip shop and the chandlers, where his real torment could begin in earnest. Danny enthusiastically led the punishment beating, as all seven Anvil crew members repeatedly kicked and stamped on the hapless, unfortunate boy.

Jay Mac watched with a casual disinterest, he had seen too many of these assaults and been a victim of a few himself, to be able to produce an emotive response. Two elderly females actually inside the shelter were upset at the incident and annoyed at Jay Mac's lack of intervention.

"Should be ashamed of yerself, young man like you watching a poor child being kicked like a football by a gang of bullies." one of them began, while shuffling her top pallet of false teeth about angrily, as if to emphasise her disgust.

"Hold 'im still!" Danny shouted, then produced his more usual tool, his razor sharp Stanley knife, ready to mark the heavily bleeding 'prey' permanently.

The boy let out an ear-piercing, gut turning scream while the grinning crew leader cut into his face with the scalpel edged blade, deftly employing a surgeon's skill, rendering a perfect deep red capital letter A on both of his cheeks.

"There y'go yer cheeky little fucker, don't come round here again with yer shit." He stepped away from the agonised 'rag doll' to allow his pack to enjoy some further well-earned sport, intending to carry out a little more personal cutting when he had gotten his second wind.

"Alright Danny, busy are yer?" Jay Mac shouted from his position outside the bus shelter.

Distracted from his work, the Anvil leader turned angrily then, on recognising his former deadly enemy, smiled grimly "Alright Jay Mac, how's it goin' lad, haven't seen yer around lately. Hang on I'll be right over, I've nearly finished 'ere." With that he abandoned any further surgical intervention, settling instead for a few rapid, violent kicks to the boy's groin.

"Takin' yer beatings a bit far these days aren't yer lad?" a smiling Jay Mac asked when the Anvil leader joined him by the grey concrete shell.

"No way Jay Mac, he was lucky I let him off because of his age. That cheeky cunt comin' down 'ere from the Brow, tryin' to sell 'is gear outside our alehouse." Danny replied, genuinely believing that his actions had been reasonable.

While they were talking Jay Mac noticed how pale and drawn the usually athletic-looking youth now was, with red blood-shot eyes and a permanently runny nose. "Are yer ill or somethin' Danny, been doin' a bit too much shaggin' or beatin' maybe, cos, no disrespect like but yer look shit."

Danny sniffed heavily drawing the shiny rivulets of mucus back up their parallel paths to his already crusty nose then cleared his throat loudly. "Nah, am sound lad, I just seem to have a fuckin' cold all the time. I'll have to stop havin' a taste of the gear for a bit. Problem is I can't leave it alone, me fuckin' heads all over the place."

Jay Mac suddenly felt an almost nostalgic twinge for the simpler days when it was all about two rival Skinhead gangs fighting each other for a piece of wasteland on the nearby motorway site. "We don't see your boys anymore comin' over for a kick-off, what's happened did we just scare yers off in the end?" he asked still smiling.

"Jay Mac, I'd fuckin' love to lead a team over to the Crown any night and give yous another good kickin' but yer must know the score already, why that can't happen no more." Danny advised expecting the Crown team player to acknowledge the legitimacy of his comments.

"Mate I don't know what the fuck yer talkin' about. Are you sayin' it's all been stopped by someone else? I'm not with yer." Jay Mac replied becoming increasingly curious.

"Fuck me, don't your main boys tell yer anythin' on that shithole? It's all been stopped alright with orders from the top, after Crag and Devo agreed how they're gonna run the north side of the city together and make sure no other fucker sells anythin'."

As Jay Mac was absorbing this revelation his garrulous, former rival continued, "Yeah, it turns out thee met up in Walton, when Crag got stuck down again after the big scrap last year, when we battered yous. Devo had been moved there from Risley to finish his time then he got out early. The only cunt who's stoppin their game is that prick Gazmo from the Barleys, he won't let them onto his ground."

It all suddenly became crystal clear to Jay Mac, finally he understood the real reason for their raid on the John Barleycorn pub; it had nothing to do with enhancing the reputation of the Crown Team but only served as a warning to those who sought to resist the drugs empire-building schemes of the crazed Devo and his equally insane imperialist, Crag.

"D'yer fancy a bit of grass yerself or somethin' stronger?" Danny asked. "I've got a stash am sellin' now from the Anvil, I'll do yer a good price." he added, ever mindful of a possible business opportunity.

"No thanks Danny, it's decent of yer but I don't ever dabble mate, it's just not for me." Jay Mac replied honestly.

"Suit yerself, I've got plenty of happy customers already. Anyway, what's in the bag, looks like yer've got yer own gear already?" Danny asked with an unknowing accuracy.

"Fuck... no, that's just me 'food,' I've got a bit of a job on tonight up at the Unicorn, am probably gonna be there for a bit." the Eagle player replied then quickly changed the subject, noticing his bus had finally appeared on the brow at the top of the road. "What's with the airgun Danny d'yer prefer that to yer knife?"

"Yer've gorra be armed nowadays Jay Mac all my crew 'ave got them, there's some bad fuckers around after yer gear, y'know worra mean? This is just a toy, am after a real shooter, am gonna get me one from the States." He paused and raised his right arm, pretending his hand was a pistol, firing his index finger at a non-specified target in the distance. "Can yer imagine that lad? An American shooter, some of their stuffs like fuckin' canons, yer could really do some damage with one of them Colts mate."

"I hope so Danny, I hope so. See yer around, take it easy." Jay Mac replied with a smile as the green Atlantean arrived at the stop, its folding doors opening with a hiss.

"I'll take it any fuckin' way I can get it. Enjoy yer 'job' Jay Mac, don't work too hard," the Anvil leader called after him as he leapt onto the half-empty vehicle, beginning the first stage of his deadly rescue mission.

"Typical." said one of the elderly ladies, "Kids today, only ever putting themselves first, no bloody thought for anyone else."

On completing the short journey to the Crown Estate, Jay Mac made his way along its lower edge in the direction of the bus terminus close to the Heron pub, intending to travel through the bleak housing development to its southern-most boundary, where the Unicorn was located. A group of Juniors where perched on the low wall outside the eponymous alehouse; on seeing the Eagle player, one of them hurried away up the steps and through the entrance door to the lounge bar.

Weaver emerged a few moments later, pint in hand, and called over to Jay Mac, "Hold on there lad, am comin' with yer."

When he had joined the surprised youth at the terminus stop he continued, "The Juniors told me what happened last night with Irish and Devo. There's no fuckin' way you're gonna pull this off without some help, so when we get there let me do the talkin', you always make things worse with yer fuckin' smart mouth."

Jay Mac feigned a weak protestation but in reality he was pleased that his psychopath team mate would be accompanying him, at least as far as the venue. He doubted that Weaver's diplomatic negotiating skills somehow matched his hammer wielding expertise, or Stanley knife dexterity. Their bus journey was only short, no more than four stops. Nothing was said by either youth as they travelled in silence, absorbed in their own thoughts.

After alighting at the nearest stop to the Unicorn they quickly made their way to the road where it was situated. On approaching the innocuous-looking former eighteenth century coaching house, Jay Mac felt an ice cold wave of fear wash over him, causing an involuntary chill shiver to momentarily seize control of his being. He did not mention his dread feelings to his team mate and they both entered into the well-decorated, relatively plush bar of the public house.

The room was fairly empty with only isolated regulars dotted about sitting at the small circular tables, either alone or in pairs. Those clientele who were in full-time gainful employment tended to do their heavy drinking on a Friday or Saturday night, or both, leaving the early Sunday evening trade composed mostly of lonely old men and those who were without any urgency regarding the coming work day.

"Stay right where y'are, the pair of yer." the dour Morgo instructed, turning from his position at the bar, where he was leaning on the counter nursing a pint of warm mild with his overweight kidnap colleague, Fat Joey, next to him.

"Joey go an get the boss." he ordered, revealing the hierarchy of command as he sent the fair haired, leather coat wearing male in his early twenties away to the lounge. Tony Joe White's version of *Polk Salad Annie* was currently playing on the jukebox and Jay Mac pretended to be casually listening to this popular hit, whilst waiting for the appearance of Devo the team leader.

"Well, well yer've turned up then Jay Mac. Some of the lads won't be too happy, we had a little bet goin' on whether yer'd show or not." Devo paused and took a drink of his large measure of dark rum from the glass tumbler he was holding. "I was right about yer after all, y'do have some guts." He turned his attention towards Weaver, "Now am not sure what's goin' on 'ere, I thought I told Jay Mac not to blab his mouth to anyone but 'ere yer are Weaver. Am I right in thinkin' this fucker's asked you to come with him to help him out?"

"No Devo, I 'eard about what 'appened from some of the Juniors, an I thought maybe I could... er... help t'sort things out like." Weaver offered genuinely.

Devo stared at him intently, scowling as he did, "Hang on, so let's get this fuckin' straight. You, a thick cunt, whose only any use for batterin' people with yer daft little hammer, who gets led round by the nose by a tit like Macca (G), you think you can come into my alehouse and start givin' it loads that yer gonna sort things out."

For the first time ever Jay Mac saw the psychopath falter and blanch as he tried to extricate himself from the mire he had stepped into.

"No... er... I don't mean any disrespect Devo... what I was thinkin' was, er... maybe if Jay Mac gives yer the gear an takes a beatin'... er... y'know like... that could square it... I, er..."

Devo interrupted angrily, "Shut the fuck up knobhead don't say another stupid word. I've always 'ad a lorra time for you Weaver, cos yer've got balls and yer can be useful sometimes. This isn't one of those times." He paused and threw back his drink. "Listen yer welcome t'stay, go in the lounge there 'ave a few pints with some of my crew, ok? But if you say anythin' else or try and get involved in any way, yer'll be endin' up in the same grave this gobshite's already dug for 'imself."

Weaver said no more and meekly walked away from Jay Mac, who was desperately trying to control his nerves.

"Right, time for the fun to begin! Morgo, Joey get a grip on 'im and bring 'im round to my office." Devo ordered and his willing henchmen complied eagerly, seizing hold of the youth by his arms before marching him away from the main bar area.

Just off to the left of the larger room was a smaller adjoining parlour separated only by a doorless, half-wooden, panelled partition, glazed above the dado; the impressive jukebox being positioned with its back to this wall. Jay Mac was led through the opening in the dark wood and frosted glass screen, then stood in front of an incongruous plain fronted, gloss black door, which opened into the rear of the building and the private quarters. Above the door was a sign which read "Office – Private." Ostensibly the domain of the landlord, though he had long since surrendered the use of the pub, offices, upstairs living quarters and, if rumour were to be believed, his much younger wife, for the convenience and pleasure of the team.

Devo produced a ring of keys from inside his denim jacket with its famed back panel insert and opened the shiny black door. "Gerrin shithead." he ordered stepping aside as Jay Mac's escort roughly pushed him into the dark room. After closing the door behind them, Devo flicked a switch bringing a single, shadeless fluorescent tube buzzing into life. Momentarily dazzled by its stark brilliance, when the youth recovered his vision fully he quickly surveyed his new surroundings. The walls were roughly plastered and whitewashed, though there were outbreaks of dark green algal bloom in various places, with black mould in the corners and particularly along the base where they met the old, uneven, cardinal red earthenware tiles. All around the air was chill and smelled strongly of damp.

Beyond where they were presently standing was another chamber, which had clearly been separate at one time but knocked-through to form an additional annexe with internal access. Although this room was shrouded in darkness, Jay Mac could just discern the outline of a desk and a couple of chairs, one of which was occupied by a crumpled figure.

"Still sleepin' hey? Am not surprised, he had a painful night, didn't he, yer dirty bugger." Devo said with an evil grin to the unusually smiling Morgo.

A horrified realisation struck Jay Mac like a violent blow to his stomach as he fully grasped the sickening meaning of Devo's words; he hoped that he had misunderstood him.

"Joey put the light on in there and wake 'Sleeping Ugly' up, he's got company." Devo laughed as he spoke.

Joey did as instructed flicking on another light in the further chamber before pulling a rough, potato sack hood from the head of the startled Irish.

"Well, say 'ello then, yer supposed to be mates aren't yer?" Devo carried on with his cruel jest, much to the amusement of his two grinning henchmen.

Jay Mac looked at his long-time friend sitting slumped on an old wooden chair, with his hands behind him tied to its back, dressed in his pale patchwork jumper, which was now darkened with deep scarlet bloodstains running from his shoulders down across his chest. Though he still wore his Fleming's jeans and heavily scuffed Airwair, his black elasticated half inch braces were hanging down and the flies of his trousers were undone. As Jay Mac struggled to take in the disturbing scene, he could hardly bear to look at the bloody pulp of Irish's unrecognisable face. Glancing away from the upsetting image, he spotted his friend's Crombie laying amidst some crates and boxes which were loosely stored around this claustrophobic room.

Irish tried to open one of his purple-black, swollen eyes and fixed his limited slit of vision onto his friend, mouthing some unintelligible words through his split lips and broken teeth.

Jay Mac spat successfully into Devo's grinning face then shouted, "You fuckin' bastard!" before being punched repeatedly in the stomach by an outraged Morgo, momentarily releasing his grip on the youth. Devo laughed loudly wiping the spittle from his battered, scarred countenance with the back of his right hand.

"Get a grip on 'im Morgo, we're gonna have some real fun with this one, he's really pissed off."

Morgo immediately moved back behind Jay Mac throwing his right arm violently around the youth's neck, whilst simultaneously grasping his left arm at the elbow with his strong, tattooed left hand; Joey stood by Irish waiting for direction.

"What's the fuckin' matter with you Jay Mac?" Devo began, "We've looked after 'im good: got 'im some chips for his tea *and* helped 'im wash them down with half a bottle of whiskey. Ungrateful cunt, threw the lot back up once Morgo got started on 'im." He paused and addressed his next comments directly to his senior player stepping close as he did, to enable him to slap Morgo on the top of his bald head affectionately with his open hand. "Yer like it rough don't yer hey? Yer randy bugger."

Jay Mac looked directly at the grinning team leader and said, "Don't tell me yer a pair of fruits, and we've been gettin' led by a shirt-lifter?"

In an instant Devo produced the razor sharp 'Fritz' and held it firmly against the youth's right cheek, cutting a thin scarlet line as he did.

"Take care shithead, choose yer words carefully, or I'll start with takin' yer fuckin' tongue out."

Irish tried to mumble a suitable response but again it was impossible to tell what he had said.

"Shut that cunt up will yer Joey, he never stops." Devo snapped angrily.

Instantly the heavyweight dark leather-coated Joey drove a powerful punch into the bloodied mush of Irish's face, silencing him once more.

"Right let's have a look in that bag yer holdin'." Devo said, returning to more practical matters, seizing the army surplus canvas bag from the youth. He tipped the contents onto an old wooden desk then sat at the more comfortable swivel chair positioned behind it, where he had been seated when the obliging Molly had 'relieved' him the previous day.

"Good stuff Jay Mac, quality gear, worth a few bob. I'll take all yer've got, no charge of course." he said with a sly grin. "Ok, search the little prick Morgo, enjoy yerself."

Happy to oblige the dour henchman set about his task, leaving no pocket unchecked, running down the outside of the youth's body from armpit to ankle, yet missing the inside of his calves, preferring to concentrate instead on squeezing his testicles painfully.

"'Ere y'are Devo, a knuckle-duster an a Stanley knife, that's it." he announced passing the items to his boss.

"Is that it Jay Mac? Nothin' else, nothin' a bit more useful, somethin' that flash cunt Floyd might have got for 'imself for real protection?" Devo asked, clearly aware that not all of the final package had yet been delivered.

Jay Mac felt ill, he knew that Devo may be insane but he was not stupid, though he replied as calmly as he could, "C'mon Devo I've done what yer asked, yer've had yer fun. Let me get Irish out of here and leave it at that, I won't tell anyone about it and am fuckin' certain he won't wanna be talkin' to anyone either".

"Hey soft lad I know yer won't be talkin' to anyone, don't try to tell me what's gonna happen." Devo replied sharply. "Alright lads, get his denim off then lash this cheeky cunt onto the table. Let's check him over again, properly."

Jay Mac's coat was dragged from him and thrown to the floor before he was roughly tossed supine onto the old wooden table, with Joey holding his shoulders firmly and Morgo grasping his Airwair encased ankles. Devo first examined the distinctive Levi's denim jacket, pausing to admire the LFC scarlet wings on its back across the shoulders.

"I like these Jay Mac, thee'd look good above me Barleycorn flag, I'll 'ave them, thanks." he said, employing 'Fritz' to roughly cut the extensive patch from its prominent position. "I think I've ruined yer denim, lad, but it doesn't matter, you won't be fuckin' needin' it anymore." After putting the 'wings' into his pocket he pulled the youth's jumper up to his chest, revealing only his white t-shirt beneath. Dissatisfied, Devo turned his attention to the lower half of Jay Mac's body. "These Fleming's are the full twenty-fours aren't thee? They're wide fuckers, yer could hide anythin' inside them and no one would ever notice, don't yer think?" he asked rhetorically then dragged up each blue denim trouser leg, with their half-inch bleached white turn-ups, to the knee of the Eagle players right and left leg. "Jackpot!" an elated Devo shouted on finding the powerful handgun taped to the youth's inside left calf. Quickly he sliced through the sticky grey industrial binding and tore the prize painfully from its position, together with a large cluster of hair from Jay Mac's leg. "Fuckin' hell Morgo I ask yer to search some cunt an yer too busy fiddlin' with his balls and dick t'find his real weapon, that's not good mate." he said with a sly grin whilst carefully handling and admiring the gleaming Colt. "Loaded is it Jay Mac, I hope?"

"It's only a fake, I was just gonna scare yer with it, that's all." Jay Mac replied, lying and quickly receiving a hard punch to his already fumbled testicles as his reward.

Devo placed the tip of the four-inch barrel onto the youth's sweating forehead. "It's a fake is it? Let's see what happens when I pull the trigger, hey?"

"Don't Devo for fuck's sake, don't do it. It's real and it's fully loaded." a terrified Jay Mac blurted out in desperation.

Devo stepped away from the table no longer interested in the youth, seduced and mesmerised by the aesthetically pleasing craftsmanship of the lethal piece, its intrinsic appeal divorced from its deadly function. "Trust that flashy bastard Floyd to get somethin' like this for 'imself." he said appreciatively then added casually, "Throw that piece of shit off my table will yers."

Morgo and Joey happily complied and launched Jay Mac unceremoniously onto the hard tiled floor, where he landed next to a stacked pile of wooden crates.

"Alright Fat Joey you can fuck off back into the lounge. I want yer to keep a good eye on that prick Weaver, he's just mad enough to try and do somethin' stupid."

After Joey had left, Morgo moved closer to Jay Mac who had righted himself into a seated position without asking permission.

"Don't you fuckin' move again, unless Devo tells yer." he warned grimly.

Devo was still admiring the weapon, passing it from hand to hand, holding it at arm's length like a child with a new toy.

"He wasn't soft old Floyd, he knew the value of fear and this beaut would put the shits up most people. His problem was he just couldn't resist posing." The grinning leader paused and looked down at Jay Mac. "Yeah, he always played his cards close to his chest but not close enough when he started doin' business with that creepy grass, Macca (G). Floyd told 'im there was a war comin' and that he'd sent for somethin' to make sure he was ready for it. Said it would be arrivin' in his next delivery and we all know where that ended up. So when Macca sent his dirty little cock-suckin' bitch to me yesterday to tell me everythin' I fuckin' *knew* you had it, yer lyin' little shit."

Irish moaned quietly and began to stir again. Morgo moved to forcibly quieten him but Devo interjected. "No, it's alright Morgo lad, I'd prefer 'im to be awake, it's more fun, yer know what I mean?" He turned his attention once more towards Jay Mac still sitting on the floor in front of him. "We've been doin' a lot of talkin' about you lad. Yer mate 'ere tells me yer a no-mark, not much use as a scrapper, is that fair?"

Jay Mac replied, "Depends on the circumstances Devo and how much I need to win."

"Good answer yer little prick. He also tells me yer into American superhero comics, an yer even used to collect them. How sad a cunt are yer?"

Jay Mac smiled and replied, "Not nearly as sad as you Devo."

"Fuckin' hell what's happened 'ere, have yer suddenly grown a pair since yesterday? Don't worry, I'll have them off yer soon enough, when we get started." He paused and looked from one youth to the other. "Irish 'ere has got a family, his Ma and Da and his brothers and sisters, people who would miss 'im. So I've decided to be generous this time and let yer mate go, after I've cut 'im a bit of course. But you, yer little no-mark, you live with yer arl uncle and his missus, yer've got no arl feller and yer Ma's a piss head, no fucker's gonna be missin' you. Its goodbye little Jay Mac, no one's gonna shed a tear for you boy."

The desperate youth suddenly blurted out "I could fuckin' have you Devo, yer shit house."

Morgo immediately booted him hard in the chest, knocking him backwards against a tower of wooden crates.

"Is that right? Yer must be really shittin' yerself t'come up with somethin' like that, I could kill yer with me bare hands if I wanted to, yer nothin'." Devo replied, much amused at Jay Mac's preposterous suggestion.

"Like I just said, depends on the circumstances and how much I've gorra win. So d'yer wanna give it a go, or are yer not that hard without yer fuckin' blade?" Jay Mac offered once again, hoping to delay the inevitable.

Devo stopped smiling "Stand that cunt up and move out the way." he ordered, placing both 'Fritz' the knife and Colt the gun on the wooden table side by side.

Morgo dragged Jay Mac to his feet then stepped away a few paces. Instantly the Eagle player sprang forward, not waiting for any formal signal to commence and thumped his right fist into Devo's battered face; following with two rapid short range punches to his body. The outraged team leader did not even flinch, grabbing hold of the youth by his shoulders and flinging him violently against the nearest wall. He jumped in close, slamming his left knee into Jay Mac's already pained groin then caught him by the hair to ensure the full force of his powerful head-butt arrived at its target, the bridge of the youth's deviated nose. Happy with the rapidly bleeding result, he reverted back to hurling, sending Jay Mac crashing into another stack of crates, bringing him and them down in a painful pile.

Despite being dazed the youth sprang to his feet, grasping one of the crates as he did then smashed it into the oncoming Devo. The grinning madman received the full force of the blow on his raised forearms and ploughed straight through the explosion of wooden shards, to grapple his bloodied opponent once more. In a repeat performance of his earlier devastating head-butt he delivered two more in quick succession, while holding the Eagle player firmly by his hair. Trying desperately to remain conscious and not slip into the pool of darkness that was opening up before him, Jay Mac was playing for time, he knew his life expectancy was being measured in minutes and he was determined to make every second count. The longer the 'entertainment' continued, the longer he stayed alive.

An ebullient Devo was indeed enjoying himself, resorting again to utilising the awesome strength his daily prison workouts and additional banned supplements had developed exponentially, throwing the limp youth from one chamber into the next. Supremely confident as he watched his opponent land painfully on the hard floor, rolling over as he did, Devo paused for a few moments, casually assessing the state of play.

"D'yer know what Jay Mac you're game for a laugh boy, I might not kill yer just yet. I could keep yer strung up in 'ere and use yer for a fuckin' punch bag whenever I fancied an easy workout." He laughed at his own suggestion then turned towards his menacing henchman, "I'm sure you'd like to 'ave him for yer own 'workout' wouldn't yer Morgo, yer dirty bastard."

"Yeah, I could really work up a good sweat on this one." Morgo replied leering and grinning lasciviously.

Devo ran forward swinging a wild reckless boot in the direction of the youth's head but his carelessness cost him the advantage, with Jay Mac catching him by his right ankle then kicking away his left supporting leg. Even as the team leader crashed to the floor the Eagle player leapt upon him, firing on all cylinders delivering a flurry of hard punches to his enemy's head, neck and upper abdomen, drawing some compensatory blood himself. Incensed, Devo spat a mix of bloodied spittle up into Jay Mac's face as the youth straddled him punching for his life.

Again pure strength won the contest and carried the day, with the supine Devo grabbing hold of the youth's waist in a reverse grip before tossing him to one side. Both combatants scrambled to their feet almost at the same instant and began exchanging bone-crunching blows like two punching automatons. Jay Mac could feel the internal blunt trauma as Devo's bricks-of-fists pounded his ribs and kidneys. He jumped backwards a couple of steps momentarily disengaging then sprang forward, producing a tremendous thrust kick catching the wild Devo in his exposed gut, forcing him to falter mid-attack.

Grunting and cursing with rage the Crown leader threw all caution to one side grappling Jay Mac around the waist, lifting him into the air then slamming him bodily onto the floor. It proved to be his coup de gras, the youth, who had been struggling to remain conscious struck his head as he landed and began lapsing from one realm to the next. Devo was upon him instantly and began delivering a bombardment of vicious punches that would each have been knock-out blows, if his opponent had been fully cognisant at the moment of their receipt.

"Is he fuckin' dead Devo?" Morgo asked disappointedly.

Breathing heavily and drenched in sweat despite the chill atmosphere, the triumphant maniac stepped away from the bloodied pulp of the unmoving youth.

"Fuck I enjoyed that." he bellowed after filling his lungs to capacity with the damp air.

"Have yer killed 'im Devo?" Morgo pressed on, "Cos yer said I could 'ave a go at 'im and..."

"Morgo, just shut you're fuckin' trap, right. Remember who's the boss... me!" Devo snapped angrily, adding "Pass me his friggin' jacket now."

Receiving the torn garment he first wiped his blood-stained hands, then his own scarlet face and sweat-soaked, bedraggled, corkscrew hair. After cleansing himself he threw the denim 'towel' down onto Jay Mac's head and upper body; there was still no movement or discernable sign of life. Irish moaned loudly in the chamber behind Devo, where he was tied to the wooden chair. The team leader surveyed the grim scene with a macabre satisfaction and said, "Go and get me a bottle of rum an a couple of glasses and be fucking quick about it, me and this Irish cunt 'ere are gonna have a little wake".

While Morgo was away on his urgent errand Devo relaxed in his comfortable swivel chair behind his 'desk' admiring both of his impressive weapons and the newly acquired stash of narcotics. The days haul and its outcome had exceeded his expectations; he was justly pleased.

"'Ere y'are Devo, yer Woods 100 and two glasses." Morgo announced, re-entering the dank, extended two-chamber room.

"Alright Morgo, leave them on the table then piss off. I'm gonna do a bit of cuttin' on this lad, now that he's back with us an I want some privacy while I'm enjoyin' meself, yer know what I mean?" He began pouring himself a drink of dark rum and also one for his intended victim, Irish, instructing Morgo further as he did. "Get yerself a pint and wait outside the door, I don't wanna be disturbed by anyone. Turn that jukebox up as well, cos it's gonna get fuckin' noisy in 'ere before I've finished."

Morgo left his boss and former cell mate to enjoy his private pleasures, knowing full well the extent of his sickening sadism and what he required to find total satisfaction.

When Morgo had been gone a few minutes, Devo strolled through from the rear chamber and locked the door to his 'office' at the front of the extended room, leaving the keys in the lock after he had done so. Irish was now fully awake and trying desperately to free himself from his bonds, while using his limited vision to observe Devo's movements.

"No need to struggle there, Irish, am gonna cut one of yer hands free so yer can join me in a drink. Cos believe me, yer gonna fuckin' need it." While speaking he leaned down and sliced through the coarse rope that was holding the brutalised youth's left wrist, then poured him a measure of the fine quality rum. "Gerrit down yer lad, it's for yer own good," he said, passing Irish the heavy glass tumbler.

With some difficulty he sipped the warming, deepest amber liquid through his swollen, split lips and damaged teeth.

"No offence but am gonna get started lad, before the mood leaves me." Devo advised holding 'Fritz' out in front of him, watching the play of light along the polished, razor edge of the otherwise dull bladed knife.

"It was all fuckin' bollocks wasn't it?" Jay Mac said softly with some difficulty from his prone position on the floor in the next chamber, having regained consciousness and removed the obstructing denim rag from his damaged, blood-drenched face.

"Fuck me Jay Mac; you can't half take some punishment, yer little shit." Devo replied, delighted at the prospect of having another victim to torment. He walked over to the injured youth, grasped hold of the neck of his blood soaked jumper and dragged him into the rear 'torture' chamber, allowing him to collapse close to his equally battered friend.

"'Ere, 'ave a swig of yer mate's drink, yer'll feel better." Devo said, taking the half-filled tumbler from Irish and physically pouring some of its contents into Jay Mac's blood crusted mouth. "Now, what were yer goin' on about lad?"

"I said you an the Crown Team, it was all bollocks. It was only ever about sellin' fuckin' drugs, nothin' else." Jay Mac forced the words from his lips, again trying to engage Devo to distract him, playing for time.

"Of course it was dickhead. Skinheads, Boot Boys, that's all me arse. I just used the fuckin' lot of yer, I look after number one, nobody else. You should know all about that, from what I've heard yer a bit of a survivor yerself." Devo acknowledged with a sneer.

"Not like you am not, I wouldn't fuck over me team mates, me friends. Yer've even had yer tongue up the arse of Crag the Kings team's top boy, haven't yer?" Jay Mac asked knowingly, struggling to raise himself onto his elbows.

"You 'ave been talkin' to some big mouth cunt, 'avent yer?" Devo replied, "Well it doesn't make any difference now, yer might as well know the lot, you won't be tellin' anyone." He paused, taking a drink of his rum then looked at Irish, "If I do let *you* go an

I ever hear that yer've said anythin' I'll be sendin' Morgo round to pop yer arse again."

Irish kept his head lowered through physical pain and the sheer weight of overwhelming shame that lay upon him.

Devo continued his confession, "Yeah I met Crag in Walton when I got transferred there from Risley to finish me time and we got on real good. He's a businessman just like me, so we decided to forget our differences that's all in the past and move on. Turns out Crag's well connected to some real top players, so he set up a meet and we boxed off how we're gonna control all the north side of the city, for starters anyway." Devo stopped and poured another drink for himself then topped up the tumbler which he was passing between Irish and Jay Mac, "Don't like drinkin' alone, it's bad luck." He motioned to Irish to take a mouthful then he poured some more of the dark liquid into Jay Mac's mouth. "Like I was sayin' these top people 'ad already warned that fuckin' idiot Gazmo not to get in their way but he wouldn't listen an kept stoppin' their dealers from sellin' in the Barleycorn, or anywhere round there. Course thee couldn't have that, so I offered to help 'im get the fuckin' message."

Devo stopped talking to down his own drink and as he sat in his comfortable swivel chair, he glanced at the colourful, mixed collection of lucrative narcotics laid out on his 'desk' close to the deadly weapon. The dull base thump of each new record from the jukebox not far away, was the only other noise that could be heard while he had been talking but in these brief interludes some of the lyrics also became discernable. David Bowie's *Life on Mars* replaced Dave Edmunds *I Hear you Knockin'* during this latest pause, while Devo seemed lost in thought.

An 'amusing' idea had been forming as he had been contemplating his captives' fates. "Still a lorra gear here Jay Mac, no wonder Macca was pissed off with yer. He said yer always kept him short, thought you were havin' a little taste yerself... So were yer dippin' into the stash for a bit of relaxation like?"

"Nah, I wouldn't touch that shite, it only fuck's yer up, yer've only gorra look at the state you're in." Jay Mac answered provocatively, mistakenly believing he had nothing to lose by displaying his defiance.

"That's what I thought yer'd say, yer tit but I don't think that's fair, yer know?" Devo began examining the assortment, selecting a random handful of square blotters and bright orange pills. "Yer've looked after the 'sweetshop' all this time and never tried the 'sweets'. Nah, that's not on, let's see what we can do about that." He rose to his feet and casually strolled over to Jay Mac as he lay propped up on both elbows. Pushing the glistening point of 'Fritz' into the soft skin immediately below Jay Mac's right eye, drawing a spot of blood as he did, he held out his left hand on the palm of which were two colourful squares and an orange pill.

"Right my friend let's give *you* a taste of the medicine, after all if yer've been sellin' it yer should know what it can *really* do. Come 'ed, open yer fuckin' mouth or I'll burst this eyeball right now, don't test me."

Jay Mac knew the sinister team leader was not bluffing and did as instructed receiving all three items at once.

Devo quickly snatched the bottle of rum from the desk top and forced the youth to swallow several mouthfuls in rapid succession, to ensure he had fully ingested the hallucinogenic narcotics.

"This'll be good Irish, watch this little prick, it won't take long with the hit I've just given him." He laughed cruelly, positioning himself behind the seated Irish, 'Fritz' still in hand, placing the half empty bottle back on the edge of the table.

Jay Mac lay down fully, initially experiencing nothing but a vague feeling of nausea, which he decided was a result of his violent beating combined with the enforced rum drinking. He was becoming increasingly aware of his own heartbeat and its quickening pace as the inside of his previously dry mouth lubricated itself with a sudden excess of saliva. Perspiring heavily while lying perfectly still he stared up at the flaking paint-covered ceiling, noticing that it was almost impossible to focus his vision, the fluorescent tube light now unbearable as his pupils dilated rapidly. Soon the emotional anxiety that accompanied these disturbing physical changes ceased, entirely dissipated with a warm sense of well-being and inexplicable calm enveloping him.

A large, mature, dark grey woodlouse fell out from a small hole in the cracked rough plaster, landing close to where the youth lay. Jay Mac casually observed the insect, who for some reason appeared to be moving immeasurably slowly at first then began progressing in rapid staccato bursts, covering great distances so fast that the youth believed he was watching a poorly made stop-frame animation film. Even more curiously whilst making his regular circuits of the room, waving his extensive feelers in front of him, the creature muttered angrily to himself in a foreign language, that

Jay Mac's deluded ear heard as an archaic Slavic dialect, like a badly dubbed episode of *'Tales from Europe'*. Why was he so angry with the world, did he have a legitimate grievance, perhaps someone should ask him; the delirious youth considered this weighty matter applying all the objective rigour of a high court judge, before dismissing it entirely from his expanding mind.

The deafening sound of metallic laughter filled his head, fighting against the insane buzzing of a thousand raging bees who lived in the dazzling brilliance that dominated the upper heavens of the now dimensionless chamber. He raised himself painlessly, floating lightly without substance until he was standing a few inches above the deepest red, gleaming floor, defying gravity. Jay Mac knew he must trace the source of this laughter, it was vital to do so but he did not know why.

Languorously he turned about as if rotating on an invisible axle without the slightest effort, he only had to think of the direction he wished to face and he drifted to that co-ordinate serenely. There it was the source of the harsh, menacing sound, crouching in a corner near a fascinating, richly grained table; a two-headed being that appeared both happy and sad at the same time.

Leaning across Irish's right shoulder the grinning Devo was enjoying this further cruel sport immensely; as he watched the hallucinating youth stagger about now completely under the influence of the mind bending drugs.

"Over 'ere Jay Mac, over 'ere, come on lad." he called watching for his reaction, hoping to see him stumble and fall.

Jay Mac drifted effortlessly towards the fascinating table or perhaps it came to him, he was not quite sure. The X, Y and Z spatial axes of the three-dimensional world no longer obeyed the constraining rules of the rational mind's physics, instead new myriad avenues, highways between dimensions opened before him, across time or abstract from it. He sensed merely by feeling the different coloured auras surrounding the two heads of the creature that beckoned him, it was both elated at his proximity and concerned by his closeness. Something on the living table was of immense power and potential danger, the youth tried to read the two conflicting messages he was receiving simultaneously from the polarised minds.

"Pick up the gun Jay Mac!" Irish managed to call through his damaged mouth.

"Shut the fuck up, or I'll put this blade across yer throat now," Devo warned, panicking as he watched the fumbling Jay Mac feeling across the table's surface like a blind man searching desperately for an item he must locate. "Get away from that, don't touch that yer fucker!" he shouted angrily, a cold fear robbing him of his arrogant confidence, with Jay Mac's fingers closing round the gleaming handgun.

Neither of their verbal impassioned pleas had any effect on the somnambulistic youth, his greatly accentuated hearing was tuning itself to a fabulous new yet familiar sound. Hawkwind's *Silver Machine* began playing on the jukebox in the room beyond the locked office door, a record that he knew well as one of his personal favourites, only now all of his heightened senses were receiving the music as a total perception experience. Looking towards the colourful cluster of glittering jewels laid out across the table's surface, though fearful of the gleaming silver and black crustacean, he knew that he must possess it, lifting it lovingly into the air, holding it at arm's length. Both heads of the crouching being emitted a dread halo as he showed them the magnificent hard shelled specimen.

The very walls began to ripple and undulate as he marvelled at the kaleidoscope of constantly changing geometric patterns; beautiful equations solving and proving all universal problems at once. Becoming increasingly indistinct against the shifting background of brilliant colours, beyond the range of the accepted spectrum, something was happening to the two-headed creature, it rose from its crouching position and began slowly drifting away from him.

"Gerrup Irish, we're gettin' out of 'ere before that fuckin' space cadet squeezes the trigger." Devo ordered cutting the remaining rope bond that held the youth to the chair by his right wrist. He dragged Irish to his feet keeping his own left arm firmly around his neck, with 'Fritz' held in his right hand pressed up against the Eagle player's face. Devo was rightly afraid, standing in front of him was a wildly hallucinating Jay Mac, with no sense of reality remaining, pointing the lethal Colt Python .357 straight at him and his hostage.

Once again rotating effortlessly on his invisible axle the youth followed the creature's movements as best as he could, now succumbing to the sensory bombardment, slipping sideways away through a widening portal in space and time, 'watching himself riding by'. The song, though ended on the jukebox remained ever present, becoming clearer in meaning, perfected through repetition, it was all and everything was it. As a growing insect army began appearing from every nook and cranny and joined in the chorus, like a grotesque of Disney cartoon anthropomorphics, fear and desperation emanating from the slowly moving two-headed being tore through his mantle of euphoria, shrouding him in darkness. He knew in that instant he must kill the creature and focused all his fully expanded senses in its direction, unwittingly squeezing the small hard central leg of the crustacean through a convenient hole in its carapace. At once the heads had become a theatrical mask both comedic and tragic, Yin and Yang, the two-faced Janus seeing all that had passed and all that must come to pass; in Jay Mac's altered perception of reality, to kill one was to kill both. He squeezed the leg again, still nothing happened, there was no sound other than the forever repeating perfect song.

Irish smashed the Woods 100 Old Navy rum bottle, which he had snatched from the edge of the table unknown to the fearful Devo, hard into his battered face, causing him to release his headlock.

Diving to the floor he shouted, "Now Jay Mac... now! Shoot the cunt!"

Even as Devo was sliding his way along the dank walls, clutching his bleeding head wound, Irish's indecipherable words tried desperately to register their meaning in Jay Mac's unreceptive, delusional brain.

Two explosive cannon bursts had already reverberated around the extended cabin, deafening both captive and captor, causing Morgo to pound on the locked door.

"What's happenin' boss is everythin' alright in there?"

To Jay Mac's third-eye vision the double-headed beast had somehow divested itself of one of its heads and all that remained was the dark entity of its total wickedness crawling slowly along the ugly, slimy walls. Jay Mac was crashing as rapidly as he had risen; depression; paranoia and all-consuming fear were upon him; he must destroy the creature even more urgently than he felt before.

Two times again he squeezed the powerful death-dealing, silver and black crustacean in his hands, without effect.

"Fuck off, please... no. Don't do it Jay Mac." Devo pleaded, shaking uncontrollably yet frozen with his back to the wall nearest the door and escape. "I'll let yer's both go, yer can even 'ave the stash, please don't do it..."

Jay Mac's fifth squeeze of the trigger silenced the talking head, exploding its evil facial features and exiting the rear of its misshapen skull in a burst of vibrant colour that spread over a disproportionate area. Finally the insect chorus fell quiet as they watched the creature slip down to the floor, a crumpled lifeless body with a cloven head.

"Devo! Are yer alright? What's goin' on in there?" Morgo shouted becoming increasingly concerned with each new loud boom from within.

Over in the lounge, Fat Joey, who had been assigned to watching Weaver, was also agitated on hearing the same repeated thuds and Morgo's worried verbal reaction. He had completely abandoned his set task, constantly rising from his seat straining to see what was happening beyond the open doorway, waiting for a call to arms from his immediate superior, Morgo.

Weaver too was poised, though sitting apparently relaxed drinking his pint, swapping tales of vicious beatings with a select gathering of the Unicorn crew. The Heron leader had made several trips both to the bar and the toilet, using each to reconnoitre what was occurring in the parlour behind the wooden and glazed screen, observing Morgo's formal guard-duty stance immediately in front of the gloss black office door.

"Devo can yer hear me?" Morgo shouted again now that all was silent then on receiving no reply advised, "I'm comin' in, am gonna put this fuckin' door in."

After two powerful shoulder barges the lock gave, detaching itself from the wooden frame in a burst of sharp splinters. Crashing into the first fluorescent tube-lit chamber Morgo froze with horror, unable to bear the sight of Devo's lifeless, slumped body and parted skull, his scarlet bathed faced only recognisable from the eyes downward. He howled in rage and pain a cry that was as equally filled with grief as Molly Brown's had been for the object of her love also. Drawing his gleaming meat cleaver from within his Crombie, he charged forward intent on killing Jay Mac who was standing blankly in the far room, with his arm still raised, hand holding the smoking gun as damning evidence.

"Fuck off and die yer rapist cunt!" Irish shouted as he sprang up from his crouching position, plunging the well-used combat knife into his abuser's groin.

So intent had Morgo been, so consumed with an overpowering desire to avenge his former cell mate, his only comfort through those long, dark nights, he had not even looked about him or considered the presence of the waiting Irish. He fell to his knees clutching at his vitals with the now ownerless 'Fritz', whom Irish had recovered when Devo dropped 'him' clattering to the floor, sunk almost to the knuckle-duster hilt into his privates most recently in action against his self-same assailant. Already on his feet even though he was still groggy from his own violent assault, Irish booted Morgo's agonised face time and again, unleashing a torrent of vengeful anger that empowered his tired legs, carrying on until his muscles ached and he was spent.

"Come on Jay Mac get this on mate!" he shouted, having stepped away from the collapsed Morgo with his bloody pulp of a face and unceremoniously dragging Devo's prized denim jacket from him to pass to his uncontrollably shivering friend. After retrieving his own filthy Crombie from the floor beneath the tumult of crates that had formed above it, when Jay Mac had been hurled into their previously neat stacks, he carefully prized the warm hand gun from his friend's clutching fingers and led him by the wrist to the open doorway.

This was Joey's moment, he would show 'the Boss' just how useful he could be he thought, darting over to the parlour determined to prove he was the equal of Morgo, rather than his subordinate. The remaining Unicorn players looked up curiously as he left the room in such haste but carried on with their drinking unconcerned when Weaver observed "Fuckin' hell, he must be dyin' for a shite, the speed of 'im, I thought he'd been blowin' off for a bit." He quickly swigged the last of his pint and rose to his feet, "Ok lads, I'm off, I'll see yers again."

Arriving at the scene of the action Joey shouted "Where d'yer think you're goin'?" on seeing Irish emerge first through the office doorway, followed closely by Jay Mac in tow. Before the startled Irish could bring the ultimate weapon into play, he was tackled round the waist and fell crashing to the ground with the Unicorn heavyweight on top of him.

Joey's moment of triumph was short lived with Weaver hammering the back of his meaty head using his primary tool, before wrenching him to one side. Even as the hopeful Unicorn lieutenant was rolled onto his back, Weaver stamped on his face and carried on after all resistance had faded.

"Irish, what the fuck's goin' on? What's happened to him? He looks totally stoned." Weaver asked, assisting Irish to his feet, adding "Where did that come from? Shit! What 'ave I missed?"

"Behind yer Weaver, look out!" Irish warned, not an instant too soon as Weaver's former drinking companions arrived as an angry eight-man posse, less than pleased at seeing their senior 'officer' having his head kicked in.

It was Irish's turn to become the saviour of all three, calmly raising the gleaming highly polished-steel finish firearm to shoulder level declaring, "Move the fuck out the way. This gun's fully loaded so only two of you shitbags even stand a chance of gettin' out of here alive."

Wisely they chose to believe his lie even though a few of them recalled hearing at least four, if not five loud booms previously.

Cautiously without taking their gaze from their stunned rivals, Irish and Weaver led the temporarily 'blind' Jay Mac out from the warm, stuffy pub into the cold, refreshing air of the night.

Why the two strangely familiar grey figures were helping him escape from the chamber of evil and death, he had no idea, deprived of his extra-sensory powers they had no auras around them for him to read. Faith was all that he could rely on now, in the end he reasoned that was all anyone really had.

Shortly after the escape of the three Crown team mates, the landlord stepped into his private office for the first time in a long while. He looked unmoved, without the slightest pity at the blood-drenched corpse of the sinister Devo, who for so long had been nothing but a plague in his life. On completing a cursory examination of the damage to his stock he quickly exited the dank, forbidding room. The wounded Morgo was nowhere to be seen. Pulling the broken door shut after him he despaired of attempting a makeshift repair to the lock and splintered frame, instead he secured it as best he could for the moment wedging it tightly shut then made his way upstairs to his repossessed living quarters. He had an urgent telephone call to make; it wasn't to the police or to call for an ambulance.

"Yeah, that's right... he's moved on... no he won't be comin' back... decided to go home for good... Yer'll send someone round will yer, to settle his bill? Thanks, I'll look forward to that." He hung up the receiver and smiled; another first in recent memory.

Chapter 11

Streets of Laredo

Sunday 14th, Friday 19th October and Saturday 3rd November 1973

Harsh words, raised voices mixed with genuine concern and relief, greeted the safe return of the battered Irish to his family. Jay Mac was admitted also being in a similar state, though less probing questions were directed at him. Mrs O'Hare wanted all the facts, every detail, she would leave no stone unturned until the youths' assailants were all identified and brought to justice, persisting in her relentless search for the truth.

"Patrick, I need the names of those boys who attacked you and John... now. I won't sleep 'til they're behind bars and they've thrown away the key."

"Ma, I've told yer a dozen times, me and Jay Mac was walkin' down from the Unicorn and a gang of rough lads jumped us from behind in the dark, we didn't see their faces and thee forgot to tell us their names, ok?" Irish replied as best he could while having his facial injuries swabbed with cotton wool soaked in T.C.P liquid antiseptic.

"Don't you start with y'cheek to me, or I'll give yer a worse hidin'." his mother replied carrying on with her home nursing, liberally applying a selection of strong smelling unctions.

Mr O'Hare, a giant of an Irishman, possessing a shock of steel-grey hair and shovels for hands, having run away to sea at a ridiculously young age and served on Arctic convoys to Murmansk and Archangel during the War as a youth, viewed their injuries as nothing serious applying the old adage 'worse things happen at sea'. He was, however, concerned about one vital aspect of their recent confrontation.

"I'm hopin' that, judgin' by the state of the two of yer, yer gave a good account of yerselves and those other fellers will be after lookin' a lot worse, like thee've done a few rounds with the great John L. Sullivan himself." He casually lit another Capstan full-strength cigarette from the dying embers of his current smoke, ensuring there was no accidental gap when his lungs may be filled with nicotine-less air.

"Are yer alright there John? Yer lookin' a bit lost, don't let it get yer down, if yer took a beatin from those boyos, as long as yer know yer did yer best and yer've left yer mark on them, that's all that matters."

"Thanks Mr O'Hare, that's great. I'm sure one of them's gonna have a hell of a headache when he wakes up." he replied trying to force a weak smile, which was about as difficult as gathering his thoughts, whilst struggling to retrieve any memories of what actually happened.

"I think yer's both need t'go to the hospital straight away, I'm goin' t'call an ambulance. God knows what's happened t'yer insides, yer could both be bleedin' to death for all we know". Mrs O'Hare was becoming more agitated by the minute and her husband decided there was only one way to calm her worried mind.

"Right, there's no need for all that, woman. The boys have had a bit of a set-too with some other boys that's all but I tell yer what I'll do to stop yer fussin' I'll pay for a taxi to take them t'Walton Hospital to be checked over, how's that? Is that good enough? Or d'yer want a letter from the Pope himself t'satisfy yer?"

Mrs O'Hare smiled smugly, folded her arms deciding not to reply as she had achieved her objective. A short time later both injured youths were dispatched in the luxury of a black cab in the direction of the nearest hospital.

"Yer can let me out 'ere mate, thanks." Jay Mac said after less than a couple of minutes when they reached the lower edge of the estate.

"Are yer sure lad, yer don't look too good and the woman who rang said to run the both of yer to the 'ossie." the more than usually concerned taxi driver asked, not wishing to be on the receiving end of a verbal rebuke from the formidable Mrs O'Hare for not following her explicit instructions to the letter.

"Am fine mate, just pull up 'ere by the bus stop." Jay Mac insisted, adding before exiting the cab, "See yer later in the week Irish."

His sullen friend did not reply. He wanted to forget the events of the past twenty-four hours as soon as possible; erase them from his memory totally. Seeing Jay Mac or anyone else from their crew ever again was the furthest thought from his tortured mind. He was trying desperately though unsuccessfully to shut out the horrific, visceral images, with accompanying smells and sounds, of Morgo's brutal assault upon him from his own mental cinema screen. Jay

Mac's actions were the cause of what happened to him and although in part mitigation, Irish accepted his fellow Eagle player had surrendered himself into Devo's cruel clutches in a foolhardy attempt to rescue him, he knew he would always blame his longtime friend. He stayed silent for the rest of the short journey to the hospital and would remain so for a long time to come.

When Jay Mac eventually boarded his bus back to the Kings Estate the few other passengers travelling through the cold October night made certain they avoided his gaze, fearing he was a wild, drunken thug. With his battered, swollen countenance covered in cuts, bruises and ill-fitting sticking plasters, wearing his filthy, blood-stained clothing and scuffed boots, no one could blame them for averting their eyes finding an interesting mark on the floor or window that required close observation instead.

Sitting on the rear seat alone enjoying the warmth seeping through from the engine, he could feel the hard metallic form of the deadly weapon tucked into the back of his Fleming's jeans, concealed by Devo's prized denim jacket. He smiled with grim satisfaction and relief that for the moment, his dilemma was resolved and the nightmare ended.

Though his aunt was awake and reading one of her usual crime novels whilst finishing her final cigarette of the day when he entered the small council flat, Jay Mac managed to remove his newly acquired coat concealing the handgun within it and hide them both in the hall cupboard filled with other redundant items.

"What's happened to your face?" she asked without looking up from her book.

"I was playin' footie with a few of the lads and there was a clash of heads, that's all." Jay Mac replied quickly.

"Yeah is that right? And I was born yesterday." She paused and extinguished her cigarette then added "I'm off t'bed, I hope whatever you've really been doing tonight you've not brought any more trouble to this door."

Jay Mac decided it was wiser not to reply, hoping that his blurred recollections of the missing segment of the evening were false, or trouble must surely be preparing to kick in that same door.

For the next five days Jay Mac remained under voluntary lockdown, only leaving the small flat to register at the Benefit Office on his signing day, the Thursday of that week. Whilst there his facial injuries attracted little attention from the other 'customers' although the over-zealous clerk wanted to know if he had acquired his cuts and bruises during an undeclared period of paid employment.

"I fell over from exhaustion walkin' round an round the industrial estate lookin' for work, ok?" was his curt reply to this suspicious civil servant's enquiry.

Apart from this brief excursion he had spent the majority of his time studying the local newspaper daily, for any reference to a violent crime occurring in or near the Unicorn public house. Surprisingly there was not even the slightest mention of any gang-related activity, let alone the fatal shooting of a known felon and team leader. By the afternoon of Friday, experiencing a degree of cabin fever and having not had a visit from the police, Jay Mac was feeling confident enough to contemplate leaving his bolt hole.

"See I told yer I hadn't been in any trouble." he called to his aunt arrogantly, pulling on his leather jacket preparing to leave under the cover of the early evening's darkness.

"Oh... right, so is that why you've been hiding in here all week is it?" she replied cynically while clearing away the dinner plates and other crockery.

After quickly giving his sufficiently restored cherry red Airwair a final wipe with the soft polish-stained cloth he always carried, he set off to catch his bus to the Crown Estate. The temperature outside was already falling rapidly with the clear moonless sky promising a sharp frost to come.

"Alright there Jay Mac, how's it goin'?" a friendly anonymous male in his late thirties enquired, casually leaning against a battered white van.

"Yeah, sound mate. Do I... er know you?" the youth replied, studying the male's thick-set features in hope of recognition.

"No, but we know you boy, we just wanted t'be sure." another deep voice called from behind.

As Jay Mac turned to look over his shoulder the first male struck him a powerful blow to his stomach, causing him to bend double in spasm.

A rough sacking hood was pulled over his head and his hands were cuffed behind his back, before he was forcibly bundled into the rear of the vehicle then driven away at top speed, the breaks screeching as they rounded the corner of the near deserted road.

Lying on the cold metal floor of the van, with head covered and arms restricted, Jay Mac was straining his senses to pick up any clue that might indicate who had abducted him, for once he hoped he was in the clutches of the police. Apart from the strong smell of petrol and oily rags, there was nothing specific that he could use to potentially identify his captors, one of whom had jumped into the rear with him acting as a silent guard.

Rolling onto his side Jay Mac decided to test the water, "There's no need for all this yer know, if yer'd just asked I'd 'ave come with yer to the station, no fuss."

"Shut yer fuckin' mouth you." was the angry response accompanied by a swift, hard kick to his stomach.

'Nothing so far to rule out the police then' he thought, though wisely keeping his views to himself.

For the remainder of the uncomfortable half hour journey both he and his travelling companion remained silent. Eventually after turning a tight corner sharply the vehicle rumbled over an uneven surface for some distance, transferring each bump vibrating painfully up from the worn suspension directly to the hard floor of the van's interior. Suddenly they came to an abrupt halt, sliding the captive youth up against a wheel arch which was being used as a makeshift seat by his guard.

"Right, c'mon shithead out yer go." he instructed, opening the double doors before pushing Jay Mac with his feet towards the exit.

Strong hands roughly grasped him by the shoulders and he was dragged out then dropped onto the damp, stone cobbles of the old back alley. Lying there for a few moments, while the vehicle was secured and his two escorts prepared to pull him to his feet, visually hampered as he was the youth sensed a certain familiarity with his present surroundings. He knew he was somewhere in the original Victorian heart of the city, in a back entry, the like of which had been one of his main play areas as a child. Quickly he was raised to his feet and marched at rapid pace in through a rear door way, across a rough flagstone yard then into a small damp-smelling room.

Thrown onto a wooden chair he could just discern through the heavy gauge, loose weave of the coarse sacking 'hood' that a single light bulb was providing the only illumination and two heavy-set male silhouettes revealed both his original captors were still present.

"Ok knobhead let's get started." his travelling companion began. "Real name, John Mack, is that right?"

The youth confirmed he was correct.

"Why did yer shoot Sean Devlin last Sunday night?"

"I don't know anyone of that name." he replied, instantly receiving a hard punch to the side of his hooded face.

"Try again, why did you kill Sean Devlin on the evening of Sunday the fourteenth?" the questioner persisted, receiving only the same response from Jay Mac.

The second interrogator took over, "What do yer know about the drug dealings of Francis Lloyd?"

"I know I need to speak to a solicitor, that's all." he replied beginning to believe he was actually in police custody.

A violent punch to his aching stomach again did nothing to alter his assumption.

"Where does Francis Lloyd get his supply from, give us the name of the alehouse?" questioner number one continued.

"Mate, if I knew what yous were talkin' about, I'd tell yers, I can stand anythin' but pain." Jay Mac replied.

Another heavy dig to the face followed immediately. On and on for close to an hour Jay Mac was subjected to relentless questioning accompanied by verbal and physical abuse. Finally after being thrown from his chair for the dozenth time and repeatedly kicked about the head, body and legs the interrogation stopped as suddenly as it had started. He was lifted back into his seated position onto the chair and his handcuffs removed, leading him to immediately rub his aching, chaffed wrists.

"Keep fuckin' still you or the cuffs go straight back on and don't even think of touchin' that hood, right?" inquisitor number one ordered angrily.

Jay Mac sat perfectly still letting his arms dangle at his sides, waiting for further developments. A door to his right-hand side opened admitting three more large silhouetted males and a strong smell of alcohol at the same time. 'I'm in the back of an alehouse am sure, I don't think these *are* bizzies, unless this is one of their own boozers.' he concluded, though not uttering a sound as the three new arrivals stood in an arc directly in front of him.

For a few moments there was only a chill silence hanging in the damp air, making Jay Mac very uneasy.

"Well John, yer've caused us a few problems haven't yer wee man?" a familiar deep male voice with a distinct Liverpool-Irish accent asked. At the same time the improvised hood was pulled off the youth's head and thrown to the floor. Jay Mac looked up blinking, trying to regain his clarity of vision in the glaring brightness of the shadeless bulb. Standing above him were three of his cousins; Niall, Francis and Tommy Mack part of a thirteen-strong army of violent siblings and leaders of the notorious Gerard Boys. Immaculately dressed as usual, in sharp tailored suits of blue or dark grey material with a certain sheen, narrow silk ties adorned with thin gold bar clips or diamond studs and expensive Italian leather shoes, they were a formidable trio and were not to be tested.

"Come through to our office John, unless yer want t'stay here in the storeroom with all the crates," Niall the elder brother offered.

Jay Mac did not reply, pleased to be leaving a room that was all too similar to the torture chamber at the rear of the Unicorn.

Once they were all seated in a small adjoining office with Niall behind a dark wooden desk, Francis and Tommy sitting on a distressed leather settee and Jay Mac in a matching arm chair, Francis the next eldest began a less painful interrogation, offering some background information as his preamble.

"Look John yer might as well know that Sean Devlin was workin' for us and we know either you or yer mate shot the crazy fucker dead." He paused to watch for Jay Mac's reaction then continued, "Yer probably had yer reasons but yer can't just go round shootin' our boys whenever yer don't get on with them."

"No disrespect Francis but as far as I know he's the only person I've ever shot and to be honest, I don't even remember doin' it." Jay Mac replied genuinely.

"Fuck! Yer a cool one, I'll give yer that John." Tommy the youngest sibling began, "Yer blow a young feller's head off an yer don't even remember, that's cold boy."

"Yeah, the fact that he'd forced me to swaller a handful of hard core drugs, so that I was off me face, might 'ave somethin' to do with it." Jay Mac offered.

Niall took over the interview, "Right John that might explain why y'pair of tits ran off and left the stash behind but we've still had to clear up yer fuckin' mess."

"Sorry about that Niall, like I said under other circumstances I would've took care of that meself." Jay Mac announced, insuring he couched his words carefully.

"No need t'worry about that, we've sent him on a little trip down the river that he won't be comin' back from." Francis advised smiling.

"He never was much of a swimmer, young Devo and those new concrete boots we fitted him with, well they can't have helped.

So it was lucky for him he was already departed when we dropped him in." Tommy added, also smiling.

Francis followed on, "Sure he's servin' some useful purpose now though, standin' at the bottom of the fuckin' Mersey like a big stick of fish food." They all laughed at the very idea, visualising the crazed former Crown Team leader being nibbled away until nothing but an angry skeleton remained.

Niall restored order, pressing on with the serious business of Jay Mac's indebtedness to their operation, "Yer see John, yer've cost us a key player, someone we recruited an was trainin' for a management position. Yer in our debt, yer owe us and we can't have that," he said menacingly.

Francis added "But here's the thing... yer family, yer blood. Yer should've come to us when yer first had y'problem with Devo but yer didn't, so what are we gonna do with yer?"

Before Jay Mac could even begin to reply, Tommy interjected "Well like Francis says, yer family and families sort their own problems. Yer gonna work for us now until yer've paid off yer debt.

Niall continued the proposal, "Ay, an when yer've done that yer'll still be doin' jobs for us whenever we need yer. Remember what's been said, yer blood and only blood can separate us." He paused allowing Jay Mac to fully absorb the meaning of his words.

"Ok, so now that we're all clear yer've no need t'worry, yer gonna be goin' away on a business trip, all expenses paid." Francis expanded, providing the actual details. "Yer always used to be readin' those daft Yank comics when y'were a kid, didn't yer John?" he pressed on without waiting for a reply, "Well now yer gonna get the chance t'buy as many as yer like, while yer over there in the States yerself."

Jay Mac was intrigued and momentarily uplifted.

"Yer'll be travellin' over by boat, a fuckin' big boat, alright, into New York then gettin' the train up to Chicago where yer'll be meetin' some of our business partners. They'll be tellin' yer what yer'll be doin' next so yer don't need t'know any more, just in case the wrong people should get hold of yer, yer won't have anythin' t'tell them."

"I'm not a grass Francis, I wouldn't tell the bizzies anythin'." Jay Mac blurted out angrily.

Tommy held up his hand as if to strike the youth but refrained, "Calm down wee man, we know yer not a fuckin' grass or yer'd be standin' next to young Devo right now. We're not talkin' about the bizzies, they're the least of yer worries."

Niall decided it was time to conclude their meeting, "Alright John, we've laid our cards on the table; we've been straight with yer. What's it gonna be, are yer gonna do the right thing and pay yer debt without fuckin' about, or do we have t'find another way of settlin' the score?"

Jay Mac, the pragmatist, the born survivor knew there was only one possible answer, "I'm in Niall, thanks for givin' me the chance to sort things out. I won't let yer down."

"Well then its jars out, come through to the bar, we'll have a little celebration drink," Niall replied with a broad smile as he slapped Jay Mac with his heavy hand on the back, a gesture repeated by Francis and Tommy also.

"Hey, Liam get that fuckin' jukebox turned up and get somethin' decent on, New York, New York or My Kinda Town, for starters, we're havin' a party, not a fuckin' wake," Niall ordered leading Jay Mac through the open doorway of their 'office' and into the bar of another anonymous drinking den, that they had recently acquired for their expanding portfolio. On entering the stifling, cigarette-smoke filled room where several of their similarly attired cronies were already gathered, Francis and Tommy joined this crew and amused themselves, while Niall sat with the youth ready to continue his informal interview.

Even as the drink flowed and the false convivial atmosphere was shared by the seemingly happy participants, wearing their fixed grin masks at all times, Jay Mac was considering how he could best exploit the fortuitous elements of his new business association and ultimately extricate himself from it. He decided he would do as directed for the time being, making sure that he aroused no one's suspicions then when the opportune moment arrived he would disappear into the vastness that comprised the Fifty States of North America.

Jay Mac knew exactly where he was going, a circuit he had long planned in his dreams. Heading out west he would visit South and North Dakota, cross into Montana then down to Wyoming. After he had enjoyed living the cowboy life in those northern regions, his southbound route would bring him to Arizona then east to New Mexico, finally arriving in the Lone Star State itself, Texas. Walking the streets of Laredo having long since traded his former Skinhead-Boot Boy denim uniform for another of similar material, though cut in the traditional, local style, he would finally swap his gleaming red Airwair for a pair of hand-tooled cowboy boots. Finding work as a ranch hand or on the rigs of the vast, expansive oil fields, he would disappear off the radar of anyone trying to find him, becoming that archetypical, anonymous, enigmatic figure of a thousand Western films and novels, the man with the hidden past.

"Are yer alright there John? Thinkin' about the States I'll bet." Niall asked perceptively.

"Yeah, I was Niall; it's a fuckin' big country." Jay Mac replied, disturbed from his mental speculations.

"It is a grand big place, sure enough, a feller could easily get lost there, if he wasn't careful." He paused to take a drink of his Guinness "but you don't need to worry about that. Yer see our business friends over there, well, they're part of an even bigger family they've got relatives all over the fuckin' place. So, if yer ever did get lost they'd *soon* find yer."

Jay Mac looked at his elder cousin as if he were a psychic, replying, "That's good to know Niall, I'll remember that."

His smiling relative quickly changed the subject, as if hoping to catch the youth off guard, "So what did yer do with the shooter anyway?"

Jay Mac smiled in return, "That's a good question Niall, like I said before I can't really remember what 'appened that night. I think I must've lashed it in the river that runs through the farmer's old field; I know I haven't got it now."

Niall looked at him sceptically, "More's the pity, yer'll need a reliable weapon when yer over there f'yer own good. Anyway not t'worry, our friends will sort yer out with somethin' suitable easy enough."

Jay Mac thanked him and his cousin moved on again, "Did yer happen t'remember the name of that alehouse where yer friend Floyd got his gear from?"

"No, sorry Niall I don't. I only went there once with him and it was all a blur, I had other things on me mind." Jay Mac replied, recalling his encounter with the obliging 'Sweet Sally'.

"I know what yer mean John, that Sherman, he's a fuckin' big lad alright and one scary cunt." He finished the dregs of his pint motioning to Liam the barman to refresh their round, continuing casually, "it was The Seafarer by the way, Floyd was a lot more talkative when we spoke to him. He gave them all up, I think he was worried about his arl feller, with him bein' in the Polis and comin' up for retirement, not too good havin' a son whose a drug dealer when yer a bizzie."

At that opportune moment Jay Mac's two abductors entered the bar, dressed in dark blue mechanic's overalls and approached their table.

"Alright boss, the van's loaded and the rest of the lads are all 'ere." the driver advised.

"Isn't that grand, I was just talkin' about the very thing." He called over once more to Liam, "Give these two fellers a measure of the good stuff before thee go."

The barman did as instructed filling two tumblers to the brim from a new bottle of Jameson's Irish whiskey.

"Slainte boys!" Niall said raising his own glass, "Make sure it's a full house before yer start, we wouldn't want t'miss anybody."

Dean Martin's *I'd Cry Like a Baby* was playing on the jukebox as the two overall wearers downed their drinks then departed on their mission.

Niall returned to outlining Jay Mac's forthcoming duties. "Ok young feller, let's make sure yer know what yer doin' we don't want any misunderstandin' do we?"

"Am all ears Niall, just tell us what yer want me to do." Jay Mac replied.

For the next half hour the senior Gerard Boy revealed and reiterated the precise arrangements for the assignment that had already clearly been set in place, in anticipation of Jay Mac's recruitment. Niall was thorough in the extreme, emphasising to the youth the deadly serious nature of their Trans-Atlantic business and that of their American partners.

"Don't even think of crossin' these fellers, no fucker ever gets away from them, ever." He paused once again letting the enormity of his words be fully absorbed. "Right here's a set of keys to the cases that'll be waitin' for yer at Southampton docks, with your name on them, so that's yer 'luggage' taken care of. Remember yer never open those cases unless yer forced to, what's inside is none of your business. Just bring a bag with a change of clothes, yer won't need anythin' else." He passed Jay Mac a large brown envelope adding, "All yer paperwork's in here, don't fuckin' lose any of it. Yer've got about two weeks till yer off, so keep yer head down, no more playin' with yer little boot boy friends and no gettin' pulled by the fuckin' bizzies, right?" He paused again to drink a mouthful of his favourite whiskey chaser then concluded their meeting. "No point in yer hangin' round 'ere then, we're done. Yer better get back t'yer shitty estate and make the most of it, yer won't be seein' it for much longer."

Niall offered his hand to Jay Mac before he left. As they shook he brought the full pressure of his mighty paw to bear in a bone-crunching grip, "Don't fuck this up John, there's more of us in you than that gobshite of a father yer never saw, remember that... Sliante!"

Jay Mac returned the salutation as he finished his own drink then left the dingy alehouse carrying his precious envelope and the keys to his mysterious luggage.

Saturday 27th October 1973

In the week that followed Jay Mac's successful employment 'interview' for a position in his relatives' family-run business, he had adhered to Niall, the 'senior partner's' friendly advice of having no contact with his usual associates. He spent most of the time by memorising the very specific directions for the different stages of his business trip and examining his few travel documents, including 'his' passport which obligingly contained a black and white photograph of the youngest Mack sibling Daniel, or 'Danny Boy' as he was known, who conveniently bore an uncanny resemblance to the Crown team player.

The first part of his journey would be straightforward he thought; all he was required to do was ensure that he boarded the 07:00 hours train from Liverpool Lime Street to London Euston then continue on the underground to Waterloo Station and board another train to Southampton. On arriving at the docks he would be met by a 'friend' who would provide him with further instructions, additional documents and the all-important luggage. Niall, though vague about the nature of the sailing vessel, other than referring to it as a 'fuckin' big boat' and the duration at sea, had been very clear regarding what he must do on disembarking in New York city.

"Make yer way t'Penn Station; wear yer Liverpool FC scarf and don't fuckin' leave that place until yer man contacts yer."

It appeared that this Manhattan local would supply Jay Mac with the remainder of his travel documentation, for the final stage of his journey to Chicago by train but only if he could answer two very specific questions about Liverpool and Everton 'soccer' clubs. The first being the reasoning behind why the gathering place for

Liverpool's most vocal supporters at their ground was named the 'Kop' and the second related to the origin of the 'Toffee Shop' or 'Tower' proudly borne as Everton Football Club's distinctive badge. Both were simple questions with the answers being that the former was named after a famous hillside battle of the Boer War, the Spion Kop and the latter originating from an eighteenth century lock-up, a landmark feature on Everton Brow known locally as 'Prince Rupert's Tower'.

Obvious as they were to any genuine 'Scouser', they were sufficiently obscure for anyone else to randomly produce the correct answers, yet innocuous enough not to arouse suspicion if asked in error, Niall boxed clever in his open simplicity.

Once again by the Saturday evening of his latest week-long self-imposed exile from the Crown Estate, Jay Mac had decided that another visit to see his team mates and tie up any loose ends could not potentially jeopardise his forthcoming mission.

Even as he strolled along the lower edge of the estate in the light, cold drizzle that was steadily falling, approaching Weaver's tenement block, he could see the dangerous psychopath haranguing a small gathering of Heron Juniors, standing in the ever-empty car park of the eponymous alehouse. Almost all uniformly dressed in white bib-and-brace overalls or white Baker's trousers and black Airwair, some having silver crescent moons or stars hand painted on them, this next generation of hopeful Crown team players seemed oblivious to the worsening weather conditions and were listening intently to Weaver's impassioned words.

"So, are we gonna let everyone think we're fuckin' finished, just cos we've lost a few players?" Without waiting for a response he pressed on, "No we're not; startin' tonight we're gonna remind every fucker we're the Heron crew. Make sure yer all tooled up, cos when we get over there into the Kings Team ground, we're gonna do some fuckin' damage, alright?" There were a few cheers but not sufficient for the new demagogue. "What's that? I can't hear yer, I said we're gonna get into that Kings crew over there in the field, settin' up their friggin' bonfires and beat the shit outer them, yeah?" This time he received the spontaneous response that he demanded and turned towards the waiting Jay Mac, actually smiling broadly for once.

"What d'yer think of that hey? Am the leader of this fuckin' crew now and we're gonna start buildin' that rep all over.

Everyone's gonna know about Weaver and the Heron crew, everyone."

"Yeah, it was a good speech mate, reminded me of Devo before we went off to the Barleys." Jay Mac replied honestly.

"Good, cos that's who I'm gonna be, the next Devo. I'm gonna start with the Kings Team then do Ravenshall. I might even go after the Barleys meself, when I've got a full crew," Weaver advised looking around at his woefully inadequate forces, none of whom were aged older than sixteen, with no senior players to be seen amongst them.

"Yer just in time Jay Mac to join us, we could do with you on board, come 'ed."

"Nah, thanks all the same but I've just come t'give yer these back and then am goin' for a couple of pints in the Eagle." He passed Weaver the heavy brass knuckle duster and the Stanley knife that he had loaned him previously, adding, "I'm... er... goin' away for a bit... goin' down South for some work... so I won't..."

Weaver interrupted him mid-sentence, "What are yer tellin' me for, I don't give a fuck what yer do?"

"Yeah, ok Weaver yer right, I just wanted t'say thanks for steppin' in that night up at the Unicorn, yer know." Jay Mac said genuinely.

"'Ey, before yer start cryin' get this straight, I got the chance to twat 'Fat Joey' from the Unicorn, that was all, nothin' else, see yer." With that he turned away preparing to lead his troops into a disastrous action, were a number of the novice cadets would be reduced to tears in their agony and pain, on being captured by their experienced Kings Team rivals.

Jay Mac watched them as they marched away around the far corner of the public house and off alongside the burned out garages below the towering, grey concrete, high-rise flats, looking like school children dressed in a bizarre, utilitarian uniform being led by a toffee hammer wielding, mad man of a teacher, about to learn a brutal lesson. He turned up the collar of his leather jacket and continued on his planned route intending to stop next at Glynn's neatly painted house, hoping to convince him that one final drink with the old crew would be of no harm.

A few minutes later he knocked on the gloss painted front door of the small residence that Glynn shared with his mother and Bristolian Uncle Ken. It was this relative who happened to answer the door to the Eagle player, "Oh it's you is it? Well Daniel doesn't want any trouble thanks, so I'll tell him you called." he announced, preparing to close the door.

Jay Mac wedged his boot in the opening, dropping his usual pleasant tone as he did, "Listen mate, I just wanna quick word, nothin' else, right? So do the honours will yer?"

"Who's at the door Ken, is there a problem? Tell them to go away," Mrs Glynn called nervously from within.

"It's alright; it's just that thug who used to bother Daniel. I'm going to call the police if he doesn't go away immediately."

At that moment an angry Glynn sprang down the stairs, "Alright Ken, you go back in now, I'll deal with this."

When the middle-aged Bristolian had shuffled away in his tartan slippers back to the living room, Glynn pulled the door open fully, leaning out aggressively towards his former team mate, "What's happened Jay Mac, lost yer way? Yer usually brown-nosin' down at the Heron aren't yer with yer rapist mates?"

"'Ey Glynn, wind yer fuckin' neck in will yer. Like I tried to tell yer uncle knobhead, I only wanted a few words with yer, ok?" Jay Mac replied sharply.

"Yeah is that right? Make it quick then, I happen to have a life." Glynn retorted.

"Listen, I'm finished 'ere now, no more Crown Boot Boys or any other shite. Next weekend am off down South doin' a bit of work and I won't be back for some time. I wondered if yer'd fancy havin' a few pints tonight, that's all." Jay Mac offered.

Glynn did not reply for several minutes as he considered what Jay Mac had told him. "Alright I'll have a drink with yer but not tonight and not in the Eagle. If yer fancy it, we'll have a bevvy in town before yer go, not this shit-hole." he proposed, now seeming more like his former self.

"That's ace mate; I'm on me way t'see Blue and Irish, so if they're up for it, we'll have a final session round town next weekend, yeah?" Jay Mac replied smiling.

"Alright mate I'll see yer next Saturday, give us a knock about eight o'clock." Glynn responded before closing the brightly painted, shiny front door.

Pleased with the outcome Jay Mac continued on his way, heading next for Blue's home. Minutes later having received no response at his corpulent team mate's residence, he quickly marched on through the driving rain to that of Irish, located further along the same road.

"What are yer doin' knockin' on my door, what the fuck d'yer want?" Irish asked angrily after opening his worn, paint-chipped front door to Jay Mac

"C'mon mate don't start, I just wanted to 'ave a quick word. How are yer anyway?" Jay Mac asked.

"How am I, what d'yer think." Irish snapped.

"Listen, I know it was bad what 'appened to yer but..." Jay Mac stopped talking as his furious, long-time friend interrupted.

"Yer know it was bad, what happened to me, that's fuckin' big of yer." He paused, exasperated, almost spitting his words. "A fuckin' queer had me held down... after five years of escapin' from all those sick bastards in the 'Cardinals', this time there was nowhere t'run, nowhere t'hide..." Irish stood silent except for the sound of his rapid breathing.

In the uncomfortable space between them Jay Mac had no words to offer knowing anything he said would be of no comfort, instead he quietly replied, "I'm goin' away... er... don't think I'll be comin' back for some time... if ever, t'be honest."

Irish stared blankly into the distance beyond, the silver rain pouring down turning orange as it was caught momentarily in the random light from the blinking streetlamp struggling to do its duty, despite being vandalised.

"Yer goin' away and probably won't be back? That's the best fuckin' news I've heard in a long time, at least one of us is gonna gerrout of this shit-hole. Just make sure yer never come back."

"I can't see that happenin'. Anyway, I only called round to ask if yer fancied a few beers in town next Saturday night. I've already asked Glynn an he's up for it, am just goin' over to the Eagle t'see if Blue's there. What d'yer say?" Jay Mac asked hopefully.

"Alright why not it might do me some good, I haven't been out of 'ere since... Yeah, yeah knock for us when yer've got Glynn and Blue an we'll gerroff into town, see yer." Irish replied seeming more amenable than of late.

Once again, though paradoxically cheered by the final result yet chastened by their disturbing conversation, Jay Mac darted past the shops and ran across the road to complete his mission, hoping to find Blue and a warmer welcome in the Eagle.

"Look out it's Jay Mac, watch what yer say, he might shoot yer." the ever chirpy, always inappropriate Blue called out as the youth entered through the swing door, into the stuffy, noisy lounge bringing the cold night air with him temporarily rending the grey-smoke veil.

Jay Mac ordered two bottles of Guinness; collected these and a pint glass from the bar then joined Blue who was sitting with: Terry (H); Johno; Brain and the two Ants.

"Alright lads, what's happenin'?" he enquired rhetorically wedging in between Blue and Terry (H). "What was that yer were sayin Blue, a funny line? Fuckin' hell who helped yer think that one up?"

"That's what they're all sayin', you shot Devo." Blue insisted, though less vocally than before.

"Who are *'they'*?" Jay Mac enquired.

"Fat Joey from the Unicorn, that's who." Blue advised, adding, "Not me though, am not sayin' that."

"Well Fat Joey better watch his fuckin' mouth or he could be next." Jay Mac warned feigning anger, continuing, "Anyway I 'eard Devo got off on holiday an won't be comin' back."

"Did yer Jay Mac, who told yer that?" Blue the gullible asked.

"Devo told me 'imself." Jay Mac answered.

"When did he tell yer that?" Blue asked, his curiosity fully aroused.

"Just before I shot 'im." Jay Mac announced with a smile, raising his right hand, pointing his index finger at Blue's head then snapping his erect thumb down.

"Bang! Just like that Blue."

They all laughed, though Blue more nervously than the rest.

Changing the subject quickly on noticing a distinct lack of background music, Jay Mac asked, "What's 'appened in 'ere, it's sadder than a witch's tit?"

"No fuckin' jukebox, its packed in. Some cunt's been messin' with it." Terry (H) advised utterly disheartened.

"That'll be Blue, so he can get a chance t'perform." Jay Mac said grinning, "Go 'ed Blue, nip 'ome an get yer pianer."

"What pianer, I haven't got one?" Blue asked naively.

"Oh sorry mate I forgot, yer more of a wind instrument aren't yer, always blowin' tunes out yer arse." Jay Mac responded, delivering his coup de gras.

Again they all laughed and the initial less-than-welcoming atmosphere altered appreciably.

As the evening wore on the crew were in good humour though Brain, once again deprived of his regular supply, was clearly depressed and out of sorts. When the opportunity occurred, Jay Mac leaned over to him and said, "Ey Brain, you look fucked without yer gear from Devo. Yer should've took me offer when yer had the chance, too fuckin' late now." A disconsolate Brain did not reply leading Jay Mac to continue, "Don't worry lad, there's bound t'be another fuckin' bloodsucker feedin' off pricks like you any day soon."

The desperate Brain actually looked relieved, cheered by the ugly truth of these cruel words.

Turning back to Blue on his immediate right, Jay Mac decided to risk telling his garrulous friend of the arrangements for the following weekend. "Listen Blue, just for once keep this t'yerself, can yer do that?"

"Of course I can Jay Mac, yer know me." Blue replied.

"Yeah I do, that's the fuckin' problem. 'Ere's the thing, am goin' away next Sunday mornin' so Irish, Glynn an me are goin' out on the town Saturday night. D'yer fancy it, just the four of us havin' a few ales and a bit of craic?" Jay Mac asked, addressing his question directly to his team mate.

"Yeah, that'll be fuckin' ace mate. Thee arl crew on the piss in town an yer know what the birds are like for me. Nice one Jay Mac and don't worry I'll keep it shut." Blue replied, genuinely pleased, already conjuring up mental images of his three favourite things: girls, booze and food, though not necessarily in that order depending on his immediate needs.

Jay Mac too was pleased the evening had gone as planned eventually and he looked forward to his final night in Liverpool's lively city centre.

Saturday 3rd November 1973

'TWO DIE IN PUB HORROR FIRE - POLICE SUSPECT ARSON' The *Liverpool Echo* broadsheet had declared the day after the burning down of The Seafarer public house in the south end of the city and the finding of the charred bodies of two unnamed individuals by fire-fighters. Jay Mac had read the accompanying brief article with growing horror, though it contained little factual detail only lurid speculation concerning possible gang involvement. He removed the clipping from the newspaper and several other subsequent stories during the following weeks, keeping them inside

an old military history journal as a macabre scrapbook of the unfolding tale.

Now while he was preparing to leave for his planned final drinking session with his friends, Jay Mac stopped what he was doing in order to scrutinise the latest instalment, in the evening paper his uncle had just passed to him saying "Look at this, the police reckon that alehouse fire was done deliberate. Some bastards locked the front doors and wouldn't let anyone out after they'd started it on purpose; two poor sods got roasted alive." He paused to take a lengthy, considered draw of his glowing, old briar pipe, "What's this bloody city comin' to? Eyewitnesses say thee was only young fellers in their early thirties who done it, bastards." he concluded.

The youth read every detail of the article line by line, how there had been a desperate struggle to escape, with violent thugs assaulting victims at the rear of the old public house as they fled into the yard. One young male regular, who did not wish to be named, described as a skilled martial artist, had apparently given a good account of himself and police were looking for several midthirties males with significant facial injuries and possible broken limbs. The identities of the two fatalities were not yet disclosed, though they were described as a large heavy-set Jamaican male and his female partner, both were said to be well-respected figures of the local community. Jay Mac already knew his cousins were violent men not to be crossed but this latest action, which he also knew they were fully responsible for, confirmed his existing view of them and reinforced his determination that once he reached America, he would escape from their clutches at the first opportunity.

"Alright am gettin' off now." the youth announced pulling on his old Crombie over Devo's famous prized denim jacket, which he had scrubbed several times to remove the deceased Crown team leader's blood stains.

"Right, ok, we'll be gone t'bed by the time you come back, so we won't see you before y'go, with yer gettin' off early." his aunt advised, adding as her parting words, "It's for the best, try to make a new start down south. Let us know how y'get on." She returned to re-reading her 'latest' crime thriller, opening a new packet of Embassy filter-tipped cigarettes, preparing for the long evening.

"'Ey, yer never were much use here, hanging round with all those gobshites. I wouldn't bother comin' back if I was you." his old soldier uncle advised sucking loudly on his pipe. "Try and keep out of trouble wherever yer end up lad." He shook hands with the youth signalling their goodbye had been formally acknowledged.

After leaving a plain, dark blue sports bag in the tiny hall containing his few travelling items and a change of clothes, he left the small council flat, intending to return briefly in the early hours of the morning, before setting off on his lengthy business trip.

On arriving on the Crown estate his first stop was at Glynn's neatly decorated residence. It was a bitterly cold, absolutely still, early November night with the acrid smell of burning wood and other flammable items filling the crisp air, announcing the premature start of Bonfire Night celebrations by some of the Juniors.

"'Ere y'are, an early Christmas present for yer but don't open it till the day." Jay Mac said passing Glynn a cereal box roughly wrapped in distinctive Liverpool Echo Sports newspaper, secured with copious amounts of sticky tape.

"Nicely wrapped mate." Glynn observed sarcastically.

"Yeah, I thought so, the pink matches yer eyes." Jay Mac replied.

"Fuck, what's in it, half a brick?" Glynn asked, feeling the weight of the rectangular package.

"Thanks Glynn, yer've ruined the surprise. Anyway keep 'old of it, it might come in useful some day." Jay Mac responded closing the matter.

Glynn took the 'gift' to his room hiding it under his bed, before both youths made their way to the houses of Blue and Irish.

Though the ever-chirpy Blue was ready, primed, doused in Brut aftershave, wearing his latest expensive leather coat and keen to be off, the dour, taciturn Irish was having second thoughts, requiring some coaxing to remove him from the security of his comfortable home.

"Come on Irish, last time ever, into town, a few beers, might even get lucky." Jay Mac tried.

"Yeah, come 'ed mate, yer've got me with yer, in me best kit, so the birds will be all over us." Blue advised, only part in jest.

"Irish, I wouldn't have bothered meself but its defo the last time so c'mon, yer might even enjoy yerself." Glynn attempted, taking the more practical approach.

Finally after sufficient encouragement and cajoling Irish pulled on his filthy old Crombie, lit a cigarette and joined them on their way to the nearby bus stop. With his dirty, scuffed, black Airwair contrasting starkly with Jay Mac's gleaming cherry-red version and his equally distressed Crombie also appearing the exact opposite of his team mate's pristine item, they looked an incongruous pair. When placed alongside Blue and Glynn who were both wearing similar smart dark leather coats, Oxford bag trousers and platform shoes, the quartet presented an eclectic mix of contemporary youth fashion, both the old and the new.

Within an hour of leaving the bleak housing estate, all four where comfortably ensconced in the relatively plush surroundings of the Mansion, having already commenced their evening's drinking in the Harp public house, one of their original favourite haunts. Now all legally allowed to drink having attained eighteen years of age, the challenge of trying to get served in different alehouses without being refused had entirely dissipated, leaving one pint in the Harp, a notorious underage drinking establishment sufficient for their purposes.

Sitting in the crowded bar enjoying studying the various female forms on display, the four youths began to relax and Jay Mac decided to reveal more of his travel plans.

"Am goin' a bit further than just down south, about three thousand miles further, to the West." he advised.

"What, yer goin' to China?" the geographically challenged Blue asked.

"West for fuck's sake Blue, not East. I'm goin' to the States" Jay Mac replied for the benefit of them all.

"That's a hell of a way t'go lookin' for work, whose payin' for yer trip?" Irish asked curiously.

"Er... it's me cousins, I'm er... workin' for them now." Jay Mac replied waiting for Irish's response.

"Are yer fuckin' mad? The Gerard Boys? Shit! Yer really 'ave sold yer soul to the devil this time." his long-time friend concluded.

"Are they the ones we met last year in that alehouse on London Road, with the flash suits an all the gold rings; cos they looked like bad cunts?" Blue asked, recalling their encounter of the previous summer.

"How did yer come to be workin' for them?" Glynn asked.

"It was all very sudden like, thee can be very persuasive." Jay Mac replied not wishing to add any further detail.

Irish, however pressed on, his perceptive curiosity aroused. "So this all came about since the night Devo got wasted, am I right?" He didn't wait for a reply pausing only to drink some of his pint, "Cos t'me that says the two things are related, as if Devo was connected to yer fuckin' cousins in some way. Don't tell me they're the ones behind the whole thing, the fuckin' Gerard Boys are the real big suppliers?" Irish has been raising his voice throughout his conjecturing, causing several older male drinkers nearby to turn and look in their direction.

Jay Mac was aware of their angry gaze, "Irish for fuck's sake keep it down mate." he urged his irate team mate, adding, "I'm sayin' no more, drop it ok?"

The convivial atmosphere chilled a few degrees requiring several rounds of drink, including whiskey chasers to resume its ambient temperature. Eventually they drifted out from the Mansion then continued along Lime Street to the States Bar, their next port of call intent on an amusing session of 'drunk watching.'

Though the small one-room bar was filled almost to capacity, leaving the four hopeful students of human behaviour forced to stand at the crowded bar, no one emerged from the zombie ranks of dead-eyed drinkers to perform for their entertainment.

"What's 'appened t'these fuckers? The borin' bastards." Irish demanded indignantly, as if he had paid good money for the anticipated floor show.

"They're either too fuckin' drunk or not drunk enough." Jay Mac concluded.

"Hang on." said Blue, passing their pints of Newcastle Brown Ale to them, this being one of the few other establishments where this popular tipple was readily available. He strolled over to the jukebox and began searching for something suitable to entice the undead from their other world dreaming. "There y'go a couple of decent tunes should bring them to life." he announced as the first of his selection loaded onto the turntable. Bobby Bloom's *Montego Bay*, a firm favourite with their original Skinhead team, began to play and the four Crown team mates watched for any signs of animation.

"Ey Jay Mac, did yer ever see that bird again that yer was always fuckin' goin' on about?" Glynn asked randomly.

"Yeah, sort of. I ran into her, or into her cousin's house in the summer, by accident really." Jay Mac replied.

"So what's the score, I thought she was the bird for you?" Glynn continued.

"Oh yeah, no doubt about it, she's fuckin' stunnin' mate." Jay Mac stated.

"Well how come yer not seein' her then?" Blue enquired.

Before Jay Mac could reply, Irish interjected "Cos she doesn't want to know a crazy Boot Boy who's runnin' around with a team of arseholes."

"Fuck off Irish." Jay Mac snapped, "That's were yer wrong see. I've even got her phone number here with me."

"Give her a fuckin' ring then if yer that sure she wants to know yer, ask her to meet yer in town... tonight." Irish suggested grinning slyly.

"I will mate, I will." Jay Mac stated emphatically, having fully committed himself, exactly as Irish has planned.

"'Ey, there's a payphone at the other end of the bar, by the bogs. I've got some change if yer need it." Blue offered, enjoying Jay Mac's awkward predicament.

"Thanks Blue, I thought yer might, yer little cunt." the ensnared youth replied, taking a handful of ten pence pieces from his grinning team mate.

Jay Mac made his way through the throng of dedicated, professional drinkers then with pounding heart dialled the number on the precious scrap of paper that he always carried in his wallet.

A few minutes later he returned to his three smiling companions, who were eagerly awaiting a full report.

"What's happenin' is she on her way?" Blue began.

"She's already 'ere mate." Jay Mac replied gloomily, "'Er Ma answered, told me she was out with her boyfriend in town and then warned me not t'ring again."

His friends all laughed, with Irish stating "I told yer a bird like that wouldn't wanna know you."

Just then Blue's third selection began to play with impeccable timing, *What Becomes of the Broken Hearted* by Jimmy Ruffin. Although Blue's accidental choice may have caused the crestfallen Jay Mac some discomfort, it appeared to be a crowd pleaser.

A solitary, toothless old crone, whose drink and cigarette ravaged features belied her actual age, took to the floor, her tatty grey, heavily stained cardigan flailing about as she gyrated in a rapid twist fashion, completely out of time with the slow tempo of the song. Stumbling several times on her old white stiletto shoes worn with skin-tight grimy once-blue jeans, turned up to mid-calf revealing a generous portion of dark stubbled leg above her loose black socks, initially she was without a partner. Fortunately a gallant regular known to everyone as J.J. a large, fat, bald-headed male, who shuffled about in a filthy pair of split Converse All Stars, stale urine-patinated, dark grey, crimplene slacks and wrapped in a foul smelling gabardine raincoat over a yellowed granddad shirt, came to her rescue. Soon both discordant dancers, though initially a respectable distance apart, joined in a passionate, romantic embrace which quickly degenerated into a stomach-turning, noisy, open-mouthed, tongue assisted kiss.

"Fuck! Am gonna puke." said Glynn.

"Shit! Why did I put this record on?" a horrified Blue announced.

"Eyesight mate, it's over rated." Jay Mac decided.

"Piss off, the lot of yer. Leave them alone, they're not doin' any harm." Irish concluded.

"Yer won't be sayin' that when he gets his cock out." Jay Mac warned, covering his eyes with his free hand.

Blue retreated to the relative safety of the jukebox and then to the bar for another round of drinks and a supply of salted snacks. When he returned he was once again grinning broadly.

"What's the matter with you, did yer get some free food while yer where there?" Jay Mac asked.

"Better than that, 'ang on a minute..."

As the bitter-sweet ballad ended leaving both dancers momentarily stranded in the silence, Blue's new selection reunited them once more reigniting their passion. *Sylvia's Mother* by Dr.Hook began to play much to the amusement of Blue, Glynn and Irish.

"They're playin' your song Jay Mac." Irish laughed cruelly.

After leaving the 'States' they spent the remainder of their night wandering from bar to alehouse, becoming increasingly intoxicated and as a consequence engaging confidently in flirtatious conversations with an array of seemingly beautiful women and girls, hoping to secure a passionate encounter with one or all of these vibrant females. Even though they remained unsuccessful in their quest, the notoriously tight-fisted Glynn still appeared to be enjoying himself, stunning his friends with a shock announcement after last orders had been called in their final hostelry.

"Listen, no point in us tryin' to catch the last bus from the Pier Head, let's find a club and keep drinkin'. We can always get a fuckin' taxi later."

"Shit! He *must* be pissed; we better keep an eye on him before he does somethin' else mental." Jay Mac advised smiling stupidly at his equally inebriated friends.

"Let's get some food first, am fuckin' starvin'," Blue announced unsurprisingly.

A few minutes later, while they were standing close to the greasy hot dog vendor's pungent mobile cart, eating their comfort food, smothered as it was in ketchup, onions and mustard, Blue who had returned for a second helping, spoke to the equally greasy short-order cook as he was being served, "'Ey mate d'yer know where's the nearest late bar or club, where there's loads of fuckin' birds?"

Scratching his backside as if to assist his memory before passing Blue his two additional hot dogs, he replied, "Well lad I've 'eard loads of punters say that new one off Mathew Street, called 'Lucy in the Sky' is full of minge."

"Fuckin' hell, thanks mate, we'll get right down there." Blue replied delighted.

All four set off at once for this venue, having received the enticement of the knowledgeable purveyor of fast food's informed opinion. He watched them as they strolled away scratching his backside once more, "I think that's what thee say, or it might be its just fuckin' mingy, I can't remember... Next."

It did not matter either way; they were already out of earshot and beyond caring.

It was not long before they literally stumbled upon the backstreet venue and joined a small queue of prospective customers. Cognisant of the fact that they would probably be critically observed by the door staff before admittance, they straightened themselves as best they could whilst awaiting inspection.

"You two alright, in yer go." said the heavyweight, scowling bouncer allowing Blue and Glynn to enter the establishment. "You two in the Crombies and the boots, am thinkin' about fuckin' yers off. If I do let yers in an I hear yer've started any trouble, I'll personally come lookin' for yers an I will kick the shite outta yer."

In this instance both Irish and Jay Mac chose not to respond in a provocative manner, merely saying "Thanks mate, that's decent of yer."

Finally, against his better judgement and after giving another stern warning, the circumspect head doorman allowed them ingress.

"Fuckin' hell, it better be good in 'ere, what a cunt." Irish observed as they passed into the semi-darkness of the stifling interior, where a live band were murdering a cover version of *Helter Skelter* from the Beatles' White Album.

The four youths forced their way through the heaving sea of the crowd towards the long bar, which beckoned them with its varied, brightly coloured optics like a homing beacon.

"There's fuckin' yards of snatch in 'ere!" Glynn shouted above the din while waiting for their golden amber pints to arrive, having successfully attracted the attention of one of the over-worked, sweating bar staff.

"There's all kinds in 'ere mate," Jay Mac replied, "From arl grannies to fuckin' jail bait." He took a drink from his pint which was served in a plastic glass, so flimsy if squeezed too firmly spillage could easily occur.

"Move away from the bar if yer've been served." the staff constantly called out, trying to break the siege that threatened to overwhelm them. All four youths pushed along to a brick-lined alcove, one of many in this recently converted former warehouse and away from the crowded counter. They took stock of their surroundings while drinking their pints, trying to hear their own thoughts.

"'Ey, look at those lads over there." Jay Mac said pointing to a group of French sailors who were surrounded by a motley gang of eager, middle-aged females, wearing far too much make-up and far too little clothing. "They're in for a fuckin' rough night." He did not realise how prophetic his words would be. Not much later once enticed outside into a nearby alley, all entente cordiale would be divested faster than the harridans' 'elevator' underwear, in readiness for their waiting 'boyfriends' to pounce on the unsuspecting matelots, mid-coitus.

"Never mind them poor cunts, check out those two fuckin' stunners who've just come in, there, over by the door." Blue called to his team mates, all of whom followed his direction.

Two very attractive girls with long dark hair and shapely figures, fully revealed in their tight-fitting dresses, were standing near the entrance, with a single smartly dressed male in attendance. Jay Mac was already walking as if in a trance towards the object of his heart's desire, instantly recognising his dream girl. With his friends looking on and taking no account of the girls' one male companion, the love struck youth presented himself before the beautiful Celeste, whose telephone number he always carried, even though he knew it by heart.

"Alright Celeste, fancy seein' you in here." he began awkwardly. "I've rang your's earlier and spoke t'yer mum."

"Sorry do I know you?" she asked coldly.

"Yeah, it's me, yer remember, yer let me hide out in yer cousin's back in the summer." Jay Mac responded, somewhat surprised.

"Oh yeah, I remember you now, what is it y'wanted anyway?" she replied without any change in demeanour.

"Am goin' away to the States for work, and I might be gone for some time so I was gonna ask yer out."

"'Ey lad, she's already out, her feller's at the bar, so do one while yer can." the good-looking, smartly dressed partner of the other silent female warned angrily.

The Eagle player totally ignored the warning, "So what d'yer think, me and you? When I come back we could start seein' each other?"

Celeste stared at him incredulously, her beautiful face perplexed. "I'm not sure what's goin' on in your head. The only 'me and you' might be in another life but not this one."

Jay Mac stood frozen amidst the sweltering temperature of the boiling cauldron, not even noticing Celeste's boyfriend's angry approach.

"What d'you want boy?" he snapped but received no reply. "'Ey am talkin' t'you. Yer better watch yerself, yer don't know who yer dealin' with."

The Crown youth turned and looked directly at the handsome young man in his well-tailored suit, "Yeah, there's a lorra that goin' round."

"D'yer wanna know who I am? I had a trial for Tranmere Rovers boy, I keep meself fit and I'm pretty handy with me fists, right?" He prodded Jay Mac in the chest with the index finger of his free hand to emphasise his point.

"Yer'll need t'be if yer put that hand on me again." Jay Mac warned, no longer smiling.

"Who is this joker?" the young man demanded of Celeste.

"Leave it Greg he's nobody." she replied, cutting the youth worse than any of his enemies' blades.

He silently walked away, being pushed and shoved by the crowd without resisting.

"Alright Jay Mac?" Blue asked when he rejoined them.

"Got blown out did yer?" Irish asked grinning slyly, adding, "Well cheer up it's your friggin' round."

"Yer'll'ave to fuckin' wait, am goin' the Gents'. 'Ere, 'old me Crombie will yer I'm roastin'." Jay Mac replied without any expression, passing Blue his coat.

"It's alright mate I'll get this one in, you can get the next round." Glynn offered generously, observing his friend's gloomy, depressed mood and proving that he was totally drunk.

A few moments later having waded through the flood of foul smelling liquid, which was overflowing from the heavily crazed porcelain urinal, with its obligatory collection of discarded chewing gum and cigarette butts blocking the metal trap in the gulley, Jay Mac stood in front of the filthy sink.

'Thee might've spent a few bob doin' the club up but this bog really is a shit-hole' he thought, whilst running some cold water into his sweating hands and splashing it on to his burning face. The flickering low-watt bulb provided only minimal illumination as Jay Mac stared at his own reflection in the grimy mirror mounted on the wall just above the sink. He stooped once more to throw another handful of water over his face. This time when he rose and looked in the mirror a horribly familiar, bald headed face was grinning over his shoulder.

"Fuck no way!" Jay Mac exclaimed, even as Morgo lay his heavy left hand on the youth's shoulder, forcibly driving 'Fritz' up to his brass hilt with his right, through the coarse denim material bearing the image of John Barleycorn, violently entering the youth's yielding flesh. Again and again he plunged the well-used American combat knife into the lower back of the Americana fan, laughing ecstatically as he did. No one had noticed the limping Morgo following them all the way from the hot dog stand, waiting for his moment of revenge.

Jay Mac let go of the chipped edge of the sink that had been supporting him, slipping to his knees then falling to the urine soaked floor, rolling onto his punctured back as he did. With his life's blood gurgling out from his slowly opening and closing mouth like a goldfish from an upset bowl gasping for air, he tried to speak.

"I need... a Catholic priest... please."

"Yer one of them are yer, I might 'ave known." Morgo paused to clear his throat. "I think I can manage some holy water for yer." He spat a thick globule of sticky phlegm onto Jay Mac's face and began a mock blessing, "Spectacles, testicles, wallet and watch."

Morgo's voice became distorted, echoing around the small chamber, his words meaningless, then all sound ceased. Jay Mac looked up at his attacker standing over him holding the bloodstained knife, he was motionless or rather his movements had slowed to an infinitesimally, barely perceptible pace. The youth focused on the hairs on the back of Morgo's scarlet hands, they seemed to sway back and forth like seaweed animated by the swirling ocean. A creeping darkness began to fill the room until it revealed the knifeman in outline only, before he too was consumed, all was now deepest, impenetrable black.

Jay Mac had slipped through the gossamer thin strands that formed the precarious net of life and had become part of the fabric of the universe. He knew nothing and understood everything at once, lying entombed in the featureless void.

When next he opened his eyes everywhere as far as he could see, there stretched a canopy of clear, azure blue. There was not a single cloud in this unblemished bright sky. He felt no pain and for the first time ever he was not afraid, all anxiety had vanished.

Away in the distance shimmering and rising out of an early morning misty veil, he recognised the iconic buildings of the Manhattan skyline, stretching from Pier 17 to Battery Park. Close by was a towering figure with its right arm raised, one of the biggest statues he had ever seen yet he was unconcerned, feeling only elation.

He gazed up at the giant, crowned with her seven-pointed halo and smiled. As he passed by, Lady Liberty replaced her fixed enigmatic expression with a warm smile in return. The torch that she held proudly aloft as a beacon of hope for the hopeless burst into flame, casting its brilliant red and gold light in every direction, bathing the contented youth in a warm glow. There on the quayside waiting for him with a beaming smile lighting her beautiful face was the girl of his dreams. Jay Mac knew without question, beyond doubt everything would be alright now.

An unseen orchestra played The Beatles' *Good Night* magnificently, filling the heavens until it too faded away...

EPILOGUE

Weaver the crazed psychopath carried on for a few more years battering his victims with his solid steel toffee hammer, always reminding them who had inflicted their injuries upon them, proudly declaring his eponymous war cry. Then in his early twenties, the worm turned, the Eagle and the Heron were both closed for refurbishments; only the one would ever re-open, leaving the lower edge of the estate without an alehouse, a focal point, a gathering place for the gangs. They moved on, found a new venue; some were imprisoned, seriously injured or killed, most simply grew up abandoning Weaver the dinosaur, violent thug to his own devices.

For the remainder of his short life he was forced to move to different locations around the city, vehemently denying his identity when frequently challenged by those who bore the scars of his savage attacks. Eventually in his thirtieth year, looking much older than his chronological age, having become a solitary, heavy drinker, he was unaware that his movements had been relentlessly tracked by someone who no amount of denials could save him from.

After staggering out of a seedy, rundown bar in a back street off the desolate Dock Road, on a moonless night with a downpour of freezing hail hammering his tired body, he stepped into a filthy alley for a much needed urination. His killer calmly walked up behind him and placed the hard tip of the cold steel barrel of his powerful handgun firmly against the back of Weaver's skull, while a steady vapour of steam arose from the growing pool at his feet. Leaning against the old Victorian weathered brick wall, trying to steady himself with one hand, holding his manhood with the other he spoke briefly to his executioner.

"Do it fucker, put me out of me misery."

The single bullet fired at point blank range exploded the psychopath's head like an over-ripe melon, finally freeing him from his raging madness, drilling through his brain, flinging a render of sticky grey matter, blood and bone fragments into the freezing air and across the aged wall.

"You're Weaver, I done this to yer, you're Weaver." were the words that passed into the ether as the former Heron player's body slumped to his knees, with his lidless mush of a head falling forward, striking the crumbling brick surface.

A couple of eye-witnesses did come forward to assist the police, although they did not see the shooting, they agreed only that a blond male, possibly of a similar age to the victim, had been loitering near the alehouse. They had never seen him before and could provide no further details.

Glynn the avenging son had thrown Jay Mac's leaving present into the stinking Mersey after walking away from the scene. Finally he smiled and was at peace.

"Three down... no more to go."

THE END

MUSIC

Chapter 1 – *Horse With no Name* **(America)**
Tony Bennett - *I Left My Heart in San Francisco*
Bing Crosby - *Beautiful Dreamer*
Frank Sinatra - *My Kind of Town*

Chapter 2 – *Mamma Weer All Crazee Now* **(Slade)**
The Temptations - *I Wish it Would Rain*
Gary Glitter - *Rock and Roll* (Part 1 & 2)
Blackfoot Sue - *Standing in the Road*
Medicine Head - *Pictures in the Sky*
Elvis Presley - *In the Ghetto*
T-Rex - *Hot Love*
David Cassidy - *How Can I be Sure?*
Al Green - *Let's Stay Together*
Little Eva - *The Loco-Motion*
The Animals - *House of the Rising Sun*
The Moody Blues - *Nights in White Satin*
Ann Shelton - *Arrivederci Darling*
The Supremes - *Automatically Sunshine*
Gene Kelly - *Singin' in the Rain*
Roxy Music - *Virginia Plain*

Chapter 3 – *Bonny Bunch of Roses O* **(Paddy Clancy)**
David Bowie - *The Jean Genie*
The Temptations - *Pappa was a Rolling Stone*
The Dubliners - *Black Velvet Band*
Chauncey Olcott - *When Irish Eyes are Smiling*
Elton John - *Crocodile Rock*
Jimmy Helms - *Gonna Make You an Offer*
The Dubliners – *The Leaving of Liverpool*
The Detroit Emeralds - *Feel the Need in Me*
Stevie Wonder - *Superstition*
Thin Lizzy - *Whiskey in the Jar*

slumped to his knees, with his lidless mush of a head falling forward, striking the crumbling brick surface.

A couple of eye-witnesses did come forward to assist the police, although they did not see the shooting, they agreed only that a blond male, possibly of a similar age to the victim, had been loitering near the alehouse. They had never seen him before and could provide no further details.

Glynn the avenging son had thrown Jay Mac's leaving present into the stinking Mersey after walking away from the scene. Finally he smiled and was at peace.

"Three down... no more to go."

THE END

MUSIC

Chapter 1 – *Horse With no Name* **(America)**
Tony Bennett - *I Left My Heart in San Francisco*
Bing Crosby - *Beautiful Dreamer*
Frank Sinatra - *My Kind of Town*

Chapter 2 – *Mamma Weer All Crazee Now* **(Slade)**
The Temptations - *I Wish it Would Rain*
Gary Glitter - *Rock and Roll* (Part 1 & 2)
Blackfoot Sue - *Standing in the Road*
Medicine Head - *Pictures in the Sky*
Elvis Presley - *In the Ghetto*
T-Rex - *Hot Love*
David Cassidy - *How Can I be Sure?*
Al Green - *Let's Stay Together*
Little Eva - *The Loco-Motion*
The Animals - *House of the Rising Sun*
The Moody Blues - *Nights in White Satin*
Ann Shelton - *Arrivederci Darling*
The Supremes - *Automatically Sunshine*
Gene Kelly - *Singin' in the Rain*
Roxy Music - *Virginia Plain*

Chapter 3 – *Bonny Bunch of Roses O* **(Paddy Clancy)**
David Bowie - *The Jean Genie*
The Temptations - *Pappa was a Rolling Stone*
The Dubliners - *Black Velvet Band*
Chauncey Olcott - *When Irish Eyes are Smiling*
Elton John - *Crocodile Rock*
Jimmy Helms - *Gonna Make You an Offer*
The Dubliners – *The Leaving of Liverpool*
The Detroit Emeralds - *Feel the Need in Me*
Stevie Wonder - *Superstition*
Thin Lizzy - *Whiskey in the Jar*

Chapter 4 – *Why Can't We Live Together?* (Timmy Thomas)
Elton John - *Benny and the Jets*
Marvin Gaye - Inner *City Blues (Makes Me Wanna Holler)*
Argent - God *Gave Rock and Roll to You*
The Wailers - *Simmer Down*
The Upsetters - *Return of Django*
Johnny Nash - *I Can See Clearly Now*

Chapter 5 – *John Barleycorn Must Die* (Traffic)
Gary Glitter - *I'm the Leader of the Gang*
Hot Chocolate - *Brother Louie*
Terry Dactyl and the Dinosaurs - *Seaside Shuffle*

Chapter 6 – *Dazed and Confused* (Led Zeppelin)
Fleetwood Mac - *Albatross*
Jimmy Hendrix - *Voodoo Child*
David Bowie - *Drive in Saturday*
Wizard - *See My Baby Jive*

Chapter 7 – *Take a Walk on the Wild Side* (Lou Reed)
Beach Boys - *Good Vibrations*
Steeler's Wheel - *Stuck in the Middle with You*
Lou Reed - *Walk on the Wild Side*
David Bowie - *Jean Genie*
Mungo Jerry - *Alright Alright Alright*

Chapter 8 – *Something in the Air* (Thunderclap Newman)
Rodgers & Hammerstein - *You'll Never Walk Alone* (Carousel)
Nazareth - *Bad Bad Boy*
Free - *Alright Now*

Chapter 9 – *Broken Wings* (Atomic Rooster)
Rodgers & Hammerstein - *You'll Never Walk Alone* (Carousel)

Chapter 10 – *Silver Machine – the other side of the sky* (Hawkwind)
The Rolling Stones - *Sympathy for the Devil*
Tony Joe White - *Polk Salad Annie*
Dave Edmunds - *I Hear you Knockin'*
David Bowie - *Life on Mars*
Hawkwind - *Silver Machine*

Chapter 11 – *Streets of Laredo* (Marty Robbins)
Dean Martin's - *I'd Cry Like a Baby*
Bobby Bloom - *Montego Bay*
Jimmy Ruffin - *What Becomes of the Broken Hearted*
Dr. Hook - *Sylvia's Mother*
The Beatles - *Helter Skelter*
The Beatles - *Good Night*

GLOSSARY

In response to the requests of some readers I have included a brief glossary of localised 'Scouse' idioms in use at that time. This is neither exhaustive nor exclusive with some of the specific expressions being more widespread, whereas others were entirely parochial.

Airwair – The name given to Doc Marten boots in this particular area of Liverpool

Arl – Old (me arl feller = my dad, my father)

Arl arse – Auld arse, old arse, = older person, usually cantankerous

Baker's – Baker's trousers, white trousers, favoured style of some Skinheads and Boot Boys at the time

Bizzies – Police (Polis – Irish for Police)

Blimping – Looking, usually taking a sneaky look

Bonfire Night – or Guy Fawkes night a celebration with fireworks and fires often burning a 'Guy' sometimes referred to as Bommie Night

Boozer – Public House, Alehouse

Brass necked – Brazened it out, bold, barefaced, daring, overconfident, impudent

Broosted – In the money, have plenty of money to spend

Chocker – Chocker-block = packed, full to capacity

Clocked – Seen, 'have you clocked this'

Come 'ed – Come ahead, come on

Corpy – Corporation = Liverpool Corporation the municipal council providers of corporation houses, their duty being the upkeep and repair of corporation houses for tenants.

D.A Style – Refers to men's hair style of the 1950s. D.A = Duck's Arse, due to the way the hair was styled.

Defo – Definitely

F.A – Football Association

Flat – High-rise blocks of flats = apartments

Geoff Hurst – rhyming slang, going for a burst meaning going to the toilet to urinate. (Geoff Hurst famous England football player)

Jib or Jibbed – To choose not to do something

Kecks – Trousers

Keds – Basketball boots (specifically Converse Chuck Taylor's All Stars)

Lash or lashed – To throw away

Last Orders – Public houses closed at 11.00pm and last orders were called before the towels would be placed on the pump handles (towels out). Last orders being the last drinks to order befor the pub closed.

Lobby – Small hallway

Magpies – Nickname for Newcastle Utd foodball team, referring to their black and white coloured strip.

Mild – A medium dark porter

'Oller – Patch of ground, where houses had been razed. (Hollow)

'Ossie – or Hossie, short for Hospital

Povo – Refers to a person with no money, poor, poverty stricken

Prince of Wales check parallels – Pair of parallel trousers with a small checked pattern

Ragged off – To rip/pull off violently

Ragged around – To be violently pushed and shoved

Sayers – A cake shop franchise based around Liverpool and North West England and North Wales.

Scouse or **Scouser** – A person born and bred in Liverpool. Many Liverpool people speak with a Scouse accent (said to be a combination of Lancashire, Welsh and Irish .influence). Scouse referring to a type of Irish stew (a staple diet of some Liverpool people. Also may refer to Lobscouse – a Norwegian/Swedish dish, similar to Irish stew.)

Scran – Food

Sound – Trustworthy, reliable

Sterrie – Sterilised milk

Tarmac – Tarmaced, Tarmacadamed thick black tar road covering

Tennies – Tenements, tenement blocks, tenement flats

Thee – Often used in place of they when talking with a Scouse/Liverpool accent.

Tramp – Hobo, Down-and-Out

Turkish – Going for a Turkish is rhyming slang, Turkish Delight = Shite (a Turkish Delight is a popular and tasty chocolate bar)

Twenty-Two inch parallels – parallel trousers with 22inch wide hems

Yer – You/your/you're (though you/your/you're are sometimes used for emphasis)

Yers or **Yous** – referring to two or more people, ie "yous two," "the lot of yers"

Printed in Great Britain
by Amazon.co.uk, Ltd.,
Marston Gate.